THE
PEOPLE'S
HOUSE

THE
PEOPLE'S
HOUSE

A JACK SHARPE
POLITICAL THRILLER

David Pepper

St. Helena Press

This book is a work of fiction. The names, characters and events in this book are the products of the author's imagination or are used fictitiously. Any similarity to real persons living or dead is coincidental and not intended by the author.

Published by Gatekeeper Press
2167 Stringtown Rd, Suite 109
Columbus, OH 43123-2989

Copyright © 2016 by David Pepper

ISBN: 9781619845121
eISBN: 9781619845138

Printed in the United States of America

PRAISE FOR THE NOVELS OF DAVID PEPPER

Praise for *The People's House*

"[L]ively, thought-provoking . . . Pepper [] writes with flair and insider knowledge of everything from gerrymandering to arrogant D.C. press aides. With speed and savvy, *The People's House* emerges as a sleeper candidate for political thriller of the year."

—*Wall Street Journal*

"The thriller that predicted the Russia scandal. David Pepper's 2016 novel is eerily similar to recent real-world political events. . . . [A] quick, lively thriller full of labyrinthine scandal and homey Rust Belt touches—reads like a user's guide to the past two years in U.S. politics."

—*Politico Magazine*

"[A] heart-pounding must-read. I almost missed a flight connection because I just could not put it down . . . an irresistible page turner that combines mystery and thrill, politics and power. When you get your copy, clear your schedule: You won't be able to do anything else!"

—*Jennifer Granholm, former Governor, Michigan*

"A great political mystery written with a clairvoyant understanding of how money, power, political corruption, technology and sex can have a corrosive effect on our democracy. Although written prior to the 2016 Presidential election, recent historical events, especially Russia's interference in that election, give this book an almost prescient mystique. Read it—you won't be disappointed."

—*Ted Strickland, former Governor, Ohio*

"A wonderful intriguing story . . . and then you realize he wrote this before all the Russian news broke. How did he know? Scary!"

—*Jerry Springer*

"[A] smart, gritty, and astute story that will appeal to political junkies. . . . An engaging tale that looks at the grimy underbelly of American political power."

—*Kirkus Reviews*

"'House of Cards' meets John Le Carré. [A] true-to-our-times political thriller. Could America's elections be stolen and its political system manipulated without anyone noticing? The answer that Pepper offers here is that it's easier than you think . . . [A] story that's both impossible to put down and important."

—*Matthew Kaminski, Executive Editor, POLITICO*

"Much like author John Grisham did for law firms, Pepper pulls back the curtain on how local political races really work. The result: A can't-put-it-down novel that's part thriller and part reason to pay attention to the election process—no matter where you live."

—*Cincinnati Enquirer*

"I love this book! Only a political insider could have written this. And only a great novelist could spin out such a page turner."

—*Jack Markell, former Governor, Delaware*

"I loved *The People's House*. Loved. It. How's that for a review? . . . This book is a revelation of state and national politics and will have readers on the edge of their seats throughout."

—*Chris Fischer, Readers' Favorite*

"[A] lively and entertaining thriller which manages to engage disturbing political issues without losing its vigorous energy or falling prey to unthinking partisanship. . . . [A] carefully-crafted thriller, a cat and mouse game between a determined, gutsy hero and a clever, manipulative villain."

—*IndieReader*

"[G]rabs you from the first page and keeps you guessing until the very end. A sleepy election in rural Ohio quickly explodes into a national scandal with global consequences. It provides a window into the real world of politics and leaves you wondering: could this really happen?"

—*Andrea Canning, Correspondent, Dateline NBC*

Early Praise for *The Wingman*

"A labyrinthine political thriller that details a plot to steal the American presidency.... [E]nergetically paced.... A cinematic and dramatic story full of delightful twists."

—*Kirkus Reviews*

"Another tour de force . . . Like *The People's House*, I loved this book. Pepper is a phenomenal writer, with great dialogue, intricate plot, subplots, and characters. And with his unique perch, Pepper deftly wraps the real issues and frustrations of modern-day politics into captivating story lines. I can hardly wait for the next one."

—*Jennifer Granholm, former Governor, Michigan*

"Pepper does it again! Believable and entertaining—just like the real news these days. What's fake and what's real?"

—*Jack Markell, former Governor, Delaware*

"David Pepper has once again managed to grab the reader in the first few pages. Not only does he intimately understand the world of politics but he has also managed to capture the inner workings of journalism and the military. With these worlds colliding, he has delivered another powerful thriller that keeps you guessing until the end."

—*Andrea Canning, Dateline NBC*

"*The Wingman* by David Pepper takes readers on a rollicking ride . . . There are the kinds of surprises readers long for and characters they will remember long after the last page is turned."

"Well-researched and beautifully crafted, *The Wingman* is a thrilling read, a story that brilliantly depicts the political atmosphere leading

David Pepper

up to the primaries. . . .The characters are superbly conceived and
developed to appear like people in real life. . . . David Pepper is a master
storyteller. . . ."

"*The Wingman* by David Pepper is an exceptional political
thriller . . . The book is well-written, interesting and, above all, suspense-
ful, and is therefore recommended to any reader, not just fans of political
thrillers."

—*Readers' Favorites, Reviews*

CONTENTS

PART THREE: INVESTIGATION

PART FOUR: DEADLINE

PROLOGUE

FEW THINGS LIFT my spirits like a good obituary.

It didn't start that way. As a junior reporter, I dreaded obit duty. When my editor assigned me my first few obituaries, I slowly punched in the phone number of the surviving spouse or child, then hung up before anyone answered. Then, I dialed again. Hung up again. Who knows how to start such a difficult conversation? Not me. Not at first.

But after I got my nerve up, I learned a valuable lesson: most folks who pass away in their later years have a story to tell. An authentic story, hidden by the passage of time and forgotten by all but their closest relatives. And few assignments in journalism are more rewarding than uncovering and retelling that story, giving the deceased one last hurrah and leaving loved ones with one final, uplifting memory.

"Ma'am, my name is Jack Sharpe. I work for the *Youngstown Vindicator*. I'm so sorry for your husband's passing, but I'm calling to highlight his life. Can you share with me how you want him to be remembered?"

That simple introduction would open the floodgates.

Who knew that 82-year-old Wilma Hubbard, who worked in a Kahn's factory to make ends meet until the day she died, had danced professionally in Europe in her twenties? Who knew that Hank George had won fourteen straight boxing bouts before settling down to raise a family and run a hardware store? Or that mechanic Joseph Battaglia was among the first soldiers to arrive at the Treblinka concentration camp, freeing thousands?

After reading my carefully crafted obituaries, everyone knew their stories. And sharing them became a refreshing break from the lives that consumed my political beat. Even gave me hope. Maybe some writer, some day, would dig back far enough to discover my exciting early years.

So after a jittery start, I came to enjoy writing obituaries—with one exception.

Lives in their prime, cut short by tragedy, can't be prettied up. The story isn't the life lived, but the untimely death. There's no way to make it pleasant.

The worst obituary I ever had to write was for a local congressman. Lee Kelly had been voted out of office, fired by his community as the nation watched. Then, three months to the day later, Kelly died on the side of a Pennsylvania highway in a high-speed, fiery crash.

"I've done this a long time," the Highway Patrol supervisor told me over the phone, "and never seen anything like it. The wreck. The fire. All from one car. Still doesn't make any sense."

The accident report he sent me was horrific to read and just as horrific to summarize, so I left out most of the gory facts. Instead, I detailed Kelly's start as a trial lawyer and county commissioner, followed by his ascent to Congress. I walked through the legislation he'd worked on and the dollars he'd brought home. I threw in praise from all corners of Ohio and all sides of politics. But in the end, there was no good story to tell, only an unvarnished tragedy. The *Vindicator* headline summed it up perfectly: "FORMER CONGRESSMAN KELLY DIES IN FIERY CRASH."

Still, even as it marked the end of his life, the obituary was not the end of the story. In fact, the sad tale of how Congressman Lee Kelly lost *his* life kick-started my own, and along the way, if I can be so bold, saved our democracy.

PART ONE
THE LEDE

CHAPTER 1

ST. CLAIRSVILLE, OHIO

November 8, Election night

"SHIT," I MUTTERED. "Gotta start over."

Only a young, bearded bartender stood within earshot. But even he wasn't listening, so this qualified as talking to myself. Again.

In the upstairs banquet room of the Iron Skillet, the nicest restaurant in his hometown, Lee Kelly's election night "victory party" was in full swing. Although Kelly was a good guy, I wasn't at the party to cheer him on. My editors at the *Youngstown Vindicator* had sent me there to cover election night, just as they had for Kelly's last four narrow victories.

This wasn't a plum assignment. Sure, the Sixth District always spawned a bloody political fight. Its design guaranteed it. The district meanders along 175 miles of the Ohio River, rarely straying more than 50 miles from the Buckeye State's borders with Pennsylvania and West Virginia. Beginning north of Youngstown, it snakes along the hills near Steubenville, through St. Clairsville, past Marietta, and all the way around the southern tip of the state to Ironton. Throw these communities together, and the district splits evenly between Republican and Democratic voters.

But for the last decade, the Democrats of the more urban and industrial northern half of the Sixth had outhustled the more conservative rural voters to win the seat. Congressman Lee Kelly had benefited each time, gutting out five- to six-point triumphs and earning the nickname "Landslide Lee."

Given this history, no one expected Lee Kelly to lose this election. Luke McCarthy, a little-known Lawrence County commissioner, had mounted a weak effort. So my election night assignment was to memorialize McCarthy's inevitable defeat.

The party started as the polls closed. For most of the evening, I sat alone at the bar, one eye on the election returns, the other on the glass of bourbon the young bartender insisted on refilling even when I didn't ask. The first set of returns are always the pre-counted absentee votes. Many seniors vote early, which means this bloc of votes is often more conservative than the rest. So when the absentee numbers came in showing Kelly up 55 to 45 percent, it boded well for his evening. And mine.

Within 30 minutes, my story was pretty much written, and the news it delivered would not be a surprise. Once I filled in the final numbers and a few quotes, it would read like all my other Kelly stories: "Landslide Lee Does It Again."

Until Landslide Lee lost.

No matter when it occurs, the precise point at which an election loss becomes clear sounds the same. One moment, upbeat music mixes with the buzz of family, friends, and supporters reliving a long day at the polls and celebrating their hard work with toasts, drinks, and laughs. The next moment—dead silence. In the ensuing seconds, awkward looks evolve into quiet murmurs. *Is it really over?* As the most seasoned in the room affirm that their year of campaigning has ended in failure, staff and volunteers hug one another, some shedding tears. Family members encircle the candidate—the spouse projecting strength, the children sobbing. Most in the room glance at the candidate, trying to size up his response to the bitter news without the awkwardness of actual eye contact. Those there for transactional purposes make the fastest exit, hoping to sneak into the winning candidate's party as if they were there all along. The quick trip, followed by a contribution within month's end, is imperative. Only the victor can dole out the deals.

The loser escapes to a quiet corner to make a terse congratulatory call to his nemesis, then returns to give a concession speech. He thanks family and friends, then vows to come back, although he almost certainly will not.

Following the speech, supporters line up to shake the candidate's hand or give him an embrace. They all say the right things. "Great campaign." "There's nothing else you could have done." "You'll be back." But they tend to whisper the words like mourners at a funeral. The visitors amble out quietly, followed by the candidate and his family. They leave banners and flyers strewn everywhere. A small cadre of campaign staff huddles over drinks for another hour or so.

I've witnessed this sad ceremony numerous times. Only two variables change—the time the moment occurs (the closer the result, the later in the evening) and the size of the upset. The more surprising the loss, the more jarring the collapse from banter to silence.

The silence at Kelly's party lasted longer than any I could remember.

First, Kelly's loss was a late one. His early lead narrowed slowly over an hour, but he didn't fall behind until after 90 percent of the votes had been counted. But once McCarthy caught him, brutal reality set in. It was over—his election, his career.

And the result was a stunner, made worse by the positive early numbers.

Most problematically for me, having already written a story with the opposite outcome, I had to start over. Given the late hour and the number of bourbons I'd downed, this was not good news.

"It's going to be another 40 minutes," I told my impatient editor, Mary Andres, in a quick phone call. "Believe it or not, Kelly lost. I've got to rewrite the story, and you may want to jump it to Page 1." Mary would do as she pleased, but I figured there was no harm in planting the seed. Even veteran reporters still enjoy a front-page byline.

I caught up to Kelly as he and his wife, Jody, started for the exit. With no easy way to ask the question, I went with the shortest version possible: "What happened, Congressman?"

"We ran a good race, but the voters wanted something different," he said flatly. "I congratulate Mr. McCarthy on a strong race." Gracious words. But his tight frown and wide eyes told the real story—that of a shell-shocked incumbent, tossed by the community that had put him there in the first place.

Then came McCarthy's turn. He returned my call from his headquarters 100 miles downriver.

"Congratulations, Luke. It's Jack Sharpe of the *Vindicator*. Are you as surprised by this as the rest of us?"

"Not at all," he shouted, barely audible over the music and chatter around him. "We called for change, and now we have a mandate for change in Washington!"

Pure pablum, but it would do for this story. Let the rookie have his day.

The Iron Skillet now sat empty, save a handful of Kelly's staff nursing drinks, probably discussing what they would do next. After all, the voters had fired them too.

I re-established my perch at the bar, pushed the empty glass to the side, and quickly redrafted my copy. I plugged in the Kelly and McCarthy quotes, filed my story, then shut my laptop.

Sensing opportunity, the young bartender swooped in.

"Another drink, sir?"

I shook my head, intending to leave within minutes, but then a soundbite from the television overhead caught my ear. An upset equal to Kelly's was in the making down the road in Cincinnati. Sure enough, within a few minutes, an underdog Republican township trustee bested long-serving incumbent Ella Smathers.

Both outcomes were so unexpected, I stayed in my seat to see if these Ohio results were part of something bigger. And in short order, Republican challengers eked out wins in swing districts in Florida, New York, and Pennsylvania. Not long after, a long-vulnerable Kentucky Democrat succumbed to defeat.

Central Time Zone states soon reported similar results. A small-county prosecutor upset the mayor of Peoria to win a fiercely contested open seat. An open Missouri seat went to a Republican, and veteran Democratic incumbents from suburban Kansas City and Milwaukee districts both lost. Oklahoma's only congressional Democrat, from greater Tulsa, also went down in flames.

The cable pundits chattered away, excited to see more drama than they had anticipated. They were almost as thrilled as the Republican talking heads they were interviewing.

An hour later, races in the Rocky Mountain states ended with more unexpected Republican pickups, and the Democrats' worry boiled over into outright panic. You could see it in their eyes as they tried to downplay the early losses.

Finally, out west, Republicans won two open California seats and knocked out an incumbent Democrat in Washington State.

All eyes turned to Tucson, where officials tallied votes late into the night. In a squeaker, the octogenarian Republican incumbent, caught in a sex scandal and having long ago lost his fastball, held on to win a 50–50 district by a few thousand votes.

I downed my last glass. Banged it, face down, onto the bar in front of me.

"That's it! Unbelievable."

The bartender and I had been talking politics for the past hour. It turned out he was a journalism major from Ohio University who'd been unable to land a news job after graduating. Probably too idealistic for the profession anyway.

"Is it that surprising?" he asked.

"Shocking."

Going into election night, Democrats held a seventeen-seat majority, and no one from D.C. to California had imagined that they would lose it. But with that Tucson outcome, sixteen of the 20 closest districts had swung the GOP's way. And most of the other close districts had done the same.

"The Republicans just took over the House—and Washington," I said to the bartender. "I'll take the check."

Minutes later, I stumbled into my dingy motel room. Despite the long day, sleep didn't come quickly. The drinks didn't help. I should have stuck with my initial decline. And of course, Kelly's loss surprised me, along with the national results.

But what kept me stewing came from deeper within. The sudden silence of the party, the look in Lee Kelly's wide eyes, the pain in his voice, even McCarthy's hollow rhetoric. They all brought me back decades. To a similar moment. A similar look. An equally long silence. And even greater heartbreak. Not for others, but for me and those I loved. It was something I hadn't discussed in years. It helped that few who would remember it were still alive. The raw memory of a long-ago election night gnawed at me for hours.

CHAPTER 2

January 3: 56 days after the election

Tom Stanton paced in the back of the stately chamber. Head down, he looked at his watch, fiddled with his phone, then ran his fingers through his jet black hair.

He badly wanted to leave the room. He hated wasting time and this meeting was sure to consume a lot of it. But, as his staff reminded him, he was the new majority leader. Walking out now would create front-page news of the worst kind—public treason on the first day of the new era.

So as his colleagues filed into the room he shook every hand he could, then fidgeted in the rear as newly sworn-in House Speaker Irwin Marshall rallied the troops.

"We've waited a long time for this moment," the Speaker said somberly. "It's time to get to work—for our friends, for ourselves, for the American people." The room of mostly white men, in their fifties or older, strained to hear the stately Southern accent that spelled out their marching orders. Not all members of the House of Representatives were in the room. Just the Republican Conference—the new majority. The only group that now mattered.

"We must work together. We must be united. We must . . ."

While the group cheered almost every sentence, Stanton didn't applaud once. The new Speaker's words offered neither energy nor eloquence. They never did.

Though it was uninspired, Stanton fully agreed with Marshall's core message. This moment presented the potential for progress on major issues. Years mired in the minority were finally over.

More importantly, for Stanton, it presented opportunity. As the new majority leader, his time to shine had arrived. If he eclipsed Marshall in the process, all the better. His ambition went way beyond majority leader. And way beyond the House.

*   *   *

An hour later, Stanton sat at the end of a long oak table in a private dining room three blocks from the Capitol. Fifteen of his colleagues, eight of them newly elected, occupied the other seats. From Peoria to Pueblo, Minneapolis to Milwaukee, the group represented a cross-section of the country.

Now this was a gathering worthy of his time. Stanton knew Marshall well and wanted to make sure this group did too. More importantly, he wanted them to know who was in charge.

"The guy ran a funeral home for decades in rural Georgia," he explained. "He operates slowly, deliberatively. The media may like that he's a statesman, but that won't work for what we need to do."

He paused to be sure they heard his next point.

"Just like I did in the elections last fall, we're going to set a different pace."

His guests looked up from their half-eaten steaks at this unsubtle reminder. Most of them had eked out narrow victories, and the media credited Stanton's spirited barnstorming as the prime reason for their wins. Even those who'd won handily owed Stanton for having orchestrated their new, plum committee assignments, secured some of their largest donations, or both. Whatever the reason, he knew each person at his table would follow his orders. This dinner signaled that he expected it.

"Election night was a referendum," he went on. "It was the clarifying breakthrough when voters approved everything we and our friends have wanted for years. And we are going to ram it all through. Each of you is here because you have a key role to play."

Stanton looked two seats to his left, at the new budget committee chair. He'd won his re-election in Tucson by one point, having survived an ugly sex scandal. Stanton had visited his district four times and directed half a million dollars in contributions his way. Pulled from the brink of extinction, this dinosaur now occupied one of the most powerful thrones on Capitol Hill.

"We'll start with the tax and spending cuts, along with the pipeline plan. That'll thrill those who put us here. Then we'll pass the election law reforms. Those'll guarantee we stay here."

He knew better than anyone that the House could easily flip back in two years. So by tightening voting rules, his planned Clean Election Law would lock in their new majority.

Stanton soon excused himself from the table, leaving his chief of staff to explain the details of their legislative game plan.

*　*　*

Minutes later, the majority leader was seated on a stool in a nearly empty room. Barren white walls surrounded him. He sat ramrod straight, stretching his already broad shoulders as widely as he could. Before sitting down, he had carefully re-combed his hair.

Only one man stood in the room with him. Stanton knew him only as Peewee, and tonight he sported a Maryland sweatshirt, blue jeans, and old sneakers. But that casual attire belied his critical role, because Peewee operated the camera into which Stanton was now speaking. With eight million viewers on the other side of the lens, this studio was hosting the most important appointment of Stanton's day.

A baritone voice bellowed through the earpiece in his left ear—Rob Stone, of FOX News.

"Leader Stanton," Stone began, "what did you think of the Speaker's remarks today?"

"Rob, as always, he inspired us all. He's why we're now in the position that we're in. And he will spearhead positive changes for our country over the coming months. I'm honored to work with him. For him."

"Many are speculating that you're the guy actually running the show. That you guided the party to last year's wins, and now you're the wizard behind the curtain."

Good. Staff had successfully planted this question with Stone's producer.

"That's nonsense. Inside-the-beltway nonsense," Stanton said, shaking his head. "But I'm proud to work with the Speaker to enact tax cuts, spending cuts, and clean up our broken system of elections. And we've got to get those pipelines approved."

Another win. He was dictating the national agenda, not the Speaker. Not even the president.

"Congressman, that's a bold agenda. Are you using it to build momentum to run for president?"

Stanton's favorite question, triggering his rehearsed response: a slight pause and a mild raise of the eyebrows, as if the question came as a surprise, followed by a trace of a frown, as if he was disappointed.

"Rob, I'm focused on passing these reforms through the House and getting them to the president's desk. There is so much to do before we start speculating on the next campaign. Plus, my wife, Irene, and I are pretty happy with our lives right now."

"Would you rule out running?"

"As I said, I'm focused on getting this important work done."

His response left exactly the impression he wanted. Iowa was less than a year away. Of course he was running for president.

CHAPTER 3

YOUNGSTOWN, OHIO
November 9: One day after the election

WITH THE EXCEPTION of a splitting headache, my drive into work Wednesday morning was the same I'd taken for years. Fifteen quick minutes that rehashed a decades-long story.

The city of Youngstown was defined by stark math: a city built for 170,000 people now housed 65,000. When the city's steel mills closed in the '70s and '80s, tens of thousands of jobs disappeared, along with the middle class families relying on them. The pockmarks left by those missing families, those missing jobs, remained everywhere.

According to the old timers, even the smell of the place changed. When the mills were going strong, the odor of burning sulfur permeated the Valley. Now, nothing. No doubt today's air was healthier, but they'd trade it any day to get the smell of that old economy back.

As for my morning commute, the 10-mile trip into town toured all phases of the loss. It started with the drive through a few city neighborhoods. These residential streets offered a smattering of houses, new and old, oddly separated by empty lots and acres of grass where other homes used to sit. After years of attempts to repopulate, city leaders waved the white flag and razed vacant homes by the thousands.

Closer to town, along the Mahoning River, sat enormous tracts of scarred industrial land. Urban planners called these sites brownfields, but they were more of a rusty gray than brown, dotted with building shells and fields of concrete. These were the gravesites of the mills themselves. Rail spurs leading nowhere were the best evidence that something substantial had once taken place here.

Entering downtown, not far from *Vindicator* Square, came the storefronts. Not all were empty, but far too many were. The most intact buildings still posted signs begging for new tenants. Others were too run down to make a credible case for commerce.

Don't get me wrong. The proud people of "the Valley"—as they refer to the Mahoning Valley region—were fighting back as fiercely as any community. I wasn't a native, so I could tell you without hometown bias that there was a gusto in the town that kept it going through the tough times. When 2008 hit, and communities struggled nationwide, Youngstown's response was: what are you complaining about? We've dealt with worse for decades. Onward. It was that spirit that kept me here over the years despite an occasional offer from greener pastures.

And that grit and energy have sparked growth of late. Ohio's natural gas industry was spurring a wave of activity, symbolized by a hulking new plant assembling steel pipes where Youngstown Sheet and Tube once rolled steel. An auto plant not far from town now churned out 1,000 cars a day. Pockets of commerce were sprouting up downtown, leading to more occupied storefronts and dining options than any time since I'd arrived here for college.

But 100,000 people gone? There was no way to paper over that.

I even saw it each morning as my commute ended, when I walked into the once teeming *Vindicator* newsroom which now sat half empty. Declining revenue first eliminated columnists, features writers, and our long-time cartoonist, wiping out much of our paper's personality. Investigative reporters went next—too expensive for anything but daily output. As departures continued, management finally removed the rows of empty cubicles altogether. The open space was awkward but less jarring than workspaces devoid of actual workers.

We survivors were each now tasked with covering more than ever, which meant the paper covered less than ever. In my world, politics, we used to have three writers and a columnist. Now I was covering it all, from the presidency to the school board. Even back in my productive days, that would have been an impossible task.

*   *   *

"I want an analysis of Kelly's loss."

I knew it was coming. The morning after the election, my managing editor, Mary Andres, was all over me. The short, plump, and cranky Andres always wanted more—more details, more analysis, more scoops.

And she barked for it like a drill sergeant. As if she didn't know what a hangover was.

"He lost, just like a lot of other Democrats. Not too much to say but that." I sipped at a piping hot cup of Dunkin' Donuts coffee. But it hadn't yet kicked in.

"Jack, you didn't expect it, and no one else did either. Readers want to know how some no-name wrestling champ with a ho-hum campaign beat an experienced congressman. So do I. Especially given what happened across the country."

"Fine. I'll get you something."

"Don't act like you're doing me a favor, Jack. It's your job!"

"10-4."

I was fried on politics. Had been burned out for years. Hell, I'd given up on politics long before becoming a political journalist, and it had only gone downhill from there.

My front-row seat made it clear—when it comes to Congress, little matters but the drawing of legislative districts every ten years. That's the whole ballgame. And what a sad game it's become. The irony is that when they designed the House of Representatives, America's Founding Fathers carefully constructed it to serve as the "People's House." With neither the United States Senate nor the president directly elected back then, they wanted the House to remain the closest to the people, which is why they provided for two-year terms and hundreds of smaller districts. Almost 250 years later, I can't imagine the Founders would be impressed by what their cherished House has become.

Through a process called "gerrymandering," today's politicians design House districts in a way that rigs the outcome of almost every election. The demographically lopsided districts, stacked with voters of one party, predetermine each election's outcome, and representatives waltz back to Capitol Hill every two years without breaking a sweat. The net effect? Modern-day elections to the People's House have almost nothing to do with the people.

Outside of a wave year, maybe 20 or 30 seats are legitimately up for grabs. These elections take place in the rare districts, scattered randomly around the country, where Republicans and Democrats possess about the same number of voters. The swing districts. So, amid the 435 House elections that take place every two years, the future of the country hinges on the less than 10 percent of races that occur in swing districts.

This is the real story of modern-day politics. But every time I tried to write about the grim consequences of gerrymandering, my editors nixed it. The readers don't care, they'd tell me. So I'd long ago lost interest in the surface-level analysis that masked what really drives politics. But that was exactly what Andres now wanted: a ward-by-ward analysis that the paper could present with a fancy graphic, liberating readers from actually reading a story. This was *USA Today* journalism at its worst, replacing real writing with cartoonish graphics and, in the process, making my job a much bigger pain in the ass.

But there was no way out of the assignment, so I set off to find something profound to say. The caffeine kicked in just in time.

My first stop? Spending. Federal reports showed that Kelly had raised and spent three times as much as McCarthy had. And the Democratic and Republican Parties spent about the same amount to support their respective candidates. So candidate and party spending didn't explain his loss. Then again, I knew that in the post-*Citizens United* age direct spending told only half the story. Well-funded groups routinely sweep into any district and change the outcome by dumping millions against a targeted candidate. Every election season, a *Citizens United* trapdoor springs open below an unsuspecting incumbent or two. Maybe that had happened to Kelly. If so, Pamela Solomon would know it. A professor at Ohio University in Athens, Pamela had become a reliable source of mine over the years, with a keen feel for local politics. A few choice quotes from her would get this useless story off my plate.

"Pamela, it's Jack Sharpe calling from the *Vindicator*. Can I ask you a few questions about Lee Kelly's loss yesterday?"

"Sure," she said gamely. "Still can't believe he went down."

"Tell me about it. I'm checking to see if you guys saw any independent ads attacking Kelly down there."

"We definitely didn't," she said. "I was wondering the same thing myself, so I checked local station logs yesterday. Nothing."

"Nothing up here either. Any issues that might have snuck up on Kelly?"

In the Internet age, political controversies erupt overnight from brush fires into wildfires, and the less astute politicians get fried before they even see the smoke. Healthcare had done that in 2010, wiping out Ohio's bench of fresh-faced Democratic congressmen.

"Not at all," Pamela said. "Kelly was in tune with the district. He was for coal, fracking, and gun rights and against single payer healthcare, so conservative Democrats, independents, and Republicans all liked him."

"Yep. That was my read too." I waited a beat, in case she had any other nuggets to share. I sensed she was doing the same, which meant it was time to go. "Well, Professor, let me know if you think of anything else."

"Will do. At this point, I can't explain it."

We hung up. Not at all helpful. And calls to county party chairs, political watchers, and a professor at Ohio University proved equally useless. By the afternoon my analysis was going nowhere. No short cut. Time to dig up the data for those fancy graphics.

*   *   *

Outside of long-term demographic shifts or a truly explosive campaign cycle, communities vote in remarkably consistent patterns.

In Ohio's Sixth District, for instance, Athens County votes for the Democrat. The area is home to Ohio University and its liberal staff and student body, and 65 percent or more of its voters will vote for the Democratic candidate. Take it to the bank.

And the populated counties of the Mahoning Valley, the northern end of the district, are where a Democrat like Kelly runs up big margins to secure victory in the Sixth. A melting pot of urban, ethnic, and labor votes—more Steeler fans than Browns fans—the Democratic candidate will win the Valley. The question isn't whether but by how much.

Further south, tiny Monroe County, surrounded by Republican counties, casts its votes for the Democrat. Not by a huge margin, but almost like clockwork.

The Republican inevitably wins Washington County, home of Marietta. And a number of other smaller counties, from Carroll County up north down to Lawrence County at Ohio's southern tip, are always red. This leaves the larger river counties of Belmont and Jefferson as the toss-ups. Whoever wins those battleground counties likely wins the race.

I set out to confirm this pattern, and that's when I found my story. In the prior day's election, the math of the Sixth District changed.

Kelly took the Mahoning Valley by the usual margins. The Republican-leaning counties went McCarthy's way. Washington County delivered a decisive 63 percent haul, a noticeable jump versus two years ago. Carroll and Noble counties delivered nice margins as well. The swing counties were split as usual, but Jefferson opted for McCarthy by just a few hundred votes—a big win for the newcomer. Kelly took Athens County, but by 61 percent instead of the usual 65 percent or more.

But what stuck out most?

Kelly had lost Monroe County.

A blue speck in a sea of red, the small, poor county along the Ohio named after James Monroe feels Republican but is reliably Democratic. The 15,000 citizens of Monroe County have voted that way for years. Not by the decisive margins of Athens County, and with President Obama as the one exception, Democrats can count on Monroe County.

The trend has long puzzled outsiders. On the surface, the communities and voters in Monroe have much in common with their more conservative neighbors. Primarily white. Rural. Struggling economically as coal mining fizzled and major manufacturing closed down. Culturally conservative. But come election time, they vote for Democrats, as their parents did, and their parents before them. When Reagan swept the country and Ohio, Jimmy Carter won Monroe County. Dukakis beat Bush there 56 to 44 percent. John Kerry won by double digits. All the county officials but one were Democrats, and Kelly had always won there.

Except yesterday.

Kelly lost Monroe County. Not by a lot, but by an erosion of votes in every ward. A county he'd won by 1,100 votes two years ago, he'd then lost by 600 votes.

That 1,700-vote swing in Monroe combined with a loss of 1,800 net votes in Athens County and 2,200 votes in Washington County. The slight shifts in other counties—Jefferson, Noble and Carroll in particular—netted McCarthy another 2,000 votes. In a swing district like the Sixth, a switch of almost 8,000 votes is all that it takes. Which is how Kelly's close win from two years ago flipped into a narrow loss.

With that, my story was good to go: "Monroe County Flips to GOP, Anchoring McCarthy Upset." The color-coded maps looked great. My editors were thrilled.

CHAPTER 4

February 2: 86 days after the election

"THE MAN SURE looks the part," Stanton whispered to the gray-haired committee chair as the two looked down at the witness table. It was not a compliment.

After weeks of buildup, show time had arrived. The chairman banged the gavel, calling the meeting to order. Just as when they'd dined over steak a month before, Stanton sat directly to his right.

Stanton tapped his fingertips on the wood desk, frustrated that he wasn't chairing the hearing. As successful as the prior month had been, the pipeline plan would propel him forward more than any other issue. But if he couldn't run the meeting directly, Stanton had at least steered it to a chairman he controlled, and now he took the rare step of attending a hearing as majority leader.

Four prominent energy executives sat at the long table before them. But one, Michael Chambers, was the reason they were all there. And that's who Stanton focused on.

Chambers ran Marcellus Enterprises, a company rocketing to the top of the industry. Marcellus had made an early, quiet bet that it could successfully drill for natural gas under eastern Ohio and western Pennsylvania, a part of the country long given up for dead. And the bet had paid off. By the time the rest of the industry woke up to the opportunity, the unknown Marcellus controlled more than 65 percent of the region's drillable land.

Stanton had arranged Chambers' center seat for today's hearing and now regretted it. Today was supposed to be all Rust Belt, no Wall Street, but Chambers' dark suit and slicked back gray hair nailed the caricature of the manicured million-dollar CEO. He sat stiffly, every bend in his body at a right angle. After having spent years on the losing side of a fierce political battle, he now carried a conquering general's swagger.

"Honorable members of Congress," Chambers began, "the natural gas opportunity in the Midwest will trigger energy independence, lower energy prices, and an economic boom in our entire nation. It's long past time that this body seize this opportunity."

Stanton cringed at the imperious tone. Sure, the Democratic House had blocked all attempts to execute the president's Energy 2020 strategy. But the good guys had won. The battle was now over. No reason to rub it in. Bad optics, bad politics.

"With the proposed pipelines, the economics work," Chambers continued. "The key to it all is the reliable and timely flow of huge amounts of natural gas to large population centers and other transportation nodes, especially our coastal ports. Without the pipelines, the economics fail. The costs, delays, and inefficiencies resulting from overcrowded roads wipe out any profit."

As they always do, the ensuing "questions" from committee members morphed into lengthy statements with only a single query at the end. Supportive Republicans tossed softballs that Chambers and the others hit out of the park.

"How many jobs will be created by this work?"

"Thousands directly in the oil and gas industry, and thousands more downstream."

"How much local revenue will this growth create?"

"Billions."

"What will this do to our overall energy picture?"

"It will make us less reliant on foreign powers."

In most of their meetings together, the politicians beg for help from the private sector titans. This hearing presented an easy way to return the corporate generosity. Stanton had instructed his colleagues not to be too obvious about it, but they were failing.

Skeptical Democrats responded as expected. Justifying their years of obstruction, they lamented the risks of gas drilling operations and pipelines spanning thousands of miles across twelve states. Earthquakes. Spills and leaks. Poisoned water.

This was the hearing's pivotal moment. *Don't take the bait,* Stanton's chief of staff, Seth West, had told the Marcellus team. *Kill the hostile questions with verbosity. Politely.* Chambers dutifully got it done, droning on after each adverse query. All smiles. Respectful. No drama.

In the end, what mattered were the votes, not the whining from the minority. And the committee passed the pipeline plan, formally known as Energy 2020, with little fanfare.

When the chairman gaveled the meeting to a close, Stanton watched as the CEOs and lobbyists huddled behind the witness table, happy with the outcome yet disciplined enough to maintain stern game faces. The congressmen who had voted their way sought them out with far less discipline, overtly congratulating their past and potential donors for the big win.

Stanton exited through a side door. He didn't need to suck up to anyone, so he walked toward the Rotunda where the press awaited him. That was the audience he cared about.

Seth West, balding and bespectacled, followed a foot behind.

"It was painful at times," Stanton said quietly, "but mission accomplished. Good coaching, Seth."

CHAPTER 5

MONROE COUNTY, OHIO
November 10: 2 days after the election

"SOMETHING AIN'T RIGHT. Monroe County would never have voted for McCarthy. And it didn't on election night."

Thursday, two days after the election, the deep, gravelly voice of Ernie Rogers bellowed through my phone.

"It didn't?"

"No, it didn't!"

If anyone else had called with that opening line, I would have found a quick exit. I had already put the Kelly loss behind me and was back to daydreaming about retirement. The last thing I needed was to waste time on conspiracy theories.

But I stayed on the line out of respect for Rogers, the kind of old-school pol who keeps my job interesting. A Korean war veteran, lifelong bricklayer, and great-grandfather, Rogers had worked his way up through the ranks of the Eastern Ohio Bricklayers Union to lead the local, and shortly thereafter took over the Monroe County Democratic Party. He'd led it ever since, even after giving up his union post. Rogers provided the face of Monroe County whenever candidates, media, and other politicos swept through. Over the years, he had met Bill and Hillary Clinton, John Kerry, Joe Biden, and a host of other candidates as they embarked on Ohio River campaign tours.

In short, Rogers was no flake. And he knew the politics of Monroe County cold.

"You know how I keep tabs on the voters down here?" he asked me.

"Of course."

"Well, they didn't vote for that kid over Kelly. I know that for a fact."

Rogers was playing his best hand. He was legendary for knowing every inch of his county, and virtually every voter of the county's 15,000.

He knew those who voted for the Democrat every time and those who voted for the Republican every time. He kept track of who showed up in presidential years, and who showed up every year. And he knew whose votes were up for grabs, and why. In fact, Rogers kept constant tabs on a handful of voters who he felt perfectly represented the swing voters of his county. He worked hard to know where they stood each and every election, talking to them and about them all the time. He called them his Monroe Weather Vane.

Old Erma Smith, the most senior member, voted for almost every Democrat on the ballot, but if one looked too eager to grab her Winchester, she would vote for the Republican. When she planted a McCain sign in her yard, Rogers correctly predicted Obama would lose the county.

William Hawsey generally voted Republican, but if a candidate came across as too distant from the working man, Hawsey would swing the other way. That's why he voted for Bill Clinton over the older Bush.

George and Jenna Smoot were true independents. They read up on each candidate, charted the relative pros and cons, and, over many meals, deliberated about the decision. Not wanting to neutralize one another, they always voted for the same person.

If a Democratic candidate risked losing Monroe County, the chairman knew. He sensed it from conversations with Mrs. Smith, Mr. Hawsey, Mr. and Mrs. Smoot, and a handful of others like them. I had seen it play out many times—his Weather Vane was never wrong.

"Trust me. Get down here and I'll show you."

*   *   *

According to the sign on the door, Traditions Lounge didn't open until 10:00 on Saturday mornings. But after my three hour drive south, I walked in anyway. If Rogers was inside, as he'd assured me he would be, it was open. I was eager to get this over with.

"Welcome back to Woodsfield, Jack!"

The chairman was not alone. His entire Weather Vane stood around a table behind Rogers, looking at me, an out-of-town reporter, like I was an alien.

A tall woman, cane gripped firmly in her right hand, had her gray hair pulled back in a ponytail. At least 80, she looked like a tough old lady. A couple in their seventies, both barely topping five feet, wore identical pairs of glasses, the husband bald as a bowling ball, and his wife sporting short, jet-black hair. A man weighing at least 300 pounds wearing a UAW cap and a biker jacket. An elegant woman looked overdressed in her long skirt, white blouse, and colorful, wide-brimmed hat. Several others joined them, each as authentic as the next.

I broke the awkward silence.

"I see you brought some friends, Mr. Chairman."

"Thanks for coming down," Rogers said, looking at me but gesturing toward his group. "When it comes to voting, these folks represent the good people of Monroe County." He turned to the small gathering. "Here's your chance, folks. Tell him your stories."

The heavyset man spoke first.

"I barely heard of that McCarthy kid, and Kelly's been here so many times. He knows us. Easiest vote I ever cast."

The female half of the couple chimed in. "The congressman and his wife are so nice. We felt like he was always fighting for what we care about."

Her husband nodded in agreement.

The overdressed woman echoed their words, saying she usually voted Republican. "He was a Democrat, but he didn't follow the party line. I respected that. We need more politicians like him. And I know a lot of my neighbors, Republican neighbors, felt the same way."

I took notes after every comment, and the rest of the group shared similar sentiments.

"Jack," Rogers said. "These are the folks I talk to before every election. If they're with someone, I guarantee you that person will win Monroe County every time. It's that simple."

They politely answered my follow-up questions, nodding as one after another spoke. This was a credible group, good people, with no ax to grind. Heck, they weren't political at all, just thoughtful citizens. That's why they were part of the Weather Vane to begin with.

After an hour or so, we all shook hands. Each smiled ear-to-ear as if they had handed Watergate to Bob Woodward. As Rogers said goodbye he pulled me into a powerful bear hug, as he always did.

"Thanks for doing this, Jack. Keep me posted."

Driving home in a steady rain after the meeting, I tried to dismiss Rogers' suspicions as nonsense. It would sure make life easier if these folks were off base. A lot less work, for one thing.

But they'd been sincere, and their narratives added up.

What if they were right? What if the official vote count in Monroe County did not reflect the actual votes of the people of Monroe County? How would that have happened? An egregious mistake made by a small county Board of Elections? A flaw in the technology? A scam?

To assure myself that Lee Kelly's loss was a fluke, and not something worse, I did something I hadn't in a long time.

I dug deeper.

*   *   *

"Ma'am, I'm from the *Youngstown Vindicator*," I said to the tall, thin woman in front of me just after nine on Monday morning. "I'd love to talk to the person who oversaw the congressional election."

I didn't have an inch on Betty Grooms. She was rail thin, and her smile revealed about 50 years of hard-core smoking, yet she proudly flashed both rows of teeth as she welcomed me into a small storefront that looked more like a barbershop than the Monroe County Board of Elections.

"You're looking at 'er. Me, Dottie, and Janice do it all."

I had no idea who Dottie and Janice were, but, still, this was not a surprise. The greatest democracy in the world delegates our elections to the smallest, most underfunded level of government in the country. In most counties, sometimes with the entire nation watching, two or three permanent staff oversee the vote-collecting and -counting process for every office up to the presidency. And they do so on the scant dollars that remain after the county commissioners have allocated most of their budget to the jail, the courthouse, the prosecutor's office, and other more politically powerful agencies.

Betty didn't seem to mind.

"I'm interested in understanding every part of the process you used to count the votes in that race," I told her.

She led me back to the small operations room that doubled as a storage area. We sat down at a metal desk, in chairs that were far too small for either of us. She nodded at me as if to say, *Fire away.*

"Could you walk me through the process you use to count votes for the congressional election, and specifically, what you did for last year's race?"

"Sure." She pointed to dozens of machines sitting on five large shelves.

"We got 28 precincts in twelve separate locations—a few churches, some schools, and a civic center. Each building houses two or three precincts. Because of our budget, we have just two voting machines per precinct, but they get the job done."

"And how about early voting?" I asked. Over the prior decade, voting in the five weeks before Election Day increasingly popular. Over 25 percent of Ohio voters now voted early, either by mail or in person, which was why Kelly had looked so good early on election night.

"People can vote early in this office up to the final weekend before Election Day," Betty said. "The lines for early voting are getting longer and longer, so we need two machines here."

"And how do voters actually use these machines?"

"It's the most up-to-date touch screen technology," she answered proudly. "After you sign in, you go to the machine and swipe your vote card. You then use the touch screen to vote in each race on the ballot."

"Is there a paper trail for every voter?"

"Sure is. We moved to that system before the last election after the state required it for extra security. Our new machines print a paper slip as each person votes, and display it though a screen on the side so that the voter can see and verify it. Those verified paper ballots are stored separately within the machine. The electronic vote is the official vote, but that paper trail lets us audit the result if there are problems or discrepancies."

"Have you done audits? Any problems?"

"We did a number the first time we used 'em. Everything checked out."

"Does your machine allow voters to over-vote?" One of the flaws of the old paper ballots was that if a voter voted for too many candidates in a race, that vote was tossed. In the old days, over-votes would lead to between 5 and 10 percent of votes being discarded. In a close election, that's enough to change the outcome.

"Nope," said Betty. "If you pick too many, the new machine tells you, and won't let you move to the next race on the ballot until you fix it."

"How about undervoting?" I joked. Betty smiled weakly at my attempt at humor. As people work their way through a ballot, from president on down, voters skip many of the contests, usually because they know so little about either candidate. I moved on. "So on Election Day, what happens?"

"We work the polls all day long, troubleshooting any problems that arise. Had a power outage one year that we had to fix quickly, but usually not a lot happens but long lines in presidential years.

"After the polls close, precinct leaders remove the machines' memory cards and drive them to the board of elections, where our main computer tabulates the totals. Everything we do is witnessed by a second person.

"As those numbers come in, we publish them online and send them to the Secretary of State's Office. Because the congressional races involve many counties, the Secretary of State adds up all the counties in the district."

I wrote down as much as I could from her rapid description, looking up after she stopped talking. "And when do you include the count from those who vote early?"

"First. When the polls close, we take the two memory cards from the early vote machines. They're the first votes put in the computer."

"How about vote by mail ballots?"

"We manually count those early on Election Day, with both a Republican and Democrat conducting the count together. The first numbers we report are the total of the in-person early votes and the mailed early votes. Then the rest flow in."

"And who does all this work?"

"We lead it all from here, but we use temps, paid poll workers, and volunteers to pull it all off. We train 'em all, but most have been doing this for years."

"Have you ever caught someone trying to vote more than once?"

"Nah. Some people have shown up to vote in person after mailing their ballots because they're not sure they sent it in time. But that's easy to sort out with a provisional ballot."

I nodded, having heard of the same thing happening in Youngstown, particularly with seniors.

"All this talk of voter fraud, I've never understood it," Betty continued. "Our precinct judges know every voter who walks into their precinct. See them every year. Even one person trying to vote as someone else, or trying to vote more than once, would stick out. Think about it: It would take hundreds doing that in this county to steal an election, thousands more in the congressional district, and at least tens of thousands in the state."

"Definitely would be hard to pull off. And you trust those machines?"

"I do, but I don't have to. Like I said, the paper trail adds an extra layer of safety."

"So what do you think about those who are saying that the votes in the last congressional race were somehow off? That Kelly actually won?"

"Old Chairman Rogers was here the other day talking like that. I'll tell you what I told him: I was surprised by the results too, but the total was the total. We did what we always do, we double checked it all, and Kelly lost. Tough break, but that's how it goes."

"Thanks, Betty. You've been very helpful."

I got up to leave, but as I did, took note of one last detail of the voting machines—the word written in the corner of each, "Abacus."

I jotted the name down at the top of my notepad and headed back north.

The walk-through both impressed me and reassured me. Hard to imagine something could be amiss in Monroe County.

*   *   *

On a gorgeous afternoon, the long drive home offered an up-close tour of the buzzing eastern Ohio economy—of the new Ohio encroaching on the old. Brigades of trucks weaved amid Amish horse and buggies. New motels, restaurants, and houses interrupted miles of aging silos and old farmhouses. Tall, steel drilling wells towered over rolling hills and fields.

Those wells were the source of all the other new activity.

As a journalist, I try to stay neutral on most things political, but the natural gas boom was great news. All the way down the river, these counties had struggled for generations. With coal fading and large-scale manufacturing disappearing, the heart of their economies had stopped beating long ago. But now natural gas was changing it all. Farmers, firefighters, county commissioners and others were getting rich overnight because of gas found deep beneath their land, and new technology that allowed it to be drilled. New millionaires were popping up in counties along the river. Young people and older ones, forced to retire early, were creating enterprises to meet the needs of their prized new industry and the new workers flocking to the region.

Good for them. Like Youngstown, these communities, these proud people, deserved it all.And with the president finally getting her way, the recent election only meant more good news to come.

An hour out of Woodsfield, after my cell phone picked up service again, Scott called.

Amid my many disappointments in life, Scott provided the bright exception.

He was an accident, the product of an alcohol-induced evening on which I'd relived a quarterback-cheerleader fling from years prior, with a woman named Roxanne. She wasn't a smart woman, or even a friendly one, but she had looked stunning that night, and the beer goggles from six Bud Lights—ugh—had only helped.

Mom and Dad were appalled that I had knocked up a woman they barely knew. But given my personal trajectory at the time, they weren't surprised. Which only embarrassed me more. I'd tried for years to lift my dad's spirits, but too often I dragged them in the other direction.

My shotgun marriage to Roxanne lasted a few miserable years, ending in a bitter divorce. But from the moment Scott came into my world, I never regretted the drunken dalliance that had produced him.

From a young age, he'd been my straitlaced, high-achieving, Type-A opposite. Class president. Phi Beta Kappa. Improv comedian extraordinaire. He was more well-rounded than I ever was, made better decisions than I had, and appeared to be blessed by better luck than mine. He took after my sister, Meredith, the aunt he never got to know. Scott went on to the University of Chicago and Stanford Business School, settling into the Bay Area as the second wave of the tech boom exploded. I knew he'd never come back to Buckeye country. His loss, I always needled him. But it was more mine. Now he was newly married and trying to have his first child. Whenever he called, I hoped to hear good news without asking about it.

"How's it going out there?" I said.

"Great. When are you coming back?"

My son did not beat around the bush. I'd visited a few times, but not enough. Most recently, about a year earlier, we'd driven down to Big Sur and spent the day hiking, with the stunning ocean view from the summits as our reward. Made me think about joining Scott out there after retiring. Maybe try writing a book on the real story of politics.

"Soon, I hope," I said, trying for nonchalance. "You know election time gets crazy. I miss you guys."

"Dad, how many times have we talked about this? That place makes you miserable. The job makes you miserable. Get the hell out of there. It's not worth it."

"Easier said than done."

"You've been saying that for years."

He was right—I had been. For Scott, my job was always a source of frustration. Too many late nights, and even on the early nights, a reporter is never off the clock. Worst of all, Roxanne warned Scott from a young age not to be like his dad, squandering a life reporting the news instead of *making* news.

"I know, Scott. I'm winding things down. I'll visit soon."

"Sounds good, Dad." But his voice trailed off as we hung up. He didn't buy it.

My ex's carping hit a sore spot, and she knew it. In my younger years, my life's ambition had been to make news. Big news. Growing up in Canton, Ohio, two things dominated my days: football and politics. I excelled at both, especially football.

The first week of my freshman year, Coach Boone stopped me in the hallway, impressed by my 6'2" frame. By my sophomore year, I started at quarterback. I was fast, tall, and strong, but Coach always said it was my intensity that set me apart, leading us to two state championships and the opportunity to start four seasons at Youngstown State.

Then seven years of glory ended in one five-second play in the second game of my senior year. I never saw it coming. The vicious hit shattered the radial bone of my throwing arm. I knew something was wrong when my right guard, the one whose slow first move had invited the helmet-to-arm collision, bent at the waist and vomited onto the field after looking my way. Feeling a sharp tingling, I glanced down. A jagged ivory-white bone knifed three inches out of my forearm; my arm looked like Joe Theismann's leg. A friend told me later that the three NFL scouts had left the stands even before the ambulance arrived.

So that was it. Season over. Career over. And the perks of youthful stardom—girls, free booze, a gift here or there—faded quickly. People still recognize me in Canton, but the brief moment of pride is usually interrupted by the same dismal question: "I always thought you'd make it all the way. What happened?"

I still didn't have an answer.

CHAPTER 6

February 21:105 days after the election

Always on the hunt for bonus media exposure, Stanton arrived at the White House before anyone else. Too early. The cameras weren't set up yet. Crews were there, but no actual reporters.

As he waited for the ceremony to start, Stanton peered into the East Room, impressed. A dark mahogany desk sat in the center of the large, ornate chamber. Three sections of white chairs, hundreds in total, were set in tight rows, facing the desk. A perfect setting for a political victory lap.

Only one month after clearing the House committee, Energy 2020 awaited the president's signature. It had passed the full House, then raced through the Senate. The Democrats from Ohio, West Virginia, Pennsylvania, and New York had whipped their more skeptical colleagues, urging them to support the best opportunity those economically depressed regions would see in a long time. In the end, only a few senators had voted against it.

Half an hour after Stanton had arrived, President Elizabeth Banfield entered the now-crowded room from the rear corner—shaking hands, gripping wrists and forearms, and engaging in small talk as she made her way up a diagonal aisle. A few feet behind her, Stanton and an entourage of officials performed the same entry dance, but with far less personal charm.

The president took her seat behind the desk as Speaker Marshall and Stanton stood to her left and right. A handpicked group of other politicians—Senate leaders, along with House members who represented the impacted areas—flanked their left and right in a single-file line.

With so many cameras pointing his way, Stanton forced a grin. As close as he stood to the president's desk, not one glimmer of the limelight would beam on him. Frustrating, especially when he was the prime reason there was a bill to sign on this day.

Instead, as she always did, the president owned the room. Her red hair and striking blue suit stood out among a row of anonymous gray and charcoal men's attire. She was still improving her delivery of formal speeches, but her energetic presence dominated less scripted events like this.

"This is a critical moment for our nation, and it's fitting that it's a bipartisan moment," she declared, making eye contact with folks across the room.

Watching from over the president's right shoulder, Stanton admired her performance. A former television anchor, she knew exactly where the cameras were, and eyed them directly for her most memorable soundbites.

"Parts of our country that have needed a boost for decades will finally get one, and the entire nation will benefit from this new domestic energy source. Beginning today, Energy 2020 is officially underway! And with it, a better, more secure, more prosperous American future!"

She opened the leather-bound booklet in front of her, lifted one of the dozen ceremonial presidential pens laying to her right, and began signing the document. She used each pen as she completed her signature. When she finished, as the room applauded, the president personally congratulated everyone standing behind her before heading back to the Oval Office.

Stanton sought out Ohio's McCarthy at the far end of the line. The rookie congressman's district stood to gain as much as any from the legislation.

"You helped make this happen, Luke. Congratulations. This will be a huge hit back home."

Stanton handed him the pen the president had given to him. McCarthy eagerly grasped it.

"Thank *you*," McCarthy said with an obsequiousness that Stanton both appreciated and disdained. "I wouldn't be here if it weren't for you."

Stanton patted the rookie on the shoulder. Although it wasn't true, he happily took the credit.

CHAPTER 7

YOUNGSTOWN, OHIO

February 6: 90 days after the election

"JACK, WHAT'S WRONG with Lee Kelly? He looks awful."

Months after the election, months after I'd dropped the Monroe County story, the same question kept coming my way every few days.

I was never especially close to Kelly. But people assume reporters know the inside scoop, especially those of us who've been around forever. And we love leaving that impression, inaccurate as it may be.

"Public rejection is rough" was my standard response, as I was trying to downplay it. But they were right. The last two times I saw Kelly, he was a mess.

Two months after his loss, when the Youngstown Democratic Party honored him in January, the always raucous crowd fell quiet as he reached the podium. There was a new slouch to his tall, broad-shouldered frame, and his previously trim physique bulged noticeably in the middle. His close-cropped brown hair, always parted carefully to the right, now plunged straight down, giving him a shaggy, disheveled air. And at the Steubenville Labor Breakfast a month later, same appearance, same reaction.

On both celebratory occasions Kelly was unable to fake it. His old smile flashed as he took the stage, but then quickly vanished. And even sitting close to the podium, I struggled to hear his brief, lifeless comments. It was hard to watch. For everyone there, I'm sure, but especially for me.

Politics had consumed my life as a kid. Dad had served for years as a state legislator from Canton, so my sister Meredith and I had grown up marching in parades, knocking on doors, and putting up yard signs. Outside of football, my other trophies in life had been photos with Nixon, Ford, Reagan, and other poobahs as they passed through the

Buckeye State. In politics, as in so many other things, Ohio lived up to its nickname: the heart of it all.

But amid this constellation of political stars, Dad remained my political hero. An old school moderate. Watching Dad had taught me that politics at its best involved good people coming together to get important things done. That was what Dad strived to do, and nothing felt better than planting "Re-Elect Sharpe" signs in Democrats' yards as well as Republicans'.

Everyone expected me to follow in Dad's footsteps. So did I, for good reason. Name recognition anchors local political success, and Sharpe was a respected moniker in Stark County. My competitive nature fired me up to win just like Dad did. Family, friends, and neighbors said I'd be a senator, governor, or even president someday. My goal was to live up to those high expectations. But out of the blue, that aspiration ended as quickly as my football career.

In 1982, Dad lost.

The Reagan wave pushed primary voters to the right that year. Dad's opponent, a far right candidate, rode the rabid sentiment, attacking every compromise Dad had ever made. Under the word "Traitor," he plastered photos of Dad with Democrats onto mailers that filled Republican mailboxes all spring. The voters took the bait, tossing Dad 60 to 40 percent.

As a matter of politics, it was arguable whether my own political future went up in smoke in that loss. Dad and Meredith always insisted I should stick with it. But what sealed it was personal. The loss, and the way it happened, shattered my boyhood optimism about politics.

We never talked about it. But the night of Dad's defeat, the moment, early in the evening, when the crowd fell eerily silent, haunted us for years. An ungrateful community dumped a good man. Dad's spirit broke that night, his brand of get-it-done politics crushed by an ideologue. He deserved better. So did our family.

When Dad's primary opponent went on to enjoy a long career in Congress, using the same tactics that had worked so well the first time, it only made things worse. For a time, Meredith's good humor and positive spirit kept the family going. But later, when we lost her, things unraveled quickly. Before I knew it, besides Scott, I was the only Sharpe left.

So yes, I knew what Lee Kelly was going through.

* * *

"You hear the news about Lee Kelly?" This time it was the chair of the Belmont County Democratic Party. The call came in right before noon, six days after I'd last seen Kelly, in Steubenville. I began my standard answer.

"Yeah, he's taking the loss hard. Saw him the other night and he—"

"He's gone."

"Excuse me?"

"Lee Kelly's dead."

I pumped him for every detail, then made a round of phone calls. Five frantic hours later, Kelly's obituary posted on the *Vindicator's* website. For my readers' sake, I sanitized Kelly's fate as best I could.

He had died 45 miles west of Philadelphia, heading west on Interstate 76. His Ford Escape had collided with another vehicle, careened off the road, and hammered into a thick oak tree yards off the highway. He was killed on impact. A state trooper found the front license plate about 30 feet from the vehicle, lying past a row of trees, crumpled but legible, and called it in. The dispatcher reported back that it was registered to a Mr. Lee Kelly from St. Clairsville, Ohio. Jody Kelly confirmed it was her husband the next morning.

But this account diluted the violence of it all. Lucky me, between the in-depth accident report and the supervisor's graphic commentary, I got to hear every horrific detail.

With no seatbelt holding him back, Kelly had catapulted forward into the windshield, thousands of tiny shards of glass piercing his flesh all at once.

"The guy turned to Jell-O," the supervisor helpfully explained over the phone.

At the same moment, the SUV exploded into a fireball.

Several passing cars had called 911 to report a large fire near the highway. Two fire trucks from nearby Elizabethtown arrived at the scene. Seeing flames enveloping numerous trees around the wreck, they called Harrisburg Fire for backup, who arrived 25 minutes later. The intense heat forced them to establish a perimeter 50 yards away. Thousands of gallons of water and 40 minutes later, they finally extinguished the flames. According to the report, the first responders initially assumed the source of the ferocious blaze must have been a fuel or chemical truck.

"We were surprised to discover it was a single-vehicle accident," the supervisor said.

The report described the grim remains: pieces of a body burned beyond recognition and virtually every part of the Escape, from its tires to its radio, melted or disintegrated into a gray, chalky ash. The tire tracks showed that a side-to-side collision a few hundred yards back had triggered the Escape's straight-line path off the highway.

"Any sense of what happened to the other car?" I asked.

"The angle of the collision wasn't extreme, so it looks like the driver of that car recovered quickly. Odd that your Mr. Kelly never did."

* * *

BELLAIRE, OHIO

Hundreds packed the Friday funeral in tiny Bellaire, Kelly's birthplace. From boyhood friends to Notre Dame classmates, from congressional colleagues to Ohio's governor and senators, the honoring of Kelly's life offered "a rare moment of bipartisanship," as I knew nearly all the news coverage would describe it. The sworn political enemies laughed together, shed a tear together, and remembered the days when they were all new to politics, when they would fight like hell on the statehouse floor, then grab a beer hours later. And all recalled that Lee Kelly had stood at the center of any cooperation that took place.

Mary Andres, my editor, didn't assign me to attend the funeral, but I stopped by out of respect. Landslide Lee was one of the good guys. As the service ended and we left the church, the hunched figure of Ernie Rogers caught my eye. He wasn't a tall man, but he still stuck out in a crowd. Seeing the chairman reminded me that I'd never followed up with him. Feeling a tinge of guilt, I turned and tried to inch inconspicuously toward the door, but moments later a forceful poke to the back of my right shoulder stopped me. Rogers could move fast when he wanted to.

"You know, Lee was looking into the voting issues in Monroe County you and I talked about," Rogers said without greeting, much louder than necessary.

"Hi, Chairman," I said.

"I waited for your story, Jack. For weeks. But when it never came, I called Kelly directly. We told him what we told you. Then he talked to Betty Grooms just like you did."

"When?"

"That's my point. Just a few days ago. He died the next day. Strangest thing I've ever seen."

"That *is* odd." I was doing my best to humor him, but I was more focused on his volume than on what he was saying. Seemed like Kelly had been polite to the old chair by hearing him out. But linking Kelly's car accident to his voting conspiracy theory in Monroe County? Now Rogers was being ridiculous. He was clearly expecting more of a response from me, but I simply nodded and slipped out through the church's doors, into the crowd.

* * *

YOUNGSTOWN

Over the years, technology has dramatically changed the day-to-day work of a reporter, and I've resisted most of it.

When it comes to note-taking, the old steno pad beats a computer or tablet. And despite our editors' encouragement, you'll never catch me tweeting stories or posting links to them on Facebook. The zeal for online "clicks" to generate revenue prioritizes sensationalism over substance. Hype over analysis. Refusing to tweet is my small protest on behalf of the old days.

But the iPhone? I'd ultimately converted. It's a veritable reporter's toolkit. It even can record interviews, putting my 12-year-old Dictaphone out of business. There's only one drawback. Thanks to my iPhone, I occasionally go days at a time without checking messages on my office line. A bad habit made worse when things get busy. After Kelly's accident, I failed to check my office messages the rest of the week. When I sat down at my desk the Monday morning following the funeral, I cringed to think of the important calls I might've missed.

Six new messages. Five were callbacks on humdrum stories. Nothing urgent. But then I listened to the first message. The oldest one. I recognized the voice at the first word.

"Sharpe, it's Lee Kelly calling."

Not a lot of people called me Sharpe, but Kelly had for years. His tone was deadly serious, but he talked carefully, softly, as if he didn't want to be overheard.

"I understand you spoke to Chairman Rogers and Betty Grooms about the voting issue in Monroe County. I did some digging myself."

A breeze and the rumbling of vehicles accompanied his words. He was standing outside when he left the message.

"Give me a call as soon as you get this to discuss."

The message was left at 12:28 p.m. Six days prior.

The day he died.

I replayed the message and jotted down every word. My penmanship was worse than usual, which made sense because my hand was trembling as I wrote. Listening to the voice of a man whose funeral I had just attended didn't bother me so much. Far more unnerving was that whatever Kelly had stumbled onto likely got him killed only hours later.

PART TWO
FIRST DRAFT

CHAPTER 8

LONDON

February 21: 105 days after the election

"B EAUTIFUL."

As Energy 2020 sailed through Congress, the man with the most at stake watched every minute of the hearings—and was pleased.

Unlike Tom Stanton and Michael Chambers, he wasn't in the room when the bill passed. Far from it.

Marcellus may have been the perfectly created Midwest company, Chambers may have been its made-for-TV CEO, but the room where all the decisions took place was located 2,000 miles away, in downtown London, hidden deep within the financial district. On a large flat-screen monitor that occupied half of one wall, the architect of it all had watched every moment of his overseas legislative success. And when it was over, after the president had signed the bill, he allowed himself a momentary celebration.

"You performed ably," he told Chambers on their teleconference call.

"Thank you, sir."

This was his biggest conquest yet—not because of its size, but because of its location. The long-sought victory moved him to reminisce like never before.

"My mother and father cheered when the old system fell," he said, talking more to himself than to Chambers, staring straight ahead. "The change came too late for them. They knew it, but they saw opportunity for their son."

He paused.

"Still, they never could have imagined this."

Celebration over.

CHAPTER 9

ST. CLAIRSVILLE
February 16: 101 days after the election

"L EE WAS STRUGGLING after his loss," Jody Kelly told me flatly. "Not at all himself. For months."

He wasn't the only one. Up close, Lee Kelly's wife appeared as a shadow of her usual self. At least ten pounds thinner. Her eyes were puffy and faintly bloodshot, her cheeks pale and thin, her black hair pulled back in a short, slightly greasy-looking ponytail. We were sitting in her kitchen, feet apart. Our conversation was off the record, so I wouldn't use any of her quotes, and she knew this. Still, I wrote down every word.

"I'm sure," I said. "My dad was a politician. Lost out of the blue in a nasty primary. We were devastated, and he never recovered." I rarely mentioned this to anyone and was feeling my way through how much to say.

"I know the feeling now," Jody said. "It was heartbreaking to watch Lee go through that. The irony is that the day before he died, it all changed."

Good. I had made the long trek down a slippery highway to gather precisely this type of detail, but I didn't want to pry. She led me there on her own.

"Is that right?" I said casually. "What happened?"

"Lee went to Monroe County all that day. Came back around 9:00. When he walked in, I was thrilled. The Lee I had married, the one this community elected so many times, was back."

"What do you mean?" I asked, leaning forward. "What was different?"

"Everything. He burst through the kitchen door, hugged me, and smiled with that old look of intensity. Then he rushed into the study and logged onto his computer. Searching for something. Reminded me of his lawyer days when he had a big case. He didn't get into bed until eleven."

The next morning, Jody explained, Lee scrambled out of the house before she got out of bed. He'd left a note saying he'd be back in the evening. By late afternoon, she hadn't heard from him and knew something was wrong.

"Even on his busiest campaign days, Lee would check in. But he didn't call once."

By 3:00 p.m. her calls jumped straight to voicemail.

"From then until midnight, I called former staff members to see if they'd heard from him. None had. I barely slept the rest of the night."

Just before 8:00 the next morning, a gray car pulled into the driveway. No siren, but a Pennsylvania Highway Patrol seal on the door.

"I knew as soon as the trooper stepped out of the car."

I jumped in, not wanting to make her relive a horrible conversation. "Mrs. Kelly, do you have any idea why Lee was on I-76 that night? Why he'd be in Philadelphia?"

She shook her head. "I don't. Whatever he talked about in Monroe County, he was pretty fired up when he got back."

"Let me be as direct as I can. Lee left me a message the day he died saying he was looking into something, something I'd also been looking into. He didn't say he'd found anything, but it seemed like he had. He wanted me to call him back, but I didn't get the message until last week. So he called me, asked me to call him, and then, hours later, he's dead."

"Yes, the sequence of things seemed fishy to me," she said. "But I didn't know who to say that to without appearing to have lost my mind. He was researching something in his office, but I haven't been up to going in there."

"Do you mind if I look around in there?" I asked. "Maybe we'll find something." This was pushing the envelope, but she seemed to want answers as much as I did.

"Not at all."

She led me to the study. It was a mess. Photos, plaques, and awards were stacked up in open boxes. Books and files were piled in different corners of the room. This was a room that someone felt comfortable in, a room that someone had planned to come back to.

"These are all from Lee's congressional office. He would start unpacking, but then get absorbed with all his old papers or memorabilia. He was just starting to make progress."

We sat down in front of Kelly's computer.

"Do you mind?" I asked.

She shook her head. "Go right ahead."

When I moved the mouse slightly, the log-in screen flashed on. Good. Kelly had never shut his computer off. It was simply in sleep mode.

"Do you know the password?"

She reached in front of me and typed it in. The screen lit up. The website Kelly had most recently logged onto appeared, a corporate page, all sharp blues and boring text, headed by a single word at the top of the screen: *Abacus.*

I said nothing. I didn't want to let on that I had failed to follow up on the most obvious lead from my own meeting in Monroe County.

"He printed out a number of pages the night before he died," Jody was saying, "but he must have taken the sheets with him."

Too bad.

But a quick scroll through the browser history showed that Kelly had researched and printed out information on Abacus. The website indicated where the company was headquartered, which also explained why Kelly had driven where he did the day he died.

Philadelphia.

CHAPTER 10

LONDON

March 7: 119 days after the election

THE TEAM, FIVE men from five different countries, met in the London boardroom two weeks after the president signed Energy 2020. Every morning, Marcellus' true CEO ate breakfast with his tight circle of executives. It was a working breakfast. He nibbled on thin slices of raw salmon and capers while the lieutenants provided updates and took orders. No food for them. Even over a morning meal, this was a top-down operation.

"How are our pipelines advancing?" the boss asked sternly.

His right hand man, a Swede, answered. "All according to plan. In anticipation of the election, we did much of the pre-work, so we are moving forward quickly."

"When will flow begin?"

"In eight months."

"That is not soon enough. We have already waited years too long. You must speed things up."

"Yes, sir."

The boss shook his head, disappointed he even had to say the words. Intense impatience had been his central management strategy since his first acquisition decades before. Jumping in line. Pushing hard. Cutting corners to get where he needed to go.

"If I displayed your lazy patience, I would still be living in St. Petersburg," he said, glaring at Andersson, then looking at the others. "With nothing."

CHAPTER 11

MONROE COUNTY
February 21, 105 days after the election

"H E WAS HERE one day, alive as can be. Then dead the next. I'm still shaken up by it all." Betty Grooms tried to be friendly, but the trauma showed on her face. I was back in Monroe County, hoping to learn whatever Kelly had, and knew a phone call wouldn't get the job done.

"I can only imagine. What did you guys talk about?"

"It was a lot like our conversation," she said, swinging a finger between herself and me, "but he really was focused on our Abacus machines. He was skeptical."

"From what I can tell, that's why he drove to Philadelphia. Can you say more about the machines?"

"We were thrilled to get the system upgrade a couple years ago, and the commissioners were excited by the savings." She explained that after the county had learned of the new federal requirement to include a paper trail for all electronic voting machines, they conducted an open bid to replace their old systems. The new Abacus system met the specifications and came at the lowest price.

"It wasn't even close."

"Do you know anything more about the company?"

"We've used them for years. In the days of paper ballots, they dominated the industry, but after the Bush-Gore mess, the technology evolved and Abacus fell behind. They lost a lot of accounts, but poorer counties like ours kept them because they were cheaper. Then They made a comeback with the upgraded system. I know a few other counties in Ohio use them as well."

"Which ones?"

"I can't remember all of them, but I know Athens County uses them.

They had the old Abacus machines like we did, then upgraded. I believe Jefferson and Washington picked them up when the new machines came out."

"How can I confirm who uses them?"

"We have to report our equipment to the Secretary of State, so they should have that information for every county."

"And do you have the records from when you purchased these machines?"

"It's all public record. Leave me your card, and I'll send you copies of the entire bid process."

"Thank you. Was there anything else that Congressman Kelly asked you that I haven't?"

"Not much. He thought it was strange that Abacus offered such a low price compared to its competitors. And that they had so many machines in his district. Not just here, but other nearby counties."

On my drive home, I dialed the Ohio Secretary of State's office, and maneuvered through a maddeningly specific automated option menu.

As soon as I wrangled an actual human, I wasted no time. "How can I find out what election equipment each county uses?"

"We update the list before every election, and whenever a county makes a change."

"Can you email me the past ten years of the list?"

"You got it."

"I need it right away. Thank you."

Funny. I felt rushed even though I faced no deadline. And no editor. That hadn't happened in years.

I flipped on the radio to distract myself. A news update focused on President Banfield's signing ceremony for the Energy 2020 legislation earlier that day. Congressman McCarthy had even attended, and he reminded the listeners back home that the bill marked his first vote in Congress.

"I received a ceremonial pen because of my role," he said. "But it was the voters of the Sixth District that made it happen, and now they will receive the benefits."

Minutes after listening to him celebrate, I passed crews working on major pipeline construction right off the road. The work site followed the highway for miles. Apparently some of the companies in the region had predicted the bill was going to pass and had started early. Lucky them. Their bet was paying off.

*   *   *

YOUNGSTOWN

The email I received the next morning contained ten years of data, listing Ohio's 88 counties and the equipment each used. The tables were inscrutable at first, but the Secretary of State's elections specialist walked me through them on the phone.

"So Monroe County used an old Abacus system for eight years," I said, "then replaced it with the new Abacus system for the past two?"

"Yes, sir. You can see right at the bottom of page 2, two-thirds of the way across the page, where that happened."

And as Betty Grooms had recalled, the chart seemed to indicate that Athens County followed the exact same pattern: eight years with the old Abacus, final two with the new.

"Same with Athens County?"

"Looks like it. Top of page 1."

Jefferson and Washington counties, also in Kelly's district, replaced their Diebold systems—Diebold dominated the election equipment industry—with Abacus systems two years ago. In the opposite corner of the state, Wood County, south of Toledo and home to Bowling Green, did the same.

"And this shows Jefferson, Washington, and Wood Counties switching from Diebold to Abacus, right?"

"Sure does."

"I think I can land the plane from here. Thanks for your help."

As I absorbed the rest of the document, several patterns emerged across Ohio's 88 counties.

First, 32 small, rural counties had used the old Abacus systems for the first eight years of the ten-year period. But two years ago, 25 of those counties abandoned Abacus for Diebold or Seiko, the second largest company in the industry. Only seven counties opted for the upgraded Abacus systems. Four of those seven were in eastern Ohio—Athens, Carroll, Noble, and Monroe counties—while another three clustered west and south of Toledo.

Second, almost all other small counties had used Diebold or Seiko machines for the entire ten years. Only a handful switched to Abacus two years ago: Jefferson, Washington, and Wood counties.

Diebold dominated the largest counties. Franklin (home to

Columbus), Summit (Akron), Lucas (Toledo), Mahoning (Youngstown), and Cuyahoga (Cleveland) all used Diebold machines for all ten years.

Which made Hamilton County, home of Cincinnati, the curious exception. Two years ago, Hamilton County had switched from Diebold to Abacus.

*   *   *

To follow up on these initial findings, I exercised some journalistic muscles I hadn't worked out in a long time. Over the years, many of my best scoops came from digging through public records. In the age of emails, public officials routinely forget that almost everything they write, text, type, or jot down is a public record. And all those records must be disclosed.

Of course, members of Congress exempt themselves from this rule, which makes them all the more vulnerable if they later hold a different office. We ended one Ohio Attorney General's career when the A.G. himself, a former congressman, had traded valuable public contracts for campaign donations, leaving a long paper trail through dozens of his own emails.

Elections records would clearly be less scandalous. But a paper trail documenting how county officials chose voting machines might prove helpful nonetheless.

Over half the counties had used the same system for the entire decade, so I set those aside. But for each county that had made a switch in election systems, and for all counties that used Abacus machines, I requested the public records documenting their bidding and decision-making process.

That afternoon, the package from Monroe County arrived. On top of the folder, a handwritten note greeted me: "Here you go. —Betty :)"

The Monroe file documented a small cash-strapped county struggling to meet what it considered an unfunded mandate.

"Our old Abacus system is not in compliance with new federal regulations," Betty Grooms had warned in a memorandum to the Monroe County commissioners. "If we do not upgrade by the deadline, we will face major fines."

Minutes from the commission meetings showed that they understood the need, but expressed deep concern about the cost. But they proceeded despite their complaining. As with all unfunded mandates, they had no choice.

Abacus, Diebold, and Seiko all submitted bids to do the county's election work. All three proposed similar technologies—touch screen voting, a verifiable paper trail, and other security bells and whistles. Abacus' upgraded system satisfied all the criteria, but the real difference was its far lower cost.

It wasn't a close call. The memo recommending Abacus touted tens of thousands of dollars in savings while ensuring a smooth transition. When the commissioners made the purchase, the savings allowed them to add a corrections officer back to the jail staff. Documents showed that the new system arrived late in the fall, easily in time for the next year's primary. And it was in place for the November election that followed, when Kelly lost Monroe County.

The other counties' responses arrived over the next week. The six other counties that kept Abacus had pursued the same course as Monroe. Each had asked for bids, and Abacus had offered its new system at a far lower cost. Game over. Then there were the three counties—Wood, Washington, and Jefferson—that had started with Diebold machines and switched to Abacus. Documents showed that Abacus had reached out proactively to promote its new technology, then had fought aggressively for the accounts. They offered one-time credits, free technical support, and other frills to convince the counties to make the change. Abacus went on to win the bid in each county.

But that's where, oddly, the Abacus aggression had ended.

I first noticed it when reviewing Adams County, a small county east of Cincinnati. Adams had used Abacus for years. Facing the same need for an upgrade that Monroe did, the county invited bids. Diebold and Seiko submitted theirs as usual. But that was it. No proposal from Abacus. And Diebold went on to grab the business.

Adams County turned out to be the rule, not the exception. In the 25 counties that replaced their old Abacus systems with either a Diebold or Seiko system, Abacus had failed to respond at all. No aggressive pitch, no cutthroat pricing. And its rivals won the day.

And then there was the oddest case of all.

Like every other large county, Hamilton County had used Diebold for years, so it didn't need an upgrade. But the county sought bids anyway. What prompted the process was an all-out sales pitch from Abacus, something it had not done in any of Ohio's other large urban counties. This time, Diebold took the threat from Abacus seriously. Ohio's third largest county operated more than a thousand machines, so the company fought to keep the account far more aggressively than it had elsewhere. Instead of its small-county price of $3,500 per machine, Diebold offered Hamilton County a price of $2,600 per machine, below Abacus' price. And as the incumbent vendor, Diebold offered lower transition costs.

Still, the county chose Abacus, ignoring the extra cost. And one man had made it happen.

From the moment the discussion began, Elections Administration Director Brett Fusco advocated relentlessly for the switch. "Diebold machines have exhibited numerous problems in recent elections," one memo explained, detailing delays, breakdowns, and long lines at polling locations. "In the past two presidential campaigns, major snafus have embarrassed the County," he concluded. According to Fusco, Diebold had broken its promises to fix the mess. "Even worse," he wrote, "the County is being nickel-and-dimed every time we have to make technical fixes to the system." When Diebold's price point came in under Abacus', Fusco implored his bosses to select Abacus anyway. Despite some heartburn about the extra cost, Hamilton County ultimately selected Abacus.

After poring over this pile of documents, I reached out to the counties that didn't switch from Diebold or Seiko. They confirmed my hunch that Abacus had never approached any of them.

So that was it. Of 88 counties, all but Hamilton County had selected the lowest bidder. Perfectly reasonable, responsible behavior. County leaders were fulfilling their duties at the lowest price possible.

But what was Abacus up to?

On the surface, its sales plan didn't look reasonable at all. In eleven counties, the company pulled out every stop to win. But in 77 other counties, Abacus abandoned the field entirely, allowing its competitors to secure account after account without so much as a proposal.

But a quick look at Ohio's congressional map showed that what made no sense as a business matter made all the sense in the world on another plane.

Abacus was playing politics.

In picking eastern Ohio, northwest Ohio, and the odd beachhead in Cincinnati, Abacus had clustered its machines in three congressional districts. But not just any districts—the only three in Ohio where close elections took place.

Abacus targeted Ohio's only swing districts just in time for the next year's election.

CHAPTER 12

SIBERIA

Six years before the election

THE TALL, WIRY figure stepped out of the black jet, walked across the snow-blown runway, and climbed into the passenger seat of a brand new Mercedes van.

"Such a desolate place," Oleg Kazarov said to the van's driver as they exited the tiny airport grounds. "Incredible to think any life exists here at all, let alone such a vast fortune."

While he rarely traveled, Kazarov wanted to see his burgeoning operation in person. So he had flown seven hours to this tiny airstrip in western Siberia and now set off for Siberneft headquarters. The road was basically straight, although the two-hour drive didn't feel that way as Yuri, his driver, navigated around an endless parade of potholes and ditches. The trek offered little to see but gray tundra and frozen marsh, with the occasional deer and caribou grazing near the road.

As bleak as the country was, Kazarov was proudest of this latest addition to his portfolio. If his initial conquests in the Urals and Central Russia had come from a mix of salesmanship, speed, and occasional brute force, this latest success stemmed entirely from Kazarov's engineering background.

For years, he had preached the same mantra to his team: *Innovation.*

Every innovation, every efficiency, every breakthrough meant finding energy where others hadn't. Finding it where others weren't even looking. It meant more gas drilled, sold, and delivered. It meant less waste. And all of this together would drive his success in the very competitive West. It was here, in what many considered the most miserable place on Earth, that Kazarov's obsession was paying off the most.

When Kazarov had first expanded into western Siberia, his company, Siberneft, discovered an oil-rich formation of shale rock more than a mile under the surface, below traditional oil wells that had been tapped for decades. The deep formation stretched across hundreds of millions of acres, but, trapped within the shale rock, was hard to access.

Unlike his predecessors, Kazarov did not walk away. Instead, Siberneft quietly experimented with an old drilling technique called hydraulic fracturing, or "fracking," which involved drilling accompanied by the forceful injection of huge volumes of water laced with a cocktail of chemicals and other materials, such as sand, to blast apart the shale and capture the oil and gas trapped within. Energy companies had conducted "vertical fracking" for decades, but the technique didn't work when a shale formation lay miles deep, as in western Siberia. Drilling deep vertical wells to access a thin layer of shale—often less than 100 feet—just didn't add up. Too many wells, too deep, too expensive, too little return on an enormous investment.

The massive Siberian shale formation required a new approach: the ability to drill through the acres of rock horizontally. So Kazarov's engineers went to work. After several years, they'd succeeded, designing a system where a single vertical well could generate numerous miles-long horizontal drilling wells in multiple directions. Once perfected, the new process produced immediate results. The company kept the breakthrough to itself and rapidly acquired as much land as possible in western Siberia.

"I've never seen anything like it. Far below barren wells, we are producing millions of cubic feet of gas per day," Yuri, Siberneft's chief of operations and today's driver, explained to his boss. "And with the new pipeline, we are now able to ship it both west and east."

"That is progress," said Kazarov. "From a dead land, we have built an empire."

More than two hours after leaving the airport, they reached the smoothest section of road of the entire trip. The two miles of new asphalt brought them to an immaculate off-white three-story building. But as they pulled up, the striking edifice was not what caught Kazarov's eye. Behind the building, as far as he could see in any direction, hundreds of silver wells jutted out from the frozen tundra.

Kazarov leaped out of the van, faced the wells, and turned his head slightly, right ear forward. His good ear. Above the howl of the wind, a low humming sounded. A faint smile passed over his face. Kazarov walked briskly into the building. Yuri jogged to catch up to him, then escorted him up one flight of stairs into a conference room. Six men quickly took their seats, and Kazarov sat down at the head of the table. Only Yuri remained standing

"Congratulations on your success, *tovarischi*. Yuri, tell me about our Western plan."

"Sir, the exciting news is that we have located an area in America with similar advantages to here."

Yuri looked down at a bearded, dark-skinned man seated to his right. "*Davai*."

Clearly nervous, the man fumbled around as he unrolled a large, rough map of the eastern United States across the marble table. In addition to the outlines of the states themselves, a shaded area spanned much of New York, Pennsylvania, Ohio, and West Virginia.

Yuri leaned over the table, removed a pen from his pocket, and pointed to the boundary where Ohio and Pennsylvania abutted each other. "American geologists have long known that vast amounts of natural gas, oil, and other chemicals are trapped in a shale formation a mile below this area. It is called the Marcellus formation."

"Mar-sall-oos?" Proud of his English, Kazarov was a stickler for getting his pronunciation right.

"Mar-*sell*-us."

"Mar-sell-us. Thank you. Please proceed."

"But like here, the depth of the formation made it economically impossible to drill there. The Americans long ago abandoned it."

"Our technology will work there, correct?"

"We have concluded that it will."

"How significant is the potential of this area?"

"Enormous. It spans more than 100,000 square miles."

Kazarov smiled broadly.

"And unlike here, Marcellus' location is strategically perfect."

Yuri nodded, pointing his pen to New York.

"That is the key. It is only hundreds of miles from New England and New York, and not much further from Chicago. About half of the U.S. population resides within 600 miles of the site."

Kazarov nodded his head slowly, taking in the good news.

"And close to major seaports as well."

"Yes. New York. New Jersey. Baltimore. But the region also sits right on the Ohio River, which flows into the Mississippi and then to New Orleans."

He traced his pen along the boundaries of Ohio and Kentucky as he spoke.

"How will our work be greeted?" Kazarov asked. Recent forays into Europe had met fierce resistance, costing him millions in bribes to move things forward.

"These are traditional mining communities that have struggled in recent decades. They will appreciate a new economic vision, especially when we adopt our generous approach."

Kazarov stood up, looking again at the map. He eyed eastern Ohio and Pennsylvania. Glanced east to the coast. West toward Chicago. Didn't say a word. Neither did the others, who only stared at their boss.

Then he cast a mischievous grin, pointing his pen at a spot back in Pennsylvania close to Lake Erie.

"What is there?" Yuri asked.

"Somewhere near there is a small city named Titusville. It is where Americans first discovered oil."

He paused, then pointed a long, thin finger at the top-right corner of Ohio.

"And this is where Mr. Rockefeller built his oil empire. Now we will unleash an energy boom back where it all began."

CHAPTER 13

YOUNGSTOWN—CINCINNATI

March 6: 118 days after the election

"TUCKER DIDN'T EVEN break a sweat," the veteran political reporter of the *Toledo Blade* told me. "He never does."

A surprising assessment, since Democrat Dwight Tucker's Eleventh District actually leans Republican. Encompassing a portion of Toledo and Lucas County, the Eleventh reaches west and south to encompass rural, conservative counties all the way to the Indiana border. Despite the strong Democratic leanings in Toledo and its suburbs, President Banfield won it both times.

Congressman Tucker did almost nothing in Congress, but he was legendary for providing the most responsive constituent services on Capitol Hill. Social Security, veterans' services, a Pell Grant, a Naval Academy recommendation, a streetlight—no service was too small. And once completed, Tucker himself penned a handwritten note memorializing each act of service. The congressman firmly believed that in his toss-up district and amid the chaos of national politics, constituent service was the best way to stay in office. Despite a few scares, his approach never failed. He had long fascinated me, but what now piqued my interest was that all four Northwest Ohio counties where Abacus had placed its machines were in Tucker's district.

But Tucker's election could not have differed more from Kelly's loss. The Republicans had recruited an opponent who initially looked to be tough and talented, and key Republican leaders had visited repeatedly. But thanks to Tucker's popularity and his opponent's late-breaking tax scandal, Tucker waltzed to a fourteen-point win.

On the other hand, Hamilton County, home to Ohio's First District, offered unexpected drama last November. Ella Smathers was expected to win the district on Ohio's southwest corner. It was a balanced district, but over her six terms, she'd always struck that balance well. She forcefully championed populist economics that appealed to the urban voters of Cincinnati, while her pro-life stance earned support in the county's heavily Catholic suburbs. Still, in a blow rivaling Kelly's upset , Pete Warner, a little-known township trustee, toppled her 52 to 48 percent.

Hamilton County stuck out in another way. Not only had it replaced another vendor with Abacus, but it had paid more to do so.

So I made the trek to the Queen City to interview the man who'd made it happen. The five-hour drive down the interstate—by the manufacturing hubs of Youngstown and Akron, past the lush fields and small towns of Central and Southern Ohio, amid the sparkling skylines of Columbus and Cincinnati—reminded me of something John Glenn used to say: if you shrink all of America into one state, you get Ohio. Which also reminded me why I'd stuck with the Buckeye state through thick and thin.

My destination, the Hamilton County Board of Elections, felt like a Fortune 500 headquarters compared to Monroe County's office. A woman greeted me as I entered the third-floor lobby from the elevator.

HAMILTON

"How may I help you, sir?"

She spoke with a slight Southern twang. Same state, different accent. She was far more serious than Grooms had been.

"I'd like to talk to Brett Fusco."

Her mouth opened slightly, but she didn't say a word. Instead, she called her supervisor, who soon emerged from an office in the back.

"What do you need help on?" the supervisor asked warily.

"I'm interested in talking to Mr. Fusco about the decision to switch voting machines."

"You'll have to talk to our interim elections administrator," she said. "Saddest thing. Brett died in a car accident several years ago."

CHAPTER 14

"W HAT IS THE problem, gentlemen?" Kazarov puffed his third cigarette of the morning.

Liam Andersson sat across from him. The 57-year-old Swede was a first-rate engineer and a slick salesman, and had been at Kazarov's side since they'd met in the hinterlands of Russia decades before. A monitor on the wall displayed a third man, the newest member of the team—an American. Both their faces froze at the tone of the boss's question. An awkward silence followed.

"Gentlemen?"

Finally, Andersson weighed in. "We still cannot get the gas out of the region. The bottleneck is extreme."

"We have discussed this," Kazarov said impatiently. "We will build the pipelines. Simple."

"It is not that simple, Mr. Kazarov."

Until several months ago, Kazarov's American rollout had been proceeding smoothly. As he always did, Kazarov had entered the Midwest quietly. He filed the paperwork establishing Marcellus Enterprises as a new private Ohio corporation, concealing his role. Doing so kept down the price of almost anything he would need to purchase while also keeping his competition in the dark.

He then recruited home-grown employees to populate the company's top echelons and plucked Michael Chambers from a dead-end career at Shell Oil. Chambers did not possess all the skills necessary to lead the new operation, but Kazarov didn't need him to. All Kazarov needed was a résumé and appearance that gave a credible face to the operation. American politicians would never turn over the vast natural riches of their Midwest to a Russian, particularly one who looked and sounded as foreign as Kazarov did.

As expected, initial tests found robust gas reserves throughout the region and confirmed that their Siberian fracking technology could access it. Marcellus signed leases everywhere they could. Soon, the company controlled millions of acres on both sides of the Ohio River.

When the wells began to flow, the sleepy slice of Appalachia exploded in gas, oil, and money. Farmers who had toiled on their land for years with little to show for it emerged as millionaires almost overnight. Vendors and contractors put more people to work. And as they started to spend more money, the secondary benefits of the boom put dollars in the pockets of retailers and restaurants, motels and malls. The region saw its first economic momentum since the height of coal. And unlike his competitors, Kazarov shared the growth broadly, maximizing the number of people on the ground who felt a stake in his success.

With all the new economic activity, government tax revenues soared. And those dollars were immediately needed. The region's dated infrastructure was overwhelmed. Counties found themselves under the gun to construct new roads, new housing, and new sewer and water systems. Local and state officials did all they could to alleviate the glut, doling out contracts with their newly-found resources.

But the most pressing need was one those local governments couldn't address: transporting enormous volumes of natural gas out of the region to big population centers and global markets.

"Why is there a problem with the pipelines? It is a simple plan. Nothing as complicated as Siberia, or even Ukraine."

Four months before, Kazarov had signed off on his engineers' recommendation to build three pipelines out of the region—to New York, to Maryland, and to New Orleans.

"The design and construction of the pipelines are not an issue. You are right. That part is simple."

"Then what is the problem?"

"Bureaucracy. America has a vast array of regulations at many levels. Our lawyers warn that the approvals required for these pipelines will take years if we follow the standard procedures."

"We do not have years to waste," Kazarov said, waving his right hand.

"We do not," Andersson affirmed. "To avoid delay, we must take the plan to the highest levels of American government for a single approval that circumvents the others. It is the only way it can happen."

"Then that is what we will do."

CHAPTER 15

CINCINNATI

March 6: 118 days after the election

A FTER THE INTERIM administrator of the Hamilton County Board of Elections filled me in on Brett Fusco's sad demise, he gave me ten minutes to ask my questions.

"Can you walk me through the thought process of switching to Abacus machines?"

"I really can't. That was Brett's recommendation, and the board went along with it."

"Despite the higher price?"

"Yep. Brett hated the quality of Diebold's work, and that settled it. No one wanted to be embarrassed during a national election. They sucked it up and paid more for the new system."

"What was wrong with the Diebold machines?"

"Again, that was Brett's thing. I can let you look at his files if you want. They're all public record."

Perfect. My pestering had paid off. I set up shop in a small conference room and looked through boxes of materials that documented the switch in vendors. What stuck out immediately was that Fusco had been lying. Several years of after-election reports described no serious issues with the Diebold machines. A power outage had caused delays in one primary. Poorly trained poll workers once tossed ballots incorrectly. There were disputes over provisional ballots and other issues. But there was no flaw with the machines themselves. Correspondence with Diebold covered many items, but never indicated that the county, or even Fusco, had complained about technical issues. Clearly valuing the account, Diebold had proactively sought feedback time and again, and nothing negative had emerged. One Fusco memorandum to Diebold said it all: "Problems have been minimal, and whenever we have needed your help, your team has been incredibly responsive."

After scouring for hours, I reached the only plausible conclusion: Brett Fusco had fabricated the Diebold problems. Having uncovered rigged public bids over the years, I'd seen this before—an anonymous official well positioned to switch out an incumbent vendor. No doubt a generous kickback had driven Fusco's single-minded effort to replace Diebold with Abacus.

Before leaving, I dug up what I could on Fusco's death. A single car wreck on I-74, heading to Indianapolis. Sounded familiar. The obituary summed up Fusco's uneventful tenure as a party activist and suburban council member followed by his six-year tenure at the board of elections. The story was short, buried at the bottom of the obituary page. Amazing. If a Cincinnati Red died in an accident, it'd be on the front page of the paper. But the man who runs Cincinnati's elections barely merits a mention.

* * *

On the long drive home, I checked in with Mary Andres, my editor, finally filling her in on what I was pursuing. Partly to get her perspective, partly to keep her off my back.

"Glad you're working on something, Jack. But that's a wild theory. Are you sure about it?"

"No, that's the problem. It all could add up to absolutely nothing. A small-county chair with a kooky conspiracy theory. A couple car accidents."

"Right," she said. "And a struggling company trying to regain lost business wherever it could, even paying people off. That happens. It doesn't mean anyone was stealing elections."

"But here's what worries me: If this is something, if the dots do connect, they only would do so on a grand scale."

"What do you mean?"

"There's no point in ousting two members of Congress, and only two, in a single state. Especially when those members, and their districts, have so little in common. This only makes sense if it's part of a far bigger strategy. A national one."

"True. But who could pull something like that off?"

"Who knows? Either this is nothing or it's something big. There's no in between, and that's what worries me."

I paused, hoping for a positive response.

"Fine. But don't waste a lot of time on this. Lots to cover back here."

With that spirited vote of confidence, we hung up.

Scott called ten minutes later, not in a good mood.

"The election's well over, Dad. What's keeping you now?"

"Scott, I'm wrapping up some loose ends on something. Shouldn't be long." I wanted to tell him I was onto something big, but held back. It would sound like an exaggeration and only make the conversation worse.

After a long pause, he spoke again, resignation in his voice. "Dad, Jana's pregnant. We've known for two months, and wanted to tell you in person, but whatever those loose ends are got in the way."

Nice job, I told myself. Way to blow this once-in-a-lifetime father-son conversation. "Scott," I said carefully. "That's amazing news. Couldn't be happier for you."

"Thanks, Dad. We'll talk about it more when you're out here."

And on that note, the call ended.

I pounded the steering wheel, certain that Roxanne had probably known for weeks.

Those two phone calls summed up my life. My editor and my son—the harder I worked to please one, the less happy the other was. I was striking a perfect balance because at this point neither was impressed.

*   *   *

YOUNGSTOWN

The three Ohio districts where Abacus placed its machines had one thing in common: they were swing districts. Indeed, they were the only swing districts in the state. The Northwest Ohio district may not have experienced a close election in November, but it was a 52 to 48 percent district, with slightly more Republicans than Democrats. Tucker's unique presence masked its toss-up status.

So the next morning, starting with these three, I searched for the 40 closest "toss-up" districts in the country. Then I called them all.

The Fifth District of Illinois comprised eight counties. I dialed the elections administrator of Peoria County, the largest county in the district.

"My name is Jack Sharpe. I'm a reporter from Youngstown, Ohio."

"The *Vindicator*, right?" said the voice on the other end. "I grew up in Cleveland. How can I help you?"

"I'm looking to see what voting machines you use for your elections."

"Like most people around here, we use the latest Abacus system. Upgraded it last year. It's a better system and much cheaper."

"Thank you very much."

I called the other seven counties of the district. Five of them used Abacus machines. The two smallest used Diebold machines.

In Colorado's Tenth, Abacus was also in five out of seven counties. In Oklahoma's Third, four out of five. Same pattern in Wisconsin and in Missouri's two swing districts.

And on down the list. Abacus. Abacus. Abacus.

Forty districts. The nation's true toss-ups. The ones that would determine the shape and direction of our nation's government. In 35, Abacus had sold its machines to almost every county.

CHAPTER 16

34 months before the election

OLIVER ARIENS III had been in meetings like this before. The cigar-smoking, big-bellied uber-lobbyist tilted back in his chair, facing the Russian billionaire across the rectangular marble table. Oleg Kazarov had flown in from London, partly to hear the plan, partly, Ariens knew, to size him up. Kazarov's silent entrance had been anything but friendly, but Ariens didn't let that change his tone.

"Welcome, Mr. Kazarov," Ariens said loudly, breaking the ice with his New Orleans drawl. "We are honored that you have chosen us to work on a project of this importance."

A translator behind Kazarov whispered in his ear. Kazarov nodded and managed the slightest trace of a grin.

"Let us present our plan to move forward," Ariens said, motioning at a screen behind him. A slide displayed the words "Energy 2020" in bold letters, with a small translation underneath. Ariens gestured to the associate to his left, who walked through a few slides outlining the technical details and maps for the three pipelines. After a minute, Kazarov muttered something to his translator. He crushed the end of his cigarette directly on the desk and immediately lit another.

"Gentlemen, Mr. Kazarov did not fly to America to hear things he already knows," the translator interrupted gruffly. "Please move on to the political plan."

Ariens jerked forward in his chair and clicked through eight more slides until the screen read, "The Plan: Energy 2020."

"Here in America, there is a hunger for jobs, for energy independence, for a return to our own greatness, just as there has been that hunger in Russia," Ariens explained. "We believe that the best opportunity to move forward on your project is to tap into that desire. To turn this project into an enormous political winner for all those who support it. And we are confident we can do this from the highest level of American politics."

Kazarov placed his hand under his chin. For the first time, the Russian appeared interested.

"This will not be about three pipelines that benefit one company. It will be a plan that secures America because it secures America's energy future."

Kazarov said nothing.

"We call it Energy 2020. Each pipeline will be named after the primary state it passes through. The Buckeye Line, the Terrapin Line, the Empire Line."

He pronounced each name slowly, then explained the origins one by one.

Kazarov nodded.

"Politicians will now have a way to create jobs, to lower the cost of gas, to compete against Middle East countries Americans distrust and dislike."

The Russian nodded again.

"Top leaders of the Republican Party, both in the White House and on Capitol Hill, share a strong interest in this project. If you approve, the president will propose it in her next State of the Union, making it a centerpiece of her re-election campaign as well as of her second term. And the Senate will usher it through."

Kazarov whispered to the translator, who then asked, "And the lower house?"

"The House of Representatives is more difficult, but there are some Democrats that will have a political interest in breaking from their leadership. Then the president will sign the bill, and we will build the pipelines."

The Democratic House would be more challenging than that, but why put a damper on the presentation with that inconvenient detail?

Kazarov nodded slowly as he took in the presentation. He never lit another cigarette. The interruptions ended.

Soon Ariens concluded: "We are confident that this plan will allow us to get the pipelines started within a year."

Before the translator even began speaking, Kazarov leaned forward and said, in near-perfect English, with only a trace of an accent, "Let's hope it's in six months. Thank you for your excellent strategy."

A knowing grin spread across his face.

*   *   *

The strategy behind Energy 2020 was classic Oliver Ariens. Consecutive careers as a lawyer, a congressman, and a lobbyist had merged into a unique approach that worked wonders for his clients.

From a prominent New Orleans family, Ariens III, like Jr. before him, had attended both Harvard and Harvard Law School. With his sterling grades and connections, he snagged a prestigious clerkship with Supreme Court Justice Rehnquist. His friends and colleagues were surprised when, after his Rehnquist year, he turned down offers from the best D.C. and New York firms to return to New Orleans.

But Ariens didn't plan to stay long.

His clerkship had given him a unique perch from which to watch the most accomplished lawyers in America jousting at the highest level, and it had altered his aspiration to join their ranks. Although intellectually interesting, arguing the nuances of law didn't energize him. Nor did the thought of spending his life serving the interests of someone else. The real action in D.C. was the practice of politics. The lawyers were just the hired help. So he returned to his hometown with a simple goal—to get himself elected to Congress. Ariens established himself as the brightest young lawyer at the best firm in the Crescent City. Eight years later, after the retirement of a long-time incumbent, Ariens outfoxed every other young political wannabe in the district to become a congressman.

Then his career took another turn. Just as clerking at the Supreme Court had dissuaded him from a career as a lawyer, a few terms in the House of Representatives squelched his political ambitions. He could count on one hand the colleagues whose company he enjoyed. The work of getting elected and re-elected included dozens of daily calls begging for $1,000 checks, flights to and from the District at least once a week, dozens of steak fries pleading for votes. The debates in committees and the floor of the House were downright mind-numbing. All predictable, shallow rhetoric. Far from the sophisticated jousting of the Harvard Debate Club or the Law School's Moot Court. It all felt beneath him.

But during his brief Capitol Hill tenure Ariens had detected a lucrative business opportunity. He had worked with many lobbyists during his time on the Hill. An unimpressive lot, accustomed to pushing unpopular ideas, their instinct was to do everything behind closed doors. Add an earmark here. Slip in a rider there. Hope the media never finds out. Together, the lobbyists were a flock of non-politicians looking to sneak controversial items into law when no one was watching.

Thanks to his time in office, Ariens believed that almost any issue could be spun to a political advantage. Each cause, however controversial, could be framed to be highly popular. Label the inheritance tax the "death tax" and before you know it, the people want to eliminate it. Erode air quality with an industry-sponsored bill, but call it the Clear Skies Act and tout it as an improvement. Go on offense, frame issues early, boldly get big things done. Don't hide in the shadows as if you're up to no good.

So Ariens resigned from Congress to put this strategy to work. He started his own boutique lobbying firm, the first of its kind to combine poll-tested public relations strategies with high-energy lobbying.

His approach worked wonders. He turned unpopular causes into politically favored and lucrative ones. When Ariens quarterbacked a project, members of Congress raked in contributions by supporting issues that also garnered votes back home. All while his clients made millions. He called it his triple bottom line.

Ariens succeeded in opening up national parks to drilling and foresting. Technology companies successfully pushed legislation that allowed them to market and sell private data. Airlines and cruise ships, banks and mortgage companies joined his long list of clients.

A few decades of turning political lemons into lemonade had made Ariens the most respected lobbyist in Washington.

So he wasn't surprised when Marcellus Enterprises called. This assignment fell right into his wheelhouse. Still, the plan he laid out was not as rosy as he let on. One formidable woman would stand in his way.

*   *   *

WASHINGTON, DC

"We will no longer sit on our hands as Middle East tyrants bilk us for the resources that fuel our economy while bankrolling their bombs," the president bellowed as her speech climaxed in its 41st minute.

"I call our plan Energy 2020. It will assure jobs, energy independence, and lower gas prices. We can't wait for government bureaucracy. It's time to get it done!"

Ariens knew it was coming. He'd spent hours crafting every word she now spoke. But he still vaulted out of his seat and applauded loudly. He had ghostwritten lines for three different presidents. But the State of the Union? In the president's final moment before the re-election campaign? This was a new thrill.

Thanks to his old friend Tom Stanton, Ariens watched from his usual spot in the balcony, behind and to the right of the president. As a congressman, Ariens had enjoyed the grandeur of the House floor, looking up at the president, but as a lobbyist this seat provided the perfect vantage point. Up high, facing the 535 members of Congress, his entire chess board was in view. He already knew what the president was going to say, so it was the members' reaction that mattered most. Her announcement of the energy initiative inspired the loudest ovation of the night, but the room was split. Half the room leapt to their feet and applauded wildly. The rest, Democrats, sat quietly, taking their cue from House Speaker Sandra Williams, who sat right behind the president. Even moderate Democrats whose votes he would need kept their hands on their laps. The mixed reaction said it all. The president had launched a polarizing political fight in an election year.

About an hour after the speech, Ariens and his top staff assembled in their K Street office. Staff stationed throughout Capitol Hill dialed into the conference line.

"The launch was perfect," Ariens said. "The proposal was the news of the night, delivered from the highest platform in politics. But you guys saw the reaction. This is gonna be a fight!"

The next morning, Senate and House leaders launched coordinated cable and weekend news appearances. Ariens rolled out high-profile endorsements, along with talking points attacking Democrats as job-killers. Poll numbers on the project started at over 50 percent, and the onslaught of free media vaulted them to 71 percent approval.

Then they unleashed a good cop-bad cop strategy targeting individual members of Congress. Law firms, lobbyists, and PACs with interests in Energy 2020 sprayed cash across the Congress. "Independent" television ads aired in districts around the country two weeks later, attacking those against the plan and urging viewers to call their offices.

When Banfield walked out of the Capitol the night of her State of the Union, 56 senators already stood with her. Within a month, that number had climbed to 64. Only East Coast and West Coast Democrats stood on the other side.

In the House, Ariens locked in every Republican from the outset. Three Democrats from Midwestern districts also supported the plan. His team's efforts coaxed a few more over in the ensuing six weeks. But then they ran into a brick wall. A more robust wall than even he had expected.

Of course Democrats from the fracking region would vote their way. They and House leadership would not knowingly sacrifice their seats in the upcoming election. Ariens had been confident that other moderate Democrats, solid energy supporters in the past, would get on board, too. But Speaker Sandra Williams got to them first.

Ariens had known that Williams would mount a fierce defense. Her history guaranteed it. She'd started her unconventional career as a stay-at-home mom who had stopped a waste dump from opening in her Portland, Oregon neighborhood. The ferocity of that effort had propelled her to Congress, where she had risen steadily through the caucus ranks to emerge as the Speaker of the House. She had remained firmly in that position for a decade. And if there was one fight from which she would not relent, it was the fight to protect the environment.

Now her defense took hold. One by one, reliable pro-energy Democrats who Ariens was counting on indicated that they couldn't support the 2020 plan. Representatives who had voted for offshore drilling, Arctic drilling, park drilling, and other pro-energy legislation were saying no this time.

Each of these members had taken thousands of dollars from energy industry PACs, from Ariens, and from the lobbyists and lawyers he associated with. They had been happy to gobble up dollars from supporters of Energy 2020.

But when it came to voting for Energy 2020, they didn't budge.

CHAPTER 17

YOUNGSTOWN

March 8: 120 days after the election

THIRTY-FIVE SWING DISTRICTS, all under Abacus control. Not a coincidence. And clearly a national story. But also a dangerous one. Two people with knowledge of the plan had died under similar circumstances. As in most tales of corruption, the sole possessor of such highly valued information has a target on his back.

It was time to get my story out as quickly as possible, so I spent all day typing the first draft.

Monroe County —Since Congressman Lee Kelly lost his re-election bid last November, Democrats in Monroe County have cried foul.

Kelly's election isn't the only one under scrutiny. Across the country, surprising upsets also led to questions from many insiders. And now, an in-depth investigation by the Youngstown Vindicator *has found that the same voting equipment company was involved in virtually every district where the races were closely contested.*

And on it went. It was my longest story in years, guiding the reader through the irregular results in the "Abacus districts."

"Jack, we can't print this!" barked Mary Andres after reading the draft. "People will think we've lost our minds. We'll lose our shirt in the lawsuits."

"Everything I've written is an absolute fact. Double- and triple-checked."

"I believe you, but you still leave far too much unanswered. You can't make allegations like these without locking down everything. Where are comments from Abacus? From members of Congress? And how exactly do you think Abacus changed the results of the election? Hell, what is Abacus in the first place?"

Valid questions. Harder to answer than she was suggesting, but definitely legit ones to ask, and I'd seen them coming. But I'd wanted to get her a draft, even an imperfect one, in order to temporarily get her off my back. And sure enough, she wasn't telling me to back off the story. Instead, she was raising the same questions I now planned to chase down answers to.

The easiest one was how, technically, Abacus had pulled it off. For that, I called the best political mind I knew.

* * *

COLUMBUS

"Thanks for meeting on such short notice, Renee. I need your help on a project."

At a packed coffee shop on the Ohio State campus, Renee Fowler and I stuck out in a sea of scarlet and gray Buckeye sweatshirts, jackets, and hats. A late winter storm had swept through central Ohio the day before.

"So I gather." Renee smiled warmly at me from behind her glasses and tucked a wisp of brown hair behind her ear. This wouldn't be the first time I'd asked her out of the blue to explain an entire concept to me in a mere half hour. With her PhD from MIT and years running analytics for national campaigns before becoming a professor, she was a political whiz like no other.

"What's up?" she asked gamely.

"You're going to think I'm nuts, but I honestly believe I've stumbled across a vote-stealing scheme that changed the outcome in numerous congressional districts last November. Might have even flipped the majority."

"I would say you're nuts," she said, "but I've always thought it wouldn't be hard to do. A bunch of us eggheads have been publishing articles for years pointing out the security weaknesses with these electronic voting machines. Only paper ballots that the voter herself fills out are safe these days, whether they're done in person or mailed in."

"What about the visible paper trail that voters can look at? The machines here had those."

"Definitely better than no paper trails at all, but still a host of problems. The right engineer could figure out how to manipulate them. And most states don't audit those paper results anyway."

"Good! I mean that's all bad, but I was worried you were going to laugh me out of here. I could use your help."

I walked through the basics, starting with Monroe County. No one knew better than Renee the particulars of each county.

"Yep. That was a stunner that Monroe County didn't vote for Kelly."

"What I need to find are any telltales of exactly how Abacus pulled it off. My editors think the story is still too speculative." I handed her the list of the counties and districts where Abacus located machines, talking her through many of them. She would do the rest.

"The data won't lie," she said confidently. "If these counties experienced rigged results, and all other counties and districts didn't, there will be some statistical evidence of it."

"That's exactly what I hoped you'd say."

CHAPTER 18

30 months before the election

"WHO PAYS A toll when the gate is already up?" Kazarov fumed.

Oliver Ariens, wolfing down breakfast in Kazarov's London office, looked up from his salmon, dumbstruck.

"Excuse me?"

"Why must I give money to those who already agree with us? Who are not standing in the way?"

"That is what they expect. Not doing so would be viewed as an insult, and we would risk losing their support."

"In Russia and most countries," Kazarov said coldly, "when you pay to remove a roadblock, the roadblock goes away. The politician keeps his promise. Not doing so would be viewed as deeply dishonorable, risking one's reputation and safety. But in America, the politicians happily take our money yet still stand in the way. So deeply dishonest."

"The dollars help, but they're not a guarantee," Ariens said.

"So I pay those politicians who already agree with me. And then I pay those who stand in the way, but they remain in the way. Your American system has no honor."

Ariens sat silently.

"So rather than sending my money through a maze of campaign donations, I will pay them directly. Surely that will get us what we want."

Ariens shook his head forcefully. "Bribing American officials is not only illegal, it is aggressively enforced. It's not acceptable in the culture of Washington, nor is it necessary. Campaign funds are the currency that matters to them—the measure of power in Washington. If you shower campaign cash on the Washington politicians, you will get your way. Most of the time."

"Mr. Ariens, I am certainly not getting my way in this instance."

"Let's be patient. President Banfield is campaigning hard on the issue. As we enter summer and fall, the political pressure should allow us to gain supporters and to defeat those who stand in the way."

CHAPTER 19

COLUMBUS

March 20: 132 days after the election

"I'M STUMPED."

A week after our first meeting, Renee Fowler called me sounding dispirited. She had looked at all 435 House district results from the prior election, comparing them to one another and to prior years. Trying to show that the outcome in Abacus districts differed from the rest in a statistically significant way.

But she had turned up nothing.

"Comparing districts, apples to apples, is proving next to impossible," she explained over the phone.

"So many factors differ across districts—the overall competitiveness of each race, the individual contours of each race, who else and what else appeared on the ballot in that district. All those factors impact the turnout and vote totals of each district in different ways. Trying to make a meaningful comparison is leading me nowhere."

Not good. I needed her to find something.

Second, she explained, it wasn't a statistical shock that many Democratic incumbents had lost, even if they had fared well in prior years. "Yes, she said, "one would have expected Democrats to actually do better in this cycle, two years after a Republican president. But a popular president sat atop Washington, and with Tom Stanton you had a Minority Whip who effectively framed the Democrats in the House as obstructionists. Maybe his spirited effort overcame the usual disadvantage?"

"Okay," I said wearily. "Well—"

"No, there's more," Renee said. The third problem was that in the closest 35 districts, it didn't take much to change the outcome of the election. "This makes it far harder to prove that something was amiss."

Finally, Fowler explained that the Abacus districts had experienced a variety of results. While Democrats had lost in most, they had held on to win in others. So across all 35 Abacus districts, it was hard to draw any firm conclusions about how Abacus had affected the outcome.

"I hate to say it, but I'm not getting anywhere at this point."

We hung up. If she couldn't figure it out, no one could. And without that proof, the story would die.

CHAPTER 20

"YOU WERE WRONG, but I don't blame you," Kazarov said over the phone to Ariens, two days after the President had easily won a second term. "It is your dishonorable politicians and your broken political system that are to blame."

While the president had cruised to victory, the makeup of the gerrymandered House had hardly changed. Two retirements and a scandal had cost Democrats three seats. A scandal on the other side had led to a Republican loss. And that was it. Stalemate.

"It seems that your House of Representatives is almost perfectly designed never to change," Kazarov said. "Despite Americans' endless lectures to the world about democracy, America's politicians have sealed themselves off from the people. They know they will never lose."

But his thinking went beyond complaining. He went looking for a solution. And found one.

To affirm his hunch, in early December, Kazarov brought Ariens to his estate an hour outside London. Kazarov was sitting on a dark leather chair as the butler ushered a disheveled Ariens into his library. Without standing, Kazarov motioned for Ariens to sit. The billionaire did not waste a word on small talk.

"I'm fascinated by the corrupt districts drawn in your country. It's an incredible system your politicians have designed for themselves," he said in his nearly flawless English.

"I can't say I'm proud of it."

"How could you be?" Kazarov asked. "Imagine what the United States would say if another country, and Russia in particular, devised a system that locked one group into power no matter how the voters voted? America's democracy does exactly that, in the wide open."

Kazarov pointed his lit cigarette directly at Ariens to emphasize each point.

Ariens simply nodded back.

The Russian leaned toward Ariens.

"What is the best way to see which districts have a guaranteed result, and which ones have real elections?"

"Everyone in Washington examines that all the time," Ariens said. "The most accurate measure is called the Partisan Performance Index, which measures the partisan breakdown of voters in each district. A score of 50 is a dead-even district. The closer to 50, the more real the election, as you say."

"I would like to see that list."

"I can get you the exact breakdown. But I can tell you that about 28 districts score close to 50. Then there are others that are fairly close as well."

Only 28 districts, Kazarov thought, out of hundreds. How foolish the Americans were—changing the leadership of the most powerful nation in the world could not be accomplished by military assault or through a powerful political leader, or even with millions of dollars. But the small number of close districts perhaps provided a convenient back door.

"I would like to see the whole list, with those numbers," Kazarov repeated impatiently.

Although he liked Ariens, Kazarov did not share his plan with him. Attacking the heart of American democracy would trouble even the most jaded American lobbyist. Kazarov would get all the information he could, then shield his plans in a tight, non-American circle.

"In America, who runs elections?" he asked. "Who oversees them?"

"They're actually run by local officials."

"Is that true even for national elections? Congress? The president?"

"Sure is. Every state in the country oversees its own elections. There are certain federal laws that must be followed, but the real work is done at the local level. The county level."

Kazarov nodded. Russia had a similar level of government, called *oblasts*. "And who pays for the election process?"

"Those same local governments. The counties."

"Even for the presidential and congressional elections?"

"That's correct."

"What if a county is so small it cannot afford the cost?"

"There are programs that help poor counties pay, but in the end, every county must oversee its own elections. Some do struggle."

"So the quality and security of an election for the president of the United States come down to the judgment, and budgets, of thousands of local officials across the country?" he asked.

"Doesn't sound too smart when you put it that way," Ariens said, "but that's how it works. Local control is an American tradition, from elections to policing to education. We've done pretty well this way."

The last sentence was the closest Ariens had ever come to arguing with his client, but Kazarov didn't mind. It was the explanation he was hoping to hear. With so much at stake, with all the riches of Washington, America left the most fundamental act of its proud democracy in the hands of the most local officials. Such a decentralized approach presented opportunities, particularly in an age of complex, rapidly evolving and expensive technology.

Kazarov shook his head. He would never run his business this way. But given his aim, he was pleased America ran its elections this way.

CHAPTER 21

19 months before the election

A<small>RIENS THREW THE</small> journal down on his desk. He knew as soon as he saw the headline: "Mystery Buyer Pulls Abacus from the Ashes."

He had represented Diebold, itself a center of controversy, for years. So the small trade journal article describing the buyout of a Diebold competitor several months ago caught his eye. Although it'd been around for a century, Abacus was a dog of a company, unable to keep up with the demand for better technology. Acquiring them made no sense as a business matter.

The overnight appearance of the buyer, a company called Digital Machines Incorporated, also raised a red flag. The mysterious enterprise had emerged in Delaware only two weeks prior to the purchase, and its leadership team comprised names no one in the industry recognized. Clearly, a far more prominent investor lurked behind the new entity—the telltale signs of a Kazarov start-up.

Ariens glanced over the portfolio of Abacus accounts, some old, some new. They had clusters of counties in Maryland and Virginia, and even more in Florida, Pennsylvania, and Ohio. Further west, they were holding their own in parts of Illinois, Wisconsin, and Minnesota. Sure enough, Abacus' footprint overlapped with a number of the nation's swing districts, the very districts on the list that Ariens had emailed to his Russian client after the election.

He called his Diebold contact for additional information.

"Whoever they are, these guys are killers," the contact said over the phone. "Within a month of the takeover, they'd swooped into some of our districts with cutthroat prices and updated equipment. There's no way they're making a profit doing it, but they're stealing a lot of our counties!"

"Are they concentrating anywhere in particular?" Oliver asked.

"Kind of random, actually. They're pushing hard in Maryland, Pennsylvania and Ohio, and making big plays out West, in Colorado, Arizona and California."

Oliver asked for more details, and once again, Abacus' expansion activity was taking place in the very swing districts he'd identified for his Russian client.

After hanging up, Ariens banged his fist on his desk. Not angry at Kazarov, but at himself. The Russian's questions months before had not been subtle. Ariens should have known then, and now it was clear. His answers had set the frustrated Russian on a dark course.

*   *   *

"Oliver, welcome back to London," Kazarov said, friendlier than usual. "How are we proceeding in Washington?"

Ariens sat in the Russian's downtown office. Between two stunning paintings of turbulent, dark green seas, an imposing portrait of Peter the Great loomed behind Kazarov, its subject staring directly into Ariens' eyes.

"As you know, we are working hard but remain frustrated by a member of . . . by certain members of Congress," Ariens said. He had not been this nervous in years and stumbled over his words.

"What is your plan to resolve the situation?" Kazarov said, turning serious.

"Our hope is that the pressure of next year's elections might move some people our way," Ariens said. Kazarov's squinted eyes showed he was not pleased.

Now Ariens sat up straight, mustering the courage to say why he had requested to meet in person. "Mr. Kazarov, there is an issue that I must discuss with you before we move any further in our partnership."

"And what is that?" Kazarov asked curtly. He put his cigarette out in an ashtray and lit another one.

"I will be direct. You and I talked in some detail last time about the conduct of American elections. It was an interesting and challenging conversation. But I now believe that you are undertaking a plan to take advantage of the weaknesses we discussed to change the outcomes in the districts that I provided to you."

Ariens expected some response to his charge, but Kazarov greeted it with only a stone-faced glare and a long silence. The Russian did not plan on interrupting him. A bead of sweat trickled down Ariens' forehead. "I have learned about the activity of a company named Abacus. That company has machines in many of America's counties, including many in the districts we discussed. I am worried that your plan is to use those machines to impact next year's elections."

More glaring. More silence.

"Oliver," Kazarov said flatly, "I have paid you millions of dollars because I was told you are the best in Washington. You have accomplished nothing, and now you accuse me of being no more than a criminal?"

"I am both your lobbyist and your attorney," Ariens said gently. "I am bringing this to your attention because I have an ethical responsibility as your attorney to advise you that the course you are pursuing violates American law. There are many legitimate ways to influence the outcome of American policy and politics, but this is not one of them."

"Legitimate?" Kazarov said, more loudly than he usually spoke. "Such as flawed districts and meaningless elections? Politicians accepting contributions as bribes yet still doing nothing? Your entire system is illegitimate."

Ariens remained calm. "I can only advise you not to pursue this path. Of course, everything between us is confidential due to our attorney-client relationship, so if you do not pursue it, the actions you have taken thus far will never be shared with anyone."

Kazarov swatted the air with his hand. "Let me repeat myself. I do not know why you accuse me of this, or what motivates you to do so. I can only tell you it is not true. You are wasting my valuable time."

As a lawyer, as a congressman, and as a lobbyist, Ariens had encountered many liars in his life. Talented ones. But he had never before faced one who looked him directly in the eye throughout the entire lie.

A slender brunette assistant appeared in the office doorway. Kazarov abruptly swiveled his chair to the left, saying nothing more. The meeting was clearly over.

* * *

Ariens flew home commercial, grabbing a first-class British Airways ticket on the next Heathrow-Dulles flight. Except for a few cat naps, the long daytime flight allowed him to wind down and plan his next steps.

His client's plot called for more than a law enforcement response.

It required the attention of the highest ranking political leaders in Washington. He would start by confidentially informing the congressional leadership of both parties: Speaker Williams, Minority Leader Marshall, and their top lieutenants.

As the Airbus passed over the southern tip of Greenland, Ariens removed his Dictaphone from his briefcase and quietly recorded all he knew about the plot: the origins of Energy 2020, the conversations with Kazarov, the Abacus activity. The next day, he would ask his assistant to transcribe his dictation into a long memorandum for House leadership.

After landing in the late afternoon, Ariens hailed a cab at Dulles. Rather than returning to his K Street office, he headed back to his century-old townhome in Alexandria, a few blocks from the Potomac. He had been living alone ever since his nasty divorce five years before, and even at his portly 265 pounds, he enjoyed walking the cobblestone streets of Old Town whenever he could.

It was a near-perfect evening, unusually warm for the spring. After dropping his bags and changing into more casual clothes, he strolled to the cozy harbor and back to get some fresh air and an ice cream. Once home, he poured himself his evening glass of bourbon. It went down smoothly, as always. So smoothly that he had another.

He entered his study and sat down at his desk. He reached back into his briefcase for his Dictaphone, planning to finalize his dictation for tomorrow's big day.

Odd. It wasn't there.

The next moment, a huge arm darted across his left shoulder from behind, grabbed the right side of his neck, and pulled him back against his chair. From his right, an equally large hand blanketed his face with a damp cloth. His eyes immediately stung, his nose burned, and he gasped, trying but failing to breathe. The coughs he managed to get out were muffled by the enormous hand now covering the lower half of his face.

Within seconds, he was unconscious.

*   *   *

CHAPTER 22

COLUMBUS

March 29: 141 days after the election

APERS COVERED THE conference room desk in The Ohio State Department of Political Science. In a frenzy, Fowler walked me through her findings. She had called Monday morning and here we were, two days later.

Although I only wanted to know how Abacus stole the election, she insisted on telling me how she'd figured it out, and she'd done me such a solid that I felt obligated to hear her out.

"I wasted a week looking at all 435 districts, which only complicated things," she said. "The statistically relevant universe was far smaller—the set of 35 districts where Abacus placed itself in the driver's seat. These 35 districts had far more in common with one another than they did with the 400 other districts, which were highly gerrymandered and generally uncompetitive."

"Okay." The less I said the better.

"Crucially," she went on, "Abacus made the decision not to win every one of the seats it controlled. This made sense as a way to mask its overall plot. If all 35 districts went to the Republican, the plot would've been exposed instantly. But by winning some and losing others, Abacus provided the statistical clues as to how it manipulated the results."

I nodded along.

"So the difference between the Abacus districts won by Democrats and those won by Republicans shows exactly how they manipulated the results. This comparison tells the story."

"And what was the difference?"

"The undervote! It's all about the undervote."

"What about it?"

"One of the least understood phenomena in politics is a voter's decision to skip races down the ballot. They don't vote in races they don't know about or care as much about. We call them drop-off voters, and they end up affecting the results of many elections."

I knew all this, but she was a teacher. Let her teach.

"It looks like Abacus took advantage of this drop-off tendency, systematically but subtly taking votes away from Democratic congressional candidates in the districts where they wanted to win. And in the close districts where Abacus has machines, a drop-off of several thousand votes can make all the difference. No one would notice this because we expect to see drop-offs, and we never know by how much. We simply assume voters are less interested in that lower race."

"So how can you prove this?" I asked, somewhat intrigued. "Are there more drop-offs in these districts than in those where Abacus doesn't have machines?"

"No, it's more complicated than that. There are actually fewer drop-offs in Abacus districts than most congressional districts. But that's because most districts are so gerrymandered they don't have close elections. So people vote less because they don't think their choice matters or because the race hasn't received the same amount of attention. Ironically, the Abacus districts have *fewer* drop-offs compared to the others, which is one reason what they did is hard to detect."

I shook my head as I imagined explaining all this to my editors. "So how can we prove they reduced votes in this way?"

"Again, because they didn't *always* reduce votes. Some districts under Abacus control were not manipulated, like in the Toledo area. They didn't want to get greedy."

"Right. Would have made their plot obvious."

"Exactly. But in doing so, they unintentionally created an apples-to-apples comparison that proves precisely *how* they cheated. And that's what I found. In the Abacus districts where Democrats held on to win, the drop off in votes was 20 percent less than the drop off in Abacus districts where Republicans won. That difference alone explains the different outcomes."

"How do you know that's not caused by natural voting behavior?"

"It's too large a difference. These Abacus districts are similar, so you would expect to see similar patterns of voting. But the drop-off differential when Democrats won versus when Republicans won is significant. But I also found several other things that seal the deal."

First, she explained, not every county in each district used Abacus machines. For example, even though Monroe, Athens, and Washington used Abacus in Ohio's Sixth District, Mahoning did not.

"In congressional districts where Republicans won, Abacus counties saw a much bigger drop-off rate than the non-Abacus counties. In the districts where Democrats won, there was no difference between Abacus and non-Abacus counties."

"Interesting."

"More than interesting. Statistically decisive. But that's not the most damning evidence."

Good. My case would have to be overwhelming to get this published.

"There was one type of vote Abacus could not manipulate: mailed absentee votes. Those create an independent paper trail that cannot be tampered with, and county staff handles and tabulates those paper ballots separately from the machine-counted others. Abacus can't simply erase the mail-in vote for a candidate like it can on its machines. In fact, Abacus never touches those ballots."

"And?"

"The drop-off rate for mailed-in absentee ballots in Abacus counties was exactly the same as the non-Abacus counties. Only the drop-off rate for the *in-person voting* was statistically different."

"Let me get this straight. There was no difference in drop-off rates for early votes that were mailed-in, but there was early votes that were cast in person?

"That's right. Because Abacus could only manipulate the in-person votes."

"And that's why Kelly led with absentees, and only lost with the later votes."

"Exactly, because they couldn't alter the mailed-in ballots. You'll find that pattern in every district where the Democrat lost."

"Good stuff," I said. "Last question. Why would the paper trail feature on the Abacus machines not capture the problem? Wouldn't the voters notice?"

"Not necessarily. Because it's all run from the same machine, that paper trail can be manipulated. One study found that most voters never even check the paper receipt anyway, so many voters might confirm a manipulated paper ballot without even knowing it. And in a close county, it just doesn't take that many lost votes to change the outcome."

CHAPTER 23

WASHINGTON, DC

19 months before the election

"WE HAVE LOST a great man, a patriot who believed in the best our country has to offer."

Tom Stanton—the House minority whip, the second most senior Republican in the House—had gone through the motions at many Beltway funerals, but those had been political performances. This was real. He meant every word he was saying. It surprised even him.

He paused several times as he wiped away his own tears. Once he recovered, his moving eulogy drew both laughter and tears from the packed crowd. They'd never talked about it publicly, but he and Oliver went back a long way.

Born and raised in the suburbs of Philadelphia, the son of a respected banker, Tom Stanton followed a long family tradition of attending Andover, the elite boarding school, followed by Yale and Harvard Law School.

In his first week in law school, Stanton met the young, chubby, and affable Oliver Ariens from New Orleans. The two shared Constitutional Law and Contracts courses in their 1L year, and as different as they were, they bonded from the start. As Stanton chaired the Law Review, Ariens served as his executive editor. The two also won Harvard's vaunted moot court competition and finished as runners-up nationally. Their competitors labeled them "The Odd Couple."

While Ariens went off to serve his judicial clerkships, Stanton started clocking time at a Philly corporate firm while plotting his political path. He was elected to the statehouse two years later, ascended to minority leader, and seized an open congressional seat several terms after that.

Along the way, he and Ariens served as best men at one another's weddings and their young families vacationed together. Ariens had flown up to the funeral when Stanton's father passed away. They were thrilled when they won their congressional seats on the same day. A dozen years after being 1Ls at Harvard together, they were once again in the same first-year class. Shortly after taking their oaths, Stanton and Ariens moved into a Capitol Hill apartment together, where they lived when not back in their districts.

But this is where their paths diverged. While both were equally unimpressed by their colleagues, Stanton tolerated the nonsense of Congress that Ariens couldn't stomach. But Stanton also had more incentive to do so.

Young, good looking, and consumed with fitness, Stanton devoured the social perks that came with being a young congressman. It was their little secret that Stanton whisked a revolving door of young women through their apartment while Irene raised their two sons and daughter back in Bucks County. For his part, Stanton was always amazed that Ariens didn't once stray from his vows, as strained as his marriage became.

Even more importantly, if he played his cards right, Stanton's path could potentially lead him all the way to the White House. So putting up with the minor league shenanigans of the House was well worth it. When Ariens abandoned his political career and moved out to become a permanent D.C. resident, the two remained as close as ever. And once Ariens' lobbying practice exploded, they formed a symbiotic bond. Ariens lined up financial support for Stanton as he rose through the House ranks; Stanton went to bat for Ariens' clients whenever they needed his help. The two met for a standing cocktail every Wednesday night at the Capital Grille to catch up and swap notes.

As they were with no one else, they had always been honest with one another. Ariens urged Stanton to dial back on the womanizing, concerned that it would come back to haunt Stanton. And Stanton worried about his friend's health, urging Ariens to take better care of himself.

So when Stanton got the call that Ariens' secretary had found him dead of a heart attack, Stanton wasn't shocked. But he felt guilty that he had not pushed his friend harder.

Four days later, he delivered the eulogy to a packed crowd. Afterward, amid a silent chapel, he walked back to the first pew, sat down, and embraced his wife, Irene, who sat stoically by his side for the rest of the service. When the funeral wrapped up, Stanton was not up for small talk, so he and Irene walked out the front, hands held, and climbed into the rear seat of his chauffeured Suburban. Their first stop was Union Station, where Irene got out to catch the next train back to Philly, then Stanton returned to Georgetown. Alone in the back, Stanton stared out the window, chin in hand, for the 20-minute ride.

Ariens' death came at a tough time, politically.

The clock was ticking on Stanton's presidential ambitions. After a meteoric rise, he was stuck behind that bumpkin Marshall in caucus leadership. Even worse, Speaker Williams' disciplined leadership trumped Marshall again and again, so they were confined to the minority indefinitely. As talented as Stanton was, who ever heard of a House minority whip running for president?

And his other potential path to the White House, a statewide run in the Keystone State, was not viable. Pennsylvania tilted too Democratic for him to make a credible run for senator or governor.

Boxed in, Stanton had often sought Ariens' advice on his options to move up. They hadn't figured out a path yet, but Ariens was his most trusted confidant on the topic. Now his best friend and best adviser was gone.

*   *   *

The next morning, a knock on the front door of Stanton's P Street townhome interrupted him as he read the *Post*. A rare home delivery. Even more rarely, he was home to receive it.

Stanton recognized the return address, which appeared directly under the box showing that two prior attempts had been made at delivery. He scrawled his signature, took the package inside, and sat at his kitchen table. Inside was a single manila legal folder. A Post-it affixed to the front of the folder implored: "Please look into this ASAP. OAIII"

Intrigued and slightly haunted, Stanton opened the file.

At first glance, the stack of papers appeared odd. Random. Not at all connected to anything he and Ariens had discussed. Articles on an election equipment company based in Philly. Abacus. Stanton knew the name. Over the years, their leadership had supported his campaigns at modest levels. (Diebold had given far more, thanks to the Ariens connection). But that was it. Handwritten notes and highlighted sentences on the clippings left a helpful trail of interesting facts. Abacus had been struggling, almost out of business. Then it had been acquired.

With new technology, Abacus was now competing fiercely to keep some accounts and gain new ones. And it was succeeding.

So what? What was the significance? No obvious answer jumped off the pages. In the grand scheme of what he dealt with every day, this seemed trivial. But then he glanced again at the note from his deceased friend: "Please look into this ASAP." Ariens would have had a purpose in sending this, to his home no less.

Stanton tossed the Post-it note into a wastebasket, put the file in his briefcase, and headed to Capitol Hill. As he strolled into his cavernous Capitol suite, his staff looked up at him from their desks. Ariens had visited the office regularly, so they all knew him, and knew how close the two were. This was the first time they'd seen their boss since.

Stanton walked past the first six desks without saying a word but stopped at the workstation of his most talented research assistant. As she looked up at him, he tossed the Abacus file onto her desk.

"Joanie, look into this company. Put together a file on everything you find, and arrange for me to stop by the next time I'm in Philadelphia."

"That's next week," his scheduler piped up from the next desk over.

"Great," Stanton said curtly, turning to her. "Get it done."

The mourning was over.

CHAPTER 24

YOUNGSTOWN

March 30: 142 days after the election

RENEE FOWLER'S FINDINGS filled in a huge piece of the puzzle.

I now knew exactly how Abacus had rigged the elections. I also dug up the long history of the company, as well as the mysterious purchase the year before by an outfit called Digital Machines Incorporated. A few final calls would round out my story.

First, I called Speaker Marshall's office and got as far as the deputy press secretary. "The Speaker isn't available, Mr. Sharpe," said a chirpy, young-sounding voice, "but I'd be happy to answer your questions."

"I don't know an easy way to ask this, but we've found that voting machines in numerous swing districts eliminated thousands of Democratic votes in last year's election. I wanted to get the Speaker's reaction to what looks to be a tainted election."

"You've got to be joking," the press aide said. "That sounds like something the *National Enquirer* would run, not a serious newspaper."

"I couldn't be more serious."

This cocky kid was why journalists consider D.C. press flacks the worst in the business. They were barely out of college, yet they always brought an attitude. I could only imagine his eye roll at having to answer to Ohio.

"We have reviewed the data for months, and it's quite clear that this occurred."

"The Speaker isn't going to respond to such a cockamamie story."

"Can I write that you refused to comment?"

I asked in an innocent tone. No good press aide would allow those incriminating words to be associated with the boss's name.

"No, you can't," the aide shot back. "Feel free to quote me saying, 'The

Speaker is proud of his party's win last year, a result of strong candidates and a clear message.'"

A perfectly hollow quote, but better than nothing.

I dialed a new number, and Ernie Rogers picked up the phone on the second ring.

"Mr. Chairman," I said, "I've got some news for you."

"What's that?" he asked.

"I looked into your questions about November's vote, and you were right. The results were rigged by voting machines."

"I knew it!" Rogers shouted. But as I went on with my explanation of the plot, the old chairman grew quiet.

"Since it was your hunch that got me looking into it in the first place, can I quote you in the story?"

"Sure." Rogers paused for a few moments to gather his thoughts.

"I fought for our country and knew many men who lost their lives doing the same," he said. "Stealing an election is an insult to every one of us who puts our life on the line to protect our incredible democracy."

He meant every word, but this was too trite to use. I'd have to try a different angle without sounding like I was spoon-feeding him the quote.

"How did you know that something was wrong with the vote count in Monroe County?"

"All I can say is a machine doesn't know the people of Monroe County like I do. As I told you that first day, our people didn't vote against Congressman Kelly. It just didn't add up."

Perfect.

Rogers hadn't just given me the story in the first place. He gave me my lede.

* * *

Over the years, one old journalistic trick of mine rarely failed: call the person implicated by a negative story last. And not just last, but as close to the deadline as possible.

The subject of a tough story will do all they can to kill the article, to cover their tracks, or to preempt the bad press. Early in my career, I had learned this lesson painfully. Twice, on the eve of a big scoop, officials had run to other journalists and spilled the beans, desperately trying to get the most positive spin out before my tougher story ran. Calling as late as possible minimized these opportunities. With everything else in place, now was the right time to call Abacus.

I dialed nervously. I'd prepared a long set of questions and had diagrammed out exactly what to ask based on the answers I received. The diagram turned out to be useless.

"I am a reporter from the *Youngstown Vindicator.* I'd like to talk to your press person."

"We don't have a press person yet. Is there anyone else that could help you?"

Yet? "Your CEO then."

"Mr. Scott is out for a few days and would only meet in person anyway. He doesn't do media interviews over the phone."

"This is somewhat urgent. Who can I speak to about an important company matter?"

"Our Chief Operating Officer is here. Let me check with him."

Tacky elevator music blared over the phone for a few minutes. Then a click.

"Butch Joseph here," bellowed a deep Southern accent. "How can I help ya?"

"Mr. Joseph, I'm Jack Sharpe, a reporter from the *Youngstown Vindicator.* I'd like to have our conversation be on the record if at all possible."

"Sure thing," Joseph said. "I've got nothing to hide. What's up?"

"We have conducted an investigation into last year's election and found that Abacus machines were located in key swing districts across the country."

"Absolutely!" Joseph said. "That's why I'm here."

Another odd response. "Excuse me?"

"Abacus kicked our ass the last few years and nabbed accounts around the country, so three months ago, we bought the sons of bitches out," Joseph said. "Those bastards undercut us all over the country. We'd had enough of it."

"Who's we?"

"Diebold! Abacus is now a wholly-owned subsidiary of Diebold. We basically bought them to buy their accounts and stop the bleeding. We don't need their technology, which they basically stole from us, and we certainly didn't need their people."

"So the old Abacus is gone?"

"Buddy, the old Abacus disappeared the day that DMI group bought them a couple years ago. DMI saved 'em by modernizing, and spent a shit ton in the process. So when DMI offered to sell for dirt cheap, we couldn't resist grabbing them."

"Dirt cheap?"

"Yeah. Fire sale. Seiko would've grabbed them if we hadn't."

"When did it happen?"

"We finalized the deal two months ago."

How the hell had I missed that? I scrambled to get back to the story. "Well, I was calling because our in-depth investigation discovered vote manipulation in last year's election, likely impacting the outcome of dozens of congressional races. All the manipulation occurred in counties where Abacus has its machines."

Joseph paused for a few seconds before responding.

"What the hell do you say after hearing that?" he asked. "We had nothing to do with last year's election. Hell, we disliked Abacus as much as anyone. You'll have to track down the prior leadership and ask them about your findings. But they got out of here right quick."

"So what can I quote you saying?"

"What I just said. That we had nothing to do with last year's election and have no idea what y'all are talking about. Nothing improper would ever happen under our watch."

"Do you have any idea how to find their prior leadership?"

"Not a clue. They were out of here the day we moved in. Odd bunch. Don't know where they came from or where they went! Just glad they're gone."

CHAPTER 25

19 months before the election

For a full day after Congressman Stanton dropped off the file, Joanie Simpson ignored it. Compared to pressing legislative items, her boss's planned visit to a local company didn't feel like a priority. Finally, late on Wednesday afternoon, she cracked the folder, planning to breeze through it before rushing to the gym. But once she scanned a few of the marked-up pages, her typical ferocity kicked in. This odd little Philadelphia company required a closer look.

The way her parents told it, Joanie Simpson kicked off her debate career shortly after learning to talk. At two years old, she first began to pepper her parents with question after question. Direct talking back followed a few months later, increasing with her ever-growing vocabulary. She argued with her siblings as they ate cereal together in the morning, took on her grade school classmates in the cafeteria, and challenged her neighbors on the playground. It only escalated from there. One-on-one. Groups. Formal venues. Family reunions. Always challenging, always prodding, always rebutting. A frenzy of facts, figures, humor, and sarcasm, all delivered ferociously. And armed with a razor-sharp mind and an intense competitive streak, she was damn good at it.

From her blue-collar St. Louis middle school, Simpson won the spelling bee championship of the county. In high school, she finished as the state debate runner-up, the only girl to make it that far in Missouri history. That performance and her near-perfect SAT opened a path out of a depressed area where few kids ever left.

Once at Williams College, she channeled her feistiness into spirited political activity. It began as a reflex to the silver-spoon liberals from fancy prep schools that dominated the place. Her dad was a construction worker, her mom was a nurse, and Joanie worked 20 hours a week in the cafeteria to help pay room and board. And these sons and daughters of Wall Street traders and Ivy League professors dared to lecture her about the needs of the working man.

That didn't last long.

Simpson founded the Libertarian Club and promptly ran circles around the other political pugilists in every debate of the college's Political Union. Most East Coast liberals dismissed conservatives as unthinking dolts. So with her unassuming appearance—thin frame, awkward gait, straight brown hair and over-sized glasses—they were never prepared for the full Simpson fusillade of facts, rhetoric, and humor.

During her junior year, the sole conservative professor in the political science department arranged a summer internship for Joanie with his old college classmate, Congressman Tom Stanton. This represented her one chance at the big leagues, and she worked furiously all summer, putting in more hours than any of Stanton's paid staff. Four years later, she served as Stanton's go-to research and policy guru and enjoyed her reputation as one of Capitol Hill's brightest stars. She now dedicated all that energy to finding something meaningful to tell the Congressman about Abacus.

The information in the file was limited, and a few minutes of reading the enclosed documents raised more questions than answers. Until recently, the company's story had been straightforward—an aging player in a rapidly evolving industry, unable to keep up and on the verge of going under. Sad for them, but such was modern-day capitalism. Survival of the fittest.

Then the story changed—someone had pulled Abacus from the ashes. Great for them, but odd. Who would swoop in and buy a voting machine company struggling to survive, only to compete against deep-pocketed players such as Diebold? A surefire way to lose millions. And the entire acquisition had been shrouded in secrecy.

Once under new leadership, the company had adjusted its footprint in a peculiar way. Joanie was a policy person more than a political person, but even she knew from the Congressman's travels that many of the counties where Abacus was adding accounts were in critical swing districts. Could be a coincidence, but also odd.

It was late, so she typed up her findings in a brief memo, printed it out, and left it in the Congressman's research inbox. As usual, she was the last person to leave, so she turned out the lights and locked the door behind her.

*   *   *

LONDON
19 months before the election

"One of the most important congressmen in Washington requested to visit us."

Andersson, in Philadelphia to lead Abacus operations, talked quickly, worry in his voice.

"Who is he?" Kazarov asked calmly from London.

"His name is Thomas Stanton. From Philadelphia, but he is the second most important Republican in the House of Representatives."

Kazarov recognized the name. Oliver Ariens had talked about him often as a key ally in the Energy 2020 effort, but also as a personal friend.

Maybe Ariens had communicated with someone prior to his death after all. But this man was also from Philadelphia, so perhaps it was unrelated to Ariens or Kazarov. Likely chasing political contributions as all American politicians do.

"Did he say what he wanted?" Kazarov asked.

"No. He just wants to pay a visit next week. His office said he was interested in seeing our new technology and how it worked."

This request came at a critical moment. Andersson and his team were in the final stages of preparation. They needed to run a few additional simulations, remove some final bugs, and then would be poised to ship nationwide. The tight deadlines put the entire operation under tremendous pressure, so Kazarov shared Andersson's apprehension about unexpected developments. But he expressed no worry. He never did.

"Let him come," Kazarov said after a momentary pause. "A visit by one congressman shouldn't worry us."

Kazarov lit a cigarette and puffed it, staring straight ahead. This was not ideal, but rejecting the visit would draw unnecessary scrutiny.

And who knows? Maybe this presented an opportunity. Perceived obstacles often did.

* * *

WASHINGTON, DC

Five days after the funeral, over lunch, Stanton picked up the Abacus research file from his desk. Once he started reading through the cover memo from his ace researcher, he forgot about his sandwich.

The history of the company was not much different from what was outlined in the original file. The company that had acquired Abacus was called DMI. It was a start-up, its backers a mystery. Not much there. But *where* Abacus had rolled out its new technology was far more intriguing: eastern Ohio, Cincinnati, Peoria, Tulsa, Tucson, and toss-up districts in California, New York, and Washington, among others.

No one knew America's swing districts better than Stanton. He had targeted them for the past three cycles. And here they were, listed as part of Abacus' growing footprint. This mysterious company had managed to place its voting machines in the exact terrain Republicans needed to take the House majority.

Stanton placed the papers back in the manila folder, smiling as he did so. No wonder his old friend Ariens had sent that package.

* * *

PHILADELPHIA

Stanton usually traveled with a flock of aides. Sometimes they were needed and helpful, sometimes not at all necessary. Either way, an entourage projected power, and was especially useful when television cameras followed in tow.

But for his visit to Abacus, except for his driver, he traveled alone. Too much uncertainty.

Abacus sat on the edge of an industrial park in northeastern Philadelphia. A dreary location, made even more miserable by the pouring rain of late spring. They arrived at 10:00 a.m. on the nose.

"I'll be back in about an hour."

His driver grunted in reply.

Stanton walked into the main entrance, confident as always. The grungy exterior disguised a new, attractive lobby. Even the corporate logo behind the reception desk differed from the stale one he remembered from their letterhead.

"I'm Congressman Stanton. I was told to ask for Mr. Miller when I arrived. Is he here?"

"Yes, he is," the receptionist said, clearly expecting the visit. "We have a room arranged for your visit. Follow me."

She walked him back through a hallway. Trailing her by a few feet, Stanton eyed her shapely legs up and down, something he did dozens of times daily in the halls of Congress. A man of his stature could get away with almost anything.

She led him to a large conference room, adorned with the technology and furnishings of a cutting-edge enterprise. Whoever had invested in Abacus had thrown in a whole lot of dough. Moments later, a tall, blonde man—looking more like a tennis instructor than a company executive—briskly entered the room. He reached for Stanton's hand, shook it energetically, and laughed out loud.

A grim aide—short, stout, darker features—followed behind.

"Greetings, Congressman. We are honored by the visit of one of America's most important leaders. I am Gustav Miller."

"I knew your old leadership well. They were good supporters of mine, and as I read about all the changes here, I was eager to see what was happening," Stanton said. "I'm so glad to see that things are improving. You're an important corporation for Philadelphia."

"Thank you. We agree!"

"Looks like you guys are overhauling this place from top to bottom. Tell me more about what you're doing," Stanton asked.

Miller clapped his hands, sat down, and reached under the table. A panel on the rear wall descended to display a large flat-screen monitor. The new Abacus logo and moniker appeared on the screen.

"We thought you'd never ask," Miller said.

The brief slideshow walked through the history of Abacus, the updated technology, the new vision for the company. All the technical bells and whistles of a modern corporate presentation were on full display. Stanton politely nodded throughout, but as it ended, he jumped to his questions.

"Mr. Miller, who is DMI, and why did they choose to invest in Abacus?"

Miller clapped his hands again.

"DMI is a group of investors looking to buy distressed companies that they've determined will shine again with better management. Abacus is a perfect example of what we want to do."

"Has DMI made any other acquisitions yet?"

"My job is to turn this company around, so I'm not an expert on their other activity. But to my knowledge, nothing yet."

"What part of the market are you focused on?"

"For the past ten years, Abacus' niche has been in the rural, less affluent counties across the country."

Stanton smiled at this glass-half-full summary of Abacus losing almost all of its large-market accounts. Sounded like too many pollsters he knew.

"Our strategy," Miller went on, "is to help those counties upgrade at an affordable price, and then to expand from there. We've successfully placed our new products in many of our old counties, and a fair share of new ones."

"You seem to concentrate in certain districts. Is there a reason for that?"

Miller paused, almost imperceptibly. "Our cluster strategy is working well for us," he said. "We don't have the resources to expand everywhere, so it makes the most sense to build our portfolio near our current accounts."

Stanton nodded as if satisfied by the answer. But it didn't add up.

"Can I take a quick tour?" he asked.

"Absolutely."

They walked from room to room, continuing their conversation. Every element was new, modern, high-tech.

The consummate politician, Stanton reached out and shook hands with each person he met. But the operation was less crowded than he expected. Those he greeted responded quietly, politely. Not as outgoing as Miller. More like Miller's quiet sidekick.

In a room labeled "Research," Miller walked Stanton through the operation of an individual Abacus machine. It looked like the Diebold machines he and Ariens had inspected on a company tour several years back.

The warehouse area stored hundreds of voting machines stacked in long lines. As Stanton scanned the planned shipments, he again recalled his Diebold tour—that facility had a far larger warehouse and loading dock, with machines lined up as far as he could see. This was a fraction of that size, and much of the warehouse sat empty.

That memory begged the question: "What's your strategy to compete with companies like Diebold?"

"So far, we are able to offer a similar technology at lower prices," Miller answered. "That's what has allowed us to win the smaller counties, which are very price sensitive."

"And how are you able to keep your prices so low?" Stanton asked, sure that Diebold's scale would allow it to keep its costs lower.

"We are intense about efficiency," Miller said.

"I see," Stanton said, grinning skeptically. Again, it didn't add up.

After an hour, Stanton walked back toward the entrance. Always on the hunt, he hoped to make small talk with the receptionist as he left, but she was gone.

"Thank you for your time, Mr. Miller."

The two men shook hands and Stanton walked out the door.

*   *   *

"Clay," he said to his driver, "keep that stop between us."

"Of course, Congressman."

From his earliest days, Tom Stanton had prided himself as a keen judge of people. As the leader of a party caucus, the most important skill he called upon each day involved sizing up people he barely knew, quickly and accurately. Lies, feints, tics. Like a good poker player, he picked up on them all. So as he drove away from the site, he reviewed who and what he had seen.

First, "Miller" was a born salesman. Not a bad thing for a company trying to revive itself. But this salesman had been disingenuous throughout their meeting. The sweeping DMI mission he had described didn't square with the fact that they had acquired only one company. Abacus could never keep costs below Diebold as he had assured. And his explanation for why they concentrated in certain areas was utter nonsense.

For the entire hour, this man had repeatedly lied to one of Washington's most powerful people. Without hesitation.

But Miller clearly served as the front man of a broader charade. Behind a façade built to impress, Abacus appeared to be largely hollow within. If anyone visited the headquarters, they would probably only stop at the fancy conference room. Maybe walk through the research wing. But they would likely never see the back end of the operation.

And that empty warehouse told the real story of Abacus.

There would be no point to invest so lavishly in the more public areas of the building but then invest so little in the inventory of actual machines. Likewise, there was no reason not to sell far beyond the locations they had selectively targeted, especially with their cutthroat prices.

The ornate entrance and rapid investment in new technology meant that a deep-pocketed investor was bankrolling the resurgence at Abacus. But the limited shipment meant that the investor wasn't eager to make those dollars back.

And one other aspect had stuck out.

Miller obviously did not hail from the United States. He had a strong Scandinavian accent—Finnish or Swedish. The woman who greeted him barely spoke, but betrayed a slight accent, just as Miller's sidekick had. The others he encountered had either said nothing or spoken with foreign accents as well.

This old Philly company, perfectly positioned to steer the outcome of elections across America, was being run by foreigners.

*   *   *

Kazarov first became fascinated by naval warfare as a child. In particular, submarine warfare, Cold War-style.

Unlike most Russian children, it wasn't the hardware that fascinated him. It was the great captains, their strategies and tactics. He refined his study of them as he built his empire.

American and Soviet submarines traveled thousands of miles, hunting one another at close range—tracking, trailing, passing, and circling one another. At any moment, one misstep meant disaster. One miscommunication among adversaries—one perceived threat, one hostile move—could trigger a disastrous sequence of events leading to mutual destruction.

While these submarines did not communicate with one another directly, they detected each other's every move. Each captain's most important skill, therefore, involved perfectly interpreting his adversary's every maneuver, while using his own maneuvers to clearly communicate his intentions, so long as they were not hostile. This symbiotic dance of maneuvers and indirect communication, of signaling and interpreting intentions, kept each hull intact and both crews safe.

Kazarov conducted his own version of that dance now.

"He doesn't believe most of what you are telling him," Kazarov said to Andersson the morning after the congressman's visit. "You can see it in his expressions, especially when your lies are most blatant."

As the politician toured the Abacus facility, cameras had captured his every step and recorded his every word. Kazarov had replayed the videos two or three times, sizing up the visitor.

"He walked through the front door of Abacus already suspicious of wrongdoing. He left certain of it."

Andersson reddened, sheepish that his performance was so transparent.

"I am sorry. What do we do?"

Kazarov lit a cigarette, drawing deep puffs and exhaling slowly, a sign that he was weighing options.

Stanton was a serious figure, powerful enough to take down Abacus. But unlike Ariens, assassinating Stanton would invite so much heat that the Abacus plan would surely unravel. Kazarov was essentially powerless to stop him.

But Stanton's visit had not signaled hostile intent, at least not yet. He had come alone. Knowing he was being lied to, he had not responded verbally. He'd simply observed and questioned, taking it all in. He too had been getting a read. He'd walked away pensively. For now, he was keeping the torpedo doors closed.

Certainly, Stanton had reasons to oppose his plan. Most Americans in his position would immediately take steps to stop it, just as Ariens had.

But Kazarov also knew enough about Stanton to know he had compelling reasons to support it. Too much was at stake to leave this to guesswork.

"He will be conflicted on what to do," Kazarov said to Andersson. "We will watch to make sure he comes to the right decision."

CHAPTER 26

YOUNGSTOWN
March 31: 143 days after the election

Woodsfield, Ohio—When Congressman Lee Kelly lost his re-election bid in a surprise upset last November, Ernie Rogers, the long-time chairman of Monroe County, immediately knew something was wrong.

"It just didn't add up," Rogers said.

It turns out, Rogers understood his own county's voters better than the computer program that systematically eliminated votes—Democratic votes—from the Monroe County election returns.

And Monroe County isn't the only place where this occurred.

An in-depth investigation by the Youngstown Vindicator found that one voting equipment company—Abacus—aggressively positioned itself to tabulate the results in the most competitive districts in the country. And in 27 of those districts, including two Congressional districts in Ohio, thousands of Democratic votes were systematically eliminated from the vote count. The eliminated votes impacted the outcome in many, if not all, of those races.

I bobbed in my chair as I reviewed my best story in years. It was finally coming together.

The article walked through every detail: Abacus' aggressive effort to control swing districts across the country. The statistical analysis proving how their machines had eliminated votes. The contrast between Abacus counties and non-Abacus counties. The difference between mailed-in ballot drop-offs and in-person drop-offs.

I quoted three sources on the record.

Renee Fowler on the certainty of the data: "There is no natural voting behavior that explains these results. They can only be explained by the machines themselves."

Speaker Marshall's press aide: "We are proud of our victory last November, and reject any allegations that it was anything but the will of the American people."

And Butch Joseph, the Abacus executive: "We were not involved in Abacus last year, and cannot speak to Abacus operations during last year's elections."

Our attorneys had advised us to stick to the facts. To head off lawsuits, they'd instructed, avoid loaded words about motive, such as "rigging," "fixed," or the like. To me, this watered down my scoop, but my editors didn't mind. The facts alone, even laid out as neutrally as possible, made for the bombshell.

The end of the story explained that Kelly had died in a car crash a few months after his election, but didn't mention that he was looking into Abacus. Again, too risky.

"Jack, that's a hell of a story," Mary Andres said as we wrapped up the final edit. "I knew there was fuel left in that rusty tank of yours."

"Don't count on it. This thing dropped in my lap." But she knew I was bluffing. This was a big scoop, and I was damn proud of it. So proud I called Scott to fill him in before he saw it in the paper.

"Dad, that's great news," he said. "Sounds like a hell of a story."

"It's a biggie, and it's what's had me working so hard these past few months."

"I'm excited for you. Maybe this is your big break."

The words themselves marked an improvement from our last call, but his flat tone made it clear he still wasn't sold.

* * *

The *Vindicator* plastered the story across Sunday's front page and a third of the paper's front section. To make the most compelling case possible, maps, charts, and diagrams accompanied the 85,000 characters of text. The editorial board penned a full-page op-ed, calling for a federal investigation and urging reform to the deeply flawed election and districting laws that allowed such a result to happen.

The next day, the front page of major papers across the country ran with it. The *New York Times, Washington Post,* and *LA Times* all credited the *Vindicator* for our investigation. The Associated Press' Ohio reporter, an old friend of mine, summarized our findings in a story that ran in smaller papers across the country. I loved imagining Speaker Marshall's press flack waking up to what Ohio media had unleashed.

Throughout Monday, national cable news outlets jumped all over the story. On MSNBC and CNN that evening, I walked through our findings with over-caffeinated talking heads. Tuesday morning, for the first time in years, I went to work thinking about my appearance—even bought a sports coat and tie for the occasion. And I spent an entire hour on NPR.

Everyone was asking the same two questions: Was this an intentional act to fix the results, or simply an error of historic proportions? And who was running Abacus at the time all this happened?

Based on lawyers' advice, I dodged the first question: "People can draw their own conclusion from our reporting." On the second, all I could say was "We are investigating that further."

Renee Fowler also made a number of appearances, walking through the data and what it meant. Even Ernie Rogers showed up on national TV, emerging as a moderate media sensation with his life story, authentic personality, and colorful answers.

But I had only a few days to enjoy it all. As with everything in Washington, the reaction split along partisan lines. Democrats jumped on the scandal, demanding a special prosecutor investigate. Minority Leader Sandra Williams, flanked by dozens of others, stood on the steps of the Capitol on Tuesday morning calling for immediate congressional hearings. I watched it from the newsroom.

"In all my years, I could never have imagined our politics sinking this low," she said in front of a wall of television cameras, going further rhetorically than I had. "We must fully investigate what happened and bring to justice whoever decided to steal an election from the American voters. And then we must change our system to never allow such a crime to happen again."

With everything to lose, Republicans took their cue from Speaker Marshall's hard denial in my initial story. Their pushback got nasty and personal.

"BREAKING NEWS: Radical Feminist Renee Fowler Is Upset That Republicans Are in Power," the House Republican Caucus' initial press release mockingly announced. According to this broadly disseminated narrative, a liberal feminist aide for former President Obama had spoon-fed a lazy, small-town reporter tainted data and he'd convinced his liberal paper to run with her wild conspiracy theory.

On Tuesday, conservative news outlets launched a full-fledged counter-attack on Renee. The lede in the *National Review* summed it up: "Radical leftists like Renee Fowler will do anything to discredit Republican leadership in Washington, especially with all the progress being made. A struggling Ohio paper is duped into reporting her nonsense, and the left-wing media is more than happy to pile on."

Marshall and his top lieutenants scoffed at the idea that Congress should waste time and taxpayer dollars pursuing a partisan conspiracy theory. Rank and file Republicans quickly fell into line. And because the majority party opposed hearings, they weren't going to happen.

To their credit, they'd wisely taken full advantage of my one big mistake. Despite our robust reporting and rock-solid findings, only talking to Democrats about the story had been a costly, unforced error. Stupidly, I had underestimated how partisan this story would become. In my mind, the facts were the facts—and we'd presented compelling proof of vote-rigging. But in Washington, it was politics. The legitimacy of the new Republican majority was at stake, and they were going to fight to protect it.

And now it was too late. As I chased down Republicans for comment, they all replied the same way: "Sorry, this is too hot. We can't help you on this one." The battle over Abacus was grinding into yet another Washington stalemate, and we were right in the middle of it.

"If they can ignore all the science on global warming even as the oceans rise, I guess politicians can willfully ignore blatant evidence of voting irregularities," Renee said as we commiserated by phone a few days after the story ran.

"They're attacking my credibility, my good name," I said. "Yours, too."

Renee ignored my anger. She was interested in bigger fish. "Jack, some group, some person paid for every dime of that Abacus operation—and it wasn't Abacus. Someone calculated it was an investment worth making."

"Absolutely," I said. "Republican politicians may have gained from the outcome. But others did too. Who would have been willing to invest millions to accomplish it all?"

"Someone who stood to gain even more millions, and perhaps already has."

She was right. Since Election Day, countless special interests had been squeezing every windfall possible out of the new House. The entity that had bankrolled Abacus was undoubtedly among them.

* * *

In the days following our initial story, a flood of emails, letters, and packages stacked up at the *Vindicator*. Every crank in the country with a political conspiracy theory had found their new hero, and, they hoped, their scribe.

I received pages detailing elaborate plots—stolen elections, assorted political scandals, every form of corruption imaginable. Some penned or typed letters that went on, single-spaced, for pages. Others sent envelopes stuffed with old clippings, every other sentence underlined, exclamation points scattered throughout the margins.

And then the hate mail arrived, accusing me of being a partisan stooge. Outside of two death threats, the nastiest letters came from the Canton area, saying my story reminded them why they had voted Dad out of office decades before.

"I always knew your damn family wasn't real Republicans," one Stark County senior wrote. "But even your dad would be ashamed of this stunt!"

Fun stuff.

But a good reporter learns that amid a whole lot of crazy come tidbits of truth and, occasionally, a major find.

So I glanced over every piece of mail directed my way. And a few interesting ones did pop up. A dozen letters came from people across the country who, like Chairman Rogers, had protested the election results in their own district. And from predictable places—Peoria, Tucson, and Kansas City. All Abacus districts. The *Vindicator* published some of these letters, doing our own journalistic touchdown dance. We also received a letter from a Cincinnati neighbor of Brett Fusco, who described how Fusco had suddenly begun spending large sums of money last year, a new sports car being the most glaring purchase. "Something seemed fishy to all of us, and then he up and died," the neighbor wrote. I put the note in a file for later follow-up.

Then, three days after the story published, the true bombshell arrived.

A professional manila envelope with my name and address typed neatly on a label. No return address, but sent from a post office in Bethesda, Maryland, a mile outside Washington. And its contents were more rigid than plain paper.

Inside, two large black and white photos clung to one another. I removed them both. A time stamp—5:05 p.m., February 6—appeared in the upper-left corner of each photo. One photo captured an impressive set of historic brick row houses lined along a quaint cobblestone street. The second photo zoomed in, making the actual house numbers legible: 1842, 1844, 1846.

Looked like a street you might see in Georgetown, or Boston's Beacon Hill. But in the wider shot, a distinct city skyline rose behind the row houses. I'd only been to Philadelphia once, but recognized the William Penn statue sitting atop Philadelphia's City Hall, along with the iconic Liberty Place skyscraper towering behind it.

Then I looked again at the first photo. The close-up. Outside the house numbered "1844" sat a gray Ford Escape. And on close inspection, I could make out the Ohio license plate. Not the number, but the Ohio flag displayed on it.

"Jesus." I'd seen this SUV before. I rifled through some old clippings and found the one I was looking for. Two months ago, February 6, Lee Kelly's gray Ford Escape crashed as he drove from Philadelphia back to Ohio.

And here it was, photographed hours before.

I'd always assumed he had visited Abacus. And maybe he had. But these pictures begged a new question. Who had Kelly been visiting in this Philly neighborhood hours before his death? And who the hell had taken a photo of it and sent it to me?

PART THREE

INVESTIGATION

CHAPTER 27

19 months before the election

S TANTON WAS A creature of habit.

The congressman left his Georgetown home every morning at 6:30. If not at a breakfast fundraiser somewhere on K St., he enjoyed a private breakfast meeting at the Capital Hilton, usually with a fellow Republican, a lobbyist, or both, every morning.

He arrived at his office in the Capitol no later than 8:15, and spent the rest of the morning there, doing official government work. Lunch took place in the Members' Dining Room, where he caught up with colleagues—in many ways, the most important part of his job.

After lunch, Stanton walked a few blocks to a nondescript building on Ivy Street. He was usually joined by any number of colleagues, often traveling in packs, heading away from the stunning edifices of the congressional campus to this bland, windowless location throughout the day, sometimes multiple times per day.

Inside the building, known as "the Bunker," rows of phone cubicles hosted politician after politician as they dialed for dollars. In and out they came, each politician accompanied by a 20-something staffer lugging binders. Their collective assignment: calling through lists of donors back home and begging for campaign contributions.

The calls from the Bunker were not long, friendly conversations. That would have defeated the purpose. To ensure effective fundraising, each call time session was tracked for its efficiency, measured by dollar raised per minute. To maximize that ratio, each staffer dialed a number, asked the person who answered to wait a few moments, and as the politician wrapped up another phone call, handed him the second phone. The staffer then started dialing a new prospect with the other phone. On and on, they kept switching. Quick calls. Little small talk. Constant dialing. Rapid-fire asking.

Stanton preached the same sermon all the time, especially to new members: If the single greatest risk to your congressional career is a willingness to work across the aisle (which invites a primary challenge in a gerrymandered district), the second greatest is failing to master, with gusto, the dialing for dollars process within the Bunker. Every quarter, if your totals are not where they need to be, the pundits will deem you vulnerable, and your colleagues and caucus leaders will call you lazy. Those labels invite viable opponents and discourage your own party from digging in to help. To avoid this fate, whenever you have a moment, you hustle to the Bunker and get to work.

Hence the steady stream of visitors all day long.

Unlike the typical Bunker visitor, Stanton had a permanent, personalized calling cubicle, and he didn't simply call home to Philadelphia donors. The minority whip spent his hours calling the largest donors in the nation, raising dollars in huge chunks for the Republican Caucus. He usually wrapped up around 4:30.

Then a round of in-person fundraisers began. Stanton would pop into three or four each evening, supporting his members as they scraped together the special interest dollars that flooded the Beltway. Even a brief appearance by Stanton paid dividends, a seal of approval that the candidate enjoyed his support, and was therefore worth investing in.

After the events, usually around 8:30, Stanton headed back to the Capital Grille for a late dinner and drinks, reviewing political gossip and rumors with his closest advisers, friends, and colleagues. And then he'd head home around 10:00, dropped off in front of his front door by the black Suburban.

But his night was not quite over.

About fifteen minutes after he entered his home, the Suburban would return. This time, it would enter the garage to drop off that night's visitor. But the congressman liked to sleep alone. So at about 1:00 a.m., the garage door opened again, and the car shepherded the now disheveled guest away.

With that departure, the congressman's daily routine ended.

Six hours later, it began again.

* * *

"The man does nearly the same thing every day," Kazarov said, more to himself than anyone else.

Kazarov's goons had reported back to London about Stanton's every move, and after three days of tailing him, they had managed to get a bug on the congressman's leather briefcase, the one he clung to everywhere he went.

From that point on, two Kazarov security specialists listened to Stanton's every conversation and meeting. While they heard a lot—deals with donors, plots with pols, off-the-record leaks to reporters, late-night activities where the young women seemed to do all the work—what they didn't hear was any talk about his Abacus visit. It was as if he had never been there at all.

Two thousand miles away, Kazarov interpreted Stanton's silence optimistically.

"We will keep listening, but he doesn't plan to stop us," he told Andersson.

*   *   *

"Did you want me to do any more research on that Abacus company?"

Stanton tried answering the question that Joanie Simpson had lobbed at him, but was at a loss for words. An uncommon occurrence. So he simply stared back at her.

"It's just so strange that they're in all the districts we've been targeting in recent years," his young researcher said. "I can't imagine it's a coincidence."

Stanton responded carefully. "When I asked them about that, they said they focus on rural areas. Those happen to have a lot of the swing districts."

"Happen to?" she said dismissively. "It's as if they purposely targeted those districts. They don't seem to be anywhere else. Doesn't make a lot of sense to me unless they're up to no good."

Stanton was silent. His instinct was to snap, but that wasn't his way with Joanie.

"Did they say anything else when you were there?" she asked. "Who is DMI in the first place? Why would they have bought a dying company?"

Finally, seeing no other options, Stanton cut her off, hoping a little anger would throw her off the trail.

"Joanie," he said. "We've got so many things to do. Chasing down conspiracy theories is the last thing we need to waste time on."

But to his consternation, she remained undeterred. It was well after midnight, so he was too tired to argue further. She'd be leaving any minute anyway. But this was a concern.

He had seen enough on his Abacus visit to guess what the company was up to. And after several days of weighing his options, he had concluded that there was little he should do to disrupt it. In fact, telling anyone would be a risk. If the plot he suspected were to take place, the person at its center would know he knew. Even worse, he or she may try to stop it.

But now someone knew.

He would have to keep a close eye on her.

CHAPTER 28

JOANIE SIMPSON WAS not about to let her hunch about Abacus go unexplored. Even though Stanton hadn't said a word since his visit, the small Philadelphia company was her new obsession. Stanton's recent scolding had only compelled her to dig further. To prove him wrong.

She had long ago accepted that certain dark arts—lobbying, outside money, attack ads, even gerrymandering and quid pro quo fundraising—were part of politics. But if her hunch was right, this went beyond that. Rigging an election? In America's swing districts? Way out of bounds. Un-American. If she could stop it, she would. And she would start by convincing her boss that she was right.

So she reached out to boards of elections throughout the country, scoured newspaper clippings, and constructed her own map of what she dubbed the "Abacus Counties." As she'd first suspected, those districts almost perfectly coincided with the swing congressional districts of the country. And as she put together the timeline of Abacus's expansion, it was clear the rejuvenated company had locked in its new accounts in a frenzy. Just in time for the next election.

What were the odds?

As she always did on deep-dive research projects, Simpson documented her findings in a long memorandum, adding maps, election statistics, and detailed findings. She also summarized years of research on the vulnerability of electronic voting machines to errors and voter fraud schemes.

Given Stanton's gruff response, she kept her additional research quiet. She didn't tell her officemates, her friends from school, or her family. Didn't even tell her equally secret new boyfriend.

* * *

Joanie Simpson lived in a small apartment, a few blocks up the street from the National Zoo, in a neighborhood called Woodley Park. It was the perfect location for a young professional in the District.

Each morning, she jogged out of her apartment building down to Rock Creek Parkway, then along the Potomac and up to the Mall. She'd usually slow her pace for a few minutes to climb the steps of the Lincoln Memorial, stopping to look up at Lincoln as he peered out over his city. She'd then continue alongside the reflecting pool, veer left at the Washington Monument, run by the White House, and make her way home via Connecticut Avenue. For a political junkie, it was the best six-mile run in the world.

To get to work from Woodley Park, she walked two blocks to the subway and hopped on the red line to Capitol Hill. Getting home was just as simple.

Her apartment also placed her only a few miles from Georgetown. While this put her close to the Georgetown nightlife, for Simpson it had a more practical consequence: the Thursday night car ride to and from Stanton's townhouse took only ten minutes. The car would pick her up around 10:10 p.m., drop her off at 10:20, and get her back home shortly after 1:00. She'd made the miserable trip for more than three years.

The congressman had first come onto her during her third week on the job, a few months after her 23rd birthday. He had asked her to come into his office to review her latest research. As she walked in, he shut the door behind her.

"Thanks for coming in," he said. "This is an important issue for me. Have a seat."

She sat in the chair across from his cedar desk, taking in the office. A bookshelf behind Stanton's desk displayed photos of the congressman and presidents going back to Reagan. Stanton had aged well—same build, same sharp features in each photo—with only a few streaks of gray marking the passing of the years. An assortment of awards and plaques hung on the walls to the left and right of the bookshelf, along with his framed Yale and Harvard diplomas.

Funny. Not one photo of his family. Within moments, she learned why.

"Do you mind reading through your conclusion and recommendations?" Stanton asked.

As she recited her findings, he eyed her legs, which she had crossed as she sat down. Unlike most men, who tried to grab a quick glimpse on the sly, he cast an uncomfortably long gaze up and down, and seemed as if he couldn't care less if she noticed.

Minutes later, he stood up and paced behind his desk. She continued her report.

He walked around the desk and behind her chair, forcing her to make a decision—awkwardly twist her neck to keep eye contact or stare forward and read her report to a wall. She continued reading.

She couldn't see him, but after a minute, could hear him—his breathing, his light footsteps, right behind her. Then he touched her. As his hands lightly gripped her shoulders, she shuddered slightly, but then held still. Looking down at her papers, she continued to deliver her report as if nothing was happening. But her heart pounded away at the uninvited contact.

A few of her friends on the Hill had warned her about Stanton, but all had instructed her in the same way: "If it happens, and you want to stay employed in such a prime-time job, you have no choice but to go along." On the road, away from their wives, toasted by lobbyists and other supplicants daily, men like Stanton felt entitled to conquests. Untouchable, her friends had explained. And any women who didn't understand this reality didn't survive long in D.C.

She had objected to this awful advice and vowed she would never go along. But then she did.

For a few minutes, Stanton rubbed her shoulders, working his way down her arms midway to her elbows, while the two discussed policy as if nothing odd was taking place. Twice, he curled his fingers a few inches forward, over and down from her shoulders toward her upper chest, but pulled back after a few seconds.

When she finished her report, he lifted his hands, thanked her for her good work, and gestured to the door. As Joanie walked through the doorway, the congressman's executive assistant looked up with wide, sympathetic eyes. The woman's expression made clear she knew exactly what had happened.

Back at her desk, Joanie breathed heavily, her hands and arms trembling, eyes gazing straight ahead at a blank computer screen. She convinced herself that all her colleagues were staring, knowing exactly what had happened and judging her for being too weak to say anything. But as her breaths steadied, she glanced around. No one was paying attention to her. They had no idea. For some reason, that calmed her down.

Minutes later, Stanton rushed out of his office for a vote on the House floor. As he hustled by her desk, he stopped and handed her a file. "Could you look into this food stamp issue for me?" he asked. She took the file, and tried to utter the words "of course." But no sound came out as he strode away.

The bad behavior continued.

At first, he arranged for the occasional meeting alone in his office, just like the first one. More unwanted touching. More silent submission.

But then the congressman began to ask her to stop by the Capital Grille at the end of the day to review issues. She'd walk over from the office. There, he insisted she drink the same drinks he did. Because they were in public, he touched her more subtly than in the office, but inevitably, he'd manage to brush her thigh, her arm, her hand. Nothing more.

At about 10:00, they'd go their separate ways.

Then it got worse. Much worse.

One Thursday evening several months after the first encounter, as she lay stretched out on her couch after a workout, Joanie's cell phone rang. A 215 area code, a number she didn't recognize. She picked up, and Stanton's voice came over the line.

"In fifteen minutes, a black Suburban is going to pull up outside your apartment," he said as if instructing her on a work assignment. "I'm going to have it take you over to my place."

She felt sick as she processed his words, deciding how to react. She had learned to tolerate the prior behavior, as bad as it was. Classic harassment, but she could handle it. This new episode would elevate things to a new level of abuse.

But she steeled herself to go through with it. She had come a long way from her rough Missouri suburb, and this was the price of the job, and the career, she felt privileged to have. She could handle this.

If she ever got fired, she would certainly tell the world. But as long she had the job, as long as she was making a dent in her hefty student loans, as long as she advanced conservative policies and worked for one of America's most powerful men, she would go along.

"Okay," she said.

As promised, a dark Suburban pulled up in front of her building at 10:10. She crossed the sidewalk and climbed in.

She stared out the tinted window the whole ride, tapping her nails nervously against the leather seat. When the car jostled along the cobblestone streets of Georgetown, she breathed more quickly. They stopped in front of a three-story townhouse, waited a few seconds, then pulled into a garage.

"That's the door there. Simply ring that bell and he'll let you in," the driver said, pointing. His dark eyes looked at her in the rear-view mirror as he spoke. She glared back. Like Stanton's assistant, he knew exactly what his boss was doing. Spineless.

She rang the bell, which produced a soft buzz and a click as the door's lock unbolted. Stanton's voice echoed through a small speaker, "Come on in, and go up one flight of stairs."

As the stairway leveled off at the second floor, she followed a hallway into a dimly lit entertainment room. She walked past a large bar to her right, stopping in front of a dark leather couch that faced the far wall. A TV hung on the wall, with two large windows on its left and right. The shades of each window were down.

Still in a suit, tie off, white shirt unbuttoned two buttons down, Stanton stood behind the bar. He flashed the biggest smile she had seen from him, a painful mix of creepy and cheesy.

"Welcome. Can I offer you a drink?" he asked.

"No thanks."

"I'm having a gin and tonic," he said. "You should have one too."

This was not a suggestion.

"Okay."

He fixed both drinks as she stood stiffly, looking out the window.

"You are so beautiful, right now and every day," Stanton said to her. He had never before addressed her in a personal way, although his voice sounded as wooden as at work.

"Thank you," she said. Normally she'd smile at such a compliment but refused to now.

"Thank you for your willingness to come over here. I have such a hard time resisting you, and I've enjoyed getting to know you better."

The debate champion considered the rebuttals she wanted to fire back his way. *I'm only here because I don't want to lose my job.* Or, *We don't know each other at all. You just rub me like a creep whenever you feel like it.*

But she held back. Too much to lose.

"Let's sit down," he said as he finished pouring both drinks.

Hoping the gin and tonic would make it all go smoother, she downed it and asked for another. She rarely drank hard alcohol, and weighed all of 120 pounds, so the second drink had her head spinning as she had hoped.

The two then sat on the couch together.

"Tell me more about yourself," he said, once again flashing the cheesy grin.

Joanie turned away, looking out the window as they talked. She explained what her parents did, talked about her childhood, her schooling, her debate victories. She spoke with no emotion, determined not to leave an impression that she was enjoying the visit, or inviting anything more from her boss.

Stanton responded to everything she said positively. "I love St. Louis," "Debating was also my strong suit," "Williams is a great school." The same smile accompanied each insincere word.

As she wound down her story, he sidled closer to her. The next moves followed quickly. His right hand settled on her left knee. Then moved up her thigh about six inches, resting there for a few minutes, squeezing gently. Finally, he lifted his right arm, put it around her shoulder, and forcefully pulled her toward him.

She never said "no," but she certainly never said "yes." She endured the next two hours as if it were a work assignment, with two more stiff drinks helping her get through it. As a clock from another room struck 1:00, he abruptly stood up.

"I'm so glad you stopped by," he said. "It's probably a good time for you to go home. I'll give you a call next Thursday."

Joanie said nothing and dressed quickly, walked down to the garage where the Suburban awaited, and sat quietly in the back for the brief ride home. Once in her own bedroom, she threw her clothes into a heap and showered, scrubbing from head to toe, and brushed her teeth furiously. Between the drinks she'd downed and the memory of those agonizing two hours, she hardly slept the rest of the night.

The routine continued. Each Thursday, the Suburban appeared at 10:05. A few drinks, conversation, followed by aggressive advances and requests, all fulfilled. At 1:00 a.m., she went home and showered.

The night visits brought an end to the inappropriate office meetings. And he never asked her to the Capital Grille again. In hindsight, those early interactions had been nothing but means to an end—tests of her willingness to go along with the Thursday visits. Tests, sadly, that she had passed.

Over time, the shallow warm-up conversation evolved into discussions about what they most had in common: policy and politics. At least the views she expressed in the visits influenced the congressman's thinking and actions back at his day job. This didn't make the situation any better, but if she buried the negative aspects of each encounter deep within, she had access to someone who could advance her conservative principles.

And now, someone who could do something about Abacus.

CHAPTER 29

"W E HAVE SHIPPED to 121 counties and eighteen different states."

Fall arrived in London, and Andersson was providing Kazarov with an in-person status report. The meeting came after Ariens' death, after Stanton's visit, after months of tailing the congressman.

"We are where we need to be," Andersson continued, "with some room to spare."

"Great news. We have certainly paid enough to get to this point."

Location acquisition and rollout had cost a pretty penny. The rapid modernization of the Abacus headquarters had totaled millions, as did the staffing, mostly transfers to Philadelphia from across Kazarov's empire. Abacus set a sale price per machine a full 35 percent below the cost of producing them. And it didn't help that they needed to rush everything.

Then there was the design work. The easy part had been stealing the vote-counting technology by reverse engineering the latest Diebold machine. The more difficult and costly part had been designing the Abacus machine to manipulate election results when and where they wanted, without detection. But this was the part Kazarov had enjoyed the most, because his engineers had manipulated the machine's paper trail mechanism—newly required to *improve* security—to do their dirty work.

In theory, the paper trail mechanism allowed a voter to verify that her vote was properly recorded. It did so by displaying to the voter a paper receipt reflecting the votes cast on the electronic screen. Once verified, the receipt was stored separately.

But a decade of research had found that voters rarely examined the paper receipt as it was displayed, and therefore rarely caught errors, particularly for down-ballot races. The Abacus engineers exacerbated that problem by designing a paper display mechanism that made it difficult to closely scrutinize each line of the displayed receipt.

To rig an outcome in a targeted district, engineers programmed Abacus machines to occasionally omit a voter's electronic vote for the Democratic House candidate from the displayed paper receipt. If a voter noticed the omission, she would assume she had neglected to vote in that race, scroll back on the electronic machine to revote, and the vote would then appear on the printed receipt. The correction would take effect. But if the voter didn't notice the omission on the paper receipt—and voters rarely noticed—that non-vote on the paper receipt would also register as a non-vote back on the memory card. The original electronic vote for the Democratic candidate would disappear, and the paper and electronic records would match up, both recording a non-vote.

"Brilliant!" Kazarov said after Andersson had first demonstrated the mechanism. "The machine allows us to induce a mistake that the voter would never have made with a simple paper ballot."

"Even better," Andersson said. "It is the act of the voter, by unintentionally verifying the mistake, that covers up the manipulation."

But these hard costs and design expenses had only been the beginning.

In small counties, Abacus' low prices and slick sales practices had won the day because their competitors had only gone through the motions. In the larger counties, Diebold and Seiko had competed fiercely to keep every account, slashing their prices as well.

That's where Kazarov's Eastern business experience had come in handy. But buying off elections officials in twelve counties to favor Abacus had cost more than Kazarov had paid anywhere else.

"These American bureaucrats are demanding," he complained.

A pittance had usually secured Kazarov what he needed in former Soviet and developing countries. The officials there made little to begin with. The Americans earned more in salary, and this was a far less common transaction for them, so they demanded a higher reward.

"They are," Andersson said. "We've only paid people when it was an absolutely essential location."

Still, Despite his complaining, Kazarov considered the $72 million a small investment for the value of his purchase.

"For control of a nation's legislature? A bargain," Kazarov said as their meeting ended.

His other investment, in the more standard expenditures of American politics, remained a complete waste. Energy 2020 remained stillborn. But his plan B would only work if plan A continued to play out on the surface, so he funded both.

CHAPTER 30

14 months before the election

"Congressman, I really think you need to look closely at what's going on with that Abacus company we talked about several months back."

Her stomach knotted tightly with nerves, Joanie could tell her statement caught him off guard. But his response was not as hostile as before.

"I had forgotten about all that," he said. "What did you find?"

"Here you go. It's all here."

She handed him the memo that she had worked on for months. She had spent the evening before editing it on paper and then had printed out the final version in the office earlier that afternoon. But she chose to share it here, in the privacy of his townhome, where she had his ear.

"It sounds crazy, but I'm convinced Abacus strategically placed its machines in all the swing districts across the country. Here's the most up-to-date list. You'll recognize every district where they have established a presence. The extent to which they went to secure these locations is incredible."

Stanton looked seriously at the list she pointed to at the back of the memo. He slowly nodded as if just beginning to comprehend her words.

"I think they're trying to steal the election by stealing all the swing districts. Nothing else makes sense."

Stanton read through the memo, page by page. When he finished, he looked up.

"I'm afraid you may be right. These are almost all the swing districts in the country. Have you mentioned this to anyone else?"

She shook her head. "I haven't. I wanted to tell you first after I finished my research. I'll leave it for you to tell others."

"Good for you. This goes way beyond party. It's an attack on the heart of our democracy," Stanton said, his eyes locked on hers. "I'm going to bring this to Speaker Williams and Leader Marshall immediately, then get the authorities involved."

Simpson smiled, her breathing eased. "I couldn't agree more. Just think of the positive press you'll get by exposing this."

Stanton shook his head and flashed a frown of disappointment, cutting her short. "This is so much bigger than my own career," he said.

They finished their conversation slightly before 11:00, about 30 minutes later than they had ever talked before. And then, another first: "It's probably best if you head home now," Stanton said. "Let's meet in the office Monday to discuss our next steps."

*   *   *

Saturday morning, iPod earbuds jammed in each ear, Joanie charged out of her apartment door faster than usual. Fall weekends were her vacation, and with the sun beaming overhead, this looked to be a perfect one. Plus, Thursday night had liberated her. The congressman took her memo seriously. They were going to stop Abacus.

A mile into Rock Creek Parkway, Joanie ran through a section of the trail that wound away from the road, under a thick canopy of trees and out of sight from traffic. Her head bobbed slightly as she was consumed with the Taylor Swift lyrics blaring through her ears.

She saw it coming, but only at the last moment.

From behind an oak tree, the thick metal barrel of a baseball bat swung toward her in a blur and then struck her square in the chest. She tumbled backward, her shoulder blades crashing down first, then the back of her head pummeling into the concrete.

Flat on her back, ears ringing, Joanie shifted her eyes toward the source of the blow. He was a thick figure, with a dark hat and mask over his head, otherwise dressed as a jogger. The man leaped past her, then reached down and clamped his large, gloved hand into her right armpit. He dragged her off the trail and further away from the road.

Joanie attempted to scream, but somewhere in her chest the air she needed was escaping—a light whistle was all that came out. The sharp throbbing in her head now gave way to the even greater pain of what felt like 1,000 pounds of pressure crushing her ribcage.

Sticks and brush scratched her face and legs as the man pulled her deeper into the woods. He stopped. She groaned as he placed his right foot on her hip and pushed down hard, pinning her to the ground. Unable to move, Joanie could do nothing but watch as the masked man raised the bat over his head, then swung again.

CHAPTER 31

14 months before the election

"DID YOU SEE that story about the jogger?" Stanton asked as he walked through his office door on Monday morning.

"Yes, it was on the news all day yesterday," his assistant said. "Awful. Looks like they still don't know who the victim is."

"Just a terrible crime," Stanton said. "Scary."

The *Washington Post* had run the Rock Creek mugging death on Page 1 of Sunday morning's Metro section. A young female jogger—white, tall, thin, brunette—brutally beaten to death on the popular running course. Cash and credit cards stolen. No hint of sexual assault. No identification found. Investigators estimated that the battered corpse had lain just off the trail for most of the day before a park ranger doing her night rounds discovered her.

Stanton sat down at his desk and picked up Monday's paper. Below the fold, a police sketch of the victim's face appeared.

He froze. Felt instantly sick to his stomach. Stared at the image for five minutes before calling his chief of staff.

"Get in here. Right away."

Seth West entered the office, closing the door behind him. The two huddled together and Stanton filled him in on the dilemma. West made a call from the desk phone, hung up seconds later, then tried again. He hung up again, then looked up at his boss.

"Straight to voicemail."

West then called D.C. police headquarters.

* * *

Two days later, at 11:00 in the evening, Stanton got the call.

"Chief Procter here, Tom. We cracked the case."

"Okay," Stanton said uneasily. "Fill me in."

"The prints on the murderer's baseball bat traced back to a guy from southeast D.C. with a rap sheet pages long. His name is Johnny Rutherford."

"And?"

The chief explained that a judge had issued a warrant to enter Rutherford's apartment. "Earlier tonight, our SWAT guys surrounded his residence, and when they tried to enter, he jumped out a window, broke both ankles as he landed in an alley, and popped off a few shots before our guys took him out."

"And you're sure it's him?"

"Oh yeah. It's him. Not only did the fingerprints match, but this idiot left the girl's car keys, ID, and credit cards in the trash bin outside his apartment."

*   *   *

When the news hit that the Rock Creek Killer was off the streets, Washington breathed a sigh of relief. Worry-free jogging could recommence.

The House minority whip, on the other hand, still nervously paced his office the morning after Rutherford died.

At first, Stanton feared the prospect of speaking at Simpson's funeral. Pulling off that performance would have challenged even him. But her family decided to fly her body back to St. Louis for the service, allowing Stanton to videotape a message instead. Bullet dodged.

But that didn't take care of his bigger concern—eliminating any paper trail back to Abacus, and doing so without raising any suspicion. The memo itself was gone. Minutes after Joanie had left his townhouse the night she handed over her startling research to him, he'd removed the two-page appendix that so helpfully listed the Abacus districts. That was a keeper. But the rest of the document was soon burning in his fireplace.

But what about her electronic files? She'd typed that memo up somewhere, probably at work.

On the Friday after her death, having waited what felt like an appropriate length of time, he made his move.

"Joanie was working on some sensitive things for me," he told West late in the afternoon when only they remained. "I would love to review her main research projects to find all the pressing stuff I need."

"We can always have a staff member do that for you," West said.

"No." Stanton shot him an intense glare. "These are very sensitive."

It helped that West knew his pattern with women staffers. Keeping his behavior from going public was a top, joint priority.

"I understand. Her documents would be stored on a shared drive, so you can go through those."

"Thank you," Stanton said, satisfied.

West sat down at Stanton's computer, clicked the mouse a few times, and brought the office's shared drive up onto the screen. "There you go," he said, standing up to leave Stanton alone at his desk. Except in true emergencies, they had an unwritten rule that Stanton cleaned up his own messes.

He scrolled through Simpson's documents. Of the 218 files stored in her research folder, none displayed the word "Abacus" in the title. Because she typically worked on issues that he directly assigned her, Stanton recognized most of the documents and skipped those. He instead focused on the titles and subjects he didn't recognize, opening memoranda and notes about topics she had pursued on her own. Farm subsidies. Clean coal. School vouchers. Ukraine. She got into everything.

Then the one-word title caught his eye.

"Epeius."

Odd name. He'd heard it somewhere before. More importantly, the document had been created three months ago, not long after he'd asked her to look into Abacus.

Stanton double-clicked on the mouse and found himself staring directly at the electronic version of the Abacus memo he had destroyed.

He looked up at the door like a nervous kid preparing to steal something, making sure no one was watching. He skimmed through the memo one last time, pushed the delete button, and watched it vanish from Simpson's research folder.

Before shutting the computer down, he went online and googled *Epeius*. That's right. Freshman year English, *The Iliad*. Epeius was the Greek soldier who'd designed the Trojan horse. Stanton shook his head, impressed yet again. Only a debate champ would see that the low-cost, vote-rigging Abacus machines were the 21st century version of the ancient ruse.

He closed down the computer, turned off the light, and walked out of the office.

For the first time since Joanie Simpson had handed him the memo, he relaxed.

*   *   *

GREATER PHILADELPHIA

All afternoon, Irene Stanton eyed them: A dozen red roses, sitting in an ornate glass vase, the new centerpiece of the marble island in her kitchen.

They had arrived just before noon with a simple note. "Love you, darling. Tom."

By four, her initial delight at the unexpected gesture had worn off. She now glared at them, at first with suspicion, now with anger.

They were too much. One gesture too many.

She knew.

Irene Stanton knew now. She had known for years.

She had heard the talk about her husband. Rumors of infidelity had circled D.C. for years. But she'd known long before any of that, before he even ascended to Congress. The way he looked at other women made it obvious. He didn't casually observe their beauty, something she would understand. She did the same thing, of men and women. Everybody did.

His look was more intense. Too intense. He eyed them as conquests, right in front of her. Right in front of their kids.

She recognized the look as the same one he had cast her way years ago. But she hadn't minded back then. A small-town beauty queen, Irene Stanton nee Rettof had grown up not far from Scranton. Her schoolgirl life was consumed by cheerleading practice all week, Friday night games, pageants on Saturdays, and Mass every Sunday. A pleasant, stable childhood in a small Pennsylvania town.

But by the time she reached her senior year, she was bored. Penn State, teeming with kids from across the state, provided her ticket out. And cheerleading for the Nittany Lions across the country expanded her sights even further. After graduating, she joined a mid-sized Philadelphia law firm as a paralegal. Dull job, but it covered the costs of enjoying big city life.

Three years and two boyfriends later, State Representative Tom Stanton passed through the firm for a fundraiser. Irene wasn't political, but when too few people outside the firm RSVP'd, the partner in charge had pulled all staff from their workstations to fill the room. Irene stood several people deep as they gathered in a semi-circle to watch this young charmer make his case.

He had spotted her halfway through his speech. Her shoulder-length blonde hair, blue eyes, and full lips always inspired double takes, but his intense gaze continued for the rest of the talk. The whole room noticed. Her fellow paralegals ribbed her for the rest of the evening.

After that, he came on strong, and she loved it. He was good-looking, wealthy, charming. People said he was a star in the making, and the potential for the limelight excited her. They married two years later.

"I should have known better," she often told her best friend, the only person she could confide in. She had scolded herself for years, and then stopped caring.

"You couldn't have known, Irene," her friend would always respond. "You're a different person now. You were a kid, looking for a ticket out."

On the one hand, her friend was right. She was a wholly different person than the young paralegal Stanton had wooed. Through her years as the first lady of Tom's statehouse and congressional districts, she had evolved into a sophisticated woman. She served on highly respected non-profit boards, dedicated to battling the related problems of domestic violence and child abuse. She became a gifted public speaker, making numerous public appearances on her own. In recent years, pundits speculated that she might seek office herself.

On the other hand, she remained angry at herself. Angry because even from the outset their relationship had been shallow—physical attraction, mutual personal ambition, and little else. During the courtship, those surface-level factors had trumped the cold reality that there was no actual emotion between them. But that reality had set in only months after their honeymoon ended.

Unsatisfying almost from the start, the marriage tumbled downhill even more rapidly after their second child was born. Irene remained strikingly beautiful, but she was no longer youthful. Apparently that's what Tom wanted because that's when he first started gawking at younger women. That's when he began to disappear for hours at a time without any good explanation. And when she talked about the issues she cared about, he'd tune her out.

Once Tom entered Congress, it only got worse. And other clear signs emerged.

Before they both went to Washington, Stanton's law school buddy Oliver Ariens had been loud, talkative, fun to be around. Irene and Oliver had hit it off from the first time they met. When Ariens and Stanton entered Congress together, she had looked forward to seeing the Arienses often. But when the two couples dined together, Oliver wouldn't look her in the eye. He couldn't hold a conversation. He appeared sheepish, too quiet. But only with her.

Whatever Oliver witnessed in their shared Capitol Hill apartment made him uncomfortable around her. She sensed what it was.

Later, when Tom moved to Georgetown, he essentially disappeared between Monday and Thursday. A morning phone call, and sometimes one at 9:00 or 9:30 in the evening, were the only times he would call during the day. She knew he was a night owl, yet he still never talked to her after 10:00.

And then there was Arlene Bradley. At Tom's side for years, she had always been such a sweet woman. So positive, so gracious. But around the time Tom moved to Georgetown, she'd changed. Like Oliver, she couldn't look Irene in the eye. Whenever Irene called, the pleasant voice that had answered became pained once Irene identified herself as the caller. No more small talk. No laughs.

Add it all up, and Irene Stanton was certain her husband was with other women all the time. At first, she'd cried herself to sleep most nights in Bucks County, eyes puffy and red as she drove the kids to school the next morning. But over time, she grew numb to it. She went through the motions of appearing together, beauty queen smile and wave always on full display, but then they lived their separate lives. Her causes kept her engaged. But except for her kids and some Philadelphia friends, her personal life felt empty. For years.

But when Joanie Simpson died, everything changed.

Irene had never met Joanie, but from the photos in the paper, she knew the young aide was exactly Tom's type. In fact, the researcher looked slightly like Irene had when he'd ogled her all those years ago. She guessed that her husband had been sleeping with this young woman up until the time of her brutal slaying. And then, within days of her death, Tom's behavior changed completely. He started paying attention to Irene for the first time in years, doting on her—and proactively, not just when he was required to.

He reached out to the kids. He added family photos to his office. He even started calling Irene after 10:00. And now, out of the blue, a dozen red roses. A sweet note.

On the one hand, Irene was thrilled to have Tom back for the first time in decades. Which is why her first response to the flowers had been a sigh and a smile, and a few minutes dedicated to putting them at the center of the table. The girl from Scranton loved the renewed attention.

But by afternoon, that had worn off. The sight of those roses now provoked the opposite reaction. And the anger boiling up clarified for her that Tom's switch had come too late.

After years of feeling helpless about her empty personal life, after years of betrayal, she now felt empowered. Empowered to even the score. To set things straight.

Irene Stanton knew something no one else did. And it was time to do something about it, White House be damned.

At 4:00, she called a private investigator and set up a time to meet. Then she walked to the edge of her backyard, faced the woods, and tossed the flowers, vase and all, as far as she could.

CHAPTER 32

WASHINGTON, DC

Three months before the election

"WHAT GIVES?" LEE Kelly asked angrily.

Stanton and Lee Kelly nearly collided in the members-only dining area at the Capitol. The two had been friendly in the early years. For a time, they had played squash every few weeks. So Stanton was taken aback by the ferocity in Kelly's voice.

"What do you mean?" he asked, raising both hands up.

"Coming to my district twice in four months?" Kelly asked. "C'mon! And those ads going after me are over the top. It's like you really want me gone. Bad form, Tom."

"Sorry, Lee," Stanton said. "It's not personal. Your party's on the wrong side of too many issues, and this is our best chance to get some big things done."

"But you know our voting records are barely different," Kelly shot back.

"It's your vote for leader that matters, nothing else. You know that."

As Stanton walked away, he chuckled.

If only Kelly knew.

By visiting eastern Ohio only twice, he had actually taken it easy on his old friend. He'd saved the full-court press for districts where he hadn't known the Democrats as well. He had initially crisscrossed the country, dropping in on each of the targeted districts. Unlike with Kelly, he'd sought out and recruited top-notch candidates. Raised money to help them. Jetted back to their districts to rally the troops. Orchestrated early attack ads, followed by really nasty mail. All much worse than what he'd done against Kelly.

It only made sense. How often do you get a preview of the next election, district by district? If the Abacus plan was going to happen, he might as well position himself to take full credit, and gain full benefit.

Sure, Lee Kelly was a good guy, so he had treated him better than most. But the poor guy was going to lose Ohio's Sixth District no matter what. So even there, Stanton needed to stop through at least twice to get any of the credit.

CHAPTER 33

LONDON

November 7: One day before the election

"WE ARE IN place in 35 districts. From those districts, we have identified the 27 races that remain close today."

On a drizzly London morning, Liam Andersson briefed Kazarov on the next day's plan while both men looked up at a large map of the United States. Thirty-five districts across the nation were highlighted in red. Twenty-seven of them had large, black checkmarks over them.

"There are a number of districts where the wrong candidate is far ahead," Andersson said. "With our machines in place, we could opt to win those districts as well. But the amount of vote elimination required would increase risk of detection."

"And we don't need those seats to win anyway," Kazarov said.

"Exactly. Winning every district would raise alarms."

"How will this look to the American people?" Kazarov said thoughtfully. "I cannot help but think that in Russia voters would smell the rat."

"The result will, of course, be a surprise. But the districts are competitive enough that there will not appear to be any irregularities. And because we control some counties in each district, we are able to spread the elimination of votes broadly enough that no county will see an extreme shift in its voting pattern."

"And the machines?"

"The early votes continue to show that our strategy works. Less than fifteen percent of the voters have noticed and corrected the non-vote on the paper receipt. The remainder unknowingly confirm it, so the vote disappears."

The wonders of engineering and patent theft. Kazarov paused for a few moments, then allowed a small grin.

"Your friend Mr. Stanton has been an enormous help."

"What do you mean?" Andersson asked. Focused solely on the Abacus operation, he had not been part of the Stanton surveillance operation.

"Having received a brief glimpse of the future, our esteemed politician has devoted the past year to campaigning with great passion in our districts. For his own political gain, he will eagerly take credit for our results. We will happily let him take it."

Kazarov paused for a moment to enjoy the thought before moving on to their next hurdle. "And how about our plan for after the election?"

"It is underway. We should be able to sell Abacus to another company within months. Any buyer will likely replace our machines immediately. Their interest will be in acquiring our locations."

Ariens and Stanton's young researcher had demonstrated that anyone looking closely might deduce the role Abacus played in the election. So Kazarov had set two priorities: to conceal the scheme long enough to accomplish his legislative goals, and to eliminate any connection back to Marcellus. As long as investigators didn't discover who was behind the company, it would be impossible for them to rescind the one legislative decision that Kazarov valued.

"The crime may be discovered," Kazarov said. "It is our fingerprints that must be hidden."

CHAPTER 34

YOUNGSTOWN

April 5: 148 days after the election

I T DIDN'T TAKE long to pinpoint the exact Philly neighborhood where the Escape had been parked. Like Georgetown, Society Hill was famous for its cobblestone streets and eighteenth- and nineteenth-century row houses.

Helpfully, the angle of the photo and the house numbers further narrowed the location. Four parallel streets enjoyed that view of downtown Philadelphia at the point where the house numbers fell in the 1800 range.

Lombard Street, Pine Street, Delancey Street, and Spruce Street.

Like any county in America, the Philadelphia County Auditor's website would provide the easiest way to find who lived at a precise street address. So I logged on and wrote down the name listed for every even-numbered house number between 1840 and 1860. The names wouldn't mean anything, but at least they would provide a universe for further research. Who knows? Maybe Jody Kelly would recognize one of them.

Lombard Street: Smith, Burghard, Thomas, Avril, Marsh.

Pine Street: Jacoby, Kennedy, Mansfield, Gomez, Ahn.

Delancey Street: Wu, Merriman, Stanton, Porter, Jefferson.

Hold it.

1846 Delancey Street. Paul M. Stanton.

Lee Kelly had been friendly with Congressman Tom Stanton over the years, so friendly that after Stanton had attacked him last year, I'd written a story about it. I wondered if Paul Stanton was any relation.

I quickly searched to affirm this was Stanton's residence. Of course, Stanton wouldn't officially live in central Philly. His district was in the suburbs. But politicians commonly keep a "district home," where they're expected to have a residence, and their real home, where they actually live. Journalists stopped caring about this deceitful dichotomy years ago, and it rarely comes up in campaigns because so many on both sides of the aisle do it.

Sure enough, Stanton had a son named Paul, and his full name matched the name of the owner of 1846 Delancey. A short online search showed that Paul Stanton had left for school in Colorado years ago and never returned. Odds were good that Tom Stanton lived in this home when he wasn't in Washington.

No big deal, except for the fact that Kelly had parked outside this secret home on the final afternoon of his life.

CHAPTER 35

April 6: 149 days after the election

SETH WEST BURST through Stanton's office door at 10:00 in the morning, the Thursday after the story ran in the *Youngstown Vindicator*.

"You're not going to believe this, but the guy that broke the Abacus story just called our office," West said.

Stanton looked up from his desk, narrowing his eyes as he heard the bad news. When the Abacus story had broken over the weekend, he'd initially been alarmed. But the Republican pushback had been so fierce that Abacus was on its way to becoming just another partisan squabble. Even better, Stanton had successfully stayed out of the fray. Until this call.

"Why would he want to talk to us?" Stanton asked. "Did you tell him Marshall was leading on this?"

"We absolutely did, but he insisted on talking to you."

"Did he say what it was about?"

"He wouldn't say. Only that he had some questions that only you could answer."

"About Abacus?"

"He didn't say it was about Abacus. But why else would he be calling?"

Stanton sat quietly. He remembered this reporter from a phone call in the fall: Something Sharpe, calling about the campaign against Lee Kelly. From Youngstown of all places. Seemed like a burnout. Stanton had actually been impressed that the same guy had shown the moxie to break the Abacus story.

"If we refuse, it may be worse," he said to West. "Tell him I have five minutes to talk. I'll just deny everything anyway."

* * *

Stanton's chief of staff called back and patched me through.

"Good morning, Congressman. Thank you for taking my call."

"You're welcome. Now that you're Bob Woodward, to what do I owe this call?"

I ignored the flattery. "Let me cut right to the chase. You and Lee Kelly were friends for years, weren't you?"

"We sure were. Such a tragedy what happened to him. Awful."

"But you fought pretty hard to get him out of office?"

"We talked about this before, if I remember right. That's my job. He knew it; I knew it." Stanton said. "But he was a good man, we went back a long way, and I still can't believe he's gone. Can I ask why you're calling me asking about Lee Kelly?"

I had set up the entire interview for the next question—talk casually, get him comfortable, get a sense of how he answers basic, straightforward questions, and then, *boom.* "Because I wanted to know why he was parked outside your Society Hill townhome only five hours before he died."

The phone went quiet. For a long time.

"I don't have the foggiest idea what you're talking about," Stanton finally said.

"I have photographs of Lee Kelly's Escape parked outside your Delancey Street townhouse the same day he died. What were you and he talking about when he stopped by?"

"Again, I have no idea what you're talking about." He uttered the words slowly. Angrily.

"Do you deny that that's your townhome on Delancey Street?"

"It's my son's, but I do stay there on occasion." Smart answer. Stanton didn't want to dig a deeper hole by lying when it was clear I already knew the answer. And technically, his response was factual.

"True. I can't imagine your son stays there often when he lives in Colorado." Getting under the skin of a pro like Stanton can be the best way to cause a rare misstep.

"Sharpe, if you're going to write an imbecile story about how I sometimes stay in downtown Philly, be my guest. As for Kelly, I have no idea what the fuck you're talking about. And you can quote me on that."

Clearly this was meant to be a closing line, but I didn't back down.

"The day Kelly died, he drove to Philadelphia. His car was seen outside your Philly townhome that afternoon. Now, you just admitted you were friends, and he told me the same last year. What a wild coincidence that he was parked one door down from your home. You guys must have talked about something?"

"I'm done," Stanton shot back. "Haven't you already gotten enough grief for your cockamamie conspiracy theory about Abacus? And now you're trying to suggest that I had something to do with the death of an old friend? Give me a break."

"I wasn't suggesting . . ."

My receiver clicked, then sounded a solid dial tone.

I retraced the call in my head. Had Stanton let anything slip?

The congressman had deftly admitted the one damaging fact I already knew. His tantrum at the end had felt like a slight overreaction. But, come to think of it, Stanton's little fit had given him a perfect excuse to get off the call as quickly as possible.

This guy was a pro.

CHAPTER 36

YOUNGSTOWN

April 7: 150 days after the election

I'D RECEIVED MY share of death threats over the years. Covering corruption will do that. But they had never amounted to anything. So the threats that came after the Abacus story didn't bother me.

But another development did.

The morning after I talked with Stanton, a dark gray Suburban with tinted windows was idling a half-block down from my home. Definitely not from the neighborhood.

Then it was parked half a block from the *Vindicator* as I walked to lunch a few hours later. The rest of the day, it remained there.

Inside the safety of the newsroom, I went about my business like any other day. Time to find out everything possible about Majority Leader Stanton.

He'd lived large in the early years, rapidly rose through Congress, and enjoyed a growing reputation as a national star. Stanton's name had emerged on the short list of potential vice presidential nominees when President Banfield conducted her search. But in the end, the low perch of minority whip had sealed his fate—compared to the senators and governors in the mix, it was not substantial enough to make the leap to national office. A few *Roll Call* articles had speculated that until Marshall retired, or the Republicans took over the House, Stanton had reached his ceiling despite his talent and ambition.

Stanton and his wife, Irene, had raised three kids back in Philadelphia. But despite what looked to be an intact family, the gossip columns buzzed about Stanton's womanizing, including preying on younger Hill staffers. A common trait in the cesspool of modern-day Washington, but rarely displayed so publicly by a man of his stature and ambition.

Overall, nothing about Stanton stuck out much. Until eighteen months ago, when two things changed.

While he always had been an aggressive partisan, Stanton had treated this past election as his own personal crusade to win the majority. Just as he'd visited eastern Ohio to stump for McCarthy—and against his old pal Lee Kelly—dozens of headlines from around the country documented similar visits.

"Stanton Back to Tucson for Third Time."

"Minority Whip Back in Peoria, Attacks Mayor."

"Stanton Stumps in Colorado Districts . . . Again"

And so on. I called a contact of mine at the *Toledo Blade* who confirmed that Stanton had dropped into northwest Ohio multiple times.

In total, news clippings showed that Stanton had campaigned in 34 districts throughout the fall, traveling to 26 of them at least twice. But as in Toledo, he'd started way before that. Stanton proactively recruited a number of the candidates in the first place and began steering dollars their way before anyone else was even paying attention. A check from his leadership PAC was the first contribution many of the candidates received.

On closer inspection, all but three districts Stanton visited were Abacus districts. (The others were a pair of districts neighboring his in Pennsylvania, and one in New Jersey, right across the river from Philly.) This was not a complete surprise, as Abacus occupied the same contested turf that any strategist would target for pick-up opportunities. Still, the overlap was uncanny, Especially since House tradition frowned upon blitzing fellow members in their own districts. But in the Abacus districts, Stanton ferociously attacked long-time colleagues. Outside of those districts, he left his colleagues alone.

Newspapers credited Stanton's effort as the key to the November surprise. The *Arizona Daily Sun* wrote that not since Newt Gingrich's "Contract with America" campaign had one House member so aggressively campaigned for his colleagues across the country. And the conservative *Washington Times* ran front-page photos of twelve of the freshman winners. The headline above the beaming faces declared: "Team Stanton."

The step up from minority whip to majority leader, and the pivotal role he played in helping so many win their races, now fueled growing Stanton presidential hype. He would be one of the front-runners, the talking heads all predicted. And he was already traveling to Iowa and New Hampshire.

Add it all up, and Stanton had enjoyed one hell of a year—politically. But that was offset by a terrible run personally.

A *Washington Post* obituary quoted Stanton praising the famed lobbyist Oliver Ariens after his fatal heart attack two years ago. And Stanton's name appeared in articles following the brutal murder of his young research aide in Rock Creek Park. I remembered the horrific crime but I'd forgotten the victim had worked for Stanton.

Some inside-the-beltway columnists connected Stanton's run of personal tragedy to his spirited campaign for the House, which began not long after the Simpson killing. The close-up view of mortality had energized him to make his mark, they speculated.

Psychobabble.

Brett Fusco. Lee Kelly. Untimely and mysterious deaths of those who had stumbled across the Abacus plot.

Now two more odd deaths. Both connected to a man who also was connected to Kelly's demise.

With all this information to chew on, I now realized giving Stanton a reason not to talk to me again had been a mistake.

CHAPTER 37

PENNSYLVANIA
February 6: 90 days after the election

L EE KELLY SPED due east about 20 miles south of the hilly outskirts of Pittsburgh. An orange sun rose above the horizon straight ahead of him, nearly blinding him as it morphed from a shiny thin line, to a dim half circle, to a full and beaming sphere. He pulled down the driver-side visor and squinted uncomfortably as he cruised along I-70. An hour later, he passed just south of Harrisburg, and by 11:15, the imposing Philadelphia skyline rose in the distance.

Kelly didn't know what he would find but was determined to take a close look. Having served on the Government Operations Committee of the House, he'd mastered America's voting infrastructure over the years. That's why what he learned in Monroe County had piqued his curiosity, and why last night's online research had further raised his suspicion. Might as well visit in person.

And if he had time, he'd see if his old friend Tom Stanton was in town. He shouldn't have let the campaign get so personal. Time to make amends. So along with catching up with a few ex-aides while he drove, he checked in with Stanton's office. The congressman's assistant said that Stanton was in the Philly office that day and might be available later.

Kelly arrived at the city's run-down warehouse district just before noon and pulled into Abacus' headquarters. The lot bustled with activity. A steady stream of workers walked back and forth from the main entrance, carrying what looked to be personal effects to and from the parking lot. Larger trucks and vans sat outside, and even more people lugged equipment and boxes into the building.

Never shy, Kelly parked his Escape and walked into the main entrance. Once inside, more of the same: boxes everywhere, people scurrying about. The lobby he entered looked to be a typical reception area, a desk at its center. But behind the desk, a large sign that said "Abacus" lay sideways on the floor. Another, emblazoned with the familiar logo for the Diebold company, hung on the wall.

"May I help you?" a woman asked from behind the front desk, dressed in jeans and a sweatshirt.

"I'm former Congressman Lee Kelly." She wouldn't recognize his name, but maybe the title would intimidate her. "I'm curious as to what's happening here," Kelly said.

"This company has been sold," she said flatly.

"Abacus has been sold?"

"Yes, it has."

"So Diebold bought Abacus?"

"I am not at liberty to tell you. This is private property. Please leave," she said. As she spoke, she reached down below the desk.

Kelly ignored her. He casually sauntered a few yards to the left, past her desk, toward an open hallway. Two men carrying boxes walked past him as he did so. He shot a quick glance down the hallway, trying to get a better feel for the place. To the right of the reception desk, a tall man appeared from another hallway. Dressed casually—jeans, sweatshirt, baseball cap—he and the woman whispered back and forth.

"Excuse me, Congressman," the man said with some kind of foreign accent. "I'm going to have to ask you to leave the premises."

Kelly turned back to both of them, ignoring the demand.

"Exactly what is going on here?" Kelly asked. He slowly walked back to the desk.

"Abacus was sold," the man said curtly. "The old staff is moving out, and the new staff is moving in. You will have to leave now."

"I'm sorry, I have some more questions."

"Sir, you have asked your questions. It is time for you to go. If you do not leave, I will be forced to call security."

This was as far as he was going to get. Not wanting a confrontation, he turned to the exit doors and walked out. But he didn't go to his car. Instead, he walked to the side of the building, and then to the back.

The whole scene looked like an escape, only confirming his suspicions. He snapped about a dozen photos with his phone.

After a few more minutes looking around, he again reached for his cell phone. But this time, he made a phone call. No one picked up, so he left a message.

He'd have to fill him in, in person, back in Ohio.

The former congressman walked back to his car.

CHAPTER 38

YOUNGSTOWN

April 10: 153 days after the election

THE DAMP GRASS seeped through every part of my sweatpants and windbreaker, but I still didn't move.

After a quiet weekend, the neighborhood was just waking up. Outside of four cars, two joggers, and a woman walking her dog, there was no sound except that of my own heavy breathing. No one had noticed as I snuck through neighboring backyards to get to the spot where I now lay. The Suburban sat only 30 yards in front of me.

As darkness gave way to early dawn, I crawled out from behind some bushes and removed my phone. I lifted it, zoomed in on the license plate, and pressed the button.

A sudden bright light flashed, temporarily blinding me. The dim morning light had triggered the phone's flash as the picture snapped. The Suburban's front doors opened, and two men—both tall, one thin, one stocky—scrambled out of the car and jogged my way.

I was gone before they got close, and was back home in minutes. The Suburban trailed me once again all the way to work. Once I was at my desk, I dialed Bill Santini.

"Chief here."

Santini was now chief of the Youngstown Police Department, but I'd first met him in his early days on the force. Bill had been a great source over the years, which I had generously rewarded with glowing coverage as he rose through the ranks. Building mutually beneficial relationships is the heart of a reporter's trade.

"Billy, it's Sharpe. I need to ask for your help. I've got myself deep into a story, and am being followed."

"Want us to come and talk to him?" Santini asked.

"No need for that yet. But I have the license plate, and would love to know who it is."

"Sure thing. Go ahead and give it to me."

*   *   *

As far as deaths go, the demise of Ariens and Simpson appeared perfectly straightforward on the surface. After all, heart attacks and violent muggings occur on a regular basis in any major city.

But so do car accidents, and both Kelly's and Fusco's were highly suspicious.

So I took a closer look at the researcher and the lobbyist who had died only months apart.

Finding anything on Simpson proved difficult. A bright young woman. Intellectual with a hard edge. Attractive. Well-liked. At least that's what the obituaries in Washington and St. Louis said. But other than that, a scant paper trail of information.

But then I remembered a trick a young reporter had taught me a few years back. Eerily, Facebook and LinkedIn pages remain online years after someone passes away. Tweets as well. And since millennials record everything they do online, those social media platforms leave a daily journal of their activity to be scrutinized, even after death—an information-packed online graveyard.

While I didn't have my own account on either LinkedIn or Twitter, I knew how to search the former, and could sign onto Twitter under the *Vindicator's* account. Nothing resembling or mentioning Simpson appeared on either platform.

I did have my own Facebook account. Signed up years ago, mainly to keep up with Scott when he moved away. After I'd first joined, old friends from high school and college reached out with great excitement. But the flurry of conversations died down after a few months, and those rekindled relationships returned to their prior status—completely dormant. So I rarely accessed Facebook anymore.

Still, I'd kept my account and now logged on. In the search box, I typed in the words "Joanie Simpson."

Dozens of entries popped up on the screen. Photos of Joanie Simpsons of all shapes, sizes, hues, and ages, from all over the country, were stacked one on top of the other. For pages.

On the fourth page, the 50-second Joanie Simpson looked like the photo from the *Post* obituary. So I clicked to that page, and there she was: Joanie Simpson. Hometown, St. Louis, Missouri. Born April 18, 1992. Single. Worked on Capitol Hill.

The most recent entry on her wall was seven months old. A dozen posts on the same day. Remembrances: "We miss you, Joanie." "We love you." "I think of you every day." "We know you are with the Lord." A few friends shared images of flowers. It was the first anniversary of her death.

A year of spam followed below. Exactly why I'd stopped using Facebook.

I scrolled past those, all the way down to the next frenzy of activity—the week of Joanie's death. Hundreds of entries captured a network of friends and colleagues responding in collective shock, in reverse chronological order, to the investigation and brutal murder that preceded it. An emotional mix of heartbreak and anger on full display.

"Glad that scumbag got what he deserved."

"He'll rot in hell."

"Joanie, they got him. RIP!"

These posts appeared the Wednesday and Thursday after she died and after the papers had detailed the Rutherford shoot out. Below those messages came two days and 200 posts of condolences and regrets.

"Joanie, we will miss you forever."

"I loved every moment we had together."

"Best friends forever!"

I scrolled through six pages of these messages, back to the moment when the outpouring began: the Monday afternoon when her colleagues and closest friends had first learned that she was the Rock Creek victim.

Before that Monday, her wall had been quiet all weekend. A single post mid-day Saturday asked Joanie if she was heading out that night; the friend, of course, was unaware that at that moment, she lay lifeless in the bushes of Rock Creek Park.

And right below that came Joanie's final post. A photo posted on Friday at 9:48 p.m. Her arms draped widely over two other girlfriends' shoulders at what looked like a dance club.

"Living it up!" read the caption.

I scrolled down from there.

Turns out, Joanie had been a voracious user of Facebook. From her later high school days up until that final photo, she documented everything she did, all day long, every day. Political commentary often linked to articles. Social activity. Tons of photos—selfies, group shots, pictures of D.C. landmarks. Even her running routes appeared on her page, so anyone could see her regular District loop.

I spent the rest of the morning scrutinizing every detail of her short life, looking for any telltale signs or patterns that might reveal something. The clearest takeaway was that Joanie Simpson was a passionate conservative. From national security to tax policy, education, and social issues, she was a die-hard. And beginning halfway through her freshman year in college, she wasn't shy about airing those views, debating even close friends and family with fierce rhetoric and sharp jabs. After she began her work on the Hill, her posts focused as much on political personalities as issues. She expressed deep disdain for Speaker Williams, celebrated the president's re-election, and regularly name-dropped other well-known politicians she admired or praised.

"Congressman Smith was fantastic on *Meet the Press* today!"

"Thank you, Senator Timken. You inspire me!"

"Awesome news! President Banfield is reducing taxes on the energy industry."

At the same time, all the way back to her college days, the page painted a picture of an intensely social young woman. As serious as she took politics, it never got in the way of fun. Out with friends all the time, she snapped and posted photos of each occasion. Her friends also routinely published pictures of her onto her wall, at bars, sports games, restaurants, and outdoor activities. Simpson kept up a ferocious social schedule.

Through the years of these vivacious posts and photographs, one feature jumped off the page. In each photo, Simpson unleashed a distinct, effusive, stunning smile.

It was wide, with both rows of bright white teeth gleaming in full view. Dimples creased deeply into her cheeks about an inch to the left and right of her sharply turned up lips. A laugh line wrinkled diagonally from each corner of her mouth to her nose. And her eyes narrowed to thin crescents, almost appearing to close. From her more awkward days at Williams to her evolution into an elegant young woman in Washington, the trademark smile never changed. And she appeared to flash it whenever she saw someone lift a camera. Every posed shot, the same joyous expression beamed. Like a reflex, but appearing natural every time.

The only photos where she wasn't smiling appeared to be when she was caught off guard. Looking in a different direction. Preoccupied with something. Eating. Talking.

With one exception.

There was a unique subset of posed photos.

The sun-drenched team shot after a Congressional Softball League game on the Mall. The office holiday party at the Capital Grille. A retreat to the historic Manassas Battlefield taken by Republican leadership and their top staff.

Unlike all the others, these photos had two features: Joanie Simpson's remarkable smile was absent. And Congressman Stanton was present. With her boss at most a few feet away, Simpson's eyes did not squint but rounded. She wasn't frowning, but her lips were pursed tightly, flat. No dimples, no laugh lines. Her overall look became expressionless, hollow.

The stark contrast with her usual beaming face gave her away: Simpson felt deeply uncomfortable in Stanton's presence.

The only exception was a group photo going all the way back to Simpson's internship the summer after her junior year at Williams. There, with Stanton standing right behind her, she flashed her usual smile.

Seeing this, I reviewed one other tidbit, something I hadn't noticed at first.

Amid all her spirited posts about political figures she admired, she never mentioned her own boss, one of Washington's most high-profile Republicans. At least not since her first week on the job.

"Honored to start working this week for Minority Whip Tom Stanton. A die-hard. A true believer."

And never again.

I sat in silence, looking up from the monitor, staring across the newsroom. I recalled the rumors about Stanton's womanizing, his fondness for young women in particular. Whispers of past harassment and legal settlements.

You can only conclude so much from photographs alone. But my gut told me Simpson was hiding a dark reality about her boss. For years. I had spent my life worked up over the gerrymandering, the pay-to-play, and the partisan nonsense. But if my hunch was right, this young woman's life and death put a tragic face to Washington's abuse of power in a way nothing else did.

Maybe this time I could do something about it.

* * *

Needing some fresh air, I walked a few blocks to grab lunch and marched back to work less than an hour later. The Suburban still idled near the office. I was so disturbed by my morning discovery I didn't care.

On to Ariens.

Lobbyists don't generally seek publicity, so I called some old friends from the Washington press corps to see what they knew.

"Oliver Ariens? Lived a big life. Drinker. Smoker. Seriously overweight. I wasn't surprised when he dropped dead," Howard Vermaat of *Roll Call* told me. "He was a forgettable Congressman, but one hell of a lobbyist."

The Hill's Nancy Pfeiffer was equally impressed. "You couldn't tell by looking at him, but the guy was brilliant. Never seen anyone tackle controversy head-on like he did and still come out on top every time. But he was struggling with his energy plan. The stress might have gotten to him."

"Any sense of who his clients were?" I asked.

"Just about everyone. At least everyone who needed major help on the Hill. Big banks. Oil and gas. Payday lenders. The better question might be who didn't he represent?"

A little digging confirmed their accounts. From the documents I found, the man had represented the *Who's Who* of unpopular industries. But two of Ariens' clients stuck out in particular. He'd represented Diebold, the largest player in the election equipment space. And he'd represented Marcellus, a dominant player in the fracking industry that had clearly benefitted from the election.

I had begun exploring those connections when my phone rang. I picked it up immediately, hoping for Chief Santini.

"Mr. Sharpe?"

"Yes."

"This is Bridget Turner of Republic News."

"Wow," I said. "Hi."

A cable television channel and online streaming site all in one, Republic News had jumped to the top of the ratings the past two years. Its 24-hour availability on every medium paired with its aggressive investigatory style revolutionized political coverage. Bridget Turner, a 43-year-old model-turned-prosecutor-turned-TV personality—armed with a charming personality and a smooth Tennessee drawl—hosted its highest-rated, prime-time show, and wanted me to appear on it.

This presented a huge opportunity. Republic had cornered the market on political corruption. Not surprising they'd be all over a scandal like this. Plus, Turner enjoyed a huge following. This would be my best chance to explain the Abacus story.

I filed away the Ariens materials, raced out to my car, and drove home to shave, shower, and don my new sports coat and tie.

*　*　*

"You're on in five. Just look right into this camera the whole time."

With blush on and a mic clipped to my tie, I sat on a wooden stool facing directly into a camera five feet in front of me.

"Gotcha."

At 7:58, Turner's deep voice spoke into my earpiece.

"Jack, so glad y'all could join us on such late notice."

"Thanks so much, Bridget. It's an honor to be on your show. I'm a big fan."

"Love it! I'll be back in three minutes."

At eight on the nose, the familiar opening music rang in my ear. Then a pre-packaged summary of my story aired, with Turner's voiceover walking through the basics.

"Just over a week ago, the whole country woke up to an earth-shattering political story. A tainted election, with voting totals manipulated by voting machines in key swing districts in the country. Today, we have the man who broke this story with us live!"

"That's right," Turner broke in, live. "Tonight we have the man from Ohio who turned Washington upside down: Mr. Jack Sharpe. Welcome to our show. Can I call you Jack?"

"You sure can, as long as I can call you Bridget."

"Jack, for our rare viewer who doesn't subscribe to the *Youngstown Beacon Journal*, please tell us—"

"*Vindicator*."

"Excuse me?"

"It's the *Youngstown Vindicator*. Akron is the *Beacon Journal*."

"Sorry, the *Vindicator*. Your little Ohio cities all sort of blend together."

These were fighting words in Buckeye country, but I let it go.

"Either way," she continued, "please tell us what you found, and how you found it."

"Well, Bridget, there was one district here in Ohio that had an election result that didn't make sense to people. So we started looking more closely, identified the voting machine company they used, which is called Abacus, and found that Abacus had managed to locate its machines in every swing congressional district in the country." I slowed down as I pronounced the last seven words.

"And?" she asked, apparently unimpressed.

"And a close look at the data showed that these Abacus machines eliminated thousands of votes in many of those swing districts, securing surprising victories all over the country."

"Wow!" Turner said as if this was the first she had heard of the theory. "So you think Republicans stole last year's election?"

No one had asked the question that way before. "I didn't say that. What we discovered is that voting results were manipulated to alter the outcome in about two dozen districts."

Turner persisted. "And Republicans won the House because of it. You're accusing the Republicans of stealing an election, aren't you?"

A bead of sweat meandered down my right temple. "I'm really not. I—"

"Do you think their leadership should be tried for treason? You're basically saying there was a coup in Congress."

She was overstating it, making my theory sound absurd. "Bridget, our story only explains that Abacus machines eliminated the votes in strategic places. We did not speculate as to who orchestrated it. It could be any number of groups or individuals. We are still looking into that. But yes, it is a very serious act."

"Who did you rely on to come to this dramatic conclusion?" she asked.

All friendliness was gone from her voice. I still tried to be polite. "Well, the data work was done by one of the country's renowned experts in political data and statistics, Professor Fowler at Ohio State."

Then I saw it. On a monitor off to the side of the camera, an unflattering picture of a young Renee Fowler appeared on a split-screen. My face took up the other half. She was at a rally, mouth wide open, her right fist lifted high in the air. To her left, a sign read, "Down with Bush!"

"Are you talking about Professor Renee Fowler?"

"Yes. She's a widely respected expert on elections and data."

"Respected by who?"

"By everyone."

Turner laughed aloud. "As a fellow journalist, don't you think we should rely on balanced sources to support such monumental claims? Even before becoming a hired gun for Barack Obama, Renee Fowler had a long history of activity in far left-wing causes. Here she is protesting President Bush."

"Professor Fowler is certainly a Democrat. But she's also a respected academic and analyst. Either way, the data on the election is the data. These are facts."

"But to prove your theory, you didn't go to 'anyone,' you went to a left-wing activist. Or did she bring it to you?"

"I went to her," I said, louder than I meant to.

"Gotcha," Turner said.

I've been in a few car accidents. They always unfold in slow motion, every second passing by at a snail's pace with nothing you can do to stop the inevitable collision. You see it all but are still helpless. This interview was beginning to feel the same way. All I could do was focus on controlling my voice and facial expression to minimize the damage.

"Let's talk about your other big source, Chairman Rogers of Monroe County."

Good. The old veteran was a big hit with the media. "Sure. Chairman Rogers was the first person to raise a concern about the vote total in Monroe County. Monroe County had almost never voted for a Republican. He knew something was up."

"Didn't the county vote for Mitt Romney just a few years ago?"

"Yes, but it's a completely white, blue-collar county."

"So you're saying Monroe County votes for Democrats except when they're being racist?"

"I didn't say that!"

"Did you know Chairman Rogers once said he wished that John Hinckley's bullet had done more damage to Reagan than it did?"

Years ago, reporters overhead Rogers say something to that effect, explaining to a local official how much better the country would have been if George Bush had ended the Reagan tax cuts earlier. The chairman was intensely criticized for the off-hand comment and apologized profusely.

"That was years ago, and he apologized. It was a terrible comment, and I know he regrets it."

"So you did know he said it? An assassination joke? And you still chose to have him *lead off* your story, accusing Republicans of stealing an election?"

"Yes, I did. He knows his county well."

"Right. The county that only votes for Democrats except when it voted for Mitt Romney." Turner chuckled at her own sarcasm. "Jack," she continued, "why should we believe your story?" Her snarky tone was more grating than the words themselves.

"Excuse me?"

"Why should we believe you? The story you wrote, if true, would have enormous implications. Why should we believe you?"

"You can attack me all you want. But the facts are clear and indisputable."

"Let's talk about that," Turner said.

What next?

"So you're saying Abacus stole elections all over the country?"

"The machines manipulated the results. Absolutely."

"Except when they didn't."

"Excuse me?"

"In Toledo, Congressman Tucker won easily despite having Abacus machines in almost every county. The same was true in other places with Abacus machines. Your own story said so."

"Right. The numbers were only manipulated in certain districts. In other districts, they were counted correctly."

"So let me get this straight. When Abacus chose to count the votes correctly, the Democrats won, and everything's okay. But if a Republican won, the votes were miscounted, and we should be concerned?"

"That's not what I said. They didn't try and win in—"

"Seems exactly like what you're saying."

I almost pulled the earpiece out and got up. But having seen politicians do so in the past, I knew it would only look worse, drawing even more attention to this catastrophe.

7:23. Six minutes to go. What else could come up?

"I see that you claim to be a Republican, so we should trust you for that reason. Is that true?"

"It is. My family members are well-known Republicans from the Canton area. My dad was even a state representative."

"Good for him. I understand he lost his election because he was too cozy with Democrats."

Jesus. I had no time to respond before she moved on.

"Why is it that you never vote in the Republican primaries? In Ohio, voting in a primary is the way you declare what party you're in."

"That's true. Once I became a political journalist, I avoided voting in primaries so people would see that I was neutral. Would make me look biased."

"You wouldn't want that, would you? So you claim to be a Republican, but you haven't voted in a Republican primary in decades. Have you ever voted in a primary before that?"

"I voted for a few before being a political journalist. I think in 1986, 1988, 1990, 1992 . . ."

My stomach tightened as I suddenly remembered.

"1992?"

"Yes. I . . ."

"You voted in the Democratic primary that year, didn't you?"

I paused. Trapped.

"Yes. My dad died that January. Almost none of his colleagues bothered to show up at his funeral. It was my small protest against the way he'd been treated."

"And that was your last primary, wasn't it?"

"It was."

"So you claim to be a Republican, but the last primary you ever voted in was a Democratic one."

"You can read it however you want. That was personal."

"Jack, I'm reading it the way Ohio law reads it."

Turner paused for a few seconds. A painful silence, but I had nothing to say.

"I'm sorry, that's all the time we have. Come back and join us again soon."

I could only imagine the sweet grin she was flashing to the TV audience as she said those words. Still, I forced a smile, knowing it would be the last image millions of Republic viewers would see.

* * *

YOUNGSTOWN

"Dad, shake it off," Scott told me over the phone. "Of course, people are out to destroy you. You're an enormous threat to many powerful interests. You handled it fine."

Half an hour after the interview, I was still cursing myself. Not at the on-air performance. But that I had let Bridget Turner do to me what I had done to others over the decades. Called me at the last minute for the interview. Buttered me up. Made me comfortable. Then *boom*. All on live TV.

"I need to be smarter. Discrediting me is the best way for them to protect themselves going forward. But I shouldn't have made it so damn easy."

Scott's pause made it clear that he agreed. "Let me know how I can help, Dad. And hang in there."

We hung up.

Fowler, Rogers, the *Vindicator*, me. We were all political now. To those in power, we posed the threat. The opposition. So the lower our credibility and integrity sank, the quicker the threat ended. And starting with the president herself, hundreds of politicians, and the powerful interests that supported them, all had a direct incentive to make that happen.

And I had just made it far too easy.

At 9:40, Fowler called.

"Honestly, Jack, it's been awful. They're digging up everything I ever did or said to paint me as some kind of socialist nut. Some of the emails have been horrific. What's amazing is no one has disproven the basic facts and data we put forward. And the media doesn't even care."

Rogers stayed up late and laughed off the blowback.

"I don't care what those sons of bitches say about me. I've been through a lot worse. We know we're right."

He was dead on.

We *were* right. Simply back up the facts from the first story. Nothing else mattered. Even more important, identify the culprit behind the scheme, and fast.

*   *   *

"What did you do to piss these guys off?"

Chief Santini called as I drove in to the office the next morning.

"Huh? What are you talking about?"

"You're being followed by some pretty serious people."

"Who?"

"We traced the license back to a Clay Dennison. Lives in suburban Maryland. We found him listed in several law enforcement databases. He's a former cop, who's worked for years as a security specialist after retiring. And get this. He's been the chief of the security detail for Majority Leader Tom Stanton for the past four years."

The tie back to Stanton didn't surprise me.

"Oh boy."

"Why in the world would someone at that level be tailing you here?

"Like you said, I think I pissed him off."

* * *

The next shoe dropped at 10:00 that morning.

"Jack, you need to see this."

Mary Andres beckoned me into her office.

"What?"

"You ever read *Scooped*?"

"Sometimes."

Scooped was an online tabloid, a media watchdog, that fact-checked stories and called out perceived bias or unbalanced sourcing. The site had a gotcha mindset, eager to get in the mud if hitting "big" media meant more clicks and online advertising revenue.

Apparently, a daily paper like the *Vindicator* now qualified as big media.

"Big story on you, and us. Not good."

"What now?"

"They rehash all the stuff Turner attacked you on. Fowler. Rogers. Your voting history. But worse, they get into your child support problems . . . .Wish we had known about those."

"What the hell? What do personal issues like that have to do with anything?"

"You've covered politics long enough to know any negative history on child support will be used to malign your credibility."

"Unreal. My crazy ex and I were fighting over terms, and I was struggling. I missed a few months, then I took care of it. That's it."

"Well, they hunted her down, and her side of the story is not pretty."

Jesus. I always knew that if I ran for office, she'd come back to haunt me. Never thought it would happen as a journalist. Andres handed me a copy of the article.

Roxanne Collins, now on her third marriage, executed a brutal takedown. "Jack was a drunk, a terrible husband, and an even worse father. He left his son and me hanging, to the point that I had to go to court to force him to pay. This is one man who cannot be trusted."

"Unbelievable," I muttered under my breath.

"Jack," Andres said, "we've decided to take you off the story. Give you some time away. Last night's interview. Now this. The publisher is worried our credibility is getting crushed by all this stuff. You look tired, beat down."

Being removed from a big story doesn't just undermine that story. It sends a signal that a reporter is in over his head. A humiliating stain. "If you do that," I said, "you're retracting the story in front of the whole country."

"People know we stand by the story," she said unconvincingly. "And we do."

"Sending its writer to Siberia kills the story. And crushes me. You need to give me more time. I have some strong leads on who was behind the plan." I was desperate and overstating my case. "If you take me out before we run with those, you're letting them get away with a smear campaign and, worse, with stealing an elect—"

"Okay, okay. Let me talk to him one more time and see what I can do."

Minutes later, she walked by my desk.

"You've got a week."

* * *

Kelly, Ariens, Simpson, Stanton.

The first three dead, all with a connection to the fourth, who was very much alive. A mysterious fifth person had sent me the photograph of Kelly's car. Clearly, this person knew something, maybe more than anyone else. And Stanton was following me. An incredibly aggressive reaction to a single phone call. Obviously protecting something.

The problem was, none of these things tied together. Only Kelly knew of Abacus. The other two knew Stanton. I needed more than that.

So I started digging further into the Ariens-Diebold connection. If

Ariens knew the voting machine industry well due to his work with Diebold, maybe he'd concocted the idea and brought it to Stanton. Perhaps he and Diebold had worked together.

He was a D.C. lobbyist, for God's sake. They're capable of anything.

*   *   *

The paper's receptionist dropped an envelope on my desk. "You got another package, Jack."

I reached for it like a kid grabbing a birthday present. The same professional package and the same typed label as the Kelly photos. Again, Bethesda post office. But the contents didn't feel as rigid. Plain paper this time.

"*CONFIDENTIAL MEMORANDUM*

TO: Congressman Stanton
FR: Joanie Simpson
RE: Abacus and Next Year's Election

   After scrutinizing Boards of Elections documents from around the country, it is my firm conclusion that Abacus, under its mysterious new leadership, is intending to alter the results of the upcoming Congressional election."

For twelve pages, the memo described the history of the company and its pattern of acquiring locations in swing districts. It read like my own story, except that Joanie Simpson had penned her memo *before* the Abacus plot took place. She'd also detailed how even the latest electronic voting machines might be manipulated to alter election results.

This was clearly a draft. It was undated, and handwritten corrections appeared on about half the pages. But they were sparse, so this appeared to be close to a finished product. A quarter-sized wine stain bled through the lower right-hand corner of the memo's first three pages, and all pages were creased right down the middle. Probably folded and tossed.

The last two pages comprised an appendix listing the Abacus districts she had identified, including the dates when Abacus had moved its machines into each district. The most recent date listed was eighteen days before her murder.

The memo raised several questions, all of which I jotted down in my notepad:

1. *What prompted Simpson research?*
2. *Did Stanton see memo? Anyone else?*
3. *Who sent this?*

The wine stain suggested Joanie had worked on the draft at home, something I might do. The fold suggested she'd discarded it after making her edits. Who would have had the ability to retrieve a discarded memo from her home? Did they discover it before she died? After? And who in the world had sent it to me?

Bottom line, this was clear proof that a second person, Joanie Simpson, had learned about Abacus. And like Kelly, not long after that discovery, she died a violent death.

CHAPTER 39

February 6: 90 days after the election

*C*LICK.

Kelly froze.

He was a lifelong gun owner, so the cocking of a revolver was a familiar sound. The cylinder that pressed against the back of his head was wide enough to be a .44. In the right weapon, a bullet that size could drop a Cape buffalo, so Kelly didn't move.

A deep voice spoke. "Start the car. Then drive out of the parking lot slowly. Don't do anything stupid. And do exactly what I say."

Kelly followed the instructions, saying nothing.

"Hand me your phone."

"My phone's dead." A lie, but it was the first thing he thought to say.

"I don't give a shit. Give me your phone. And no more talking."

Kelly reached into his left pocket, took out his phone, and lifted it back over his left shoulder. A hand snatched it out of his grip.

"Now follow every instruction I give you."

He did so, driving off the property. After a few miles, the intruder spoke again. "Pull over here."

Kelly slowly turned into an empty parking lot off the road, weighing his options.

Crash the car and hope to recover more quickly than his unwelcome passenger.

Jump out, run like hell, and roll the dice that the gunman was a poor shot.

Attempt to overpower him.

Or cooperate and hope for the best.

Right when he decided the second option offered his best chance of survival, the gun barrel crashed into the back of his skull.

CHAPTER 40

YOUNGSTOWN-WASHINGTON

April 11: 154 days after the election

"D o you know anything about Lee's relationship with Tom Stanton?"

I was just south of Pittsburgh, on my way to D.C. In between Buffett and the Eagles, I had dialed Jody Kelly.

"They were close before Tom changed. Both were moderate, working across party lines to keep the extremes in their party at bay. We went out to dinner with Tom and Irene a few times in D.C. and always had fun. That's why Lee was so furious about Tom's visits late in the campaign, and how nasty the attacks got."

"Do you know if they talked since the election?"

"I'm not sure. Lee felt bad about how ugly it got between them. He wanted to make amends."

"Do you know if he did?" I asked.

"Not that I know. Tom was from Philadelphia, right? Do you think that's who Lee visited the day of the crash?"

"I really don't know. But I have some evidence that he might have. Looking into it now." I switched topics. "Do you remember when you first tried to call him that afternoon?"

"Yes. It was about four. My calls kept going straight to voicemail the rest of the evening. Lee always kept a charger in his car, so I knew something was wrong."

Four would have been around when Kelly's Escape sat outside Stanton's home. So his phone had already died by then. But it had clearly worked earlier, when Kelly left me his message.

"Do you have access to his phone records?" I asked.

"Lee's? Of course, we had a family account."

"If you're okay with it, can you see who he called that final day and send it to me?"

Minutes after I walked into my Hampton Inn room in suburban Maryland, she called back.

"I went online and checked our bill. The morning drive was so early, he didn't call anyone for a few hours. At 9:30 a.m., he called a couple former aides, but it looks like he just left messages. It also looks like he left a message for his brother, who lives in Jersey.

"At about 10:45, he had a twelve-minute call with a 202 number. Then in the early afternoon, he made two calls. Both about two minutes long. One was to Youngstown at 12:28. I assume that was to you."

She read the number.

"Yep. That's my office line. And the other call?"

"The other was to a 215 number. He called that number about 30 minutes after his call to you—at 1:05—again, lasting about two minutes. It was the last call he made."

Philadelphia area code.

"Can you give me that full number?"

"Sure." She read the ten digits. Sitting on the side of the motel bed, I scribbled them down on a Hampton Inn notepad.

"Thanks so much. I'll keep you posted."

As I settled down, I flipped on the television set. The volume was off, but I scrolled through the channels.

And there she was. Channel 34. Republic. My new favorite channel.

Roxanne, my ex-wife, talked into the camera. The caption beneath was not subtle: "Reporter's ex: 'You can't trust him.'"

CHAPTER 41

February 6: 90 days after the election

WHEN LEE KELLY came to, he was still in the car, looking directly ahead through the windshield. A pungent chemical burning his nose forced him to cough violently. Unlike before, it was dark out. Must have been out for a few hours.

As he gathered his bearings, three horrific realities set in. He still sat in the driver's seat, but his Escape was speeding up at an outrageous rate. His right foot was on the accelerator, but as he tried to remove it, he found that both his foot and the pedal were bound to the floor. And his hands were tied, bound with some type of thin twine to the steering wheel, which also was locked in place, directing the SUV straight ahead.

The speedometer indicated 45 miles per hour. Then 50, 55, 60. He jerked his arms and right leg frantically, trying to free them, but to no avail.

He next smelled the strong stench of gasoline throughout the vehicle. Even felt damp himself.

Bang!

From his left, a sedan smashed into the driver's side of the Escape. Not too hard a collision, but enough to jolt his heading 20 degrees to the right. The Escape continued speeding up. With the wheel stuck, Kelly was helpless as he shot diagonally across several lanes of highway.

The speedometer topped out at 87 when he flew off the road.

The Escape jostled violently as it tore through the guardrail and over a strip of high grass. Just behind the grass, amid the darkness, Kelly first made out the silhouette of a row of tall, wide trees. Seconds later, he spotted the broad base of an enormous oak tree not far in front of him and closing quickly.

The long grass slowed the Escape slightly. But not enough. The speedometer still showed 78.

Too fast.

Too late.

Kelly didn't utter a sound.

CHAPTER 42

WASHINGTON, DC
April 12: 155 days after the election

DRIVING DOWN CONNECTICUT Avenue from my hotel, I weaved among fancy cars cruising into the District from the million-dollar Maryland suburbs. High-priced lawyers, lobbyists, and consultants, all rushing to get back to the government that fueled their lucrative practices.

Once in D.C. proper, I passed through neighborhoods teeming with young professionals. Jogging, walking dogs of all sizes, entering the subway, and sitting outside of coffee shops catching up before the day began. These were the worker bees of Washington—crammed in apartments, or in large houses they rented together—who staffed the lobbyists and the government decision makers. Ironically, in their first and second jobs out of college, thrilled to graduate from unpaid intern status, many of these kids performed the research and made the recommendations that led to the riches that their older, out-of-District neighbors enjoyed. Only in the unique dysfunction of the nation's capital do millionaire K Street lobbyists huddle with recent college grads in the august halls of Congress as the lawmakers sit in dreary call centers dialing for dollars back home.

Then came Joanie Simpson's old playground, Woodley Park, with the famous Uptown Theater to my right and the Washington Zoo to my left. I passed a string of restaurants and then crossed an ornate bridge high above Rock Creek Parkway. Joggers and bikers scurried far below, only a mile or so from where Joanie Simpson died.

I pulled into a parking space blocks from the Capitol and walked to the House entrance, through security, and up several flights of stairs. A long row of portraits welcomed guests to the House leadership suites. Sandra Williams, Paul Ryan, John Boehner, Nancy Pelosi, Dennis

Hastert, Newt Gingrich, Tom DeLay, Jim Wright, Tom Foley, and a few others in color, followed by many more white men in black and white. Amazing how many had ended their tenure in disgrace or had fallen into it later. Regardless, their photos stayed forever.

I opened the door to Tom Stanton's suite and entered a waiting room. A young woman at a reception desk, so young she may have been a college intern, smiled up at me.

"How can I help you?" she asked politely.

"I'd like to meet with Chief of Staff Seth West. Is he here yet?"

"He normally gets here around ten 'til. Who can I say is here?"

"Jack Sharpe of the *Youngstown Vindicator*. He'll know who I am."

I sat down and waited, reviewing my carefully prepared manila folder one last time. Re-checked my phone.

Working over the chief of staff provided the best pathway in, but would be difficult. Politicians love being in the news, but the smart ones know that the adage "all press is good press" is nonsense. This interview would bring all risk, no reward for the congressman—making it a no-brainer to decline.

I'd have to play it just right to flip that equation on its head. And I'd have only a minute or two to do it.

*   *   *

Just after 9:00, the door opened.

"Mr. Sharpe, I'm Seth West, the congressman's chief of staff. How can we help you?"

Short little guy, bald, West didn't smile at all. His assignment was to get rid of me as quickly as possible, and it showed.

"Is the congressman in today?" I already knew the answer, having confirmed before leaving Youngstown that Congress was in session. Stanton would have to be there, at least during the day.

"I'm not at liberty to say."

Here we go. "This is a public office and a public body that Mr. Stanton leads. His schedule is not a state secret." Already taller than this pipsqueak by a good eight inches, I stretched my 6'2" frame as vertically as I could to intimidate him. But he simply looked up. No response, no expression. "The House is in session today," I said. "I can't imagine he's not in Washington, and I would like to talk to him for a few minutes."

"Let's save us both some time," West said, sneering. "You will not have an opportunity to interview the congressman today, or any day."

"But he is here." A statement more than a question.

West just stared. So I did the same back. He finally broke the silence.

"Mr. Sharpe, haven't you embarrassed yourself enough? You're giving small-town papers a bad name. The shaky story. The outlandish accusations. Your personal baggage."

"I'm sure you were stunned by those stories, Seth." I couldn't help myself. No doubt Stanton's office had spoon-fed Turner opposition research on me. His smirk confirmed it.

But then I laughed back. The jab by West had opened the door, so I went for the kill. "If you want to talk about baggage, let me bring up a whole crateful of baggage."

I spoke loudly, making the conversation as uncomfortable as possible with young staff nearby, then went in for the kill. "I have evidence that Mr. Stanton was engaged in a sexual relationship with Joanie Simpson before she died, and that it took place for her entire time as an employee. We are prepared to print a story on this scandal, but it's up to you."

I raised my hand to chest level, displaying the manila folder as if it were chock full of evidence. I was going way beyond what I knew with certainty, but being this direct would smoke him out. Then I went silent for a few seconds. Let the choice sink in. "Although we know people are eager to read it," I continued, "that type of scurrilous behavior is not what I want to write about. I'd rather talk to him about more important matters. But again, it's up to you."

"Mr. Sharpe, there you go again," West said, a slight tremor in his voice. "This is ridiculous."

"You go tell your boss what I just told you. Come back, and we can proceed. Again, it's up to you."

West looked at me, considering my offer. A lot rode on this decision, for him, and for Stanton. Merely consulting with Stanton would signal that I was on firm ground. But letting a reporter walk away without the boss weighing in also presented a huge risk, one that was not his to take alone.

A few more seconds passed.

"I'll be right back."

Soon West re-opened the door. "Come on back."

Round one was mine.

*   *   *

We walked through the entire length of the office. Young men and women sat at their desks, typing away on their computers. Iconic photos of Philadelphia covered the walls, along with maps of the district, Phillies and Eagles paraphernalia, and photos of Stanton with the last three presidents and numerous foreign leaders.

It was all so predictable I almost missed the one authentic element in the whole office. A large framed photo of Joanie Simpson.

Once I saw it, on the far wall to my left, I stopped. Handwritten messages filled the white matting between the photo of his deceased aide and the frame: "We miss you," "We love you," and the like. I stared at her for a good ten seconds. Wonder what Stanton thought every day when he walked past this humble memorial. Seeing the stunning smile that he had never witnessed in person. Hope it pained him.

At the back of the suite, we walked past a workstation where a middle-aged African-American woman looked up at me for a moment, then quickly looked back down. Wonder what she knew about her boss' harassment of a young staffer. As the sentry posted right outside his office, probably far too much to have said nothing for years.

We then walked through an open door into a spacious office. Seated behind a large desk at the other side of the room, facing the door, was Stanton himself. As I entered, West hung back a few feet and closed the door.

Awards, more photos with presidents and foreign leaders, and framed newspaper articles occupied most of the bookshelf behind the majority leader. To Stanton's left, at about his shoulder level, sat a framed photo of the congressman and his wife. To his right was another photo, this one of his all-American family on a beach somewhere. Happy husband and wife bookended by two proud sons and a daughter. The first lie of the interview.

Stanton didn't budge. "What the fuck is your problem?" he asked.

Confidence and attitude offer the best response to a politician in a bullying mood. Projecting strength gets their attention. So that's what I threw back at him.

"What's my problem? My problem is that I'm trying to get to the bottom of this Abacus scandal, and people are doing all they can to stop me. Makes me think I must be onto something really big." I chuckled as I said this, wanting Stanton to know I was enjoying the moment. That

I could give a shit if he was mad. In a town of ass-kissers, this would've been something he rarely experienced.

"Congressman," I continued, "let's go off the record for a few minutes. But I'm going to take a few notes if you don't mind."

"Fair enough."

My aggressive reply had worked. Stanton eased back in his chair and motioned for me to sit down. West sat to my right, facing us both. I took out my reporter's notebook and my new Hampton Inn pen.

"We know about your inappropriate relationship with Joanie Simpson," I said nonchalantly. "You covered it up well for it to not come out after she was killed."

"That's ridiculous," Stanton said. I wouldn't be sitting there if it was ridiculous, but Stanton felt the need to at least mouth the denial.

I waved off his comment. "We don't have an interest in covering the relationship, as unseemly as it was. And we have no interest in reporting on any other inappropriate harassment that took place here, but we do want to dive deeper into the Abacus scandal."

I smiled. As direct an offer of journalistic blackmail as I'd ever made in my career.

"I told you, the first I heard about Abacus was what I read in your story."

"But you've received checks from them in the past?"

"Don't be an idiot. They're a Philadelphia company, so I know them. I meant the first I heard of your conspiracy theory."

"I see. So you had no idea what Abacus was up to before my story?"

"For the record, I don't think Abacus was up to anything. But the theory that they were? Never. What nut would dream that up?"

The perfect question. "Well, your star researcher—the one you were sleeping with until she was beaten to death, the one smiling on your wall out there—sure seemed to know a lot about it. Did you?"

Pay dirt.

His head jerked back and his eyes widened. Even Stanton's poker face couldn't mask his alarm at this one-two punch—a bombshell fact followed by a painfully direct question.

"Excuse me?"

"Joanie Simpson knew all about Abacus. She figured the whole plot out a year in advance."

I let the sentence hang out there. Stanton stared back as if studying my face intensely enough might coax out what else I knew.

"Now how would you even know such a thing?" he asked, uttering each word slowly. Clearly trying to regain his composure.

Wrong question.

"I have a memo she wrote to you, before she died, walking through the whole thing. I'm happy to refresh your recollection of it."

The look of dread returned. Even more exposed than before. This was quickly becoming my favorite interview in years.

For the first time, West also looked worried. He simply stared at the floor.

"I'm not sure what shit you're peddling, Sharpe. I have no idea what a junior researcher would be dreaming up in her spare time. We certainly never discussed anything with her about Abacus."

"Do you want to see the memo I have?" I asked. A trap question. If he had never seen the memo before, "no" was the wrong answer. Of course he'd be curious. But saying "yes" presented its own dilemma—minutes of play-acting the role of the surprised reader.

"Sure, I'll take a look at it," Stanton said, as if he had just agreed to let me punch him in the face.

As I pulled the memo from the manila folder, Stanton eyed the folder itself. He could see other materials were inside. Like a lawyer conducting cross-examination, I wanted to leave him wondering what else I had. How much I knew.

I handed him the memo, and Stanton leafed through it, performing well. Whatever was going through his mind, his expression made it appear that this was his first look at the document.

"It looks like this is a draft. All these corrections still to be made. That probably explains why I never saw it. She must've died before completing it."

"Looks like she was down to her final edits and it was a couple weeks prior to her death. Are you sure you never saw it?"

"Yes, I'm sure."

New angle. "Why do you think she researched this in the first place? How would she have known to look into Abacus?"

"I have no idea. She was a curious person. Who knows?"

"What do you think of what she's written there?"

"Seems as off the wall as your story. She was a great researcher, but her intensity could get the best of her at times."

"You're not curious if this really happened?"

"I know that it didn't. We worked our ass off in that election, and that's why we won. The people wanted new leadership. This is fantasy."

"But she wrote this before you worked your ass off, Tom." I relished using his first name, knowing this was a moment when he couldn't correct me. "You campaigned in all of these districts. And she predicted the election results exac—"

"No, she didn't. Not exactly."

A slip. He'd stated the words too quickly, too casually, too knowingly. This was something he had thought before.

"Excuse me?"

"A lot of the Abacus districts from your story did not go the Republicans' way. That's been covered *ad nauseum.*"

A quick cover for his mistake, but not enough to undo the damage.

"Did you have a chance to look at the appendix?"

"Yes, I looked at it."

Bullshit. I had watched closely—he'd only glanced at it for a few seconds. Not enough time to take it all in.

Now the congressman turned to it again.

"You see, of her 31 districts, Democrats won a number of them. Tucker held on in Ohio. Brewer in California. And so on. Your Abacus theory is not right, and Joanie didn't get it right in this memo."

"If she had brought this to you, how would you have responded?"

"I would have worked to verify it. If I thought it were true, I would've stopped it."

I turned to West, trying to catch him off guard.

"Could we look to see if this memo is still in your system? That would confirm what the congressman is saying."

"It's not there," West said, too quickly.

"How do you know?"

"Our staff reviewed all of Joanie's files, and then we divvied up her work among others. If anything like this had shown up, we would have known."

"Don't you think looking for it now makes sense? To back up what the congressman is saying?"

"There's no file to look through now. We dispersed all the documents to others."

"So there were never any Abacus-related documents here?"

"Only if she kept them on her person. We never found anything like that."

I turned back toward Stanton.

"So you've never seen this memo?"

"Not before today."

Time to move on.

"Congressman, I want to talk again about your old friend Kelly."

"Jesus, Sharpe. Haven't we talked enough? I've got votes to get to."

"It's your choice. The Simpson sex scandal and now this memo would be a bombshell."

Stanton shook his head, slumping a little further into his chair. I had all the leverage.

"When was the last time you and he talked?" I asked.

"A few weeks before the election. He called me whining about my campaigning in his district."

"You never talked to him again?"

"I didn't."

"Did you hear from him again?"

"Nope."

"As you know, the day of his crash, he drove to and from Philadelphia because he too had stumbled across the Abacus plot."

"I knew he was driving back from Philly when he crashed. That's it."

"We tracked down his phone records from the day he died. Guess what we found. He had a ten-minute call with a 202 number as he drove to Philly in the morning. We tracked the number to this office. Can you explain why he called here the morning he died?"

Stanton glanced at West, looking for a life preserver to be tossed his way.

"I have no idea. All I know is that I didn't talk to him. I wasn't even here, as I recall. Seth, did you?"

"I didn't."

"Where were you, Congressman?"

"As I remember, I was in our Philly office that day."

That admission came a lot easier than I expected.

"Which brings me to my final question."

"Thank God," Stanton said, his most honest moment of the meeting.

I reached into my folder and slapped the two photos on the desk.

"Here is Kelly's car parked right next to your Society Hill townhouse, on the day he died. Do you still deny seeing him that afternoon?"

Stanton stared at the photographs, clearly more frazzled than at any time in the interview.

"I don't know his car, but, obviously, that's my townhouse. All I can tell you is that I never saw him, or saw him parked there."

"That's his car. You can even make out the Ohio plates. And you never heard from him? Met with him?"

"Sure didn't."

"Thanks for your time, Congressman. As we put together another story on Abacus, I will be sure to call you for an on-the-record reaction."

"And the other stuff?" he asked.

"I will write nothing about the affair—I mean the abuse. Although I am sickened by it and this entire office." I shot West a nasty look as I said this. He had allowed it to happen. The truth is, there wasn't enough evidence of the relationship to write about it anyway. "It might help your cause if you kept my personal stuff out of this as well," I added. "My trigger finger on scandals gets real itchy when people go after me."

"You'll see nothing else. I swear."

"Good. By the way, good luck in your presidential run. I guess I'll see you in Ohio."

I stood and nodded at Stanton. No handshake. I walked toward the door, West trailing a few feet behind.

But before reaching the door, I reached down in my pocket and retrieved my phone, as if I was checking my messages. But that's not what I was doing. While waiting outside, I had pre-dialed into my phone the 215 phone number from Jody Kelly—the final number Lee Kelly ever called. It was still displayed now.

As I passed through the doorway, I pushed the phone's "call" button and simultaneously muted the volume of my receiver. The phone rang the mystery number, flashing the words "Calling Mobile" on my screen.

As his assistant stared up at me, I heard exactly the noise I'd hoped to—consecutive bursts of vibrations against the wood of Stanton's desk. A cell phone ringing. His cell phone.

A moment later, I could hear Stanton through the door.

"Hello, Tom Stanton speaking. . . . Hello. . . . Hello?"

My phone began counting seconds.

:01 . . . :02 . . . :03 . . . :04 . . .

"Damn it. Who the hell . . ."

West closed the office door behind me.

The words "Call Ended" flashed on my phone as I exited the suite.

* * *

The name was the first listed on the directory at 1801 K St.: the Ariens Group. Stanton's early availability had left me extra time for a bonus visit before heading home.

The elevator took me to the tenth floor, home of the priciest lobbying shop in Washington. But for all the hype about Ariens and his high-powered clients, it was a modest office. Modern and professional but not extravagant.

"I'm a reporter from Ohio," I said to the young intern manning the front desk. "My name is Jack Sharpe, and I was hoping to talk to Janet Compton." Quick research had shown that Compton had taken over the firm after Ariens died.

"Let me see if she's available."

Minutes later, a heavyset woman in her mid-fifties, her dark hair pulled back in a tight bun, marched down the hallway and reached out to shake my hand.

"The famous Mr. Sharpe!" she said, echoing her predecessor's New Orleans drawl. "I'm Janet Compton. Welcome. I hope you're not accusing *us* of stealing that election!" Compton laughed as she said it.

"Only a strong suspicion. Here to confirm it."

"For what it's worth, I thought you held your own against Turner the other night. She had you by the balls, set you up, but you were good. I was impressed."

"I appreciate that." And I did. "Can you write a note to my less-than-enthusiastic bosses saying that?"

Compton walked me into a conference room down a hallway. It was essentially a shrine to the firm's late founder. Photos of Oliver Ariens stared out from all four walls. With presidents, senators, foreign leaders. And there was one prominent photo with his old friend, classmate, and roommate, Tom Stanton, looking a lot happier than he had 20 minutes ago in his office.

We sat down.

"Seriously," Compton said. "How can I help you?"

"I was in D.C. to follow up on my story and thought I'd stop by. Can I speak confidentially with you?"

"Mum's the word," she said.

That was almost certainly not the case.

"Mr. Ariens was uniquely positioned in Washington, D.C. If someone were out to try to rig last year's election, he likely would have known one or more of the players, and perhaps some of the plan's biggest beneficiaries."

Compton's smile disappeared. Her tone wasn't angry, but firm.

"Mr. Sharpe, I know you are doing your job. A core Ariens principle is that we respect and work with the media so you can do your job. But as you can tell from these walls, we hold Mr. Ariens in great esteem. He was a wonderful man, a generous man, with a deep sense of right and wrong. That is what guided him through ethically challenging situations over the years."

An ethical lobbyist—novel concept. I edged slightly forward in my chair, planning to respond, but she raised her voice, making it clear she did not intend to be interrupted.

"I can assure you if Mr. Ariens had any notion that something inappropriate was taking place, he would say something, and then work to stop it."

"Do you think that's what he did?"

Compton paused, considering my question thoughtfully. "Mr. Sharpe, I have no reason to think he knew about the plot you have described."

Then came the biggie.

"I ask all this because he was close to people who I believe knew about the plot. And I have found that most who discovered the plot, at least those who were not the ones perpetrating it, ended up dead."

Compton took a moment before responding.

"Mr. Sharpe, we are verging on unhealthy conspiracy theory here. Mr. Ariens was a large man who lived a large life. Up until his final day, he worked eighteen hours a day, smoked too much, drank too much. He traveled weekly—hell, he flew to and from London in his final 24 hours on this Earth. So his death was tragic, but no one, including his doctor, suggested anything but an honest-to-goodness heart attack."

I pushed a little further, perhaps one step too far.

"Let me provide an example. I know you guys have represented Diebold for a long time. Certainly they would have the expertise on—"

"Mr. Sharpe, let me stop you. I will not discuss client relationships, let alone accusations against our clients."

"Understood. You've been very gracious." I was wearing out my welcome, and her glance down at her watch confirmed it. "If anything occurs to you along the lines we've discussed, please let me know."

"I will do so," she said.

I passed her my business card, a gesture she did not reciprocate.

As we stood up and walked out of the conference room, we faced a second set of memorabilia adorning the hallway wall. A trail of framed newspaper and industry journal covers describing major Ariens legislative achievements, guided us back to the front desk.

"Industry-Led Water Initiative Sails Through Senate."

"National Parks Drilling Gets Green Light."

"Airlines Celebrate Reduced Restrictions"

Only a Washington lobbyist would display such ignoble headlines with pride.

As the wall ended at the front lobby, the last three framed newspapers touted each successful step of the firm's most recent and high-profile achievement.

New York Times: "After Three Years, Energy 2020 Passes House."

Washington Post: "Senate Clears Energy 2020; Pipeline Plan Awaits Presidential Signature."

Wall Street Journal: "President Signs Energy 2020 Legislation."

The irony.

In the public domain, lobbying firms do all they can to keep their clients and projects a secret. But show up at their office, where they're trying to impress potential clients, and they helpfully plaster the evidence of their handiwork all over their walls.

*   *   *

Even though the current occupants of the District leave a lot to be desired, the architecture of official Washington will take your breath away. Always does mine. Only a few blocks away, the White House beckoned me before heading home.

On the way, I mulled over Ariens' office. Ariens hadn't merely counted Marcellus as a client; he had played a major role in the high-profile Energy 2020 push. No issue had hung in the balance more in the election, and Stanton had actively promoted it in the fall campaign. Could this have been the motivation for the Abacus plan? Old friends Stanton and Ariens working together to get the pipelines built? It was my best theory so far.

I reached 16th and Pennsylvania and walked along the tall White House gate. At the dead center of the White House, I turned toward the stunning façade and stared in silence. For those few moments, with my boyhood idealism in politics flashing back, I missed Dad.

After getting my fix, I turned around to look at Lafayette Square, the historic park directly across the street. Apparently, I'd pivoted quickly. Thirty yards away, standing by a tree in the Square, a slender, dark-haired man in a brown suit was looking directly at me while talking on a cell phone. He quickly looked away.

The man's furtive movement was too obvious to miss. I pretended not to notice, staring straight ahead into the Square. Moments later, I started walking back to K St.

I reached the garage in ten minutes and entered the elevator. Having parked on the fifth floor, I pushed the button for five, but also pressed three as well. As the third bell rang on the way up, the elevator stopped, the door opened, and I stepped out. The door closed behind me and continued up to five.

I walked to the far corner of the garage. Anyone intending to follow me would wait for me on the street, either behind or across from the garage's exit. So from three floors up, I glanced over and looked for someone positioned accordingly.

There he was. The slender man from the park paced back and forth at the far sidewalk near 21st Street—again on his cellphone. He stopped, calmly stood at the sidewalk's edge, and then turned his head to the left as traffic approached. Seconds later, a vehicle pulled up beside him, the man opened the passenger door and hopped into the car.

The vehicle pulled a U-turn and idled half a block behind the garage's exit. But more than its illegal traffic maneuver, the far more important data point was that the vehicle was the same dark Suburban that had followed me around Youngstown for a few days. While I'd been belting out the lyrics of "Take It Easy" and "Margaritaville" in the dark, the Suburban had trailed me all the way to Washington.

Stanton really was relentless.

But then it dawned on me. This wasn't Stanton's doing. At our morning meeting, Stanton and West had been caught off guard. They'd had no idea I was paying them a visit, meaning They weren't the ones having me tailed.

And if they weren't, then who the hell was?

* * *

I looked up as soon as I heard it. The deep, long blaring of a truck's horn, clearly intended for my ears. I swerved back onto my side of the road just in time to avoid the oncoming semi.

Long before texting came along, I had mastered the prehistoric version of distracted driving—steering with my left hand while using my right to leaf through my reporter's notebook, occasionally scribbling down a note or two. Despite the occasional close call, it was still better than letting vivid interview details fade.

So a few seconds after the near miss, I again looked over my Stanton interview notes and jotted down the key points emerging from our conversation.

First, West and Stanton's reaction confirmed that the congressman had carried on a sexual relationship of some sort with Simpson, giving me the continued leverage I needed.

Second, the phone number Kelly had called before his death was clearly Stanton's cellphone.

And third, while Stanton had valiantly tried to read the memo as if he hadn't seen it before, he'd slipped up. When he stated so quickly that Simpson hadn't predicted all 31 districts correctly, it confirmed that he'd reached that conclusion previously.

"Thirty-one districts," I muttered to myself. Stanton had been explicit. Thirty-one districts!

My research had uncovered 35 Abacus districts. But when reviewing Joanie Simpson's memo, Stanton had said the number *31*.

How had I not noticed that her memo was four short? My folder rested on the passenger seat, and I reached over and grabbed Simpson's memo from it. I turned to the appendix and looked over it once more.

"Wow."

The chart wasn't numbered. Simpson had simply listed the districts, un-enumerated, for two pages. I had never bothered to count them up. Now that I did, one at a time, the total was indeed 31. I counted through again just to confirm it.

I had watched him closely. The congressman's quick glance through the Appendix had not given him enough time to count all the districts as I just had. There was only one way that he knew that the memo listed 31 districts.

He had seen it before.

He had counted them before.

* * *

Dunkin' Donuts coffee in hand, I was planted at my desk the next morning before 8. Anxious to confirm my theory from the previous evening, I pursued two big questions.

First, which four districts had Simpson overlooked in her research? A quick review showed that she'd failed to identify the two Abacus districts in Missouri and the two in Florida. And my own records showed why. Those four counties had switched to Abacus only after her death.

Next, I retrieved my prior research on Stanton. The first time around, I had found that Stanton had campaigned in 34 districts over the course of the election. Excluding the three districts that neighbored his own, 31 out of those 34 were Abacus districts. Then I compared my prior research with the list in Simpson's memo. The congressman had traveled to every district of Simpson's 31.

I then scoured every account of the Florida and Missouri congressional races that had taken place in the Abacus districts—the ones Abacus had secured after Simpson died. And again, I found what I suspected. While a visit by the House minority whip would have inevitably drawn media coverage, not one newspaper described a visit by Stanton to any of the four districts.

The son of a bitch hadn't just reviewed Simpson's list. He'd used it as his campaign roadmap.

* * *

The call came in at 1:00 p.m.

"Sharpe, there's a woman calling from Washington. Says she met you yesterday, and that it's critical she talk to you."

That was fast. Janet Compton must have thought of something.

"Patch her through." The line rang, and I picked up. "Janet, good to hear from you!"

"Hello?" The voice was not Compton's. It too was Southern, but thicker and far less confident. Wavering. "Is this Mr. Sharpe?"

"It sure is. Who am I speaking to?"

"This is Arlene Bradley. Congressman Stanton's administrative assistant. I was sitting outside his office yesterday when you two met."

I remembered her instantly, her facial expression in particular. She had looked uncomfortable as our meeting began, and downright miserable when it ended. If I'd read her correctly, this call presented an enormous opportunity.

"I remember you well," I said. "How can I help you?"

"I don't have much time. I'm on my lunch break away from the office. But I have some information involving what you talked about yesterday."

"Okay. And let me assure you, everything you tell me will be strictly confidential."

"Thank you. I can't have anyone know I'm calling you. When's a good time to call you after work?"

"Why don't you try me at 6:00, at this same number?"

"I will. Thank you. I have to go."

The phone clicked.

Her call brought risks and opportunity. It could easily be a trap. If Stanton listened in on the call, he might discover what I knew, and where I was taking the story. But all that was evident already. On the other hand, cultivating her as a source—the woman who sat right outside Stanton's office every day—presented an enormous opportunity. And she struck me as authentic.

Definitely a risk worth taking.

I spent the rest of the afternoon digging further into the Energy 2020 angle, the years-long fight, and the lead role Marcellus, and apparently Ariens, had played in pushing the pipeline plan.

Last year's election outcome had finally unleashed the 2020 Plan, so Marcellus and other energy companies must've celebrated the outcome. But would a company that had done so much good for the region have gone as far as stealing an election to further its goals?

Unless I could penetrate Marcellus more directly, there was not much more to learn. So I tracked down the corporate headquarters, located over the border. Titusville, Pennsylvania. Interesting choice. I put in a call to the Marcellus offices and left a message with the chief public affairs officer.

* * *

"I'm not even sure where to start. There's so much to say."

Arlene Bradley called at 6:00 on the nose, using her brother's home phone. I had to strain to hear her halting voice.

"Well, start where you're comfortable."

"Okay. First, they know that you called his cell. Minutes after you left, the congressman asked me where the area code was from. So when I found it was Youngstown, they knew."

I nodded. It was obvious they'd figure it out. Could've used a burner phone, but the truth was, I didn't care.

"How did you get that number anyway?" she asked.

Why was she asking questions? Maybe this was a trap after all. I paused for a few seconds, not wanting to give anything away. Thankfully, Bradley interrupted the silence.

"The reason I ask is that's his private cell phone. No one has that number but family and staff. He was amazed you had it, and so was I."

"Let's just say I found it somewhere it shouldn't have been," I said.

"Fair enough. Well, what I wanted to tell you was that I was the one who took the call from Congressman Kelly that you asked about."

"Which call?"

"I overheard you say that Congressman Kelly called our office the morning that he died. I'm the one who took that call. Congressman Stanton was not in, and Mr. Kelly and I talked for a short time. He was always the nicest man. Given that he died that day, I've been haunted knowing that I was one of the last people he ever talked to."

"Do you remember what you talked about?"

"Yes. We caught up a little bit on life, and then I told him the congressman was not in. He mentioned he was in Philadelphia that day and wondered if Congressman Stanton happened to be there too. That he hoped to patch things up."

"And?"

"The congressman was in the Philly office, so I encouraged him to call him there. He said he planned to. And ever since, I've worried that my advice cost him his life."

Indeed, it may have, but I kept that to myself. "Of course you didn't, Ms. Bradley. That was just a tragic accident."

"Seems a lot fishier than that now."

"I guess it does. Did you happen to give him the number to call?"

"No. He said he already had his cell phone."

"Did you talk about anything else?"

"No, we didn't. He just wished me luck, and I did the same."

"Did you tell the congressman about your conversation with Congressman Kelly? Did he know he was in Philly?"

"I emailed our office director right away that the congressman should be expecting Kelly's call."

This was crucial information from an incredibly well-placed source. Probably all she called to tell me, but I desperately wanted to keep her on the line. "Ms. Bradley, I'd like to ask you another question if I could."

"Yes?"

"And it's not an easy one."

She paused for a few seconds. "Is it about Joanie?"

"Yes, it is."

Silence.

"Did you know?"

A quiet sniffle.

"Ms. Bradley?"

"Of course I knew," she said with anger in her voice, although I sensed it was directed at herself, not me. "Half the people in the office knew. Not about Joanie in particular, but that Congressman Stanton harassed young female aides over the years. But no one was torn apart by it more than me. I'm the one who had to witness these young ladies go into his office, watch that damn door close, and then watch them come out 20 minutes later looking lost. I thought I'd get numb to it but never did. It was awful. And whenever they stopped going into that office, something else happened. Maybe worse. Because those women kept wearing that lost expression until the day they stopped working there."

Her anger evolved into a sob.

"I think when they stopped coming into his office, he had them come over to his townhome. He called them from that secret cell phone you dialed, and his security team picked them up and drove them there. That's what the rumor was."

"Terrible. And why—"

"Why didn't I do anything about it?" The anger had returned.

"Mr. Sharpe, I grew up in abject poverty in Alabama. As a little girl, I was one of the first African Americans in a white public school. I worked my way through secretarial school waiting tables and cleaning homes. And then I made it all the way to Capitol Hill. My husband passed a decade ago, and I still raised two great kids. Congressman Stanton knows I can't give all this up. I think he purposefully selects young women, like Joanie, who face the same pressures I did, ones unwilling to step off the path to power they think they are on, and willing, in the end, to pay the price he makes them pay to stay on it."

"Is it still happening?"

"I don't know. Joanie's murder scared him. In the weeks after her death, he and Seth were in a panic, clearly worried his womanizing would catch up to him. That's when he put his family photos back on his desk. They hadn't been there in years. No, there are no longer encounters. At least in the office. Who knows what he does late at night? Only his driver would know that."

I tried to keep her talking without scaring her off the phone. "Did you think her death was suspicious?"

"Joanie's? I never did. Muggings happen in Rock Creek Park. Lord knows good people die every day in Washington, but the big shots never care. But this recent stuff, and Stanton's frantic behavior, make me think maybe Peter's been right all along."

"Who's Peter?"

"Peter Kreutzer. He was dating Joanie when she died."

"She had a boyfriend?" I asked, nearly yelling into the phone. A boyfriend hadn't been mentioned anywhere.

"Well, they had been close friends for a while, and then it turned into something more. They hid it from almost everyone, but I could tell. It was special. He was a legislative aide for Congressman Jackson, the next office over."

"Why would they hide—?"

"Given the situation, of course they did," Bradley said. "She clearly didn't want the congressman to find out. Who knows how he might react? And I think she held Peter back from getting too close because she didn't want to explain why she was not available certain nights."

"So Peter didn't believe it was a mugging?"

"From the day the police ID'd Rutherford, Peter insisted it didn't happen the way the police said. That someone else did it, and not as a mugging. People dismissed him, so he stopped talking about it. He's a highly respected staffer."

"Do you think I could talk to him about it?"

"He finally seems to have moved on, but maybe. He now works for Senator Lewis of Indiana."

Jotted down both names for follow-up. "Ms. Bradley, I have one more question for you?"

"Yes."

"Do you remember any interaction Mr. Stanton had with the company Abacus, the one I have written about?"

"I don't. I'm not his scheduler, so I wouldn't be aware of many visits he made. But after your story, I went back to his calendar over the last few years. I never found anything on it regarding that company."

"Could they have erased it from the system?"

"Of course. Or they may have never put it on that calendar in the first place."

"Who is his scheduler? Would she talk?"

"Sadly, she died about a year ago. Horrible skin cancer. She was gone about five weeks after they discovered it. Only 45 years old."

"How sad. Ms. Bradley, you've been an incredible help. I cannot thank you enough for calling, and for your honesty tonight."

"I'm glad. I know it was terrible I didn't stand up for Joanie when she was alive. I will never forgive myself."

I said nothing back. As helpful as she'd been, I couldn't forgive her either.

CHAPTER 43

April 13

156 days after the election

"O<small>N ZNAET</small>?" K<small>AZAROV</small> asked in his native tongue. "Does he know we are following him?"

Boris Popov, Kazarov's chief of security, answered, also in Russian. "He knows someone is following him. He has known for days. But he doesn't know *who* is following him."

"And what does he know?"

"He knows about Stanton. That is clear. And he is bold. He went directly to his office to confront him, driving six hours to do so. I like him for that alone."

"So why are we meeting?"

"Because he is now digging into Marcellus."

Kazarov took a moment to let this sink in. Disappointing. He thought they had sufficiently hidden his enterprise's involvement. "And how do you know this?" he asked.

"He visited Mr. Ariens' office. The next day, he put in a call to Marcellus headquarters, wanting to talk to our public affairs person there. Left a message."

"Have we called back yet?"

"Not yet."

"We should. Let's learn what he knows, and what he wants to know. And to be prepared, let's find out more about him as well."

CHAPTER 44

YOUNGSTOWN

April 14: 157 days after the election

HOW TO APPROACH Peter Kreutzer?

Calling into a senator's office unexpectedly posed risks, especially now that Republicans detested me. And Indiana's Senator Lewis was as rock-ribbed as they came. So instead of calling, I returned to Joanie Simpson's Facebook page and re-scrolled through pages of posts and messages. There was one simple post from a Peter Kreutzer, five days after her death: "Joanie, you will always be with me. I miss you every moment. I will fight for you. Heartbroken, Peter." An assortment of photos of the two together appeared over the prior four months, always surrounded by others. If they were romantically involved, they certainly didn't let on in public.

Unlike Joanie's page, Kreutzer's blocked access to anyone who was not a "friend," so there was little more I could learn about him. I hit the "message" button and typed a few brief sentences. *Mr. Kreutzer. I am a reporter looking into Joanie Simpson's death. Look up the* Youngstown Vindicator *to confirm. I understand you have concerns. I will keep them confidential. Please call me.* I added my cell number and pushed send.

Less than a minute later, my computer sounded the distinct ping of a returned message.

I know who you are. When can we talk? Kreutzer wrote. A quick answer. Good. No time to waste.

I'm free now.

Ten minutes later, the phone rang.

"Mr. Sharpe?"

"Is this Peter?"

"Yes, sir. I probably shouldn't be calling you. You're the most hated man in Washington, at least among those I associate with."

"It's important that you called," I said, trying to appeal to the young man's sense of duty.

"Yes."

"I'm so sorry about Joanie's death. I can't imagine what you went through."

"Thank you," he said. "It still hurts."

My leading question, and Kreutzer's heartfelt response, confirmed that Bradley was right about their relationship. "I understand you have real concerns about Joanie's cause of death. I have questions as well, and I was hoping you could share your concerns with me. Everything you say is completely confidential."

"I actually told a lot of people my doubts, including the police, so I'm not surprised you heard about them. I stopped bringing it up because people acted like I was crazy. But I'm telling you, she was not killed by that Rutherford guy."

His confidence impressed me. "Who do you think killed her?"

"I have no idea. But it wasn't a mugging, and it wasn't that guy."

"What makes you think that?" I asked.

"So much. First, Joanie had been spending a ton of time working on something she wouldn't talk about. Some research project. She was so intense about it for weeks. And nervous too. Not nervous about her safety, but stressed, consumed. It was a big deal, more than any issue she'd ever looked into. It didn't feel like just politics."

Clearly the Abacus memo.

"And?"

"And then finally, the day before she died—that Friday—she finally relaxed. We had lunch that day, and it was clear she must have completed the project. She seemed so relieved. Then she's killed the next day. I always figured it was related to that research."

Simpson likely finished the memo late in the week. Stanton must have seen it on Thursday or Friday, and she was dead in less than 48 hours.

"Was she relieved Thursday too?" I asked, trying to narrow the window.

"She was a basket case most of Thursday at the office. We talked a few times, took an afternoon break like we always did. She was tense. I didn't talk to her at all Thursday evening. We would do our own things Thursday nights. Then Friday, all good. She lived it up that night, as happy as I'd seen her."

"Okay," I said. "This is helpful."

"There's more. The day she died, I stopped in her apartment about four that afternoon."

Holy shit. "You did?"

"Yes. She'd given me a key in case I stopped by when she was already asleep. I'd tiptoe in and crawl into bed. So when she didn't answer calls all Saturday, I stopped by." He paused for a few seconds. "Mr. Sharpe, someone had been in her apartment."

"How do you know that?"

"Well, there weren't any obvious signs. Nothing was broken. No footprints. But you have to understand Joanie. She was meticulous about order and cleanliness, to the point of being obsessive. She was like a Marine making a bed. Had to be perfect. We would always laugh about it, but it was true."

"So?"

"So anyone sneaking into her place, no matter how careful, would leave an obvious trail of disorder versus how she would have left it. For example, she had a little desk in her bedroom. That afternoon, a few papers on the desk were out of place, laying a little crooked. Compared to how Joanie would leave her desk, it looked sloppy. I noticed it right away. I think someone had been looking through those papers."

Needed more than that. "Anything else?"

"Yep. Same thing in her kitchen. When you opened the cabinet doors below the sink, two bags were mounted on the door. They looked the same, but the one on the left was for recycled paper, the one on the right was for garbage. They weren't marked or anything, so you'd have to know Joanie's system. And she was religious about recycling every shred of paper. "When I stopped by, I opened that cabinet door, thinking maybe there'd be some sign of when she'd been there last. I didn't find anything new, but what I did find were a number of pieces of paper in the bag for garbage, and they were on top. Joanie would never have put them there. Someone had dug through her recycled papers and put them back in the wrong bag."

This kid was good.

"So you think someone searched her apartment?"

"Definitely. They obviously were looking for some type of papers or documents."

"Can I ask you a strange question?"

"Sure."

"Would Joanie ever work from home, possibly over a glass of wine?"

"Always," Kreutzer said. "She liked to edit her work on printed pages. She'd curl up on her couch, read it over with her red pen, often with a glass of wine next to her. Then she'd type her edits into her computer and bring it to the office the next day. Why do you ask?"

As Kreutzer explained this, I looked at Simpson's Abacus memo sitting in front of me, folded in half, marred by that wine stain. This is clearly what the intruder had been looking for, and found, probably in the recycling bag. But I never liked to give away too much. "I wanted to confirm something I had found. Peter, tell me about Rutherford. Did you look into him?"

"Of course. It just never added up. The guy was a career criminal, but his crimes were always pretty minor—usually drug-related, disorderly conduct, stuff like that, in his own neighborhood. He had no profile committing worse violence, and had never ventured far to commit a crime."

Kreutzer's voice was getting louder as he continued.

"And why the hell would anyone leave a baseball bat, with prints, at the scene of the crime? But then that same person leaves no trace of his visit to her apartment? Then he stupidly dumps her stuff in a trash bin outside his apartment complex for the entire world to find? Give me a break!"

He was right. None of it added up. Someone had set up Rutherford. "Why did they pick Rutherford?"

"I could never figure that one out," Kreutzer said.

"Not sure how you could," I said. "You've been a huge help. I'll keep you posted on what I find."

I meant it. This was a breakthrough.

Someone killed Simpson within 48 hours of her having handed in that memo. Someone, likely the killer or an accomplice, then marched into her apartment within hours of the killing, using her own keys to enter, rifled through her papers, and found her Abacus memo. And while carefully hiding his own tracks, the killer then planted a trail of evidence pinning the crime on a man who had nothing to do with any of it.

*   *   *

Before looking into the Rutherford angle, I jumped back on Facebook to see if Simpson's page verified Kreutzer's story. It did. And while there, I discovered a pattern that had eluded me earlier.

When she wasn't at work, Simpson had posted all the time: where she was, what she was thinking, what she was doing. These personal snippets, tracing her every move and thought, would routinely go on until about midnight every night. Her friends and followers would react to every post, making her page a real-time group diary of every day's and evening's activity. Must be a generational thing. If I had been so open about my comings and goings in high school and college, I would have been expelled from both.

But on close examination, something new stuck out. An absence.

The Thursday night before she died, unlike most evenings, her Facebook page went atypically dark. For most young people, Thursdays are the beginning of the weekend. And if she went out, Simpson would have certainly posted about it.

But that night, she reported nothing. Based on Kreutzer's account, this must've been when she finalized the memo and handed it to Stanton. And based on the rumors Arlene Bradley described, she probably did so in the privacy of the congressman's townhouse.

To confirm this, I looked at both the Wednesday and Friday posts. Wednesday described a laid-back evening—gym after work, early casual dinner with a friend, home from about 9:00 p.m. on. And Friday was a big night out, culminating in the last post of her life.

But Thursday? Nothing. Clearly delivering the research that had gotten her killed.

Before logging out, I delved deeper into her page. I was haunted by Bradley's theory that Stanton brought Simpson and others back to his townhome regularly. If her online silence revealed her visit that Thursday evening, how about prior weeks? Kreutzer had said they never spent Thursday nights together. Sure enough, the same pattern occurred month after month. Dozens of posts, constant activity, six days a week. But silence every Thursday.

I had to scroll back almost a year, during the heart of the presidential election, to find several posts on Thursday evenings. On those nights, Stanton would've hit the road campaigning, liberating Simpson from an otherwise dehumanizing routine.

As much as Simpson celebrated the president's re-election, the campaign's end also meant the end of her escape from Stanton.

*   *   *

Over the years, I'd gotten to know policing as well as anyone short of a cop, judge, or criminal. Chief Santini and I talked all the time, and I was friends with our crime reporters. Plus, from embezzlement to drug dealing, more than a few of the politicians I'd covered ended up on the wrong side of the law.

From all this, I'd discovered what few Americans ever figure out, something that the officers and the criminals realize but about which the average citizen is clueless: Outside of a small percentage of cases and crimes, the entire system is a treadmill.

All the players in the system are running in place, week after week, rarely moving forward. Whenever cops don that uniform, they're on that treadmill—they just happen to be risking their life in the process. And unless criminals commit a truly heinous crime, they too are running in place. The treadmill exists because states and cities have created a laundry list of laws that require arrest for all sorts of behavior. And lawmakers at all levels are always adding to that list. You don't win elections by subtracting.

The list is so long that it generates an unsolvable math problem: Far more people commit crimes than local jails have space or funds available to hold them. So police officers make constant arrests for this vast array of offenses, bring the offenders in, and, short of a homicide or excessively violent crime, those offenders are back out within days. Over and over again.

The repeat transactions create an odd familiarity among the players involved. The same officers see the same offenders all the time. Get to know them by name. Even build friendly relationships with many of them. Some of those offenders become their best sources, informing them about other offenders' misdeeds.

But when they re-violate one of those many laws, the officers arrest them again, book them, go to court to testify against them, and watch them walk back out. And with every arrest, the arresting officer dutifully fills out a form at booking, naming the criminal, checking off the appropriate boxes, writing in his badge number, describing the circumstances of the arrest. And then he signs his name at the bottom. It's all part of the treadmill.

After talking to Kreutzer, I called the D.C. Police Department looking for such records for Johnny Rutherford. It turned out Johnny Rutherford was a treadmill champion.

"Rutherford? That guy was our top frequent flyer until he killed that girl," the clerk said when I mentioned the name. "I mean, we're talkin' seven, eight times a year."

"Can you send me over his record?"

"Sure thing. Be sure your fax machine is full of paper!"

Seventy-eight pages came through half an hour later.

Rutherford lived on Atlantic Avenue in Southeast, a tough part of town. And rarely a month went by without Rutherford committing some type of crime. Usually serious enough to require arrest, sometimes jail time. But never serious enough to require more than a brief sentence. Much of his time behind bars came from failure to make bail. The first page of the pile was typical. After a trespassing charge and arrest, Rutherford spent a few days in jail because he couldn't make bail. Run of the mill stuff, in his own neighborhood, just as Kreutzer had described. So after Rutherford pled guilty, the judge sentenced him to time served.

The rest of his arrest record followed suit. Breaking and entering. More trespassing. Drug paraphernalia. Drug dealing. Resisting arrest. A couple assaults, but none too violent—street fights, bumps and bruises. No behavior consistent with a brutal slaying of a young woman on the opposite side of town.

He was a career criminal, not a murderer. Exactly as Kreutzer had said.

Having leafed through the records once, I took a closer look at the first arrest. Beyond the crime itself, I studied the whole arrest form. A new detail, one far more important than the crime itself, jumped off the page. The bottom of the page.

While the arresting officer's name wasn't typed, the signature appeared in large, round cursive letters. Highly legible. And the name was familiar.

Clay Dennison.

I grabbed my notes from a few days before. Yep, it was the same name Chief Santini had identified as Stanton's security chief. The one he thought was following me. The former D.C. police officer.

Dennison had arrested this guy. He knew him.

I quickly scanned all 78 pages again. Sure enough, 21 times in five years, Dennison's distinct signature emblazoned the bottom of Rutherford's arrest forms. For more than half Rutherford's arrests, Congressman Stanton's current security chief had signed as the arresting officer.

I shook my head in disgust. Ruthless.

When looking to frame someone for Simpson's hit, Stanton and his security apparatus didn't just find their man. They already knew their man. And with his extensive record, they knew he was the perfect man. Everyone would believe he was the culprit.

One reality about the treadmill—when a criminal's been on it his whole life, he doesn't get the benefit of the doubt.

CHAPTER 45

13 months before the election

Back at her kitchen table, Irene Stanton read through the arrest record one page at a time.

This was the sixth package she'd received from the private investigator, a former Philly cop. The prior files had confirmed that her husband had harassed young female employees for years. There also appeared to be some mild corruption in her husband's office.

But this latest batch of information was far more startling. Johnny Rutherford's arrest record was inconsistent with the brutal murder of Joanie Simpson. But Clay Dennison's name appeared as the arresting officer dozens of times. She immediately recognized the name as her husband's security chief.

Irene buried her head in her hands. What had her husband become?

PART FOUR
DEADLINE

CHAPTER 46

April 14: 157 days after the election

I SAT BACK IN my dad's chair and took it all in. The cool lake breeze flowing through the screen windows. The soothing aroma of the cedar walls and floors. The choppy, white-tipped waves of shallow Lake Erie.

This was my escape, and I needed it. Arlene Bradley and Peter Kreutzer had provided important new information, and the Dennison find was a breakthrough, but my narrative remained scattered. Many loose ends. With only days to go, time to focus.

My family had owned a small cabin near Geneva-on-the-Lake since my childhood, and after both my parents passed away, I'd inherited the property. It had served as my getaway ever since.

My family had endured many ups and downs over the years, and this place brought back the ups. The positive memories. The old family photos on the wall, back when all were healthy, happy, and hopeful. The pencil marks on the door tracking my and my sister Meredith's growth spurts over the years. Trophies on a bookshelf, still boasting top achievements decades later. And some of Dad's favorite political paraphernalia and photos, hung before we'd all become so disenchanted. Even the old photos of Meredith brought a smile.

She was born four years after me. As photos and the pencil marks captured, she too was tall, with long brown hair, hazel eyes, and high cheekbones. People always said she could've been a model. In her 29 years, she always was the apple of Dad's eye. Mine too. We called her the family angel. She made us all laugh from the time she'd hit seven months old. If I mimicked Dad's political interest and intensity at a young age, Meredith had inherited the interpersonal charm that made him such a good campaigner. Her intense, uninterrupted gaze, warm smile, and gentle manner lifted everyone lucky enough to be on the receiving end. Her disposition anchored the family when times got tough. When Dad lost his election, when my own life fell apart, when Mom succumbed to breast cancer, Meredith kept the family going. She was the rock.

But she made one terrible mistake—she married the wrong man. As much as we loved her, and communicated with her on a regular basis, neither Dad nor I had detected the signs. Years of abuse hidden beneath her pleasant exterior. Years of bruises and broken bones masked by makeup, creative explanations, and assurances that all was okay. A complete mirage, we would later find out.

When we got the call, Dad and I were watching an Indians game in his living room, back in Canton. "Mr. Sharpe," the cop said, "we need you to come to the Clinic right away. It's an emergency."

We raced up I-77, arriving at the hospital shortly after she fell into a coma. We hardly recognized the bruised, disfigured body lying in the hospital bed. Almost every inch of her face was a horrific hue of deep purple or blood red. Her broken nose bent unnaturally to the left, her swollen right eye was sealed completely shut. Her arms and legs were tattooed with additional dark blue and purple bruises. We both grasped her right hand because her left was mangled, fingers splayed in opposite directions due to fractured bones beneath.

She stopped breathing shortly after midnight, overwhelmed by the internal bleeding. The doctors were amazed she had held on that long.

The homicide detectives later pieced together the crime scene. Spurred on by a disagreement over money, her husband had beaten her for hours, at first with his fists, and then with other household items. The autopsy also revealed a history of broken bones, including an eye socket and a collarbone in recent years. And Meredith had never told a soul. In hindsight, I wasn't surprised. She never asked for help, she was always the one helping others.

The jury sentenced her husband to life in prison, but for us it didn't assuage a personal sentence that felt far more painful.

Dad passed away four months after the trial. I never doubted that the heartbreak of his daughter's brutal death, of blaming himself for not being there for her, had driven Dad's health downhill quickly.

I felt equally guilt-ridden. The big brother, who physically towered over the monster who killed her, had failed to protect her. I rarely spoke of Meredith again.

In only one place in the world, Geneva-on-the-Lake, did Meredith's spirit remain. There, and only there, the photos of Meredith beaming from the walls overwhelmed the vivid image of my dying sister that was otherwise cemented into my memory. So after arriving at the cabin, I did what I always did. I grabbed a Yuengling, sat back in Dad's old rocking chair, faced the lake, and soaked it all in. A few moments to recall the good old days. To feel the way I did back then, before Dad's loss and everything that followed.

But this time, as I glanced up at the photos of Meredith, the framed photo of Joanie Simpson in the Capitol Hill office also flashed in my head.

*   *   *

I had made enormous headway, far beyond my first story, but so much of it was off the record, unsourced. Even worse, there were still so many loose ends. So I made a list of them to keep from feeling overwhelmed:

1. *Who did Stanton work with? Abacus plan required major investments.*

2. *What role did Ariens play? Did he know of Abacus? Was he the connection back to the investor(s)?*

3. *Who sent the information on Stanton? Insider? Or someone else aware of plot?*

4. *Who was following me?*

Just as I finished jotting down my list of unknowns, my cell phone rang. A Pennsylvania area code.

"Mr. Sharpe?"

"Yes. This is he."

"My name is Michael Chambers. I'm the CEO of Marcellus. I understand you want to talk to our company. When can we meet?"

*   *   *

It took me two hours to get to Titusville, where a sign at the run-down town's entrance displayed the town motto: "The Valley That Changed the World." Couldn't tell from looking at it. But then it occurred to me that the slogan was accurate. The world had indeed changed thanks to Titusville—just not to the benefit of the little town itself.

I continued on to the Marcellus headquarters, located south of town, only miles from where oil had first been discovered and drilled more than 150 years before. At the security gate, the guard waved me through to the stunning site. I had expected a nice new building, but not an entire campus of them. Five silver buildings, each eight stories tall, spaced out in a semi-circle and all facing the same pristinely landscaped green in the middle. These people were printing money.

After a quiet elevator ride, a woman at the top floor reception desk greeted me. She led me into a large conference room and promptly left. I looked out the large window to see the impressive campus from above, tiny Titusville sitting humbly in the distance. And a few miles west of town, a large fracking pad burst skyward, taller than any structure in the town itself.

A deep voice interrupted from behind. "Jack, thanks for coming so quickly." I turned around. "I'm Michael Chambers," said the man as he reached out his hand to me.

This guy took slick to a whole new level. Chambers was my height, wore a perfectly fitting dark suit, light blue shirt, and cuffs monogrammed with "JSM." His hair was combed straight back. His teeth shone white, his face a deep tan. A hybrid between Mitt Romney and Gordon Gekko.

I reached out and shook his hand, which was weak and oddly cold.

"Thanks for calling me back," I said. "I was surprised you were the one who returned the call."

"Given what you've been writing, I thought it best if we talk directly. Must be important."

Odd answer. Entirely inconsistent with how most corporations respond to press calls.

We sat down across the table from one another. Chambers leaned back, lifting his hands to the back of his head, angling his elbows out, and crossing his legs. They must coach these guys on arrogant, obnoxious poses.

"Mr. Chambers," I began, "I'm a political reporter and not a business reporter, but I'm so impressed by what Marcellus is doing. You're changing the face of eastern Ohio, bringing hope back to so many communities that had lost it. I've never seen anything like it."

A guy like this loves buttering up, but I meant every word.

"Thank you. We've worked hard to become a good community member. It's been our pleasure every step of the way."

"I'm sure it has," I said, looking at Chambers' gold cufflinks and white-gold Rolex. "But I'm interested in digging deeper into our story about last November's election."

"I figured, but I have no idea why you'd be calling us."

He sounded completely sincere.

"We have come to believe"—"we" made my assertions sound far more conclusive, and also provided a blanket of protection from anyone tempted to think that eliminating me would make a nettlesome story go away—"that your lobbyist Oliver Ariens may have been part of the vote-stealing plot."

This greatly exaggerated what I knew, but I hoped an earth-shattering statement like this would throw Chambers off his game.

"Are you joking?" Chambers asked. Laughing heartily, he looked genuinely surprised.

"I am not. Can you tell me about your relationship with Mr. Ariens?"

"Oliver was a great friend of Marcellus and the best in the business. I'm sure you know that he was the leader of the Energy 2020 effort that is so critical to our long-term success."

"Yes. I can only imagine how important the election was to you."

"It was absolutely critical. The American people finally woke up and got rid of the knuckleheads standing in the way of progress. We were thrilled with the outcome."

Apparently, Chambers didn't think much of my Abacus theory. But even if willfully ignorant, he was disarmingly honest. He had just volunteered Ariens' Energy 2020 leadership role and then embraced the tainted election outcome with glee. His answers left little room for follow-up questions.

"Were you concerned when Ariens died?" I asked.

"Of course we were. Ariens was the key to the whole plan. We were sick to our stomachs when he died."

"I mean did you find his death suspicious?"

"Oh. Not at all. He was huge. So out of shape that he had it coming. But it was a real setback for our efforts."

What a heart. "Mr. Chambers, wasn't the Energy 2020 strategy a complete failure until the surprise of last November's elections? Nothing happened until then."

"I don't know, Jack. I'm not a politician, I'm an oil and gas man.

Whether it's in the ocean, the desert, or here in the Midwest, I care about making investments that lead to outcomes. It took a while, but we got the job done. And now we're changing this place, just as you said at the outset."

He was shooting straight. No bullshit at all. But as I glanced out the window, and recalled the systematic Marcellus rollout in eastern Ohio, something didn't feel right with this guy. Something didn't add up.

"How long have you been in charge at Abacus?"

"Excuse me? What's Abacus?"

Momentarily confused, I realized I had asked about the wrong enterprise. But Chambers' answer was telling. He sounded as if he had never heard of the company.

"Sorry, I meant how long have you been in charge at Marcellus?"

"Since our founding," Chambers said. He sounded defensive, as if I had questioned his manhood.

"And what did you do before this?"

"I worked at Shell Oil, vice president over new source development. Perfect for this role."

"Where did you work at Shell?" I asked.

"All over. The Middle East. Texas. The Carolinas when we expanded our offshore work. And I traveled a ton. How is this relevant?"

"Just curious. Always want to know folks I talk to. How did you end up here?"

"I was recruited by the private investors that formed Marcellus. They wanted the best, and they got it."

"And you run the show?"

"Of course. What about the words 'chief executive officer' do you not understand?"

A question worth ignoring. "What's next for the company?" I asked.

"We will keep growing. With the new pipelines in place, we will finally get our products to market quickly and efficiently. Our prior growth will look small compared to what we're about to experience."

"And what's been the key to your success?"

"Hmmm," he said, pausing, then looking out the window. "Many things have been critical. Can't say one in particular sticks out."

"Well, you've certainly done about everything right."

"Thank you."

"So you don't think Oliver Ariens was trying to change the outcome of an election to help make Energy 2020 happen?"

"That's the most absurd thing I've ever heard." Chambers laughed again as he said it. The thought had never occurred to the man.

"And you mentioned Marcellus' private investors. The ones who hired you. Who are they?"

"They're private for a reason," he said, folding his arms. "And they want to keep it that way."

So I'd gotten all there was to get. "Thank you for your time, Mr. Chambers. Big weekend plans?"

"Back to the city!"

This was not a phrase you heard around western Pennsylvania or eastern Ohio. "Which city is that?"

"New York," he said matter-of-factly. "Still get home almost every weekend."

*   *   *

My trip back to the cabin allowed me to reach three conclusions.

First, Chambers had answered forthrightly about Ariens, Abacus, and last year's election. He knew absolutely nothing, barely recalling the company's name.

Second, this didn't surprise me, because Chambers appeared entirely incapable of pulling off the Abacus scheme.

Third, for the same reason, Chambers was neither the architect of nor the brains behind Marcellus.

I'd had a front row seat to it all. The Marcellus rollout in eastern Ohio had involved a combination of strategic thinking, cultural sensitivity, and raw efficiency the likes of which I'd never seen. The company had developed an enormous technological advantage, moved into the area swiftly yet quietly, and devised a bottom-up identity that eclipsed companies that had operated there for generations. It was a household name, a positive one, but anchored locally. Such planning and execution could only have been orchestrated by an authentic, visionary leader, a master strategist, armed with a broad set of skills. And the man I had just sat with for an hour was most certainly not that leader. Chambers had no doubt gained solid experience at Shell Oil, working steadily up the ladder of a large, bureaucratic corporate culture. But that would not have lent itself to the stealthy, entrepreneurial, but ultimately overwhelming rollout that Marcellus had executed so effectively.

Chambers' answers on the reason for the company's success, and its future after Energy 2020, had appeared entirely sincere. But shallow, and not at all impressive. He failed to display any of the strategic thinking that the leader of such a revolutionary enterprise would possess. Like he said, he was an "oil and gas guy" who made investments and watched them pay off. But Marcellus operated in a far more sophisticated and aggressive way than that.

And while Marcellus had shown an ability to meld with the culture of the old Midwest, nothing about Chambers suggested he could pull that off.

Never mind that everything about the man communicated that he wanted to spend as little time there as possible. More telling had been his response to my initial comment. Whoever had masterminded the deep investment into local communities up and down the Ohio River had done it with careful attention, as a central element of Marcellus' overall strategy. But Chambers' statement about being a "good community member" had been a throwaway line, uttered without passion.

Finally, while Chambers had a working knowledge of the Energy 2020 strategy, he showed none of the political sophistication you'd expect from a CEO working hand-in-hand with the nation's top lobbying firm. Marcellus had spent years forcing an enormously controversial bill through Congress, yet Chambers came across as a political neophyte.

Yes, someone very impressive ran Marcellus. Just not its CEO.

*   *   *

GENEVA-ON-THE-LAKE

It rained most of Saturday, so I huddled inside, typing away on my laptop. After starting to draft a memo to convince my bosses to keep me on the story, I turned it into the actual story instead. My focus was on the Stanton connection:

> *Few politicians worked harder in last November's election than Congressman Thomas Stanton, and few benefitted more from the surprising outcome. The new House Majority Leader is now among the three most powerful people in Washington and appears on every short list of viable presidential contenders.*
>
> *Throughout the fall, Stanton campaigned heavily in almost every one of the districts in which the Abacus company altered the results*

in last November's elections. And a Vindicator investigation has found that this wasn't a coincidence—Stanton, as House minority whip, knew more than a year in advance virtually every district where Abacus had located its game-changing machines. And that's exactly where he campaigned.

I kept it simple, reciting the facts I could support. This would keep us out of a losing lawsuit and head off a quick veto from my editors. I took a stab at describing Simpson's death.

The researcher who composed one memo for Stanton outlining the plan was murdered just as she finalized the memo and a list of Abacus districts. Several anonymous sources questioned the rushed conclusion of the murder investigation, especially given the suspicious timing of her death.

A separate Vindicator inquiry found that the suspect in the murder, Johnny Rutherford—who died in a gunfight with police as they attempted to arrest him—had a direct connection with Stanton's chief of security. As a police officer, that security chief had arrested Rutherford on at least 21 occasions.

I was intentionally offering up tantalizing facts. My editors would require far more before publishing them, but there was nothing wrong with whetting their appetite with this draft.

As I typed up the story, one gap became clear: there was no evidence proving that Stanton was *part* of the Abacus plan, as opposed to simply being *aware* of it. A crucial difference. The killing of Simpson, and all his lies, suggested he was covering up something he was part of. But I still needed something concrete to nail his role down.

I added this shortcoming to my list of unknowns.

At about 4:30, after the rain tapered off, I took a short break. Since childhood, I had jogged along the same dirt road by the lake, running three miles east, and then heading straight back, often into the sunset. In my prime, I used to cover the distance in under 41 minutes. I now averaged 48, still a decent clip, and that was my pace today.

Reaching the turnaround point at 25:08, I sped up on the way back. But halfway home, at 36 minutes, my phone buzzed. It was Scott, so I picked up.

"Dad, someone is following us," he said, nearly shouting.

I slowed my pace from a jog to a fast walk. "Why do you think that?"

"Jana and I had brunch in that spot we love in Sausalito." They had taken me there once, via the ferry. A stunning view from the little bayside town. "When we took a walk afterward, we noticed that a car that had been sitting a few houses back when we left home was parked right near the restaurant where we ate. Some big dude was sitting in the car, trying to look occupied, as we walked by."

"What kind of car?" I asked, my temper already flaring.

"A Toyota SUV of some kind, California plates. Had a little Hertz sticker on the back."

"Did they follow you back?" I started walking faster, pissed off and preparing to do something about it.

"We couldn't tell if they did. I'm sure the guy was rattled as we walked by. Didn't see the car as we drove back home. But they clearly know where we live."

"Keep checking and see if you can see them. Also, call a friend and have them drive by and see if they see the car there. They're probably parking a little further back now. And keep me posted."

"Good idea," he said. Scott would never want me to see him scared, but I could hear the nerves in his voice. "Will do."

＊　＊　＊

I sprinted back toward the cabin, livid.

I had become fatalistic about this story. I knew what was at stake, and I had intentionally crossed the threshold into true danger, so I was prepared for whatever they tried to do to me or say about me. I could take it. Hell, I'd asked for it.

But Scott? And his young wife? Tailing them was low. Spineless.

I entered the cabin's side screen door, letting it slam behind me. I paced back and forth across the creaky wooden floor a few times, then marched back outside, this time bursting through the front door.

The Suburban had trailed me up to the cabin. Earlier that morning, I had spotted it laying low at the end of the dirt driveway, so I walked briskly in that direction. Yep, there it was.

I marched up to the side of the driver door and pounded on the window. Although the glass was tinted, I could see that the driver was startled.

"Get the fuck out of this car!" I yelled.

The driver looked through the window, and put his arms up shoulder high, palms out. He then lowered his left hand, opened the door slowly, and stepped out of the car.

The man stood an inch shorter than me but was thicker at every level of his frame. Must have weighed 40 pounds more. Black turtleneck, dark pants, short cropped hair. An imposing character, but my temper overwhelmed my judgment.

"Who the fuck are you?" I said. "And why the hell are you guys following my son? He has nothing to do with this."

The passenger door opened, and a shorter, thinner man got out from that side of the car. "Mr. Sharpe," he said calmly, "if you know what's good for you, you will go back to your cabin." *Meester Sharpe . . . You weel go back to your cabeen.*

His thick Slavic accent caught me off guard. "Who the hell are you guys? Why have you been following me, and why are you following my son?"

The driver looked at me with a hollow stare.

"Mr. Sharpe," the passenger said again, "for your own good, you will want to return to your *dacha* now. I will not warn you again."

"I want you to take me to the man who pays you to follow me. I want to speak with him directly. I've put up with this long enough."

At this point, I stood just to the left of the driver but looked directly at the passenger doing the talking. And the passenger, while still looking my way, responded with a foreign word.

"*Poschli.*"

"Excuse me?"

Instantly, and painfully, I realized he wasn't talking to me. The goon to my right whirled his arm toward me and struck the back of my head with a hard object.

Everything went dark.

*   *   *

"We should have killed him," Popov said to his boss. "No one has ever confronted my men like that and survived."

"Killing him would not end this, which is why I ordered you to keep him alive in the first place. Sharpe is not a one-man newspaper. They know about Ariens, and they know about his tie to Marcellus. He said so himself. A death now would only make them more suspicious."

Popov nodded, chastened.

"Allowing his son to see he was being followed was another mistake, Boris. Your men are getting sloppy, and their repeated mistakes make our task much more challenging."

"But you said you wanted him to see he was being followed."

"Sharpe, yes, while in Ohio, but being spotted in Washington, D.C. was a terrible error. And now the same thing has happened with his son. Sloppy. Yuri talking to him directly was inexcusable."

As always, Kazarov's tone remained calm, even. He did not need to show his anger for his subordinates to grasp his displeasure. Plus, he too had made a mistake. Tasking Chambers to engage the reporter had backfired. It was clear from the tapes that Sharpe had left the interview skeptical of his American CEO.

"Outside of an extreme circumstance, we cannot simply eliminate Sharpe. Did you at least put a bug on him?"

"Yes, his cell phone is now both tapped and bugged. We will hear every conversation he has, in person or by phone."

"Anything else?"

"They could not get into his computer, but there were many notebooks next to it. They emailed us the photographs they took of all the pages."

"I'd like to see the notes myself," Kazarov said.

"*Konyeshno,*" Popov said. Of course.

*   *   *

The full moon, high in the sky, cast a beam straight to the water's edge. It was the first thing I saw when I opened my eyes.

I found myself seated back in Dad's rocking chair, facing north, out the window. My stopwatch was still running from the jog, at 7:36 and counting. I'd been out for almost seven hours.

Simply angling to look at my watch hurt. My entire head throbbed, only made worse by waves of sharp pain emanating from behind my right ear. I reached back and yelped as I felt a tender bump about the size of a ping-pong ball. Flakes of dried blood fell away at my touch.

An awful odor invaded my nose. I reached up, touching something gel-like clinging to the edge of my nostrils. I wiped it away with my left sleeve, and the smell and sting faded. Didn't appear that I had any other injuries. They had clearly knocked me out with a blow to the head and kept me out for hours with some type of substance. But at least it looked like they'd left. Thank God.

I leaned back in the chair, reconstructing it all.

First, the skinny guy, the passenger, was the same man who had followed me from the White House. Slavic accent, probably Russian. Why in the world was a Russian following me around Ohio as I covered an American political scandal? And the driver. As he'd emerged from the car and stared me down, his bewildered expression had made it clear he spoke little or no English. The passenger commanding him in a foreign language had only confirmed this. But even more telling had been the man's appearance: the build, the outfit, the hair. The perfectly executed blow to the head. And then the substance that knocked me unconscious. All the trappings of a goon, but a *professional* goon. All of this reminded me of my conversation with Chief Santini. He had indeed asked the right question. Who in the world had I pissed off that professional henchmen from Russia were tailing me, and now Scott?

I woozily walked back out the front door and up the driveway. My head pulsed with each step, but seeing that the Suburban had left eased the pain slightly.

I lumbered back into the cabin and flipped the lights on. Nothing looked to be missing. My computer was in sleep mode, exactly where it had been when I'd gone running. My phone lay right next to it, also in sleep mode. My notebooks, scattered messily across the wooden desk before the jog, remained scattered now. No doubt two professionals would've taken the opportunity to look around once they dragged me back inside, but there was no clear sign of what they had looked through or found.

My phone flashed a red light, indicating new messages. I typed the four-digit password to get out of sleep mode. There were nine missed calls and three messages. Scott had made most of them, so I called him right away before checking the messages.

"Dad? Where the hell have you been?"

"I'm fine. Are you okay?"

"Yes. I worried that you were going to do something crazy, so when you never answered, it scared the hell out of us."

"Well, let's just say I had a tough conversation with the people following me about the fact that they are now following you. And they ended it bluntly." I briefly went through the details, downplaying their roughing me up. "Scott, be careful," I said. "These people are both serious and dangerous. The good news is, they didn't kill me, and it wasn't because they're squeamish about murder. They made that decision for a reason. Whatever it is, we need to keep it that way."

"Dad, are you sure you're not in over your head? I'm all about your story, but maybe it's not worth it."

"I hate this as much as you do, Scott. But I'm in it deep at this point. If they were going to do more, they had every chance to. The most dangerous thing would be sitting on this story. That's when getting rid of me would make it go away for good."

CHAPTER 47

LONDON

April 16: 159 days after the election

"HE KNOWS STANTON is heavily involved, and deeply distrusts him," Andersson said. "But he suspects he must have been working with someone else, someone who could fund the enterprise."

Kazarov and Andersson had been staring up at a large overhead monitor for almost an hour, Popov having entered halfway through. Andersson gripped a mouse in his right hand. He scrolled through large photographs capturing the reporter's individual notebook pages. With each click of the mouse, a new photograph appeared on the monitor. Then he zoomed in closely on each.

Kazarov, looking at a later page, added, "And he is looking for a piece of evidence that shows that Stanton did not just know of the plan, but took part in it, led it. He is eager to make the connection."

"He also is still unsure of Ariens' role," Andersson said.

Andersson paused for a few seconds, and then added, "He has little to say about Marcellus."

"True, but"—Kazarov reached over and scrolled a couple slides down—"here are his notes following his visit with Chambers. As I predicted, he does not believe that Chambers is capable of running Marcellus. While he was simply fishing at first, that meeting has raised his suspicion that we may be involved."

They turned to Popov, and Kazarov asked him a few questions.

"Did the photographs in his phone tell us anything?"

"Only that he cares a lot for his son," Popov said. "There was one photo of the Suburban's license plate, but we already knew about that one."

"And his phone calls?"

"He mainly talks to his son and a few times with the professor. He has talked several times with Kelly's wife. He had a conversation with a congressional staff member who we don't know, but are now looking into. And he called the Stanton private cell phone number—and it looks like he did so during their meeting."

Kazarov smiled. "I like this man from Ohio."

Of course, he had liked Ariens too.

CHAPTER 48

THE PAIN OF my goon-induced injuries was largely gone by 10:00 the next morning, so I tried to put the finishing touches on my Abacus follow-up story. But I couldn't focus. My mind kept wandering back to the fact that a Russian-speaking thug squad was on my tail. Who would hire them, and why? Plus, Scott had only been tailed *after* my Titusville meeting. So were the brains behind Marcellus the ones keeping an eye on my every move? And had they broadened it after the Chambers meeting to include Scott? It was a hunch worth pursuing.

I had installed an internet connection at the cabin four years ago, knowing that my parents would view this as sacrilege. The cabin hadn't even had electricity 20 years ago, but I'd had to modernize for times like this.

I googled the words: Russian, energy, oil, gas. Numerous entries appeared for Gazprom and Lukoil, the two largest oil and gas enterprises in Russia. Not useful. These were enormous bureaucratic organizations, far more like Shell than Marcellus.

I added "fracking" to my search terms, generating a new set of results. The first four entries referred to a large shale formation in western Siberia, the site where horizontal fracking first succeeded in extracting oil and natural gas. Good.

I dug deeper. Who initiated fracking there?

The company was called Siberneft, and had conducted the first horizontal fracking tests there ten years ago. Wisely, Siberneft had then kept its initial success quiet while acquiring huge tracts of land. Before anyone knew it, the young company had drawn gobs of oil and gas from beneath old oil fields long ago abandoned as dry.

Sounded like the Marcellus story in Ohio.

And who was behind Siberneft?

I searched further. One name came up again and again. Oleg Kazarov.

I printed out everything I could find in English about the murky oligarch and then spent the next two hours reading the materials.

Like many of Russia's richest men, Kazarov had been the perfect age at the perfect time in Russia's history. As a young engineer, amid the lawless privatization of the mid-1990s, his first move was to wrest control of a gas company in the Ural Mountains by swindling peasants out of their valuable auction vouchers, and then outwitting his partner, an old party boss, to seize full control. He then initiated a number of start-ups and acquisitions across Russia, other former Soviet satellites, and ultimately Europe. Each time he used the same pattern—keep a low profile, perfect the engineering technology required to succeed, and share the riches generously with local communities. And the formula worked every time. His various companies raked in billions while winning over the locals who helped make it happen. He now lived in London, and despite remaining in the shadows, had earned the respect of Western financiers along the way and become known in some circles as the stern Russian with the Midas touch.

This was no doubt the man behind Marcellus. Well disguised, too. Throughout all my looking into Marcellus itself, the name Kazarov had never once appeared. But the parallels gave it away.

I jammed all these materials in a file folder and pulled my running clothes back on. Before heading home I was hell bent on completing the full jog from the day before. I hit the turnaround point at 23:14 and brought it home in 23:40. My best pace in years.

* * *

"Where the hell did that bump come from?" Andres asked the next morning, pointing to the back of my head.

"Just part of my commitment to the paper. But I guess I should have had my head examined a long time ago." I laughed at my own joke. She didn't. Then I explained what happened.

"Jesus," Andres said. "I'm not surprised you've pissed some people off. But being followed and then knocked out? That's scary stuff."

"It is. But I'm onto something big. And they know it. Following Scott is pure intimidation. They could tell I'd stopped caring."

"Well, we'll chat at 1:00. Be ready for some tough questions from the top."

"I'll show my bump as Exhibit A."

I walked to my desk, where a large yellow envelope greeted me. It was from Bethesda and looked like the prior ones, solid, unbendable. Like the first package.

I opened the envelope and pulled out five 8.5" x 11" color prints. A little grainy, like something you'd see on a security camera. Time-stamped. Between 9:00 and 10:00 a.m., almost two years ago. The same man appeared in all five pictures. Jet-black hair. Tall. Thin. Well-dressed. I recognized him in an instant: Tom Stanton.

Walking into a lobby entrance.

Sitting in a meeting room with someone whose face was blurred.

Walking through another hallway.

Standing in a much larger space, a warehouse. I could see a large loading dock in the back corner, and boxes stacked up, ready for shipping.

And the last one? A photo of Stanton examining a machine of some sort.

I paused at that one, looking closely at the machine.

My god. The congressman, now majority leader of the House, was eyeing the same machine I had observed in the Monroe County Board of Elections months back. An Abacus voting machine.

I jogged down the hallway to the photo room, grabbed the small magnifying glass our photographers used to crop photos, and rushed back to my desk to take a closer look. Under the lens, the Abacus logo was plainly visible on a screen in the meeting room. And it appeared on the dozens of boxes awaiting shipment near the loading dock.

Back to the first photo. I didn't even need the magnifying class to see that the wall behind the lobby's reception desk displayed an Abacus logo. I had been so focused on Stanton I hadn't noticed it the first time.

Unbelievable. The guy had toured Abacus months before he'd ever seen Joanie Simpson's memo. He had reviewed the whole operation first-hand.

Finally, this was my proof that Stanton had not only been aware of the Abacus plan thanks to an eager staffer, but had participated in the plot himself. And it explained everything that had followed. The killing of Simpson once she'd figured out what her boss already knew. The killing of Kelly once he'd done the same. Stanton was in on it from the beginning, had everything to lose, and responded accordingly.

*   *   *

The draft I turned into my editors Monday afternoon packed a punch. It was mostly what I'd drafted at the cabin, with an additional paragraph closing the loop on Stanton.

> *Photographs obtained by the* Vindicator *show that the Majority Leader himself reviewed the operation of Abacus, in person, nineteen months before the election. From examining the vote-counting machines close-up to looking at its shipping operation, it appears that Stanton was directly involved in overseeing the Abacus operation . . .*

The story still didn't mention the Marcellus connection. That remained only speculation, nothing I could prove. But it did walk through the deaths of Kelly and Simpson after each had discovered the Abacus plot, and described each victim's connection to Stanton.

Andres and the *Vindicator*'s publisher, Dennis Davis, said nothing as they read my draft. A silver-haired veteran newsman who'd seen it all, Davis was someone we reporters rarely heard from directly. His stories taking down prominent mob figures had earned him nationwide respect decades ago, along with years of personal, armed security. Given that experience, few stories shook him.

But now he looked at me with alarm. "My God," he said quietly. "Is all of this true?"

"Actually, there's a lot more than this," I said tentatively. "Those are just the facts I am 100 percent certain of, with strong sourcing."

"Stanton must've been working with someone, right?" Andres asked.

"I'm looking into that as we speak. Have some good leads, as you'll see from that stack of papers on my desk."

"We definitely need that answered to move forward," Andres said.

"I used to think so, too," I said. "But think about it—the House majority leader, and a contender to be the next president, participated in a vote-rigging scandal. That's the story either way. Whoever he collaborated with is secondary. Sitting on it would be like holding up the Iran-Contra story because you didn't know what shipping company they used to move the weapons."

"That's a fair point," Davis said. "Stanton is the story. But we should hunt the partner out anyway. Closes the circle."

Easy for him to say. Still, I decided to be agreeable. "I'm on it."

"I'm not sure what to say about including the two deaths," Andres said. "That may be a little much."

"I've simply reported the facts, which speak for themselves."

Andres looked over at Davis. The publisher looked back and, a second later, nodded his head.

Andres turned back to me. "Good work. Give us your final draft by Thursday."

CHAPTER 49

YOUNGSTOWN

April 17: 160 days after the election

BACK AT MY desk I made two calls.

First, to Stanton's office. Seth West. "Seth, I hope you had a good weekend," I said after he picked up. "I have to do an on-the-record interview with Stanton immediately."

"It's not going to happen, Jack."

"It will take five minutes. Your choice."

He couldn't say no. "I'll be right back."

Stanton clicked onto the line. "What do you want now? I told you everything already."

"Not exactly, Congressman. What are the odds that the person blamed for killing Joanie Simpson was arrested by your man, Clay Dennison, 21 times in five years? They knew each other."

"Clay mentioned that. When it comes to hardened criminals, it's a small world, I guess. What's your point?"

A much calmer answer than I expected. "It doesn't strike you as odd?"

"Of course it's odd. But when you're in my business long enough, odd things happen all the time. I don't know what you're getting at."

He'd navigated that one surprisingly well. But now came the fastball at the head. "Congressman, I have clear evidence that you toured the Abacus facility long before November's election. Please tell me what in the world you were doing there." I wanted to scare him, but didn't want to reveal how damning the evidence was.

"I don't know what you're talking about." His voice lacked the confidence of his prior answers.

"You don't remember being there?"

"Being where?"

"Abacus."

"Of course not. I don't know what you're talking about."

"So 'I don't know what you're talking about' is your official answer.'"

"Yes, it is. That's your five minutes."

*   *   *

On to my second call.

When Janet Compton of the Ariens Group came on the line, she wasted no time. "Mr. Sharpe, I'm very busy," she said. "How can I help you? And please make it fast."

That had been my plan anyway.

"Okay. You mentioned that the day before he died, Mr. Ariens traveled to and from London in a 24-hour window. Was he visiting Oleg Kazarov?"

A pause. "Excuse me?" she asked.

"When he went to London, was he visiting Oleg Kazarov?"

She regained her footing. "I told you before—I'm not at liberty to discuss our business at that level of detail."

"But Mr. Kazarov is a client, right?"

"No! I'm not confirming or denying anything. I'm done with this harassment!" And with that she hung up. Short call, but I'd gotten what I needed.

Given Chambers' lack of political sophistication, someone else at Marcellus must've worked closely with Ariens on the Energy 2020 political plan. When we'd met in person, Compton had mentioned that Ariens had traveled to London the day before he died. And Kazarov lived in London. Maybe the Russian himself had directly led Energy 2020 with his lobbyists.

And this call made that appear even more likely.

Compton's response was entirely appropriate—she should not have discussed client relations with me. But Oleg Kazarov was a shadowy figure. Outside of Russia, at least, he effectively kept himself unknown to all but a small circle of direct reports. Which is what gave Compton away. Amid her protest, Compton failed to ask one fundamental question: "Who is Oleg Kazarov?"

She knew exactly who the Russian was.

*   *   *

LONDON

An early riser, Kazarov switched off his reading lamp and lay down to sleep just after nine in the evening. Minutes later, the phone rang. It was Andersson.

"We just picked up a call Stanton made to our Ariens people. He knows who you are. He knows Ariens visited you in London the day before his death. He knows!"

Kazarov asked to listen to the recording of the call. Andersson played it through the phone. "He is close," Kazarov conceded. "He is still fishing, but yes, he is too close."

Kazarov sighed. Sharpe had come a long way from the notebooks of a few days before. And it was exactly what he'd feared would happen after his henchmen's flubs. Days ago, this small-town reporter had been desperately searching for some Marcellus connection to Abacus. Now he knew Kazarov's name.

But Kazarov remained surprised, pleasantly, by two things. First, Sharpe did not know that they had bugged his phone. And even more importantly, except for the call to the Ariens Group, he had not mentioned the Marcellus connection to anyone, including to his editors.

Kazarov patched Popov onto the call.

"*Ceichas*," he said to the two men. *Now. It is time.*

* * *

YOUNGSTOWN

Around six, as I prepared to leave the office, my work phone rang. Another 202 number. Washington.

"Is this Jack Sharpe?"

I recognized the voice right away.

"Yes, it is."

"It's Janet Compton. From Ariens Group. I'm calling from our secure line."

That last tidbit piqued my curiosity. "Hi, Janet," I said, tentative.

"I couldn't say much earlier today, but I want to talk more about your question," she said. "Can we meet in person?"

"What do you want to talk about?"

I was on guard for traps, but this had the potential to be my biggest break yet. A question or two might smoke out the difference.

"I want to tell you what I know about Kazarov," she said gravely. "His role in Marcellus. In Energy 2020. But I can only do it in person."

Here we go.

"Why don't we meet in the middle?" I said. "There's a Pennsylvania town called Breezewood a few hours from D.C. and not too far from me. Why don't we meet there?"

"I've driven through it a bunch myself," Compton said. "There's a Bob Evans right off the road. Let's meet there. Does 8:00 a.m. tomorrow work?"

"Sounds good. See you then."

This was a high-risk rendezvous. But every risk I had taken so far—confronting Stanton in his office, crawling up on the Surburban, trusting Arlene Bradley, even confronting the Russian goons—had paid off. And Janet Compton was perfectly positioned to fill in the final gaps in my story.

CHAPTER 50

BREEZEWOOD, PA

April 18: 161 days after the election

"You want a seat, young man?"

It never fails.

I've eaten Bob Evans omelets for decades, and every time I enter the iconic red and yellow buildings, the hostess, usually in her more senior years, offers the friendliest greeting of my day.

Gladys, as her nametag identified her, hit the mark this morning, welcoming me with a sweet smile and warm hello. I always try to return the kindness, but today was far too serious to pull it off.

"Actually, I'm meeting a woman here—"

"Well, lucky her!" Gladys said cheerily.

I smiled. "I think she's probably already here."

I was ten minutes late, thanks to a rain-soaked and foggy drive through the Pennsylvania hills. Looking around, I spotted Compton sitting alone in the far corner of the restaurant.

"There she is. I'll just join her."

"Great. Enjoy! A server will be right over."

Compton looked up at me, raising her right hand limply. I nodded back and walked toward her booth.

I'd taken only a few steps when her expression changed from a polite smile to a grimace, then to a frown. Then I sensed them. One large body behind me, another to my right. I had focused so closely on Gladys and Compton, I hadn't bothered to look around. And now it was too late.

A small, solid object pressed forcefully into my back. The man on my right spoke—the same voice as the passenger at the lake.

"Mr. Sharpe, you will come with us. Do not make any quick movements."

"I'm supposed to meet her."

But one more look at Compton and I knew. I'd trusted one source too many. Her expression remained a deep frown, same as before. She did not enjoy witnessing this. At the same time, she did not look surprised.

"The lady will be fine. Come with us."

The gun barrel pressed even harder into my back. "Okay, okay. I'm coming."

As we walked back toward the door, I smiled at Gladys as if all were well.

"What's the matter? She not like you?" she joked, none the wiser.

"Just met some old friends on the way to her table," I said. "Tell her I'll be right back." The man to my right, hearing my words, flashed Gladys a big grin.

As we set foot in the parking lot, I glanced at a car window a few feet away. The reflection confirmed my fear that the man behind me was the driver. The large driver.

"Look straight ahead," his smaller counterpart warned.

We marched across the lot to the back of a White Castle next door. The familiar Suburban now came into sight.

Somehow, I had crossed a line. My casual followers were now my captors. Based on Compton's reaction, it had clearly been my call to her, and no doubt my mention of Kazarov, that had flipped the switch. She must have tipped off the Russian—her client, after all—who instructed her to set up the morning meeting. I had walked right into the trap.

The key question was whether my captors now intended to be my assassins. I hadn't yet shared my theory about Marcellus with anyone. Oleg Kazarov might have concluded that this presented his point of no return—his last opportunity to eliminate me and still get away with it, along with everything that he'd done before.

*   *   *

Ever since childhood, watching high-profile news events, I had always imagined how I would respond to the prospect that another person planned to take my life.

I so admired the actions of the passengers on United Flight 93 on September 11, who seized control of their plane once they'd realized their fate.

And when I saw terrorists behead victims on television, I was surprised, even disappointed, when those victims did not put up a fight.

Faced with that same threat, I imagined myself turning around and tackling the hooded terrorist, pounding him endlessly before someone else put me out of my misery. Same outcome, but seemed more noble than helplessly letting someone take everything from you without even a fight.

So I had long ago committed not to walk the plank peacefully. If I faced imminent death, I would resist until the very end. "Let's roll" would be my mantra.

But as these two men guided me to their car, I now realized this lifelong promise to myself was easier made than fulfilled. I now felt what those hostages, the ones who died without resistance, must have felt.

First I felt doubt, a hopeful doubt, that perhaps, despite all appearances, these men didn't aim to kill me after all. And if that wasn't their intent, resisting might compel them to do the very thing they weren't planning to do, which meant going along was likely the better route to staying alive.

Second, with one man to my right, and another behind me, I felt—I was—surrounded. Resisting seemed so futile. So irrational. Suicidal.

But one factor settled my wavering. Over the years, Chief Santini had explained that among the variety of armed incidents, the statistics paint the bleakest picture about my predicament. Victims of routine armed muggings usually live to tell about it. Same with bank robberies, convenience store hold-ups, and even home break-ins. But getting into a car at gunpoint? Unlike the others, the majority who do so don't return from the ride alive. "Whatever you do," Chief Santini had always warned, "don't get in that car. You won't live to tell about it."

And here I was only feet away from that fatal threshold.

So, weighing it all, I made my decision. And my move.

The big guy offered the more strategic target, the more lethal foe. He had a gun in hand, but he could likely kill with his bare hands too if he needed to. He was behind my left shoulder. Fortunately, to keep our exit from Bob Evans uneventful, he had lowered the gun after the initial shoves to my back. It was either still in his right hand facing down or within inches of the hand's reach. Either way, that slight shift in position provided a split-second opening.

The hard corner of my elbow would be my best weapon. Knowing that a wind-up would give too much notice, I traded the power of a full blow for the surprise of an instant one. Spinning left, I whipped my arm back and up and struck with the elbow exactly where I hoped—into the big guy's left cheek and nose. The loud crunch meant I'd snapped at least his nasal cartilage or cheekbone, and he instantly lunged forward in pain. Anticipating this reflex, I grabbed the back of his head, accelerated its downward trajectory with a hard shove, and at the same time thrust my left knee upward, once again smashing solid bone into his already bloody face. Another crunch. He fell to the pavement, hands cupped over his nose, writhing in pain.

Now in a slightly crouched position, I focused on the smaller man on my right, who, thankfully, had been slow to react. With the luxury of a full wind-up, my right elbow struck the man's stomach with even greater force. I had planned to use my left fist to knock him down, but he was already crashing backward to the parking lot asphalt, choking and gasping for air. I had clearly knocked the wind out of him.

I dashed away, desperate to get back to my pick-up. I cleared about 35 feet before I heard the two men yell actual words, in pain and in Russian. I glanced back. The goon was getting up, and the smaller man was still writhing on the pavement, coughing.

I had parked on the other side of the Bob Evans from the White Castle, which was a good thing, because once around the building's corner, I was out of the gun's direct line of fire. As I made a bee-line toward my now-visible truck, I reached into my pocket for the keys and pulled them out.

And then I saw the tires. The truck was sitting on its rims, all four tires flat. Now I needed a quick plan B.

Beyond the Bob Evans was a Days Inn. I sprinted to its entrance and charged through the front door. With six people gaping at my noisy, wet entrance, I ran down the hallway toward a stairwell, entered it, and loudly slammed shut the stairwell door. I bounded up two flights of stairs, leaping multiple steps at a time.

I reached the third floor and opened the stairwell door, raced down the hallway to the stairwell furthest from the lobby, opened and shut that stairwell door carefully, and descended those stairs as quietly and quickly as possible. Once back on the ground floor, I found myself only feet from a door exiting the motel. I pushed it open, held the handle as it closed, and dashed away as fast as I could.

My spur-of-the-moment plan had been to draw my abductors into the motel and convince them I was hiding upstairs somewhere, and it appeared to have worked. I ran away, looking back every dozen yards, and I never saw them exit the motel.

I sprinted through parking lots, driveways, and sidewalks, relieved that adrenaline and my recent lakeside runs were giving me much-needed stamina.

The last stop before the interstate entrance was an Applebee's. I darted in, planning to hide in a booth and make a few phone calls to get out of this jam. Only when I sat down did I realize how wet I was from the combination of rain and sweat. My left elbow and knee were both throbbing.

First, I called Chief Santini. "Chief, I'm being chased by the two that have been following me for days. They mean business. What should I do?"

"Where are you?"

"At an Applebee's in Breezewood, Pennsylvania. About three hours away."

"What in the world are you doing in Breezewood?" Realizing how unhelpful this question was, the chief didn't give me time to answer. "I'm going to call the chief there right away. Stay put unless you think you're in danger."

"I *know* I'm in danger, but will do."

I next tried to call Scott, to make sure he was okay. If they were closing on me, maybe they were going after him as well. No answer, but not a surprise. It was still early out west.

Soon sirens blared from a distance. They grew louder and three Breezewood police cars sped into the Applebee's parking lot. Just before I stood to greet the officers, my phone buzzed with a text. A number I didn't recognize had sent an attachment.

On seeing its contents, I now realized the third reason that people facing imminent death don't resist their captors. The most compelling reason.

Family.

The attachment was a photo of Scott and Jana, time-stamped from the evening before, happily enjoying dinner together. The ramifications were clear. The phone buzzed again with a new text. *Don't Be a Fool: Keep Them Alive.*

I lowered my head. Those words ended my resistance.

What do I need to do? I texted back.

Simple: go back to White Castle in 5 minutes.

Okay.

I thought of texting Scott but didn't. It was too risky to do anything but cooperate.

As the four police officers ambled around the restaurant calling my name, I buried my head in the menu. Seconds later, the phone rang again—Chief Santini, surely calling to see where I was. I let the phone ring until it stopped. Minutes later, the officers left the restaurant and drove away, sirens off.

I slowly walked out of the restaurant. Defeated. Walking the plank. I soon passed my immobilized truck at the Bob Evans, and could see through the restaurant window that Compton was gone. I walked to the back of the White Castle and peered right.

There they were, only yards away. Sitting in the Suburban. Engine on. The thin Russian sat in the back seat, behind the passenger seat. Perfect—in mob movies, that's the guy who always shoots or knifes the passenger.

"Get in the car," he said through the half-open window, gesturing toward the front seat.

I opened the door and sat down. The driver's face was smeared with half-dried blood, both from his nostrils and a gash on the side of his nose.

As I leaned back to fasten my seatbelt, the driver plunged his enormous right fist into the center of my abdomen and yelled something loudly in Russian. The clenched hand struck like a mallet, with more force than any sack I could remember. I doubled over, temporarily suffocating from lack of oxygen, gasping to find air, coughing furiously.

The driver uttered something else in Russian. His comrade responded curtly. The car pulled out of the White Castle as I continued to gasp.

We didn't turn back onto I-70 either toward Washington or Youngstown, but hopped on a small road, State Route 30, heading west. The middle of nowhere, definitely an ominous sign. Chief Santini's warning echoed through my head.

"It seems you have gotten the message, Mr. Sharpe." The voice came from behind.

"Yes. You thugs have made it clear."

"You have a choice: you can make this easy, or you can make this difficult."

"I walked to the car and got in, didn't I?"

"You did. Now keep cooperating. It will make things far more comfortable for you, and for Scott."

Hearing him say Scott's name made my blood boil. "Don't you ever mention his name again."

"Don't do anything that requires us to. Please pass me your cell phone."

I passed it back over my right shoulder. This ended all conversation for the next half hour, as we drove west, up and down western Pennsylvania's rolling hills through the steady rain.

As signs indicated that we were approaching a town called Bedford, the man in the back spoke Russian to the driver. I discovered that when you think you're being driven to your own death, every unknown word scares the hell out of you. The car exited off the main road and made a series of turns on smaller roads. The man behind me was clearly giving exact directions. Recalling the fates of Ariens, Kelly and Joanie Simpson, I assumed they were driving me to my gravesite.

CHAPTER 51

April 18: 161 days after the election

T HE MORNING AFTER his abrupt, painful telephone interview with Sharpe, Stanton sat behind his desk, stewing.

He had ably run over, around, and through every obstacle that had ever threatened his career. And there had been many. And now some jaded, small-time reporter was going to take him down just as he was closing on his ultimate goal? Not a chance.

They needed a plan to stave off the damage. To do that, he'd have to come clean with Seth West, so he called his chief of staff into the office for an impromptu meeting. When West walked past Arlene Bradley and into Stanton's office, his eyes opened wide at seeing Clay Dennison already seated. Stanton's gruff security guy rarely made appearances in the actual Capitol.

"Seth," Stanton said, "we've got a major problem, and I need your help."

"What is it?"

"That reporter Jack Sharpe figured out that I visited Abacus before the election. He's clearly going to write about it."

"What's he going to say? You just walked through, right?"

"The truth is, from what I saw, it was pretty clear what they were planning. I put two and two together quickly. But I had nothing to do with any of it. I didn't tell them or anyone else that I knew, and I didn't communicate with them again. Now Sharpe's saying I masterminded the whole thing. Which is complete horseshit."

West stared at his boss stone-faced. "You mean that you knew Abacus was going to steal the election, and you didn't do anything about it?"

"Don't lecture me! I had a hunch, and it turned out to be right. Then

I campaigned in places I would've campaigned in anyway. None of that's a crime! Now do your job and help me solve this."

"What do you have in mind?"

"Our best defense is a good offense. If we can expose who was behind this, they will rightfully take the blame. Who bought Abacus, ran it for two years, and then sold it to Diebold? Who was that Swedish guy at Abacus, Miller, who kept lying to me? And who's sending the reporter dirt on me? Someone put this whole thing together. We have to find them and beat Sharpe to the punch!"

"Well, how are we going to find all this so quickly?"

"I can tell you where to start. With Ariens. The whole reason I went there was a note from Ariens." This was also something he'd never shared before.

"Are you kidding? Ariens tipped you off to it?"

"He sure did. Must've been one of his clients. Ariens either was in on it or figured it out."

"Congressman, he represented so many special interests, and we helped so many of them." West paused. "So Simpson's memo was real, wasn't it?"

"Yes, it was." No point in denying it any longer.

"And did she really die shortly after giving it to you?"

"Yes, she did." He shook his head as he said it, knowing how bad the timing was.

West paused again, looking like he wanted to ask the obvious follow-up question. But never did.

"And no, I had nothing to do with it!" Stanton shouted.

*   *   *

As soon as he left the boss's office, West called Janet Compton to set up a meeting. The two had worked together for many years, and in recent months, Stanton had been a huge help to her clients. That afternoon, they met at a Starbucks a few blocks from her office. He was sitting at a small table, coffee in hand, when she walked through the door and strode directly toward him.

"How are you, Seth?" she said cooly.

"Busy as always. You?"

"Great."

The pleasantries ended.

"I have something serious I need to talk to you about," West said.

"What is it?"

"The congressman is very concerned about last year's election."

Compton's head shot back. "I thought you guys said that was all some conspiracy theory."

"We did, but I'm afraid it's not. In fact, before he died, Oliver sent the congressman a note about Abacus."

"Excuse me? You can't be serious."

"Dead serious. Oliver sent a note telling Tom to take a look at Abacus. He knew something was happening. And the congressman wants to know if you know any more about this."

Compton narrowed one eye skeptically. "And why would the congressman have kept this to himself until now?"

"He says he didn't know what to make of what Oliver wrote. And when he passed away, Stanton never focused on it again. Obviously, the *Vindicator* story changed that."

"Well, this is the first I've heard of it."

"My question is, among your clients, is there anyone who would've been tempted to rig the election? Who had the capacity to do it? Oliver must've been tipped off by a client."

"Seth, you know I cannot reveal client confidences."

"Janet, this is more important than your client relations. This is about our democracy. Among your many industry groups—the oil and gas people, the banks, others—can you think of any that might have done this? They all got so much out of our win last year."

"Seth, I'm not going to speculate about any of them. But I can confidently tell you that none of our clients is threatening our democracy."

"So Oliver didn't mention this to anybody?"

"No. But you know we represented Diebold for many years. Maybe this tipped him off to something irregular. Diebold lost a lot of accounts to this Abacus outfit, I know that."

West knew this was nonsense, but he was impressed that she was sticking to her guns. Compton would clearly tell no one about who was behind the plot. Was even willing to lie before doing so.

As they wrapped up, she ended on a cordial note.

"Tell the congressman we want to be helpful, but we aren't going to hang any clients out to dry. I also want to make clear that Oliver Ariens would never have been a part of any plan attacking our Congress, our democracy. He believed deeply in our system."

"Of course we know that, Janet. Thank you for your help."

The two parted ways.

He reported in by phone as he drove his BMW up Independence Avenue back to Capitol Hill.

"I pressed her hard. She's a vault. Won't say a word."

* * *

"You figure out who did it?" Stanton was still in his Capitol office when Seth West returned.

"I didn't, and I don't think we'll have time to. But I have an idea."

"It's obviously one of Ariens' clients," Stanton said, impatiently.

"Maybe. Maybe not. I just met with Janet Compton. She clammed up quickly. And the problem is Ariens had so many clients, there's no good way to figure out which one might have done it."

Stanton rubbed his hand through his hair, still agitated.

"So what's your big idea?"

"We don't need to know who did it. We can just say Ariens did."

"Blame it on Oliver? You're talking about my lifelong friend here!"

"Why not? We know he knew about it. He represents some of the most disliked industries in the world. We can say he was at the heart of the plot, call for an investigation by Congress, and let some special committee do the digging from there. If we do it ahead of Sharpe, we take away his story."

"Why would anyone buy that Oliver did it? Seems far-fetched."

"Are you kidding? The only people despised more than politicians are lobbyists. And he was the king of all lobbyists, representing the worst industries. The press and voters want to burn guys like Ariens at the stake. Trust me, if we point the finger at him, it will stick. Then we call for an investigation of all his clients. Shit, we may actually find out who did this."

The congressman calmed down. He weighed the unappealing prospect of betraying his best friend against the benefit of getting out of a nasty jam. As the latter began tipping the scale, he nodded slowly. So much for loyalty when it conflicts with survival. Plus, Oliver was six feet underground.

"It's probably the best shot we have," Stanton concluded. "Let's think through how we do this, and talk later this evening."

"The key is to beat Sharpe to the punch. Get the Ariens theory out there first. Everything Sharpe writes after that gets lost. But we have to frame it all first, and fast. And I've got a plan on how to do it. Let me make a few calls."

Stanton still doubted whether this would be enough to trump Sharpe's story. In addition to targeting Ariens, they might have to silence the reporter some other way. But that was a conversation to have with Dennison, not West.

As West stepped out of Stanton's office to put their plan together, the ex-cop stuck around.

CHAPTER 52

PENNSYLVANIA

April 18: 161 days after the election

TRAPPED IN A car in the middle of nowhere. Armed Russian henchmen to my left and behind me. The fatal moment felt imminent. After all, Kelly had also met his brutal demise in a car in the middle of the Keystone State. And why the hell else would we be driving into Bedford, Pennsylvania?

The sudden roar of jet engines overhead answered my question. With thick clouds hovering only hundreds of feet off the ground, I couldn't see the plane, but it was clearly low, either taking off or landing. Small signs along the road now pointed the way to the Bedford County airport, and the Suburban followed them all.

Thank god. We were heading to an airport.

"You are going on a long journey," the man behind me said. "But don't worry; if you cooperate, it will be a comfortable trip."

"Thanks for the suspense," I said, not caring if he understood.

We turned and drove up a dirt driveway, past an open gate, and directly onto the tarmac. A small fleet of single- and double-prop planes sat in two rows. I was a plane buff, and recognized some old Cessnas, a Cirrus, two King Airs, and a couple Pipers. Standard for a small airport.

Less standard, sitting off on its own, was the black Gulfstream, which was clearly the plane that had just landed, and as sleek and luxurious as a private jet could get. Fifty million at least. The car stopped a few feet from the jet. The guy in back climbed out of the car and boarded the plane. A tall, blonde man greeted him inside the open door. The two talked briefly, and the Russian passed my confiscated cell phone to the blonde. He then descended the stairs and climbed back in the car.

"We will stay here," he said. "Please board and Mr. Holmberg will join you for the journey, along with the pilots."

The blonde man greeted me inside the plane's cabin, out of the rain.

"Welcome, Mr. Sharpe. I am Stefan Holmberg, and will be with you for our flight."

"Nice to meet you. What is your accent? Doesn't sound Russian like the other two."

"No questions, please. Come back and have a seat. Please make yourself comfortable. There's a loo if you need to use one, and a towel to dry off. And the seats fold into beds. Our flight will last around six hours. We will be taking off in five minutes."

"Whatever you say."

I took him up on his bathroom offer, toweled off a morning's worth of rain, sweat and blood, and sat down halfway down the cabin, in a left window seat. Then I looked around. Just like the outside of the plane, the inside gave no indication of its owner. But with lush carpeting, dark leather seats, a pullout desk, a mini-bar, and a large monitor at the front of the cabin, it was the nicest mode of transportation I'd ever traveled in. Hell, it was the most luxurious *room* I'd ever been in—it just happened to have wings attached to it.

After a turbulent takeoff through the thick clouds, I kept a close eye on the map displayed on a cabin monitor. We were heading northeast at 475 knots, backed by a 90-knot tailwind, soon passing north and west of Wilkes-Barre and Scranton.

While the map didn't show our destination, the relevant data all pointed in one direction.

Six-hour flight. Heading northeast. 600-knot groundspeed.

London.

Kazarov.

* * *

LONDON

A hard knock on the door woke me.

"Mr. Sharpe, I will return in 20 minutes."

It took a few seconds to get my bearings—that I'd slept almost the entire flight, that we'd landed in the countryside outside London and driven to this palatial estate in a black Rolls Royce. The voice at the door was the same butler who'd escorted me to this room hours before.

I quickly showered and shaved, and put on the black slacks and light blue shirt that lay folded on a chair next to the bed. Both fit perfectly.

The butler knocked minutes later and opened the door.

"Please follow me."

We walked back down the ornate hallway I'd walked the night before, past the grand foyer, and into a library. The butler motioned toward a couch on the opposite side of the room. I sat down, sinking deeply into the soft leather cushions.

Dark wood bookshelves were built into three of the four walls surrounding me. One displayed books about Rockefeller, Armand Hammer, Steve Jobs, Bill Gates, John F. Kennedy, and Ronald Reagan. Another held great works of literature, from Tolstoy and Pushkin to Melville and Hemingway. Somewhat out of place was the Tom Clancy novel *The Hunt for Red October*. But overall, this was a library fitting of the architect of Marcellus.

Minutes later, a large door from the side of the library creaked open, and I could see immediately why Michael Chambers was so important to Marcellus. A man with these extreme features could not have sold Energy 2020 to America. He stood at least 6'1", but was wafer thin, so he looked taller. Awkward. His skin was so pale it was hard to see where his white shirt cuff ended and his wrist began. Oily black hair, slicked back, covered a small, round head, and his tiny, dark eyes were set unusually far apart. From the front, his nose looked narrow and indistinct, but from the side it jutted prominently and ended in a severe point.

I rose to greet him, but he waved me off and gestured to a nearby couch. He sat in a chair facing my couch, crossed his right foot over his left thigh, and flashed a hint of a smile.

"Welcome, Mr. Sharpe." An elegant accent, mixing British and his native Russian. Sophisticated, but cold.

"Thank you. I assume you're Mr. Kazarov."

He removed a cigarette from his shirt pocket, a lighter from his pants pocket, and lit up. He took a slow puff, and exhaled equally slowly, appearing to enjoy the first drag immensely.

"I am," he said. "I hope you enjoyed the journey over."

"For a kidnapping, I must say, it wasn't bad."

Kazarov ignored the sarcasm.

"You have a fascinating library," I said.

"My parents were both professors in St. Petersburg, so I read from a young age: literature, science, history, poetry."

I gestured toward his Western books, directly behind him.

"Along with American business and politics."

"Yes. The great inventors and businessmen of America were my heroes. While Soviet leaders instructed us to fear capitalism, I dreamt about its wonders."

"It looks as if those dreams came true."

"Indeed," he said, looking back over his shoulder for a moment. "I learned much from these men."

I didn't say anything else, hoping this would end the small talk.

"I brought you here," he said, "to discuss your Abacus story. It is an important and historic story. I want to make sure you have the correct information."

I'm sure you do. I watched him closely.

"We are concerned that you believe that our Energy 2020 team played a role in the plot you so wisely discovered."

More up front than I would have thought, a directness I respected. "I hadn't reached that conclusion yet, but the circumstances that brought me here certainly have raised questions."

"I brought you here to clear Mr. Ariens' good name, and to assure you that we would never engage in such behavior."

I nodded, amused that the Russian was making this about his dead lobbyist as much as himself. "Kidnapping me, threatening my son's life—none of this boosts my confidence in your adherence to the law."

I was testing how far I could push him, but he responded calmly.

"I apologize if Eastern business tactics are rougher than those in the West. Of course, you have your own forms of crime and corruption. But you will agree that this was the only way to get your attention."

"A free Gulfstream ride to London would have gotten it done," I said. He didn't smile.

"Mr. Sharpe, we know you have questions about Oliver Ariens. We do not. He was a good man. We were impressed by his integrity and saddened by his death. It was a huge blow to our efforts on Energy 2020."

I said nothing. If Kazarov had something to tell me, I'd let him do so.

"You may be interested in something he sent us shortly before he died." Kazarov held up his right hand and rotated his second finger in a small clockwise circle. Through a speaker on the wall behind me, a voice spoke in a distinct New Orleans accent. Ariens. Had to be.

"*I have closely watched a near-defunct company called Abacus over the last few months*" the voice drawled. "*Based on my experience with Diebold, their behavior establishes a very suspicious pattern . . . .*"

I was speechless.

The speaker was only a few feet behind me, and it was as if Oliver Ariens were calmly talking in my ear, answering one of my final remaining questions. The lobbyist had discovered the Abacus plot but he had not been part of it.

"*They were acquired by a mysterious buyer, dramatically invested in new technology, and turned around a wholly new product in record time. But then they have aggressively marketed this product in only a few places. And sold at a price that guarantees a substantial loss on each sale.*"

Kazarov held his open palm up in the air, and the voice stopped. "Oliver sent us this tape days before he died," he said. "We believe this information is what got him killed, and that he sent it to us knowing his life was in danger."

"Can you play more?"

"Of course."

Kazarov circled his finger again.

"*The plan is to position voting machines in dozens of swing districts around the country. There is no reason to do this except to alter the results of next year's election. The Abacus business strategy makes no sense. But the political strategy is brilliant, nothing short of a coup in an otherwise unwinnable election.*"

Kazarov twirled his finger counterclockwise, and the tape rewound to its beginning. Ariens again: "*This memo should be sent to both Speaker Williams and Minority Leader Marshall as soon as possible.*" Kazarov held up his palm one more time.

Another key data point. Ariens had not only figured out the plot, he'd decided to stop it. This also confirmed that his death, happening when it did, had not been a natural heart attack.

Kazarov read my mind. "It seems clear that Congressman Stanton was behind his death, just as he orchestrated the entire Abacus plan, as you have discovered."

Of course, I had never mentioned the name Stanton. "But is there any part of the tape where he mentions Stanton's involvement?" I asked.

"No. I don't believe Oliver knew who was behind Abacus. But we believe he shared these concerns with Stanton, his oldest and closest friend, who then arranged for his death."

"How would you cause a heart attack?"

"Simple biology, Mr. Sharpe. There are ways for that to be done, and then to be hidden. You must know that the CIA mastered such techniques decades ago."

I had no idea such an assassination technique existed, but Kazarov clearly did. And wasn't shy about it. But I moved on. "Why would Ariens have sent this tape to you?"

"He and I spent many hours together, including in this very room. We discussed politics at great length and built a good friendship. He knew that if he was concerned about such a plan, we would be concerned as well. He was our lobbyist, after all. Our eyes and ears."

"And why would Stanton, after reaching the pinnacle of power, decide to become a murderer as well as a traitor?"

"You can guess as well as I can, but it appears that frustrated political ambition drove him. He had not reached the pinnacle he sought, and knew he never would without a dramatic change. Your system of politics is so broken, he probably realized that only an intervention would bring him to his ultimate goal."

I nodded. Fair assessment. "Why do you say our system is broken?" I asked.

"Oliver and I talked at length about your political system, and how deeply flawed it is. Your corrupt districts make it impossible for any change to take place through elections themselves. And in between elections, it also makes your politicians act in such silly ways. In England, in Russia, we would never stand for such a paralyzing system."

I almost laughed aloud, but then remembered I'd made the same arguments in the newsroom for years, of course excluding Russia from my examples of more upstanding democracies.

"But," Kazarov went on, "Stanton figured out that the very system that guaranteed the outcome of elections in most districts also opened a path to steal an election. Alter the results in a handful of districts and, voila."

"So why didn't you intervene when you received this tape from Mr. Ariens?"

Kazarov crushed what remained of the cigarette into a small bowl next to him and promptly lit another. "We were unsure whether it was true, and I did not feel that it was our place to interfere. Oliver's death came as a shock, and we had to work hard to keep 2020 moving ahead. When the election turned out the way it did, it appeared he had been correct. And when your story came out a few weeks ago, we were certain."

"But you must have been thrilled by the election results. It was exactly what Marcellus needed to move forward."

"Indeed. We finally can advance our plan to help the communities that we work in. To provide clean, low-cost energy to our customers. To build success for them, as well as our workers. As we have done all over the world. Even your town has benefitted—look at the new factory producing pipes for our wells."

This man was clearly the brains behind Marcellus. If Chambers had given that answer, I probably wouldn't be sitting here right now.

"But now that your story has revealed the Abacus plan," Kazarov continued, "our greatest fear is that because of its clear benefit to Energy 2020, poor Oliver and our good company will be blamed for the Abacus coup."

"So you've kidnapped me, hit me over the head, threatened my son, and followed me for weeks, all to convince me how innocent you are?"

"Indeed, but you are unharmed, are you not? This is very important to us. How is Scott, anyhow? He seems like a fine young man."

I gritted my teeth at the mention of his name, an implicit threat. "Indeed he is," I said evenly. "Thank you. Do you have children?"

"I do not, Mr. Sharpe. My business activities have kept me too busy to create a family."

"That's too bad," I said. "I consider being a father my most important role."

Kazarov grinned for the first time. But it was not a friendly look. "Your ex-wife does not seem to agree with you."

So I had gotten under his skin. Time to dig deeper. "Mr. Kazarov, how long have you watched Mr. Stanton?"

"For some time. We know you have your suspicions that he killed both his research aide and Congressman Kelly. We share that view."

Again, I had never mentioned these suspicions, which meant they must have searched my stuff thoroughly, tapped my phone. Probably both. "And how did you figure this out?"

"Looking at the same facts as you have. After Oliver died, the congressman became our greatest champion in last year's election. Now we know why."

"I've received several envelopes in the mail that have been very helpful in developing my story, like the tape you just played. Did you send these?"

"What envelopes?" Kazarov asked, with what seemed like genuine interest. "What was in them?"

"Photographs implicating Congressman Stanton. A memo from his research aide. Critical pieces of evidence."

"I know nothing about these things."

Earlier in the meeting, when he'd been disingenuous, it had shown, but now he wasn't setting off my bullshit detector. If he was lying, he was damn good at it. "I ask because whoever sent them was close to the Abacus plot. Most likely a partner or accomplice in the plot itself. For example, the memo could only have been acquired by someone who entered the aide's apartment after she'd been killed, and that would only be possible if they used the keys taken from her as she lay in the park dying."

"Perhaps a comrade regrets being part of it, and is now willing to turn Stanton in."

I chuckled. Or perhaps that "comrade" wanted to pin it all on Stanton and get off scot-free.

"Mr. Sharpe," Kazarov said, leaning towards me, "I know you realize the historic opportunity your story provides."

"Enlighten me."

"You and your publication could fix America's entire political system."

"Is that right?"

"Of course. You have found that one of the most important officials in Washington stole a Congressional majority due to the weakness of your nation's electoral system. The—what did Oliver call it—the gerrymandering. Your insecure elections. Once exposed, the outrage at this political scandal may offer the best chance America will have to reform itself."

I had casually considered this previously, but never as clearly as this foreign observer had just described it.

"As you know," Kazarov continued, "the Watergate scandal led not only to Nixon's resignation, but to reforms of the American political system. Your story is bigger than Watergate. The demand for reforms will be bigger as well."

He was right. But somehow I doubted this man's sincere commitment to reform.

"You are being distracted by your hunt for secondary accomplices," he said. "They will only diminish the story's impact. Congress and the politicians would eagerly blame someone else for their broken system. But your story now, focused on Stanton, makes it clear that the blame is entirely on the system itself. The politicians will have no choice but to fix it."

This was an incredibly convenient theory from someone who might be the accomplice, or the mastermind. But of course, I had told my editors the exact same thing two days before. "You may be correct," I said. "But justice also demands anybody involved in the scandal be held accountable."

"It does indeed, if there is evidence proving that person was involved. But mere speculation only lets the politicians off the hook."

I began to reply, but Kazarov talked over me. "Mr. Sharpe, I have read about your father and his noble career."

Like the mention of Scott, the reference to Dad grated my nerves.

"The current system is what keeps true servants from entering or surviving in politics. Men like your father."

"I agree with you. But it's the system we have."

"That is the same thing that Oliver said to me. But in the end, he tried to do something about it."

His tone suggested that Kazarov had sincerely admired the dead lobbyist. But then again, Ariens was now six feet underground, and the Russian had just identified the poison that had put him there.

* * *

As we left the library, Kazarov waved off his silent, hovering butler and escorted me to the front door, where he bade me goodbye.

"You have been most pleasant company, Mr. Sharpe. I had looked forward to your visit, yet you still exceeded my expectations. Best of luck. We will be watching closely."

"I believe it," I said.

I flew home unaccompanied except for the pilots, and settled back in my seat after the plane reached cruising altitude. Of course, Kazarov was right. The biggest fish in the story was Stanton. His involvement would prompt demands for full-scale reform. I'd finally have my bombshell story on gerrymandering, and it would actually do some good. Kazarov was also correct that Stanton and other political hacks would do all they could to deflect blame elsewhere. If they could make another person or entity the bad guy, they would do it in a heartbeat. Just look at what those jackals had done to me. At the same time, whatever the consequences, journalistic ethics required me to pursue and report if others had been involved as well. But the reality was that I had no hard proof connecting Kazarov and Marcellus to Abacus. Yes, the signs all pointed to Kazarov. The theory made perfect sense. But as the Russian clearly understood, it was all speculation. Nothing solid enough to publish.

In fact, Kazarov had demonstrated that he had a strong defense. Ariens, his chief lobbyist, the architect of Energy 2020, was not only *not* part of the plan, but had discovered it and planned to blow the whistle.

Kazarov's closest American ally had stood in the way. And had paid for it with his life.

CHAPTER 53

April 19: 162 days after the election

I SQUINTED AS I stepped through the plane door into the bright Pennsylvania sunshine. On the airport tarmac, only yards from the plane, my truck beamed, shining from an apparent cleaning and boasting four new Firestones. I reached into my pocket to see if I still had my car keys. They jingled, still there. Nothing like a hot wire, car wash, and tire service all in one.

Before I descended the stairs, the pilot tapped my shoulder. He handed back my phone.

"Thank you" was the only expression I knew in Russian. "*Spasiba.*"

It was 1:05 p.m., and I drove directly back to Youngstown. I charged my phone and checked my messages. Two from Scott, one from Mary Andres, and a bunch from Chief Santini. But the most interesting one came from Arlene Bradley: "Mr. Sharpe, I have some information to share with you. It's urgent."

I called Santini first to let him know I was fine. "In all the drama, I lost my phone," I said uncomfortably. "Had to get a new one."

"Whatever, Sharpe," he said. "You scared the shit out of me."

I then called Arlene Bradley. No answer, but she returned my call minutes later. She started talking so quickly I had to ask her to slow down.

"Congressman Stanton is really worked up," she said, "terrified of your story. He met with his chief of staff and top security officer yesterday."

"Dennison?"

"That's him. How do you know him?"

"Research."

"They know your story will run soon, and they plan to shift the blame from themselves. To identify others who were part of the scandal."

"That's helpful, Ms. Bradley," I said. "Thank you, and keep me posted."

Exactly what Kazarov had guessed would happen. To beat them to the punch, I would have to move. So I made three quick calls, taking notes as I drove.

The first was to Speaker Marshall's office, the second to Minority Leader Williams. First, to confirm that neither had received the dictated memo from Ariens two years ago. Second, to get their reaction to Stanton's involvement in the Abacus plot. Their responses to my first question did not surprise me. Their answers to my second did.

The next call, back to Abacus, marked my final attempt to identify Stanton's accomplice.

"Butch Joseph here. Don't you have someone else you can pick on?"

"Nah. You guys are my favorite target."

"Well, you sure made our newly acquired brand famous. Thanks for the great marketing."

My first story must have cost them millions in damage control. "You're welcome," I said. "I did have one question I wanted to ask. When you purchased Abacus, did you interact with the people you bought it from?"

"Honestly, it was the oddest transaction. They were hesitant to meet in person, and gun-shy about overlapping as we moved in."

"So you never met?"

"Nope. We never had a face-to-face meeting. Like two ships in the night, they finished moving out the day that we moved in. Then they were gone."

"How about names? You get their names?"

"Sure. I interacted with a few people. The main guy's name was Gustav Miller. Only talked to him on the phone. Come to think of it, I don't even know who else was involved. A lot of foreigners. Strange outfit."

"And was anything left behind after they moved out?"

"No, they took everything. They were rushing to clear out."

"I received some photographs that were taken before you guys moved in. Was there some kind of security camera system set up when you moved in?"

"No, they'd taken their system out by the time we got there." He paused, thinking. "But we would've added our system the first day. When bad guys see folks moving, that's when security risks are highest."

Just what I'd hoped to hear. "So you might have recorded things that day?"

"I can't imagine we didn't. But we were installing those cameras all day, so not sure how much footage we would have gotten."

"If it's not too much trouble, I would love to view those tapes."

"Why don't I email you the files, you have your people review them, and if there's any material you find noteworthy, call me back. My only request is if it's proprietary, that you don't use it in a public way."

"We can agree to that."

I chuckled at the concept of my "people" reviewing it.

* * *

I pulled into the *Vindicator* parking lot at 3:30 p.m. and sat down at my desk minutes later. The emails from Butch Joseph had already arrived, and included footage from six cameras, labelled one through six.

Camera 1 began recording at 9:48 a.m. The subsequent cameras were installed and turned on about every 45 minutes thereafter, with a lunch break in between. I viewed footage from camera 6 first and worked my way back. Camera 6 was mounted in the loading dock area. It began operating at 2:15 p.m. Six trucks delivered boxes and large equipment via the loading dock over the ensuing four hours. Camera 5, in the research room, turned on at 1:32 p.m. New boxes and equipment were also visible there, but no one walked in and out from 1:50 on.

Lots of activity appeared on cameras 3 and 4, which were mounted outside the building at 11:15 a.m. and 12:18 p.m. Trucks, smaller cars, and vans driving in and out. People walking back and forth, lugging equipment, furniture, boxes from vehicles, into the building, then coming back out for more.

Camera 2 was back inside and peered down from the end of a long hallway. It began capturing footage at 10:38 a.m. I fast-forwarded through the hours of activity, primarily people from the parking lot delivering materials to the offices and other rooms that adjoined the hallway.

Finally came camera 1, the front lobby camera. It provided the exact same view as the photograph of Stanton when he entered Abacus two years ago. Installed at 9:48 a.m. Like camera 2, video footage showed a flurry of activity. Two men took down the old Abacus logo behind the desk, laid it on the floor, and replaced it with Diebold's. A woman dedicated several hours to organizing the front desk. Lots of folks walking through the lobby, hauling items back and forth.

I fast-forwarded to noon and paused as a sole figure walked into the lobby from the outside. Even from the back, I knew the man—from his height, his build, his shock of brown hair, his gait, even his clothes—khaki pants with a light blue sports coat. I'd seen that outfit before.

The man approached the reception desk and spent a few minutes conversing with the woman standing behind it. He wandered a dozen feet to the left of the desk and peered down a hallway. Another man, slightly taller, walked in from the right side of the lobby. He wore a baseball cap along with jeans and sweatshirt. He first talked to the woman, and then the three engaged in a short conversation from about a ten-foot distance. Finally, the visitor walked back toward the desk, turned toward the exit, and walked back outside. The camera finally captured a direct view of his face.

Lee Kelly.

Of all the days to show up at Abacus, Kelly had arrived on moving day. Stumbling into this frenzy of activity, a rushed effort to clear the scene, must have confirmed Kelly's hunch that Abacus was up to no good. And that explained his call to me shortly thereafter.

I quickly re-ran the footage from cameras three and four. Kelly's Escape was already in the parking lot when camera 4 was installed. Must have been parked there for some time prior to the camera turning on. And at 12:33 p.m., Kelly returned to the Escape, not directly from the lobby, but from another part of the parking lot. Probably had been looking around the outside premises. That's when he'd called and left his message, only minutes before getting back in the car. I watched Kelly open the door and climb in. Four minutes later, the car drove off the lot.

This footage made three things clear:

Kelly had stopped by Abacus before heading to Stanton's.

He'd driven away in his own car.

And if Kelly had shown up a few days earlier, or even a day or two later, he would still be alive.

*   *   *

I spent the early evening finalizing my draft. I added the quotes from Marshall and Williams, and from Ariens' dictated memo, which Kazarov had agreed to let me use so long as I didn't disclose where they came from. After explaining the other connections to Stanton, I added a new section:

> *In addition to Simpson, famed lobbyist and long-time Stanton friend Oliver Ariens also became aware of the plot early on. Only days before his death, Ariens dictated a note that he intended to deliver to Speaker Williams and Minority Leader Marshall describing precisely what Abacus intended.*

I quoted the note.

> *Although he shared it with at least one close confidant, the memo was never delivered to its intended recipients. Ariens died before he had a chance to send it. The coroner deemed the death a heart attack.*

*　*　*

As I wrapped up just after 8 p.m., my cell phone rang. A 202 area code. Despite how angry I was, I picked up.

"You have a lot of nerve to call me," I said.

"I'm so sorry," Janet Compton said. "Working with foreign clients is challenging, as you can imagine. I told them not to, but they thought it was the only way to get the two of you together in complete secrecy."

"It's still a crime, and you were complicit."

"Well, I hope you at least picked up some important information. I'm calling because I wanted to pass something along to you."

"Yeah, I bet you do. What is it?"

"Seth West, Tom Stanton's chief of staff, wanted to meet. So I did. Met for about an hour. He's asking all the same questions you were."

"Was he trying to figure out who was behind Abacus?"

"He's trying to figure out who to blame for it. They know they're up a creek, desperate to get ahead of your next story."

"I had another source tell me the same thing."

"Even worse, they're trying to pin it all on Oliver. West told me that Stanton first learned of the plan from him, that Oliver sent a note around the time he died."

"Did he really admit that?" This—Stanton's office acknowledging they received Ariens' note, just as Kazarov had said—added a critical piece to the story. Stanton had heard about Abacus from both Ariens and Simpson, both of whom died shortly thereafter.

"He just offered that up," said Compton. "But he said they ignored it until your story. Now they want to know who was behind the plot, and I worry Oliver's going to be their fall guy."

"Thanks for the heads up," I said coolly. "And don't worry, I have clear proof that Ariens didn't participate in the plot, so that won't go anywhere."

"Good. Thanks, and glad I could be helpful."

"You're still digging out of a deep hole, but I appreciate it."

We hung up, I re-opened my story, and added an additional sentence.

Although he shared it with at least one close confidant, the memo was apparently never delivered to its intended recipients. Ariens died before he had a chance to send it. The coroner deemed the death a heart attack.

But a source close to Stanton stated that the congressman—a long-time friend of Ariens—also received a note from Ariens about the plot.

Just as I finished up these edits, and after a few rounds of phone tag, Arlene Bradley called once again.

"I think Stanton and West have finally hatched their plan."

She walked through the calls West and Stanton had asked her to make. It was exactly the approach I'd expect out of them.

"You've been an enormous help," I said. "I can't thank you enough."

She did not respond with a simple "you're welcome." But with a long sigh.

"Mr. Sharpe, I thank you. I pray for forgiveness every day. Forgiveness because I did nothing to stand up for Joanie," she said. "That's why I keep calling you. I think this has been God's way of answering those prayers. He gave me a second chance to stand up for her, and for what is right."

"Goodbye, Ms. Bradley."

With Stanton trying to beat me to the punch, I began furiously typing away, not at my story but at an email, a long one, under the subject line "Highly confidential." It summarized the key findings of my weeks of research—the Simpson memo, the 31 districts, her death—but it also described facts I'd left out of my story, things that I had promised not to write about: Simpson's Facebook page, the years of abuse, the secret boyfriend. I also provided a link to Simpson's Facebook page, and attached a scanned version of the Simpson memo along with the photographs of Stanton visiting Abacus.

After completing the email, I rifled through some scrap pieces of paper scattered across my desk. I found the one I was looking for, typed in the email address at the top, and pushed send.

With that, having started in London, and come home to Youngstown via Bedford, Pennsylvania, the longest work day of my life ended.

*   *   *

I turned in my story at 9:30 the next morning, knowing that my editors would want all day to review it. Beyond all I'd previously drafted, the story now quoted both Irwin Marshall and Sandra Williams.

In my interview with Marshall, he had made it clear that he'd had enough of Stanton. This was the Speaker's chance to find a new majority leader, someone who wouldn't always be nipping at his heels, so his quotes thrust a knife into Stanton's gut.

> *"I am deeply concerned by the evidence tying Congressman Stanton to the Abacus plot," Marshall said. "We will immediately investigate all aspects of this matter to get to the bottom of it."*

Williams also took Stanton to the woodshed.

> *"All Americans should be appalled that the majority leader of the House of Representatives took part in a scheme to undermine the will of the American people. If these facts bear out, Congressman Stanton must be brought to justice."*

The story ended with Kelly.

> *The ties between Stanton and Abacus continued even after the election.*
>
> *Congressman Lee Kelly lost his re-election bid last November, and his district was one where Abacus machines eliminated thousands of Democratic votes. Having conducted his own investigation, Kelly discovered the Abacus plot. He traveled to Abacus' Philadelphia headquarters and arrived there the very day*

that those who had pulled off the election heist were abandoning the facility. Kelly called to alert the Vindicator of his concern, and called Congressman Stanton shortly thereafter.

After his car was spotted outside Stanton's Philadelphia townhouse later that afternoon, Kelly died in a fiery car crash later that evening. Despite photos of Kelly's Ford Escape parked in front of his townhome, and phone records showing calls to both Stanton's office and cell phone that day, Stanton denied any communication with his former colleague the day that he died.

Normally I relax when I turn in a draft. But this time, I paced back and forth in the newsroom, hoping to receive a reply to the prior night's email. The reply never came.

*   *   *

Just after 2:00 p.m., Mary Andres called me into Dennis Davis' office.

I walked in, my heart racing. This was a bombshell, and bombshells scare the hell out of both publishers and their lawyers, which means delay. But delay, now, would kill my story, allowing Stanton to preempt it with his own "investigation."

"Jack, I think you've done it!" bellowed Davis, rapping me on the back like a little league coach celebrating his star player's home run. "We've been on the phone with our lawyers, and with a few word changes they think we're on solid ground. We want to review the story with you one more time, and then we can put it to bed."

"Well done, Jack," Andres said. "Best story we've ever run. Historic."

I tried and failed to keep the grin off my face, feeling relieved, righteous, and on the brink of exhaustion. With our Cleveland-based lawyers patched in over a conference line, Andres and I spent the next two hours in her office walking through the copy one paragraph at a time. I explained my source for each factual assertion, and they approved each claim. It was painstaking work, but I happily did it, knowing we had the ball at the five-yard line and were poised to score.

"We're good to go," Andres said finally. "This will post right at midnight on our website."

"And tomorrow's paper?" I asked.

"The entire front page. You'll also like what our graphics and layout people have done. On the front page, and online, we're going to include the photos of Stanton visiting Abacus."

"Wow," I said. This would be a public prosecution, with the most damning evidence presented on the front page of the paper.

"I have one more thing I need to tell you," I said.

"What is it?"

With an eye on her closed door, I explained the email I'd sent the night before and the larger plan it was part of.

"It's risky, but I think it makes sense," Andres said when I finished, apparently too happy about my scoop to care that I hadn't come to her before taking such liberties. "Let me know what you hear."

When I returned to my desk, I checked my e-mail one last time to see if there was a reply.

Nothing. Maybe the plan wasn't going to work after all.

*   *   *

At 5:00 p.m., I walked back to my car, exhausted from the long week.

I hadn't been tailed since returning from London, so I didn't worry when I first saw a Suburban idling near the parking lot. But then the car followed me. Bizarre. This one was slightly darker than the other one but had the same license plate.

So I didn't return home. Definitely not safe. If Kazarov was tailing me again, he might be playing for keeps. I did all I could to ditch the car. Ran through a few yellow lights right as they turned red. Maneuvered to get cars between me and my tail. Several sudden, unsignaled turns. But every move failed.

I started to sweat. Here I was, on the verge of my breakthrough, and someone was still trying to stop me.

"Chief?"

"How's it going, Sharpe?"

"I'm being followed again, and they may be going for the jugular this time."

"Jesus. I'm starting to think you're the boy crying wolf, Jack."

I still had never explained the Breezewood disappearance, but I wasn't about to now. "I know, Chief. I'm sorry. But this time may be for real. Can you have someone pull this guy over so I can get away?"

"Sure."

"I'm at South and Lakefront, heading north. I'll go pretty slowly so your guys can head us off."

"Gotcha."

Minutes later, two Youngstown squad cars, sirens blazing, drove up behind the Suburban. It pulled over. Problem solved.

* * *

"You're going to want to come in here."

"What is it, Chief?"

"Trust me. Come to the station right away."

I had just walked into my favorite local dive, Dooley's. I needed a television set all to myself, and had found one in the back.

"Okay."

"Please save me that corner booth if you can," I said to the bartender on my way out. "Need to watch something at 8:00."

Minutes later, I walked into the chief's office. A dark-haired, heavyset man sat on the leather couch opposite the chief's desk. Looked to be in his early sixties. Gray suit. Square jaw. Tough-looking guy. I didn't recognize him.

"Jack, meet Clay Dennison."

I did a double take. "As in Stanton's Dennison?"

"You know who I am?" he asked.

"Of course I know who you are," I said. "You're Stanton's goon."

"Slow down, Sharpe," Chief Santini said.

"What do you mean, slow down? This guy's up to his ears in rotten stuff."

"Sharpe, cool it," Santini said. "I think you're going to want to listen to the man."

I stopped talking.

"Mr. Sharp," he said. *Shap.* Pure Boston. "The congressman sent me here to kidnap you."

I was too stunned to say anything. Santini watched me as it sunk in.

"He's worried sick about what you're going to write," Dennison said. "But don't worry. I'm a former cop. I wasn't going to kidnap you."

"What was he going to have you do after kidnapping me?"

"I don't think he knew. But he needed you to disappear for a while."

"So my story doesn't come out? And his does?"

"Exactly."

"And you got cold feet?"

"My feet never factored into it. I do security. I drive. I don't kidnap. As soon as he told me to do it, I figured I'd drive here and tell you myself."

"Why didn't you just call instead of scaring the hell out of me?"

"You never know who's got who bugged in my business."

I nodded, trying to think all of this through on the spot.

"I've actually got a lot I could tell you about Stanton," he said, unprompted.

At any other moment, I would've grabbed my reporter's notebook and feverishly taken notes. But I needed to get back to Dooley's by 8:00, and it was already 20 'til. "I need to get to something that's pretty urgent," I said. "Why don't I have the paper put you up at a nearby hotel, and we'll meet first thing in the morning?"

"That works for me."

I rushed out of police headquarters and raced back to the bar. Walked in at 8:00 on the nose.

Right on time for the Bridget Turner show.

*   *   *

West and Stanton sat in the green room, going over their game plan one last time.

The chief of staff pumped his boss up. "Remember, you're outraged that someone tried to overturn the will of the American people."

Stanton responded with even more faux outrage. "Absolutely," he said. "This is above party politics. This is about the essence of our democracy."

"And even if it means calling out your old friend," West said, "and undermining the very party you lead, your duty is to put your country first."

"So we're calling for an immediate investigation into Abacus and Oliver Ariens, and Ariens' clients?"

"Yes. Leaving no stone unturned. You do this right, and you'll get universal praise for standing up when everyone else is ducking."

"I'm ready to go. This is brilliant, Seth. Turning the tables on ⊠em."

"Just need to pull it off. And you will. You're a big game performer."

Someone knocked on the door. Then a young woman, a production assistant, stepped into the doorway. "Congressman, you can follow me to the studio," she said. "The interview starts in five minutes."

"Yes, ma'am," he said. "Happy to follow you anytime!"

She ignored the comment and walked out of the room. Stanton trailed her down two hallways to the live studio. He sat down behind a V-shaped desk, and the woman clipped a mic onto his red tie, a few inches below his collar.

"Look into that camera when you're introduced," she said. "But after that, just talk to her as if you're having a regular conversation. She'll sit there as the show starts."

"Sounds good." He'd been through this drill many times. "Thank you." He reached out to pat her lower back as he spoke, but, seeing the hand coming, she jumped away just in time.

"Good luck," she said.

A deep male voice came over the studio's speakers "Ten, nine, eight . . ."

Following the opening music, the familiar voice of Bridget Turner echoed through the studio.

"Last month, a story about a stolen election rocked our nation's capital. But then it spiraled into controversy. Was it true? Was it some kind of left-wing myth? Today, we are joined by Congressman Tom Stanton. Our new majority leader—and who knows, maybe our next president—says that not only is the story true, but he knows who was behind this attack on our democracy."

As Turner's voice spoke to pre-recorded audio, Stanton enjoyed watching a monitor displaying images of him in action. Turner herself then appeared from behind a wall, slipped into the cozy studio, and sat behind the other wing of the V-shaped desk. As the recording continued, she gave Stanton a spirited thumbs-up along with a big smile.

"That's right," she broke in live, looking into the monitor with a green light illuminated below it. "We have the second most important man in the House here to explain what happened. Majority Leader Tom Stanton."

Stanton looked into his camera and displayed a huge, all-teeth grin.

"Welcome back to our show, Tom!"

"Thanks, Bridget. Good to be back!" He looked over to his host, feeling confident. They'd worked together on many stories, including getting her that brutal research on Jack Sharpe and his sources.

Turner's face slipped from serene to serious in a nanosecond. "Tom, these are disturbing allegations. Tell us what you think happened."

"Unfortunately, I think people got greedy. They prioritized power and money over respect for the will of the American people. And since the first story ran, too many in Washington have turned the other way. I decided to put party aside and get to the bottom of it."

"Who do you think was involved?"

"Well, we don't know all of them, but we think we've found the ringleader. His name is Oliver Ariens, and sadly, he was a friend of mine and many others. Probably the most powerful lobbyist in Washington. But it looks like he was the man who orchestrated this plan, for one or several of his major special interest clients."

"How do you know this?"

"He sent me a note gloating about it before he died of a heart attack."

"He did?"

"Yes. And then the exact plan he alerted me to happened. He didn't live to see it, but whoever he was working with clearly pulled it off. Which is why I'm calling for a full investigation of his firm and his firm's clients."

*   *   *

"Damn."

I cursed at the screen. Exactly what Kazarov had predicted. The show was off to a terrible start. I'd never heard back from the email I'd sent Turner, so I had no idea if anyone at Republic had even read it. And now what I'd feared would happen was taking place. Stanton was pulling off his scheme masterfully—beating me to the punch.

*   *   *

With the interview off to a perfect start, Stanton relaxed.

Turner followed up with her next question. "And what did you do after you heard about this from Mr. Ariens?"

"I didn't believe it," Stanton said proudly. "It sounded nuts. And once he died, I was more concerned with grieving my best friend's passing. But after the *Vindicator* story came out, it was clear that his group had done exactly what he'd told me."

"So you never did anything with the information?"

"I had my team look into it at first, but it never went anywhere. I wish I had done more. Maybe I could've stopped it."

Turner jumped into a new line of questioning, glossing over his answer.

"Tom, I want you to look at that monitor over there. Our viewers are seeing it as well. You see that?"

He recognized the photo instantly. It was the Abacus lobby, the company logo clearly visible. Worse, there he was right in the middle of the shot, from his visit years back.

"Is that you, Tom?" Bridget asked.

"Um." Stanton's heart raced. Where the hell had that photo come from? And how did Bridget Turner have it?

"How about this photo?" Turner asked. "This looks like you're looking right at . . . What is that, an Abacus machine? And this one looks like you overseeing some sort of loading or shipping process."

"That is me," Stanton said quietly, his mouth suddenly dry. "As I said, we looked into it a little . . ."

* * *

"Yes!" I raised my arms to signal a touchdown. She'd definitely gotten my email! Her next questions got only nastier.

"This looks like more than just 'a little,' Tom, doesn't it?" she said.

"Well, I checked out their facility near Philly," Stanton said, "but I had no idea what they were up to."

"Looks like you're getting a pretty *close* look, Tom. And this was well over a year before last year's election, wasn't it?"

Even through the bar's television set, Stanton's face looked dumbfounded as Turner let the brutal question linger unanswered. Then she moved to another.

"Tom, can you tell us who Joanie Simpson is?" Here we go, I thought.

"Uh, yeah, she was a research assistant for me a couple years back. Tragically, she was killed jogging in a Washington park."

"Is this a photo of her?"

A close-up shot of Simpson appeared on the television monitor. It was the Friday night Facebook photo. Turner's team must have followed the link I'd emailed, the one connecting to Simpson's Facebook page.

"It sure is," Stanton said, obviously feeling like he was back on solid ground.

"This is the night before she died," Turner said. "It's from her Facebook page."

"So sad." Stanton shook his head, a reaction so insincere I nearly felt sick.

"She's beautiful, isn't she?" Turner asked.

"I actually try to avoid thinking in those terms when it comes to staff."

"Is that right?"

I smiled, knowing Bridget was setting him up for a major takedown.

"Absolutely."

"Well, I think she's beautiful."

"Others did, too."

"Do you know what's funny, Tom?"

"What's that?"

"Whenever we found her in a photo with you, she never smiled."

Silence.

"Is that strange?"

"I don't know."

"You don't know? She always smiles, except when you're nearby?"

"Maybe she was professional in the workplace or nervous around authority?"

"Nervous around you?"

"Not me. People in authority."

"Oh. By the way, although she always posted things on Facebook, Joanie never posted on Thursday nights. Can you think of a reason for that?"

She was going further than I ever thought she would.

"How would I know?"

"You don't know how she spent her Thursday nights?"

"Of course not."

"We talked to her boyfriend at the time she died. He's a good young man, a Republican. Would it surprise you to learn that he thinks you forced her to come over to your townhouse on Thursday nights?"

"I have no idea what you're talking about."

"Well, we're going to interview him on our program tomorrow night, so we can learn more then. You may want to watch."

Long pause.

"Speaking of your staff members," Turner went on, "do you recognize any of these women?" Next a series of photos flashed on the left half the monitor, all young women. I didn't recognize any of them.

But Stanton did. He stared at the screen, dumbstruck.

"Tom?"

"They all worked for me. Good workers all."

"Nothing else you want to say about them?"

Silence.

"We'll talk more about them later—all of them. But I brought up Joanie Simpson because she stumbled upon this Abacus plot as well. Did you and she ever discuss it?"

"Yes, we did. Briefly. After Ariens told me about it. Like I said, I had my staff look into it."

"And did she tell you about the detailed plan?"

"Um . . ."

"Actually, if you look up on the screen, we have an image of a memo she sent you—a copy generously provided by the *Youngstown Vindicator*—that explained what was going to happen in Abacus districts. A pretty amazing document. Do you recognize it?"

She even plugged us. Nice.

"My staff prepares a lot of memos. As I told the *Vindicator*, I'd never seen it before they showed it to me."

"But Tom, this was a big one. Are you sure you don't remember it?"

"Never saw it."

"Well, it laid out 31 swing districts where Abacus had its machines. Here they are on this map on your screen."

An outline of the United States appeared on the screen, highlighting the 31 districts that Simpson mentioned in her memo.

"Tom, should it strike our viewers as a coincidence that you campaigned in those 31 districts last fall?"

"No. Of course I campaigned in the key districts."

"But you didn't go to other swing districts that she didn't have in the memo. What are the chances of that?"

"I have no idea!"

"Pretty incredible odds. You went to the same 31 districts outlined in your murdered staff member's memo, but no others. It's like her memo served as your guide for the election cycle."

Stanton muttered something in response, but it was unintelligible.

"Well, we're running out of time for my questions. I know you had some ideas on who was behind this. Who do you think was behind the Abacus plan?"

"His name is Oliver Ariens," Stanton said, still barely audible.

"And he died two years ago?"

"Sadly, yes."

"But he was able to pull off this elaborate plot from the grave?"

"He sent me a note about it, yes. Then it happened as he described."

"Maybe he was telling you about it to warn you. Maybe he expected you to stop it."

Stanton leaned forward, clearly trying to regain his footing. "He represented some of the most controversial industries in the world, Bridget. One of them paid him to undertake such a scheme, not stop it. And they clearly pulled it off, even after he died. That's why I'm proposing a committee to investigate it."

"Tom, does it haunt you that people died so quickly after telling you about the Abacus plot?"

"I've had a difficult couple of years. Lost some important people. People I respected. But I don't think it had anything to do with Abacus or me."

"Sure seems strange. More to come, I guess. That's all the time we have for tonight. I really appreciate you coming on. I also want to thank the *Youngstown Vindicator* for their partnership on this story. They will have more of the details beginning at midnight tonight."

As she said this, a chyron of the *Vindicator*'s website appeared on the bottom of television sets all over the country.

"I have no doubt there will be investigations following their story," she continued. "You're welcome to come back anytime! Good luck as you decide whether to run for president." Turner addressed the last sentence right to the camera, smiling as she spoke directly to millions across the nation. Stanton might as well not have been in the studio.

"Good night."

Another round of music closed out the show. I leaned back in my chair, clenched my right fist, and tapped it three times against the wooden table.

* * *

Turner walked out of the studio without saying a word. Stanton gazed straight ahead for a few moments, shell-shocked. He reached up to unclip the mic.

"Can I help you with that?" The young woman, the one he'd tried to touch only 30 minutes before, smiled sweetly as she waited for his answer.

"I got it," he muttered, looking away.

He walked slowly down the hallway, back to the green room where he'd left his briefcase and where West was waiting. Stanton was eager to talk damage control with his chief of staff. He opened the door, spotting his briefcase on the floor right where he'd left it.

West was gone.

*   *   *

Irene Stanton watched the interview in tears.

Seeing her husband skewered for all his transgressions was wonderful, but the fact that she enjoyed his comeuppance reminded her how broken her marriage was. And she knew this night marked the end of three lost decades. She ignored all the incoming phone calls. Friends and wives of Tom's colleagues calling to express their sympathy. Her kids, who had stopped caring about their dad years ago, checking in to see how she was handling it. Her best friend calling to cheer.

She ignored them all as she packed her bags and loaded them in the minivan. She backed out of the garage at 10:30. She planned to head south to D.C. for a day, then out west to spend time with her children.

Time to start over.

*   *   *

I tried to sleep, but my adrenaline had other plans. After tossing and turning for nearly an hour, I turned on my TV and logged onto my laptop. The wave had already started.

Bridget Turner's interview of Stanton had exploded as breaking news on every cable show. Up and down the dial, pundits replayed and analyzed clips of the usually unflappable majority leader flubbing answer after answer—sweating at the sight of Joanie Simpson, freezing when confronted with the photos of his Abacus tour, and melting down under Turner's barrage of haymakers.

When midnight hit, the *Vindicator* posted the story. Thanks to Turner's plug, my handiwork quickly became the bible of this scandal. The story itself, the photos, the Simpson memo, the 31 districts, the Marshall and Williams quotes, and the Ariens transcript—all there to be scrutinized and parsed. Within an hour, every major newspaper rehashed the plot on its own website, faithfully crediting the *Vindicator* for the game-changing scoop.

New York Times: "Youngstown Paper Finds Stanton at Heart of Vote-Stealing Scheme"

Washington Post: "Majority Leader Part of Abacus Scandal, Paper Finds"

Wall Street Journal: "Speaker Calls for Answers as Stanton Tied to Abacus Election Scandal"

The incriminating photo of Stanton examining an Abacus machine served as the centerpiece of every story, always with the *Vindicator* credit.

After the initial surge of reporting, I managed to catch some sleep in the early morning. When I awoke at 6:30, the story and Congressman Tom Stanton were the talk of the country. By then, the *Times* and *Post* had already added online analytical stories from their premier political writers. Both explained how the extreme gerrymandering of districts and a weak system of elections had combined to allow such a scandal to happen. Both called for dramatic reforms.

The *Today Show* led off that morning's program with a long story describing the Abacus scandal and Stanton's role. In an interview, Speaker Marshall promised to get to the bottom of it all. His tone made it clear that he meant it.

After getting dressed, I checked my messages from the night before. All congratulations and thanks. Jody Kelly sounded ecstatic. Arlene Bradley, thrilled. Peter Kreutzer said he was inspired to come forward now.

Scott had sent a text as well. "Awesome job, Dad! You did it!"

And I'd received one other text, this one from a longer number, one I didn't recognize at first. But as I opened it, the prior two messages from the same number appeared.

Simple: go back to White Castle in 5 minutes.

Don't Be a Fool: Keep Them Alive.

Someone from Kazarov's operation, if not Kazarov himself.

But this new text was more positive: *Well done, Mr. Sharpe.*

*   *   *

I'd learned my lesson—I wouldn't be the story this time. Wouldn't even try. No interviews. No appearances. Let the politicians and the D.C. pundits talk this one through. Stay in the background and watch things unfold from afar. In fact, what a perfect time to escape west to see Scott and Jana. It had been far too long. I'd head out there over the weekend. I'd earned it.

Only a few things to do beforehand.

First, I walked into Dunkin' Donuts just as Clay Dennison's Suburban pulled into the parking lot. We sat down at exactly 8:00, each with a dark coffee and glazed donut in front of us.

"Holy shit, Sharpe," he said. "I can see why Stanton wanted you kidnapped."

"I guess our little story packed a punch, huh."

"Sure did. But it was a long time coming."

"Not sure what you're willing to tell me, but I appreciate you meeting with me. And I especially appreciate you not making me disappear."

"My pleasure."

"So what did you want to share?" I asked.

"First, the guy is a serial abuser of women and a complete asshole. You've done our country a favor by taking him down. The man should not be president and now won't be, thanks to you."

"Did you see it all for yourself?"

"Of course. I hate admitting this, but I did most of the driving a few years back. A different girl every night. I played the chauffeur. I took them to and from his home in Georgetown. Some of them seemed to enjoy it, but most of them rode home miserable. I'm ashamed that I played the role I did, and I was in denial most of the time."

"What made you change your mind?"

"After that girl, Joanie, was killed, the night visits stopped. The boss was spooked people would catch on to him. And then one day I saw her photo hanging in the office hallway—so happy, so pretty. Looked like a different person than the girl I'd driven home every week. The contrast woke me up. So I vowed never to do it again if he asked me."

"And did he?"

"Once. I refused. If he started the visits up again, I wasn't part of it."

"Anything else?"

"I was with him the day he visited Abacus. I knew something was up when he wanted to go there alone. Then when he came out after an hour, he sat quietly most of the trip home. Cursed about a 'lying Swede,' but didn't say a word after that. I think he knew exactly what was going on there. No one else understood why he was so unnerved when your story came out. But I knew exactly why."

Good. A guy with a front-row seat was confirming two key elements of my story. But a few other questions lingered. Dennison beat me to the punch.

"Sharpe," he said, "how the hell did you know who I was? And why did Chief Santini know my name?"

"Well, I was followed here for about a week. When we ran the license plate, it came back to you. And because you're a retired cop, Santini was able to figure out who you were."

"My plates were on another car? Jesus. That explains why my front plate was stolen a few weeks back."

"I actually learned more about you than just your license plate."

"Yeah?"

"Yeah. Like the fact that you arrested Johnny Rutherford 21 times. The same Rutherford who was blamed for beating Simpson to death."

"Try 28 times. Crazy, huh? That was either one hell of a coincidence or someone really was trying to screw Stanton. It's the main reason Stanton was so freaked out after she died. I told him about the connection once I heard Rutherford was the suspect, and he figured someone was out to get him. But then things died down."

"So you didn't put Rutherford up to it?"

"Are you kidding? I wouldn't be part of a murder. Tell you the truth, I don't even think he did it. And if he didn't, someone sure set it up so it looked like he did."

At this point, I didn't know who to believe, but that ended the serious talk. We spent the rest of the breakfast sharing crime and cop stories.

* * *

I headed to the *Vindicator* after breakfast, parked in my usual spot, and made the same short walk into the cavernous building that I had made every morning for decades. I took the stairs to the second floor and trudged down the dark hallway toward the newsroom. The *Vindicator*'s most historic front pages hung on the walls to either side of me.

"Allies Cross Channel, Land at Normandy."

"Kennedy Shot, Killed in Dallas."

"Ohio's Armstrong Walks on Moon."

Each headline spanned the top of the front page in large capital letters, below the ornate *Vindicator* masthead.

After the 2008 banner headline proclaiming Obama's victory, a new frame appeared. Although it occupied what had been the last empty spot on the left wall, I was almost past it when I noticed it. Its shiny glass and polished wood frame stuck out from the others. And unlike the worn, yellowish copies preceding it, the page encased in the frame was brand new, white as ivory. The photo still had its full color.

"Majority Leader Caught in Vote-Rigging Scandal," shouted the headline. I stared proudly at the framed paper. My first trophy since college.

Standing at the edge of the newsroom itself, I now heard a bustle within. As I entered the room, a large crowd erupted in applause. Greeting me first were my two ecstatic bosses, Davis and Andres. Lined up behind them were dozens of fellow reporters, photographers, editors, assistants, along with Santini and a few retirees and old friends.

"You did it!" Davis said.

"You really did," Andres added.

The two of them hushed the crowd and then spoke, praising my game-changing scoop. Game changing for the paper, and for the country.

"Jack, you've put us on the map nationally," Davis said.

Andres was equally thrilled. "Our website has had more hits in the last nine hours than we've had in the past year combined."

I said a few words of thanks, and then made my way back to my desk. Colleague after colleague shook my hand, slapped my shoulder, and congratulated me.

*   *   *

We stayed glued to our television sets all morning.

By noon, talk of reform consumed Washington. As nefarious as the plot may have been, the pundits agreed that the ease of stealing the congressional majority was a scandal in and of itself. They were demanding change. And leadership.

Speaker Marshall and Minority Leader Williams jointly appeared in the Capitol Rotunda, surrounded by their top lieutenants. All four networks, as well as cable television stations, covered it live. A flock of reporters pressed forward and against one another, jockeying for the best position. The clicks of cameras started as soon as the two leaders made their way to the podium.

It marked their first joint appearance in years. Marshall spoke first, Williams standing behind his right shoulder. "We talked to the president

20 minutes ago," he said, "and we all agreed—we will pull together a bipartisan commission to look into two issues. Districting reform, and election security. We can never again allow our democracy to be at risk from such a scheme."

Williams stepped to the podium and followed. "Majority Leader Stanton will certainly be held accountable for his actions here," she said, "along with anyone he worked with. But more fundamentally, we must fix the badly broken system that allowed this to happen in the first place. I pledge that we Democrats will join with the president and speaker to get this done. We need districts that give our voters a choice, and we need clear national standards that guide how we run our elections, including ensuring that these new technologies are safe."

As she finished her statement, dozens of reporters asked questions at the same time. Bridget Turner stood in the front row, and Marshall called on her first.

"Mr. Speaker," Turner said, "are you even the Speaker anymore? If this election was really stolen, how do we walk back the results?"

"That's a great question, Bridget. Minority Leader Williams and I are already working to create a joint leadership caucus for the time being, as we sort out how to implement districting reforms. And of course, we will hold a new election next year in those new districts, and with the new election safeguards in place."

"And what about laws that have already passed?" Turner asked.

Williams stepped to the podium. "We've reached a compromise. It would be nearly impossible to undo all the legislation enacted since January, so what was passed and signed will stay in place. But our joint leadership caucus will govern for the rest of this term. Any legislation that the president has not yet signed will be suspended and screened by the joint caucus. Unless a majority of both parties' caucuses agree to a bill, it will not move forward. And this will occur until the elections next year. Finally, due to his involvement, the divisive voting legislation that Leader Stanton authored will be scrapped immediately."

"What will happen to Stanton?" another reporter shouted.

Marshall returned to the microphone. "The president and I have written him a letter calling on him to resign. He will also be subpoenaed to testify before Congress on his involvement. And he will be held accountable for his actions."

God, I hope so, I thought. For *all* his actions.

*   *   *

The rest of the day, I returned calls.

Arlene Bradley was thrilled by it all. Neither Stanton nor West had shown up at work, and Irene Stanton had called to let her know she'd left her husband.

Jody Kelly cried during our call, but she assured me repeatedly that they were tears of joy. As awful as her husband's death had been, at least he'd died on an important mission. Still tragic, but heroic too.

Peter Kreutzer gushed about his scheduled appearance on Turner's show. He finally had an audience, so he planned to turn the screws on Stanton even more as well as vindicate Joanie for doing all she could to stop the Abacus plot.

And Scott celebrated not only the story but my idea of visiting. "Dad, we couldn't be more proud of you. Your story is going to change our country."

He meant every word. And every word felt great.

Ernie Rogers also left me a celebratory message. "You nailed that son of a bitch," he rasped. "Always hated that guy."

I called Bridget Turner just after three.

"Well, that was one hell of a joint venture, Sharpe," she said. "You sent me that stuff just in time, and boy was it nuclear. How did you know he was coming onto my show?"

"Just had a hunch."

"Sure. Well, we make a good one-two punch. I'm still heartbroken about that Joanie Simpson. Horrible how he treated her, and the other women. That was an incredible find."

"It really was horrible. And atoning for what happened to her kept me going despite the ups and downs."

"Really sorry that our prior interview was one of the downs."

"That's fine. We Ohioans know how to get back up after being knocked down. Plus, you forced me to dig deeper, and you more than made up for it last night."

"Thanks to you. By the way, we'd be happy to have you on next week to walk through more of the details."

"No thanks," I said. "I'm stepping away for a few weeks. Figured you and everyone else can take it from here."

"Great. And enjoy."

"Will do. Good luck with Peter Kreutzer tonight. Great kid. You might give Jody Kelly a call. She'd be great as well."

"Will do. Speaking of politicians' wives, Irene Stanton has some new information on Simpson's death. She's eager to talk. We're running a two-hour live special tonight."

CHAPTER 54

YOUNGSTOWN—ILLINOIS

April 22: 165 days after the election

I woke up early Saturday and packed a few bags. Loaded a tent, sleeping bag, and some fishing gear into the truck in case a nearby river or stream called my name along the way.

Two thousand five hundred miles, almost entirely on the same road that I enter ten minutes from my home. I'd head across I-80. Through Toledo, then Chicago, Des Moines, and Omaha. Then into the Rockies, through Cheyenne, Salt Lake City and on to Reno. Then past Sacramento and into the Bay Area.

Exactly my kind of trip. Eagles, Buffett, some Beatles, all loaded up and ready to play.

At 6:20 a.m., I made one stop before heading out of town: Dunkin' Donuts. Coffee from the drive-thru. I was hoping to get to San Fran by Sunday night. Maybe we'd eat in Sausalito, on the water.

* * *

The first few hours of the drive were uneventful. Light traffic. No cops.

But as I crossed into Indiana, the adrenaline rush of publishing the story, of beating Stanton to the punch, of hearing the accolades, began to fade.

On the one hand, I had wrapped a tight bow around my story. A clean narrative, a seamless theory, one that the national media and politicians accepted whole hog.

But now my second-guessing began.

The first tinge of guilt had begun to kick in the day before, about what my story hadn't reported, but the events of the rest of the day had lifted my spirits and shielded me from my nagging self-doubt. Deep down, though, I knew. My story, as published, wasn't quite right. The impression it left was off in critical ways. Some facts had run against the grain, and would have undermined the narrative, so I had purposely excluded them and set them aside in my own mind.

First, one of my most important finds cut both ways. Discovering that Stanton had campaigned in the 31 districts, and *only* the 31 districts, outlined in Simpson's memo, had been a breakthrough. It showed Stanton had been lying through his teeth. That he had seen Simpson's memo long ago. But the "31" breakthrough also introduced an important limitation to my narrative. Stanton had *only* known of the districts Simpson enumerated in the memo. He had been unaware of the four others in the Abacus footprint—the ones Simpson herself hadn't known about. This meant Stanton had wholly relied on his aide's memo when he chose where to campaign. If her memo alone had provided his roadmap, then Stanton hadn't had a deep knowledge of the overall plot, or key details. He must not have known which districts Abacus covered until Simpson's memo helpfully listed them for him.

But if you were part of planning the operation, those districts would be the first thing you'd know. They would be your targets, so you'd know all 35. And if you were part of planning the operation, Simpson's memo wouldn't have provided any new information whatsoever. Based on where Stanton had campaigned, her memo had provided *all* he knew.

So although Stanton had visited Abacus months before he got Simpson's memo, he was likely only observing it, as an outsider. That's why he'd been so quiet on the drive back from his visit, as Dennison described. Yes, the photos of him touring the place provided damning evidence that he was part of the planning. But the fact that he'd only campaigned in 31 districts—not 35—showed he was not.

Yep, I had left this part out—on purpose.

Then there was Kelly. In recent days, it had also become clear to me that Stanton didn't kill Kelly, and that Kelly hadn't visited Stanton's house in Philly, at least of his own volition. Hell, he hadn't even called Stanton. The tapes of Kelly leaving the Abacus facility filled in a big piece of the puzzle. Kelly had stopped by Abacus before visiting Stanton. The two stops were connected. But the time sequence also made clear that what happened was more nuanced.

Jody Kelly had been clear, and she knew her husband's habits. He would always call her back once he returned to his car, once he had recharged his phone. But on the video, he had climbed back into the

Escape at 12:28, which was later parked in front of Stanton's at about 4:00. In all that time, he never answered his phone. Nor did he call his wife. For some reason he wasn't *able* to call her back, and it wasn't because his phone was dead. His phone had worked before he got in the car because he had called me only minutes before. And once in the car, he could have charged it.

The only logical answer was that Kelly wasn't alone as he drove away from Abacus. The four-minute delay before putting the car in reverse had struck me as odd the first time I watched it. And then he didn't call Jody after driving off. Or ever again. So Kelly had driven under duress or perhaps didn't drive at all. And that meant the person in the car with him had been the one who ensured the Escape appeared in front of Stanton's townhome, for a photo that conveniently pointed the finger at Stanton.

And then there was the phone call, the only call Kelly made after getting back in the car, about 30 minutes after he drove off the lot. The last call he ever made. To Stanton's private cell. Kelly himself could not have made that call. Even Arlene Bradley said that the number Kelly dialed—the one from Kelly's phone records, the one I had called that Stanton had picked up—had rung Stanton's highly confidential line, the one for family and staff. And apparently the women. But no one else.

When Kelly told Bradley he had Stanton's cell, he must have been referring to a different number. Any number possessed by one of hundreds of congressmen, and one of the other party, was certainly not the closely kept one.

But his captor, the one in the car, somehow had it. And that person either dialed the confidential number himself on Kelly's phone or instructed Kelly to dial it. Why? To point the finger at Stanton. Again.

It all added up to a ferocious attempt to lay the entire Abacus plot, including the murder of Kelly, at the feet of Stanton. The photos of Stanton's tour, the photo in front of Stanton's townhouse, the call, all implicated Stanton. And these bits of evidence had all been dropped in my lap.

Stewing as I entered Illinois, I then recalled my conversation with Dennison over donuts. That brief discussion had raised even more red flags.

Kazarov's men had gone to the trouble of stealing the security chief's license plate in order to make me believe the congressman was the one following me. That was serious attention to detail. Aggressive. But it also meant that Kazarov's crew had followed Stanton, discovering who

Dennison was. And from our conversation, Kazarov's crew had certainly wired everyone. Me. Stanton for sure. Maybe even Simpson. Kazarov simply knew too much.

This also meant they'd likely overheard the conversation where Simpson handed her memo to Stanton, and they knew enough about Stanton's operation to dig into Dennison's past, and to have located and framed Rutherford for Simpson's killing—once again implicating Stanton.

And there was one final red flag. A glaring one. Raised high.

It was something Dennison had said over coffee. As much as I wanted to get west quickly, I couldn't let it go.

* * *

To satisfy my curiosity, I pulled over at a rest stop an hour west of Chicago. No Dunkin' Donuts around, but a Bob Evans.

A gray-haired woman named Gracie greeted me at the door with typical Bob Evans sweetness and walked me to a booth. I ordered my usual: omelet, biscuits, and a slice of ham.

Awaiting the order, I took out my laptop and signed onto the *Vindicator*'s email system, searching emails from two days before, specifically from Butch Joseph, of Diebold. I opened the emails containing footage from Diebold's cameras, number 1 and 2.

Hurrying to beat Stanton to the punch, I had rushed through both videos the first time around. And after the bombshell of seeing Kelly enter and exit the lobby, the main story had occupied the rest of my day. But now, with more time, I reviewed the videos closely to find something in particular. Someone in particular.

On camera 2, the camera focused on the hallway, no one of interest appeared in the camera view for the entire afternoon, so I opened the camera 1 file.

"—Omelet, biscuits, ham. Enjoy!" Gracie, kind as can be, set down my plate.

"Thanks so much."

On camera 1, from between 10:32 a.m. and noon, nothing new emerged. And of course, right around noon, the camera captured Kelly entering from outside, talking to two staff, wandering around, and then exiting. Just as I had seen before.

And then I watched again. More slowly this time. Watched the other man, the one with the baseball cap, who entered from the side and had a few words with Kelly.

I had barely glanced at him when I first observed the tape, distracted by Kelly. But now I eyeballed him more closely. The cap hid much of his face, but he looked familiar. Height and build especially. I fast-forwarded the tape, trying to find him again. And at four o'clock, he reappeared. No cap, but the rest of the outfit was the same. He was leaving the building, a decent-sized bag in his right hand. Blonde hair. Buzz cut.

I recognized him immediately. It was my air-mate to London, Stefan Holmberg.

This was the first and only direct evidence connecting Kazarov and his operation to Abacus. And it was definitive.

His look and accent had made it clear that he was Scandinavian. So when Dennison had mentioned in passing Stanton's complaint about a "lying Swede," Holmberg's face had immediately popped into my head. And lo and behold, here he was, overseeing their last day at Abacus, keeping intruders like Kelly away, and cleaning out any evidence linking the vote-stealing plot back to Marcellus. Back to Kazarov.

*   *   *

I calmly shut my laptop and took my time savoring a meal I'd eaten a thousand times before. I even ordered another biscuit for the road, along with another cup of coffee.

As I paid at the counter, the banner *Chicago Tribune* headline lying a few feet away screamed the latest on the scandal: "Irene Stanton Bombshell: Husband Tied to Staff Death; Harassed Aides for Years." I didn't buy the paper, but good for Mrs. Stanton.

Instead, I walked outside after Gracie handed me my change. Climbed back in the pick-up, and got back onto I-80. "Take It Easy" echoed through the truck. I drove west. No turning back.

Of course it had its flaws, but in all other ways, my story was perfect. It did everything I wanted done, everything I needed done. It took down a scumbag who deserved everything he got from the Turner-Sharpe one-two punch, and whoever else was now piling on. Stanton was the worst kind of partisan, just like the guy who'd beaten Dad years ago. He mistreated women, abused women—his own staff. As one of the most important members of Congress, he'd watched gleefully as a plot to steal an election played out. And he'd pursued every ounce of benefit possible from that plot, including a path to the presidency. And then at the last minute, to try to get out his jam, he'd tried to frame an honest man, his own friend, who likely died trying to stop the scandal. If I'd rushed the final days of the story to head off Stanton's desperate attempt to preempt it, Stanton had no one to blame but himself for the slightly inaccurate result.

Would Stanton ever be convicted for either Simpson's or Kelly's death? Of course not. No one would be. Professionals had clearly killed them both—professionals who'd left no trace of their handiwork and no connection back to who'd hired them. But if the scandal permanently cast a dark shadow over Stanton, he deserved it, even if he hadn't ordered the killings himself. His unwillingness to stop the plot had led to those deaths.

At the same time, the story—my version of the story—preserved the new economic hope of the Valley and eastern Ohio. The pipelines, the growth, the jobs would continue to move forward. This was great news for the communities up and down the Ohio, as long as the environmentalists were wrong, and as long as the region avoided the same fate as Titusville. If Marcellus went down in the scandal, all that potential would fade.

Equally important, I finally had my story on gerrymandering, and it had kick-started the best chance for real reform in decades. When we'd talked on the phone, Marshall and Williams had struck me as deeply committed to fixing things. Their joint press conference had left me with the same confidence. This was the best moment, offering real hope, in a long time. The kind of bipartisanship Dad would've led.

Kazarov was right. Complicating the clean Stanton storyline with the jarring introduction of a foreign-led plot would end the rare chance at reform before it even began.

And Scott was safe. Scott and Jana and the little one coming. The story as written guaranteed that. Too much nuance would have guaranteed the opposite.

Finally, heading west into Iowa, the final words Arlene Bradley had spoken to me echoed in my ears. That God had granted her a second chance to stand up for Joanie Simpson. To make up for her failure.

She was right.

This story, written exactly as it was, had given me my chance too. The chance, after so many years, to stand for something. For Joanie Simpson. For Meredith. For Scott, and his safety, his family. For myself. For a better politics. For a better country.

And for Dad.

Yes, it had its flaws. But I wouldn't change a word.

EPILOGUE

LONDON: 14 months before the election

T HE SUN WAS on its way up in London. An unusually pleasant Friday morning.

Oleg Kazarov and Boris Popov worked through their breakfast. Small slices of orange salmon and green capers on dark squares of bread occupied most of the circular plate between them. It was their usual gathering time and Kazarov's usual meal, but this was a far more important meeting than most.

Kazarov shook his head in disappointment and swallowed a bite of toast. "This man is weak," he said. "I expected more from a powerful congressman. Someone who wants to be America's president."

They had just listened to the tape of the conversation between Stanton and his young researcher from hours before. She had explained the plot, handed a written report to her boss, and left without it on her. She had been visibly relieved on the ride home.

And they had listened as Stanton, always within range of his briefcase, had done nothing after she'd left but mutter to himself.

"She is smart," Popov said. "She figured out so much of it."

"And he is spineless," Kazarov said. "He does not have the strength to stop our plot, but he also does not have the strength to eliminate her. We will have to do his work for him."

He disliked the prospect of more violence. But this also posed a critical moment for another reason. Just like Oliver Ariens, the girl had figured out their plan.

"Someone will discover Abacus, and the role it will play," Popov said. "That is nearly certain. We must prepare accordingly."

His security chief had already read his mind. As Kazarov talked, Popov scattered large photos from Stanton's Abacus tour on the table where the two men sat. Kazarov was now doubly pleased that Stanton had visited the facility, and that they'd recorded every moment of his visit.

Kazarov placed a long, thin finger on one of the photographs, about an inch below Stanton's face, pointing directly at the congressman's chin. "How have discussions proceeded with his security man and the chief of staff?"

"Both are demanding," said Popov, "but both despise the man, which will help. The security man is a former police officer, a true professional. He has already been helpful. Of course, each will look out for themselves first, but they can be trusted to help at key moments."

"Good. Please keep me informed," Kazarov said. "We have observed him for long enough."

Harking back to his naval warfare lore, Kazarov described the moment when a torpedo, seeking a target, homes in on the heat of the closest vessel. It is the moment where one vessel is sure to be destroyed, and any other vessels, even those nearby, are spared.

"After the election, a torpedo will surely launch," he said. "It will seek a target. It may circle near us. But beginning today, and after the election, we will project enormous heat onto Mr. Stanton. When he finally discovers he is the target, it will be too late."

As it always did for Oleg Kazarov, everything from that day forth went almost exactly as planned.